The
Rogue's
Wager

ALSO BY
CHRISTI CALDWELL

The
Rogue's
Wager

Christi
CALDWELL

Montlake
Romance

Published by Montlake Romance, Seattle

www.apub.com

Amazon, the Amazon logo, and Montlake Romance are trademarks of Amazon.com, Inc., or its affiliates.

ISBN-13: 9781503940628
ISBN-10: 1503940624

Cover design by Michael Rehder

Printed in the United States of America

To Alison Dasho and Lauren Plude.
As a young girl, I always dreamed of writing stories.
As a young woman, I dreamed of seeing my stories
published.

In all those dreams, I could have never imagined a more
amazing editorial team than you, Alison and Lauren.

Thank you for helping make Robert and Helena's story
what it is. This one's for you!

London, England
Winter 1809

Prologue

He'd been summoned.

And when the powerful, austere, unforgiving Duke of Somerset summoned one, one answered that call.

Particularly when that man controlled the proverbial strings of one's finances and status.

Even more so when one was hours away from marrying and, as such, very much in need of those funds.

Lord Robert Dennington shrugged out of his cloak and turned it over to his grandfather's butler, Carmichael, with a murmur of thanks. "My grandfather . . . ?"

The aging servant averted his gaze. "Is in his office, my lord." Color filled the man's cheeks.

Of course he was in his office. Robert pulled off his gloves and stuffed them inside his jacket. Was there another place for the powerful peer? The duke controlled every aspect of the Dennington family with the same grasping control he showed in every manner of business.

The butler shifted back and forth. "May I show you to H-His Grace's office?" Carmichael gulped.

The unflinching, smooth-faced servant, who'd served the miserable duke since Robert had been a boy of five, had never so much as cracked a smile, frown, or laugh. And he certainly did not swallow in that loud, troubled manner.

Nervousness seized him. There had been the curt summons to come on this day of all days . . . the timing was too precise, and His Grace, cold and unfeeling, never had been, nor ever would be one of those devoted, loving patriarchs who actually desired his grandson's company. No, the same man who'd used traitorous servants to uncover Robert's love for the nursemaid, and then coldly called his grandson a "bloody fool," didn't have a spot of warmth in his heart.

He knows about the elopement.

"M-My lord?" Carmichael interrupted Robert's panicky thoughts.

Robert tugged his lapels and forced a smile. "I will see myself to His Grace's office." After all, at one and twenty, he was hardly a boy to be cowed by anyone—including the equally feared and revered Duke of Somerset. "I've certainly been called before my grandfather enough to know the way," he added in a desperate bid for levity.

Instead, Carmichael gave a juddering nod and then bolted in the opposite direction with a speed better reserved for a man two decades his junior.

That isn't altogether true, a taunting voice whispered at the back of his mind. *If you were unafraid of him, you'd not be planning to elope this very night and would instead give Lucy Whitman the very public ceremony she deserves.*

Forcing his legs into motion, Robert started down the hall and beat a familiar path to his grandfather's office. The truth was, everyone was more than a little afraid of the man. After all, he'd cut off his daughter, Robert's aunt, for marrying a servant, as easily as if he'd yanked the thread dangling from his jacket.

No, such a man would never, ever tolerate Robert's marriage to a nursemaid. A governess, who'd come from a respectable family, *mayhap,* but never a nursemaid. He dried his damp palms along the sides of his trousers. The duke was too emotionally dead to ever see a servant as an equal, or at the very least, as a human being. As such, he could not know the goodness of Lucy's soul. Or the way she teased and blushed and smiled. Not in the way Robert did. Robert, who daily, through her dealings with his sister, Beatrice, saw more than a maid or servant. He saw the young woman who cared more for him than his title, and wanted to be his wife because she wished to share a life with him and not because she'd be a future duchess.

Now, to make his grandfather see reason. Because there could be no doubt that the Duke of Somerset, who saw all and knew even more, had called Robert here because of the elopement he'd planned for that evening.

Robert came to a stop outside the dreaded office.

Searching for the strength to face the mighty Dennington patriarch, he drew in a deep breath, and ran his hands over the front of his lapels once more. Before his courage deserted him, he raised his hand to knock . . . just as a low, agonized groan penetrated the wood-paneled door. He paused, his hand suspended.

Another tortured moan, one that iced Robert's veins, filtered into the hall—the sound of *death*.

By God, he'd never loved the man, but neither would he ever wish him on to the hereafter. With swift movements, Robert pressed the handle and frantically opened the door to reach his aging grandfather. He jolted to a stop.

As he stood motionless, a dull humming filled Robert's ears. He blinked several times but no matter how many times he blinked, the horror remained and through it Robert remained rooted to the floor: an outside observer in a sordid scene of sin and ugly. Sprawled on her back, with the duke pumping away between her legs, Lucy ran her fingers down the old man's back, urging him on. "You are so good, Your

Grace," she panted, lifting to meet the duke's quick thrusts. "I want more of you."

Bile burned the back of Robert's throat, and he shot out a hand and caught the edge of the doorway. *Oh, God, no. Not Lucy.* She'd been the only bloody woman to see him, and not a future duke. Surely he'd not been so very blind, so flawed in judgment, that he'd given his heart to a rapacious schemer? Except . . . how else to account for the licentious display before him now?

His grandfather looked up. He may as well have been evaluating his ledgers for the precise, methodical glint in his steel-grey eyes. "Am I better than my grandson?" he demanded, breathless from his exertions.

Lucy moaned in reply. "Oh, yes," she panted.

"And you'll leave him as you said and be my duchess."

"Anything," she cried out, arching her back.

Robert's stomach lurched, and he pressed his eyes closed. *I am going to be ill.*

With an abrupt movement, his grandfather straightened. "That will be all," he said with a thread of ice coating his tone. At the jarring cessation, Lucy lay prone on the desk. She creased her sweaty brow. "Your Grace?"

The lyrical quality of her voice that had once captivated him jerked Robert back from the edge of madness.

"You are late," the duke snapped, and Lucy swiveled her head sideways.

A gasp spilled from her lips, and the color leached from her cheeks. "Robert."

As his grandfather adjusted his garments, he stepped around Lucy. Lucy, the one woman who hadn't given a jot whether Robert would one day be a duke. Lucy, who'd so wholly captured his heart. He fisted his hands at his sides so hard, his nails ripped the flesh jagged, and blood coated his palms. "You summoned me, Your Grace?" he said with an ice to rival a winter freeze, one that even his grandfather would be hard-pressed to not admire. All the while he deliberately kept his gaze averted from the crying, pleading lady who hurried to right her garments.

"Robert," she cried out.

"Silence." The duke's quiet directive had the power to command with a greater strength than any thunderous shout. "I warned you about her." He waved a hand at Lucy. "This one would have made you a terrible bride."

A cynical laugh rumbled up from Robert's throat. Those were perhaps the only true words this man had ever spoken. "Indeed," he drawled, proud of that smooth deliverance, when inside his heart iced over, freezing him from the inside out.

"Robert," Lucy pleaded once more, making to rush past the duke, but the powerful lord easily stepped between her and the path to Robert, cutting off her forward movement.

"There is something wrong with the blood in this line that you are all drawn to the inferior blood of your lessers." His mouth tightened. "First, my daughter and the damned footman." He inclined his head. "It was easy enough to sever her from the family. There is little need for a daughter beyond the connections she might make. But you," he continued over Lucy's copious weeping.

His heart hardened all the more. Those false tears of a lying whore.

"But you, Robert, will one day be duke, and I will be damned if I see a whore perpetuate the bloodlines." Not pausing to take his gaze from Robert, the duke stuck his finger at the door. "You're through here, Miss Waltman." The old bastard had bedded her like a common whore on his desk, in midday, and didn't even know her name. *Then, isn't that what she is?* A shiver of disgust coursed along Robert's spine. For the duke, for Lucy, and for himself in seeing a maid and believing in her station. She'd been different than all the ladies of the peerage, this woman he'd given his heart to and would have given his name, in a few short hours. His Grace spoke, cutting into Robert's musings. "My man-of-affairs will see to your payment."

Her payment. Again, Robert's stomach pitched and he fixed on the hatred building inside like a slow-growing cancer, anything but the gradual, endless cracking of his heart.

Cheeks damp and red from the force of her tears, Lucy rushed around the duke, and came to a quick stop before Robert. "Robert," she begged. "He promised me I would be his duchess."

I would have made you my wife and you would have been my duchess . . . Except, her greed too great, her grasping even greater, she'd been unable to wait for this man to kick up his heels. Robert sneered. Then, there was still his father, who in robust health would have never seen this woman a duchess . . . not anytime soon.

"Surely you understand, Robert. I-I am no governess. I am not of noble birth, I've always—"

"I have nothing to say to you," he cut in. Incapable of looking into those treacherous brown eyes, he looked beyond her shoulder and held his grandfather's stare.

"I'll not ask you again, Miss Waltman," his grandfather said in bored tones the way he might ask a parlor maid to apply an extra coat of wax to his treasured desk. "If you don't leave this instant, I'll advise my man-of-affairs to see you have nothing."

That sprung her into movement. Without another look, or so much as a backward glance, Lucy Whitman stepped out of the room, and out of his life.

His grandfather moved to his sideboard and poured himself a glass of brandy. "You hate me, and that is fine, but I saved you from yourself," he said as he carried his drink to his desk.

Robert stood, hands tightly clenched still at his side. "I am touched by your devotion." Hatred laced his tone, and the duke pursed his lips.

"As a duke, and in your case a future duke, you'd do well to remember, the only risks worth taking are in matters that can grow your wealth." His lip peeled derisively. "We do not make decisions with or for our hearts. So you may have your tantrum and hate me for now, but someday you will thank me for this."

Never.

Except, even as the silent protestation sprung to mind, he tamped it down. Even if he'd wed Lucy and become a cuckold, the greatest fool, he'd never thank his grandfather. Not for this. The duke claimed his tall-backed chair and sprawled in his seat. "I am not your father, my foolish son, waxing on about romantics the way he did with your mother."

No, the duke's soul was stamped black, in ways his only son's never had been, nor ever would be. When the duke had cut his own daughter from the fabric of the family for marrying a footman, Robert's father had shown them kindness and support. It had been that act which had made him hope . . . nay, *believe* . . . that Robert could have an honorable union, built of love, with Lucy. The muscles of his stomach clenched. *Fool. Fool. Fool.*

"My son has a good head for business, but he's a foolish heart." He made a sound of disgust. "He's done you no favors by presenting a weak, romantic view of women and marriage."

The truth of his grandfather's harsh words hit him. No, the romantic notions his father had instilled in him *hadn't* done him any favors. His parents had found love, but Robert was now facing the stark reality of how very rare their bond was.

"You'll do well to remember the lesson of this day, Robert." Then in a dismissive movement, the duke set down his glass, grabbed his ledger and pen, and proceeded to work.

The audience was over. Robert collected himself. His heart might be shattered, but his grandfather had taught him an invaluable lesson. The only sincerity he could hope for in marriage would be to a woman of the *ton*. He'd previously scorned them for their coldheartedness. Now he appreciated the ruthless sincerity of those grasping creatures. At least, with their hungering for his future title, they were clear in their desiring.

Unlike Lucy, who'd given him nothing but lies, and who would have sold her soul for the title of duchess if the Devil had offered that barter.

The duke glanced up from his work. "Is there anything you require, Robert?"

He flattened his mouth into a hard line. "Go to hell," he said quietly, and not allowing the man just below a prince another word, strode from the room. He didn't bother to close the door in his wake, but made his way steadily and purposefully from this hated home.

He'd been wrong earlier.

In two regards: First, he did, in fact, wish the Duke of Somerset dead. And second, women were not to be trusted.

St Giles, England
Winter 1820

Chapter 1

Rule 1
Never set foot on the gaming floors.

Entering the breakfast room, it took but one glance at the Duke of Somerset, with his healthy pallor and the casual sipping of his coffee, for Lord Robert Dennington, the Marquess of Westfield, to confirm one very important detail—his father was most certainly *not* dying.

Robert paused in the doorway and narrowed his eyes. It was not that he was *unhappy* about his father's vigorous health—quite the opposite really, and not simply because he'd long reveled in the freedom afforded him as the ducal heir.

But rather, he genuinely loved his father, which was saying a good deal in a Society where any emotion was rare, and even strongly discouraged.

What Robert did not love was the underhanded efforts of his father—who'd recently hosted a summer party with one, very specific purpose—to marry his son off.

His father looked up from his copy of *The Times*. "Robert," he drawled, acknowledging his son in a strong, healthy, and decidedly not deathly tone before promptly returning his attention to the paper in his hands.

A muscle jumped in the corner of Robert's eye and fury ran through him. He'd spent the whole of his summer at his father's estate, with his head in his hands, devastated by what he thought was the impending death of his sire. Only to find now, in this very casual way, that he'd been duped. Fooled. Tricked. All for the purpose of seeing Robert marry. Another muscle twitched near his eye. Then, hadn't the previous duke demonstrated that same power of influence over a person's life? "Good morning." Yanking off his gloves, Robert tucked them inside his jacket pocket. "*You* are the picture of perfect health, Father," he said and started for the table.

"Afternoon," his father called, not taking his gaze from the front page of *The Times*.

Robert waved off a servant who rushed over and pulled out his chair. "Pardon?"

"It is well past morn."

Ah, this. Again.

Reclining in his chair, Robert layered his palms on the arms and tapped his fingertips. "I was—"

"At your clubs?" His father lowered his paper slightly, peering at him from over the top with a pointed, knowing look.

And perhaps if Robert were most men, and hadn't been reared from the nursery to perfect that same ducal stare, then that look would inspire . . . something. Alas . . . Robert shrugged. "I daresay we have more to discuss than my visit to White's?" He motioned over a servant and the liveried footman came forward with a pot of steaming coffee. He accepted the drink from the footman and blew into the hot contents.

"And what would we have to discuss?" his father asked in bored tones that set Robert's teeth on edge.

Robert took a small sip of the bitter brew. "I don't know?" From over the rim of his glass, he lifted an eyebrow. "Perhaps your sudden and miraculous recovery?" A recovery that followed countless months of the duke's *impending* death.

His father at least had the good grace to flush. He glanced at the handful of servants present, and taking that silent cue, the liveried footmen quickly filed from the room. "Dr. Carlson is amazed," he said as soon as the door closed behind them.

"Oh, I would say he undoubtedly is." Robert infused a dry edge to that retort, which raised a frown from his father's lips.

"Regardless, we weren't discussing my health."

"Your abruptly restored health," Robert amended, setting his glass down.

"But rather *you.*"

Had they? Robert really thought they'd been debating morning versus afternoon greetings. Alas, all conversations with his father inevitably followed the same, familiar trajectory.

"You are three and thirty, Robert," his father began.

"I am aware of my age, Father. An age that I feel compelled to point out is still quite young. " Robert braced for the impending lecture. His father could spout on about finding his future duchess and doing right by the Somerset line, but Robert was quite content to continue to live the same roguish, carefree, and unmarried life he'd adopted in the past years.

Marriage and securing the family line were all endeavors he would see to. Eventually. When he did, there would be no shortage of prospective brides. Women, of the *ton* and the serving class, had all demonstrated a remarkable avarice for that vaunted title. For now, however, with his father very much alive, he was quite content living just as he'd lived for the past twelve years.

Twelve years to the date.

Instead of a well-structured argument, his father sat in silence, skimming his paper, and occasionally pausing to sip his coffee.

Robert drummed his fingertips on the arm of his chair. He'd never sat down across from his father at a gaming table. His father vehemently disavowed all forms of gaming, often saying that if the current duke *did* take his pleasures there, the man deserved to lose his ducal shirt. The tight lines at the corner of his sire's mouth, and the manner in which he leaned forward in his chair, hinted at a person who very much wished to say something.

"Do you know, Robert, the day you first noticed your sister's nursemaid, I was not displeased."

Robert stilled as his father's quietly spoken pronouncement turned the table. He'd not spoken of Lucy in more than ten years, and then, only with his one friend in the world, Richard Jonas. He'd never breathed a word of his romantic affection for the fiery-haired servant, whom he'd intended to elope with, to anyone else.

In fact, mayhap he was the worst of the Denningtons in terms of wagering, for he would have wagered his very life that his father hadn't even *known* about the young woman who'd captured his son's heart. Unlike his commanding grandfather, who'd made it a point in life to control everything remotely concerning the family. A black, still-potent rage for that now long-dead patriarch gripped him.

"And when your grandfather came to me and told me he'd learned of your plans to elope," he continued on through Robert's silent tumult, "I was . . . happy." He grimaced. "Perhaps that is why I'd failed to realize the implications of both his discovery, and my approval, of your relationship with Miss Whitman. The duke would have never supported such a match."

No. He would have rather dueled the Devil than dare taint the Dennington line. Robert gave his head a disgusted shake. How very naïve his father had been to that late duke's evil. Then, hadn't Robert himself been guilty of that same weakness?

The duke looked at him with sad eyes. "You are quiet," his father needlessly observed.

"I did not realize you required a response," he drawled, as the young man proceeded to pour him a cup. Time for a discussion about Lucy Whitman, and the late duke's hand in Robert's future, had long passed. Not that he cared to discuss that afternoon twelve years ago with this man, or anyone really. Even Jonas had received nothing more than a curt recounting of the lady's treachery. The shameful details, he'd opted to withhold.

His father continued in too casual tones. "Then I believed this summer you'd chosen Lady Diana Verney."

Ah, Lady Diana Verney. The Duke of Wilkinson's cherished daughter. That supposition only proved how oblivious his only living parent had always been about his son. "Gemma Reed."

The duke angled his head.

"I would have married Gemma Reed." His sister's bluestocking friend had, at the very least, been interesting when every other woman inspired tedium. In the end, the lady had married Robert's best friend, Richard Jonas. Which was all rather fine. Robert's heart hadn't been engaged. And his heart had long since been protected—he'd intentionally hidden it away.

"You do not say," his father said to himself.

Robert tipped back on the legs of his chair. "I've not ruled Lady Diana out as a prospective match. I just thought given her tender years, I would wait until she at least made her Come Out before I formally offered for her hand."

Surprise flared in the older man's eyes. "You *do* intend to marry Wilkinson's daughter, then?" After all the less than discreet attempts at throwing Robert together with that young lady at the summer party, was it a wonder whom he'd ultimately settled on? "I had no idea," his father said, and his mouth turned down at the corners.

Robert shifted in his seat. "Yes, well, she will do." The last state he cared to speak on was his marital one. His marriage would be one based on practicality and proper connections; a cold union that offered the only true honesty afforded to the peerage. As such, Lady Diana would do . . . as well as any other well-bred lady. Their marriage would unite two ducal families with a history of friendship that went centuries back. Hearts wouldn't be involved. Instead the match would be built on structured arrangements of land and money. It was a situation that the current duke thoroughly approved of.

"Robert . . . ?" For a brief moment, pain contorted the older man's features, twisting them with so much regret and sorrow that Robert had to look away. "I am sorry about Lucy Whitman," he continued in hushed tones. Most dukes would never offer words of compunction. Certainly not the last man who'd held the Somerset title.

That simple apology softened the edges of Robert's stoicism. The current duke had never been like any of those other lords. An affectionate father, a loyal and loving husband, a devoted brother, he'd demonstrated an idealistic way life should be lived. Yet, he'd also been weak . . . as had been evidenced by the late duke's manipulation of Robert. *I would have never been so weak.* For his someday children, Robert would slay dragons, and certainly never allow a villainous bastard like the late duke mastery over his family.

His father stared intently at him, and Robert shifted under that probing regard. "There is nothing to apologize for," he said tightly. At one time, he'd possessed an equally strong resentment for his father having allowed himself, his son, and all the Denningtons to be so controlled by the late duke. With the passage of time, he'd let go of his anger and considered himself fortunate to have been saved from a mistake he would have regretted the whole of his life. Now his sole living parent would drag up years' worth of resentment and bitterness?

"There is everything to apologize for."

Yes, there was.

Inside, he chafed at the pity glinting in his father's eyes. He didn't need pity for having given his heart to a woman and having it ripped from him in that very shameful display his grandfather had subjected him to. "It was better I knew her intentions." And that was the rub of it. Had he not stepped into that office twelve years ago, he'd have married a woman with lies on her lips and ruthless aspirations the only thing in her heart.

"You misunderstand me," his father amended. He set down his paper, and neatly folded it, then smoothed his palms over the surface. "I was pleased the day you noticed her because it spoke of a gentleman who saw beyond the titles and saw to a person's worth."

A cynical chuckle rumbled from his chest. "I showed a remarkable lack of judgment," he said, wanting to say nothing else, wishing he'd never stepped inside this dining room, wishing his father had left that day long buried. Preferring it when he'd moved through life believing his father knew nothing about any of it.

"Yes, you did," his father conceded.

It was a mistake Robert would never again make. Not in the name of that fickle, false emotion of love.

"But," the duke said, lifting a finger. "You also showed remarkable judgment in desiring love and respectability above even rank."

This time a sharp bark of unexpected laughter exploded from Robert. His father was the only peer in the realm who'd be praising his son for loving beneath his station.

His father frowned, and fixed a stare on him that was very much the late duke's practiced look. "You have, however, shown an even more remarkable *lack* of judgment since."

Ah, at last, the lecture. All dukes inevitably worried after the state of the title, and at three and thirty years of age, Robert had taken many more years for his own pleasures than most noblemen, and no doubt all dukes. "I'm not reckless," he said through tight lips. "I wager no more than most gentlemen. I keep one mistress and I'm careful to never beget a bastard on those women." Through his methodical list, his father's frown deepened. "I visit White's and Brooke's, and hardly ever the more scandalous clubs." Though in truth, he did frequent several of those establishments and *always* on this particular day.

There was something about intentionally taking a risk on the anniversary of the day that had cost him everything that kept a gentleman grounded.

His father leaned forward further, and his seat groaned in protest of the shifting weight. "What you fail to realize," he said quietly, settling his elbows on the table, "is that I'm not worried about you being the *same* as other noblemen." He paused. "I worry about you setting yourself apart from them."

Unnerved by the powerful glimmer in those blue eyes nearly identical to his, Robert returned his focus to his coffee, blowing into the already cooling brew. He'd never sought pride or praise from anyone. Rather he'd been content with the person he'd become. He didn't litter the countryside with his bastards and had considered himself a devoted brother, and respectful son. To have his three and thirty years called into question so abruptly shook him in ways he despised.

"I am not disappointed with you," his father added when Robert still said nothing.

"Thank you."

Did his father hear the wry edge to those two words? Or mayhap it was that he didn't care.

"I am disappointed with your lack of living."

His lack of living? A rather powerful lecture, on this day of all days. "I'm content with my life," he said simply. And he was. The hopes he'd once carried, of love and family, had been unrealistic hopes not afforded one of his station. It was the death of a dream he'd made peace with.

The duke waggled his eyebrows. "Ah, but content is not happy."

Robert paused. Was there truth to that charge? He'd not given it much thought—until now. He moved through life, his company sought after by nearly all, the recipient of attention granted for the future title that would come to him. His life was . . . safe.

"It is time you find purpose."

Robert kicked back the legs of his chair and flashed another half grin. "And here I believed my whole purpose was to make a respectable match and provide the necessary heir and a spare."

"Ah, but you've not even done that."

The accusation rung loudly off the walls. Just as it had with the blasted summer party not even three months ago, all matters inevitably came round to mention of a proper bride. Settling the legs of his chair on all fours, he leaned forward, matching his father's pose. "Is this about me doing my requisite duty? Or is this about me being a man of greater worth and value?"

"It is about both," his father softly returned.

Robert's neck went hot. It was not every day that a gentleman's honor was called into question—by his father, no less. Should he expect anything different from a man sired by the late duke? "I learned every lesson you taught about the estates and properties. I visited properties with you and have made myself current with the profits and the state of affairs for our tenants." Even with that, it wasn't enough. Mayhap his father was more like the late duke than he'd ever believed.

In an uncharacteristic break in composure, his father dragged a hand over his face. "This is not about me questioning your capability as the future duke."

"Then, what is it about?" he shot back. Because somewhere along the way his sire's words had all become muddled.

For a long while, the duke said nothing. Just passed his piercing, solemn eyes over his son. Robert sat frozen through that silent scrutiny, prepared for another moral diatribe. Then his sire gave another sad shake of his head. "If you do not know or understand, I'm afraid I can't tell you, Robert. It is for you to find out who you are."

Weary of lectures and lies at all the Dukes of Somerset's hands, Robert finished his coffee and then set his cup down. "If you'll excuse me? I have an appointment I must see to." Which included attending that scandalous club, as he did every year at this time. On the heel of that was a niggling of guilt. *You only prove your father correct, in going.* Shoving back his chair, Robert climbed to his feet. "I am pleased to see your health restored." He turned to go.

"Our pockets are nearly to let, Robert." Those quietly spoken words managed to thunder around the breakfast room, and brought him slowly around.

"What?" Surely he'd misheard.

In another remarkable break in composure, his father scrubbed a hand down one side of his suddenly haggard face. "We are in quite deep," he said, confirming that Robert's ears were not in fact faulty.

He scoffed. "Impossible." They'd one of the oldest, most landed titles. *Then, what would you truly know of it? You've been living a roguish, carefree existence for more than ten years, now.*

"Oh, I assure you," his father said, and then in a maddeningly calm manner, sipped his coffee. "Quite possible."

A knot formed in his chest, and he waited until the pressure eased. Given the Somerset dukes' longstanding history of manipulating their children, Robert wouldn't be so much as a fool to fall victim to another scheme. "I do not have time for any more of your games," he said tightly, and started for the door.

"Why do you think I, who has touted a love match above all else, should arrange a summer party to try and make advantageous matches for my children?"

The words cut Robert in his tracks, words that echoed of truth. He balled his hands reflexively, and when he trusted himself to speak, turned back, and tried once more. "If this is merely to see me married, then—"

"It is not that, Robert," his father neatly interrupted. A flash of something lit his eyes, but was quickly gone so Robert didn't know if it was merely a turn of the sun's rays penetrating the floor-length windowpanes.

On wooden legs, he stalked over and reclaimed his vacant chair. "What happened?"

His father cradled his glass of coffee in his hands. "You knew your grandfather." *All too well.* "His wealth, power. It was never enough. At the end of . . ." He stared into the contents of his cup. "At the end, he was not lucid. He cut me off of all financial discussions and allowed his man-of-affairs to make large investments."

Robert dragged his chair closer to the table. "In *what*?" His mind spun, as with every revelation, his father confirmed the state of their finances.

"Steam."

"Steam?" he repeated. His always-proper grandfather had dabbled in trade?

"Borrowed against the estates." He grimaced. "A lot. Too much. As such I've been seeing the tenants do not pay for the crimes of my father."

And the Denningtons were in dun territory for it.

He peered at his father. Mayhap this was as false as that goddamn summer party?

"It is true, Robert," his father said, unerringly following his thoughts. "It is *one* of the reasons I wished to see you both married."

Robert sank back in his chair, flummoxed. "One of the reasons?" A cynical laugh escaped him. "Never tell me, *love* being the most important?"

His father frowned. "Yes. I had so very much hoped that you and your sister could make respective matches that brought you love and improved our finances." He coughed into his hand. "Now you know."

Now I know. A black curse burst from his lips. Guilt . . . at his own self-absorption, at his failing to take an active role in the estate, all of it, assailed him. And annoyance . . . that his father believed the only way Robert could improve their circumstances was through landing a wealthy bride.

The duke's gaze strayed to the doorway. "Your sister cannot know."

"No," he agreed. For the fury at being deceived by his father, they were of like regard where Bea was concerned. Suddenly, the discussion of the past, the revelations of today, was too much. He needed away from this townhouse. Robert abruptly shoved back his chair. "If you'll excuse me? I intend to take rooms at my club." At least for the evening he could seek escape from his ugly reality. Robert braced for a fight. Welcomed it.

Instead, as he should expect, his father was as convivial as always. "Good afternoon, Robert." Good afternoon? There was nothing remotely good, or even fair, about it.

With the duke's powerful stare boring into his back, Robert hastily beat a retreat. He made his way through the corridors, the very same halls he'd avoided as a child, and then hated as a young man who'd had his heart broken. He gritted his teeth, the irony not lost on him. Twelve years ago, on this day, his life had fallen apart. And now, it had been ripped asunder once more.

His father would turn him into a goddamn fortune hunter. Then, given his carefree existence these years, why *should* he expect Robert capable of righting the mess of their finances?

Robert reached the foyer.

His sister, Beatrice, stood with her hands propped on her hips, blocking the entrance—or in this case, the exit—of the Somerset home. She knitted her blonde eyebrows into a line. "Robert," she said, with the regal tones befitting a queen instead of a younger sister. "Where have you been?"

"Bea," he said with a forced smile.

Having made her Come Out four years earlier, his only sibling was as of yet unwed, grasping and clinging to that great hope of love. Alas . . . She'd yet to realize and accept that the Denningtons were not slated for that sentiment. Especially not now, given the change of their financial circumstances. The world, lords and ladies, servants and paupers, could never, would never, see past the ancient title. Now that truth might save them.

"I am here about Father. He is—"

"Well," he supplied for her, as he reached into his jacket and pulled out his gloves. He tugged them on. "We just . . . spoke," he settled for.

She furrowed her brow. "No . . ."

"Yes," he said, as the butler, Davidson, rushed over with Robert's cloak. Thanking the servant, he shrugged into the garment. "He is quite the picture of health."

Beatrice cocked her head. God love Bea. She'd only ever seen the best in everyone. Robert knew the inevitable day would come when that innocence would be shattered. Robert also knew that when it did he would end the bastard responsible for hurting his beloved sister.

When Beatrice still said nothing, Robert took pity on her. "He was trying to marry us off." *To refill the depleted coffers.* At the very least it now made sense. Yet why had he not confided in Robert before? Instead he'd sought to manipulate him. Just as everyone ultimately did.

Beatrice opened and closed her mouth several times. Then . . . "Surely not." She spoke those words as fact. "I saw him."

Yes, they'd seen precisely what the duke had wished them *to* see. "He wants us married, Bea," he said, gentling his tone.

His obstinate sister brought her shoulders back. "Not enough to *lie*." The emphasis placed on that particular word could only come from a woman who'd never seen the whole ugly that existed about them.

Robert cuffed her under the chin. "I assure you, he is quite hearty and healthy, and I could not be happier." Robert might resent the man for forcing him to look at the life he lived, and less than subtly placing doubts on him, but he loved him, still. It was hard not to. Particularly when one saw the manner of beast the late duke had been.

"You're certain?" Bea pressed. "He is not simply saying he's feeling better for our benefit?"

"I'd wager all my funds on it," he reassured, except as soon as the words left him, panic reached his core. Their lives were nothing more than a castle made of sand.

Her shoulders sagged, and he found some solace in her blitheness. "Oh, thank God." Then a slow, wide smile split her cheeks and she stepped aside. "You may go, now."

Davidson rushed over and pulled the door open. Desperate to be free of this house, and alone with all the admissions made by his father, Robert hurried forward.

"Oh, and Robert?" Bea called, staying his movements.

He shot a questioning look over his shoulder.

"Behave."

He winked. "I always do."

His sister rolled her eyes skyward, and with a half grin, he started for his horse.

Chapter 2

Rule 2
Never visit the gaming hell during the midnight hours.

Since Helena Banbury had been a small girl, her "brothers" had teased that she was better at reading numbers than people.

Given her remarkable lack of exposure *to* people, she rather thought their words said in jest made a good deal of sense.

This particular moment was no exception to her rather predictable, if safe, days—and nights—inside the Hell and Sin Club.

Tucked away in the small office at the back of the Hell and with her spectacles perched on her nose, Helena ran her gaze over the neat columns of numbers. Bellowing shouts sounded outside the doorway, and she continued working through the brawl taking place beyond the heavy wood panel. There was something to be said for having a solid oak door between you and danger. Until her rescue years earlier by her brother, Ryker, she'd had nothing to protect her from the perils of the world. That was the precarious lot of a motherless and fatherless child on the streets of London.

Chewing at her lower lip, Helena swiftly tabulated the weekly liquor expenses.

Fifteen cases of whiskey.

Fifteen cases of sherry.

Twenty cases of brandy.

A bothersome strand of brown hair escaped her tight chignon and fell across her brow. Noblemen and their bloody drinks. Not pausing in her writing, she blew back the tress and marked a final note in the column. Working a quick gaze over the numbers she silently cursed. They required far more brandy. She stretched in her chair, rubbing her lower back. Her bloody obstinate brother insisted on only purchasing the finest French spirits, despite Helena's insistence that any cheaper brandy would do just as well. The swiftly depleting stock of spirits that week was proof of that.

A wry grin pulled at her lips. Yes, her four brothers of the street. Though she only shared blood with one of them, the bond between them all was no less strong. What most failed to realize was that if you knew how to read them, numbers could tell you a good deal about people. And the glaring details in the neat rows of her ledger said all number of unfavorable things about noblemen: they drank too many spirits; they spent too many pounds indulging in their liquor. And they demonstrated a remarkable lack of self-control.

Granted, those failings of character had resulted in the triumph of the Hell and Sin Club. And having risen from the dust and ash of the streets to become leader of the glittering underbelly of St Giles, her brother, the majority owner of the club, expected nothing less than even greater wealth and power. There was, however, always room for greater success. Dipping her pen in the crystal inkwell, she proceeded to add the cost of those pricey bottles. Helena drummed the back of her pen on the smooth mahogany surface of her desk, all the while contemplating the columns.

Footsteps sounded in the hall, and she jerked her head up just as the door opened. Raucous laughter from the floor of the Hell spilled into the room, only to be muffled moments later, as her brother Calum stepped inside.

The tall, bearish man, with a jagged scar at the corner of his mouth, who stood at the front of the room would have terrified most women. "Your brother wants the figures."

Then, she wasn't most women. The jagged scars crisscrossing her back were proof of that. "Which brother?" she said, infusing a bored note into her question.

Calum snorted. "You know."

Yes, she did. The jest was that Ryker had his hands, and head, in nothing *but* the club . . . and if he had a heart, then that would be in it, too. Long ago, however, the head of the club had demonstrated his cold, calculated approach to everything . . . and everyone—including the siblings he'd grown up with on the street.

Helena returned her attention to her columns. "Tell him, I'm not done." She directed that pronouncement at the page, as she considered the area to best reduce expenses.

"Not good enough," Calum drawled, and she looked up, a gasp escaping her.

"Christ on Sunday." The pen slipped from her fingers. "Must you sneak?" Several inches past six feet, and broad across the chest, a man of his sheer size had no right to be so stealthy. It had served them well when he'd been one of the most skilled pickpockets in all of London, but it proved a bother when one was trying to focus.

He rested his hip on the edge of the desk, and stared pointedly. "The numbers, Helena," he said, fanning her exasperation.

For as fortunate as she was to not be any bastard-born child whoring in the streets, a deep-seated irritation simmered inside for the still-powerless role that came with being a woman in her twenty-fourth year with so little influence.

"Does he want them now?" she snapped, pulling her spectacles off and tossing them on the desk. "Or does he want them correct?"

Calum grinned. "He wants both."

Pointing her eyes to the ceiling, Helena threw down her pen. "Very well." She shoved back her chair.

Ignoring the way Calum shot his dark brown eyes to his hairline, she started for the door.

"Where in hell are you going?"

She froze midmovement, and wheeled back. "To see—"

"Ryker is on the floors," he interrupted, all earlier hint of amusement gone, replaced with a dark scowl. And with reason. Even the prospect of Helena setting foot on the floors, or outside the club, at the height of the early-morn gaming hours, was an act that had been expressly forbidden. It had also seen one careless guard fired, when she'd wandered onto those floors ten years earlier.

Helena folded her arms at her chest. "I live here." The place she'd lived for nearly half her life.

Calum snorted, and then matched her pose. "I know where you live. Do *you*, Helena?"

She gritted her teeth, and tamped down the endless barrage of questions and pleadings she'd put to all of her brothers through the years—to no avail. There were valid reasons for her to stay tucked away, but also, as a grown woman, in charge of the finances for the club, there was a grating restiveness inside her. What power did she truly have? In a place where lords ruled the polite world and ruthless men led the underbelly, women were left on the fringe of both. "I swear you'd all have me a prisoner in my own home," she muttered under her breath. She cast a covetous glance at the door that shook under the force of the ribald laughter from the floor below.

Calum settled a large palm on her shoulder, and she stiffened. "There are rules for a reason," he said, with gruff gentleness.

Since Ryker had rescued Helena, a girl of six, from Diggory's clutches, he had ingrained into her the necessity of rules. There were only, and always, rules. She lifted her gaze and held Calum's stare with an unflinching directness. "I am not a girl, anymore, Calum." And yet, they all still saw her as wee Helena, in need of protecting. Now, just three inches shy of six feet, she towered over most men.

"No, you're not a girl. You're something far more dangerous." He cuffed her under the chin. "You're a woman."

With a sigh, she started over to her desk. Yes, she was a woman, who straddled two worlds. She'd never belong amongst those toffs on the gaming hell floors, but neither would she be viewed wholly as a member of the Hell and Sin. Not as the youngest, protected sister of the lethal Ryker Black. "He'll need at least ten more cases of brandy before the week's through."

Calum whistled.

His otherwise silence spoke more words than a Shakespearean novel. Helena's ears burned with heat and she swallowed back the defensive words on her lips. In their world, you didn't make excuses. You took ownership of your decisions and actions. Even if you weren't *entirely* to blame. Still . . . "I advised him to buy a cheaper quality, and larger quantity." Even as the words left her mouth, the futility of them registered.

Calum gave her a pointed look that only sent further warmth spiraling to her pale cheeks. Blasted pale skin.

"Ryker expects the best."

She firmed her jaw, Calum's meaning clear. Ryker expected the best for his clients, and accuracy from his employees. And her status as sister to the ruthless owner meant naught. What mattered was that all saw to their responsibilities and the establishment ran with a fluid efficiency that plumped the owners' pockets.

Calum started for the door, and she called out. "Perhaps if I were permitted on the floors, and able to evaluate the habits of our guests—"

"No." The steel in that one-word utterance should have killed her efforts.

"But—"

"Use the goddamn numbers, Helena." Calum quelled her protest with a glare.

She tipped her chin up. Be it a brother or powerful lord, she'd not let a single person cow her. Just as Ryker, Calum, Adair, and Niall took pride in climbing from the mire of London's streets to build an empire of wealth and power, so too did she find satisfaction in all she'd accomplished. The once snarling, cursing, illiterate girl from the Dials had developed a head for numbers that even her indomitable brother could never hope to rival.

Releasing her stare, Calum looked away. His gaze snagged upon the ledgers, and he motioned to them. "You don't need to go on the halls in the midnight hours, Helena," he said with gruff gentleness. "You have free walk of the floor during the day, and during the evening you have the books to tell you everything you need to know."

Yes, those numbers taught her everything about the inner workings of the club . . . but nothing about the world beyond these increasingly suffocating walls. Helena fisted her hands at her side. She may as well be spitting in the wind with all of her protestations. "Tell him I'll have additional numbers for him in the morning."

Calum nodded, and started for the door.

"And Calum?" she called out. He turned back. "Also, tell him that he'd be wise to consider finding a new supplier. His liquor provider now is fleecing him and delivering broken bottles."

A wry grin twisted his lips. "You may be frustrated with your circumstances, Helena, but you are deuced good at what you do."

"I expect Diggory has gotten to his supplier."

All hint of amusement fled, replaced with a somber set to his features.

Diggory, the leader of a gang who'd also risen up from the Dials, now ran The Devil's Den. Where the Hell and Sin catered to all—merchants, nobles, and sailors on the street—Diggory's hell catered only to the lowest rung of humanity.

"I'll let Ryker know."

She nodded, grateful when he took his leave. As soon as the door closed, she let the tension seep from her shoulders. Though Calum's parting words and confidence would have inspired pride in most, for her, they only grated. Letting out a curse that would have shocked most thieves in the Dials, she began to pace. How she despised Calum's too-astute statement. If he sensed her frustration, then so too did Ryker, and every other owner, guard, and prostitute in the club. And she hated that they saw . . . hated it mostly because they recognized that she herself wanted more than the gilded walls of this protective cage.

As much as she'd learned the reason to fear the streets of London firsthand as a girl, there was also her growing need to look at the world as a woman grown and have *some* control. Control that extended beyond her brother's protective influence.

She came to a sudden stop, and as her modest green satin skirts fluttered noisily at her ankles, Helena stared blankly at the door.

How many years had she been ordered about and away? She had a decided role to fill, just as each sibling did . . . and they were to not look beyond those responsibilities.

Do not do it, Helena . . . Do not . . .

Ignoring the logical litany echoing around her mind, she strode to the door and pulled it open. The distant rumblings of ribald laughter and cheering filled the corridor. Before her courage deserted her, or logic was restored, Helena started down the corridor.

She held her breath, and stole a glance about. Alas, her private offices were strictly off-limits for even the most loyal workers at the club.

Guards were stationed at various entryways and stairwells to prevent wandering lords from reaching the main living quarters and offices.

"You are not doing anything wrong," she muttered under her breath.

No, what harm was there in stealing belowstairs and discreetly evaluating the actual consumption habits of the guests? The *same* guests who were making a bloody mess of her calculations. Helena reached the end of the corridor, and started down the stairwell. She blinked several times, struggling to adjust to the dimly lit space. Ominous shadows, cast by a handful of sconces, danced off the white plaster walls. Panic rioted about her mind. Mayhap it was the earlier talk of Diggory, the demon of her past, but an icy shiver worked along her spine. *Do not look. Do not look* . . . Except, like a moth drawn to that fatal flame, her gaze strayed to the crimson tip of a candle. The acrid scent of smoke and burning flesh flooded her senses, and she grabbed the stair rail.

Helena sucked in slow, even breaths as memories assaulted her. The vicious agony as Diggory melted her flesh with a burning candle . . . her own screams and pleas . . . *Stop!*

A loud cheer went up, jolting Helena back to the moment. She slid her eyes closed as the boisterous excitement within the club continued to filter up the stairway, calming and safe. Ordinary sounds that blotted out remembered cries. Helena brushed her palms along her skirts.

Is this why Ryker kept her hidden away from the gaming floors and outside world? Did he see that for what she'd managed to survive all those years ago, there was this weakness in her, still? Firming her resolve, she pushed away from the wall and resumed her determined march downstairs.

The wood creaked under her footsteps; however, the increasing din on the gaming hell floor drowned out all hint of sound. She reached the bottom landing and wiped her hands on her dress once more. One of the guards quickly turned. *Blast and damn.* The day had apparently come where she, once a skilled pickpocket, couldn't escape the notice of a handful of guards. Her mouth soured. How bloody frustrating to have had more freedom of movement as a child of five than a woman nearly two decades older.

Oswyn frowned. "Miss Banbury?"

"Hello, Oswyn." All of the women employed at the Hell and Sin had perfected a distracting, whispery smile. By the pained twist of her lips, Helena's attempt was really more a grimace than anything. The tall, muscled guard scratched at his bald pate.

Her tongue grew thick in her mouth. *He's going to have me sent abovestairs.* And once again she'd be shut away while the world carried on around her. *Say something. Say anything . . .* "Ryker wished me to evaluate the inventory of spirits for the remainder of the week," she said quickly. Which wasn't altogether untrue. After all, she *had* been instructed to calculate the numbers. Those calculations, however, had in no way merited a night visit to the floors. Not by Ryker's estimation, anyway. In Helena's, well, she required more judicious movement in the club . . . and beyond.

With a nod, Oswyn stepped aside.

She hesitated. How many times as a young girl had she sat at the top of those very stairs, trying to make order of the discourse and laughter from those powerful peers below? Surely it could not have been *this* easy to gain entry? Oswyn looked questioningly at her, and that sprung her into movement.

Helena hastily stepped past the guard, and entered the hall. A cloud of cheroot smoke hung heavy in the expansive room, stinging her eyes. She blinked several times and continued to take in the club during the height of activity. The crystal chandeliers cast a bright glow upon the floors that lent an almost artificial sense of day to the nighttime scene. Hastily skimming her gaze over the crowded floors, she did a search for Ryker. With no hint of her fierce brother, she started along the perimeter, taking care to avoid gazes and notices . . . an easy feat given the well-placed pillars constructed about the hall. Heart pounding, Helena borrowed shelter from one Scamozzi column and surveyed the guests.

Alcohol flowed freely, with the tinkling of crystal touching crystal as bottles were poured. The women of the Hell and Sin Club moved between tables, providing additional spirits to the *revered* patrons. Helena did a quick inventory, silently counting. One, two, three . . . "At the very *least*, fifteen cases of whiskey," she muttered to herself. And that was still being conservative in numbers because of her frugal brother.

She studied the gentlemen freely tossing cherished coins upon the card tables, and gave her head a sad shake. Granted, their freedom with their purses provided her and every other employee within this hall a livelihood. Yet, even with that, distaste filled her at the wastefulness of it all. Was life so boring and empty for these men, that this was all the joy there was? Recalling the task at hand, Helena gave her head another shake and did an inventory of the tables within eyeshot. Silently counting the bottles and glasses, she shook her head in exasperation. Her brother might fault her for the erroneous supply count, but the foxed lords deep in their cups consumed spirits the way a man stranded in a desert, who'd stumbled upon water, might.

How am I supposed to know that, unless I observe the proclivities of our guests . . . ?

In a bid to view additional tables, she took a step and then stopped. Her gaze collided with a pair of sapphire blue eyes. Time stood still in a charged moment, with the nightly revelries carrying on around her in a whir of muffled noise. In a world in which she was invisible to all, the burning intensity of the stranger's stare stripped away her anonymity, and there was something so gloriously heady in being—seen. Her heart skittered a beat. *Mayhap this is why Ryker keeps me shut away.* Not with worry of the harm Diggory might do her, but rather to keep her from experiencing this irrational pull that robbed a woman of logic.

And then she registered the blankness within the fathomless depths. A profound sadness, and pain so deep, it stretched across the room and held her frozen.

In ways that moved beyond the beauty of his chiseled features and aquiline nose, the stranger's barely concealed anguish made him stand out amidst the gaiety of the other patrons. He was a solitary figure, one who belonged even less than she did in this room. The golden-haired lord grabbed a bottle of brandy, and swiftly poured himself a drink. Then their eyes met once more. This time, there was no sadness but rather a piercing intensity that made her pulse race through her veins.

She swallowed hard. No gentleman had a right to be so gloriously golden and masculinely perfect. Even with the distance between them, there was an aura of commanding strength to his broad shoulders and square, noble jaw. The faintest cleft lent a—

A dandy in burnt orange satin breeches stepped in between them, and jerked her back to the moment.

Cheeks ablaze, Helena gave her head a hard shake, and continued on. After all, her visit to the floor had nothing to do with a too-handsome-for-anyone's-good lord, and everything to do with the responsibilities she saw to in the Hell and Sin. For all the worries her brothers had for her well-being and safety, Helena had grown up in the streets. She might speak like a lady and read with an ease that would have impressed an Oxford scholar, but she could protect herself better than most men.

From across the club, a faint buzz went up, and she followed the attention. Ryker cut a path through the club. His face set in a hard, unyielding mask, he strode past gaming table after gaming table. One horrifying moment stretched on to eternity as she waited for him to notice her. Only when he stopped to speak to Calum without even glancing in her direction did she breathe again. *Thank goodness.*

It was one thing to embrace your freedom and a sense of control, but it was an altogether different matter to openly defy that man. Brother or not, Ryker Black would never tolerate broken rules—not in his club, and most definitely not by his sister.

Chapter 3

Rule 3
Never overindulge in spirits.

If Robert Dennington, the Marquess of Westfield, was manipulated, maneuvered, or deceived by one more Duke of Somerset, he was going to lose his bloody everlasting mind. As it was, he opted for the welcoming distraction of drink.

Particularly as it prevented him from thinking on all the stares directed his way . . . and all because of the lie perpetuated by his conniving father.

His lips twisted in a cynical smile. It was his lot to be manipulated . . . and by those he trusted most. Older matrons, marriage-minded misses, of late, eyed him with an increased interest aspired to that coveted ducal prize. With the papers reporting on the impending demise of the duke, well, the most relevant news in the whole of England happened to be: Robert's marital state.

Robert took another swallow of his drink. Or mayhap he already had lost his bloody mind. It was also why, at this moment, with a bottle of brandy before him, in a club that was decidedly not polite or respectable, Robert intended to get bloody soused.

After his third glass, he'd ceased to feel the burn or sting of the fiery spirits.

Then he was already well on his way to the everlasting goal.

"My regards for your father, Westfield."

Oh, bloody hell. This? The polite, murmured greeting pulled his focus away from his noble task of getting foxed to the gentleman who stood at his table. Lord Hubert, was it? He furrowed his brow. Or Lord Halpert? After four snifters of fine French brandy, it was really hard to sort through the man's identity. Lord Something-or-Another stared expectantly back.

Lifting his glass in appreciation, Robert murmured the expected, appropriate words of thanks one would give a person sharing regret about the impending demise of your father. After all, there were social expectations that went with being a future duke . . . and that included acknowledging polite company when you'd much rather send them to the Devil, and be on your own business.

Grateful of the other man's departure, Robert downed his drink and reached for the bottle.

One would correctly argue that there was nothing acceptable about a duke getting drunk in one of the most disreputable, notorious gaming hells in St Giles.

Then, certain liberties were permitted to dukes. Even more liberties permitted to marquesses whose fathers were close to meeting their maker. His lips pulled in disgust. Not abandoning his father's side during the summer, Robert would have struck a deal with Satan to prolong his father's life. But then, perhaps he had. For all his devotion, for having pledged to marry and do right by the Somerset line, he'd been repaid with this.

Through all the treachery of Lucy Whitman and his grandfather, he'd now add his father to the list of those who'd betrayed him. For even as those two men had sought to protect Robert, they'd done so in a way that was so wholly manipulative, it could never be truly forgiven.

Granted, in his youth, he'd been too blinded by the illusion of love to listen to his grandfather's reasoning. However, he was no longer that same callow lad. Had his father possessed the decency to speak with him on the solvency of the estates, he'd have listened. Instead, his sire had developed an underhanded scheme better reserved for the late duke.

At three and thirty, Robert well knew the responsibilities expected of him. He'd just failed to realize the extent of those responsibilities—until today. *Then, that isn't truly your father's fault.* He fisted his glass so hard, the blood drained from his knuckles as on this day, of all days, that betrayal stung all the deeper.

Lightening his grip, Robert swirled the contents of his glass in a circle. For the past twelve years, he had lived for his own pleasures, a rather carefree, roguish existence. How very different his life would have been had it continued along a different trajectory, with Robert wedded that long-ago night. He'd even now be married, and most likely a father. He'd not be riddled with matchmakers and scheming misses.

Lifting his gaze from his drink, Robert skimmed it over the mindless revelry being celebrated throughout the gaming hell. He was no father. He was no husband. And by his father's admission today, Robert, with his sudden shift in financial circumstances, was not unlike every other bored gentleman losing a fortune at his respective faro table.

And there was something so very humbling in that truth. Tightening his mouth, he refocused his energies on his drink. Tomorrow he could focus on the expectations the world placed on him. Now, he'd spend the night fanning the long-buried resentment and regrets for what had almost been and what would never be because of the title he'd been born to.

A young woman, with thick blonde hair and an invitation in her eyes, sidled up to him. "Would you like company, my lord?" she purred on a throaty whisper that promised carnal delights.

He eyed the lush beauty. On any other night, if he weren't maud-lin and more eager to lose himself in the mindless amusements of the club and the fine French brandy, he would have followed the nameless beauty abovestairs. She grazed her fingers over his sleeve, and leaned close.

Not this night. This night, he'd come for but one purpose. He waved his hand. At his clear dismissal, her plump, red lips formed a small moue of displeasure, and then she moved on to some other patron.

Raucous laughter and the clink of coins hitting felt gaming tables resonated through the halls of the club, that revelry mocking Robert with the carefree levity of those around him. He raised the tumbler to his lips once more and froze. The slightest movement at the edge of the gaming hell floor snagged his attention on a woman on the fringe of the entertainment. Perhaps it was the splash of her mint-green dress amidst the mostly black coats, that color pale and pure against the gar-ish canary-yellow and burnt-orange waistcoats of the dandies circulating the club.

Robert swirled the contents of his glass and studied the woman as she skirted the tables, weaving between wagering gentlemen and fierce-looking bouncers. But for the vicious scar down the right side of her face, there was nothing immediately remarkable about her. Her hair drawn tight at her nape accentuated too-sharp features. Her gown hung on a too-slender, narrow-hipped frame. Nay, she hardly possessed any kind of beauty that beckoned. Rather, it was her sly steps that gave him pause. The woman didn't walk, nor sprint, nor stride. But rather . . . *tiptoed* about the room. Occasionally she paused, and cast furtive glances about.

She came to a stop beside a pillar and scanned the room. Her full, bow-shaped lips moved, as though she were talking to herself.

And in that moment, all previous melancholy lifted, replaced with a sudden intrigue. Did she seek to lift a man of his coin? Or search for a bed-partner?

He cursed as a tall figure stepped directly in his line of vision, obliterating the hint of the mysterious woman. Robert leaned around, searching for a glimpse of the fey creature—

"You look like hell."

Well, that wasn't the standard polite greeting he'd gritted his teeth through for nearly a month now. Through dry eyes, he snapped his gaze up at the interloper, and blinked several times. Richard Jonas stood before him. Which really wouldn't be shocking for most gentlemen . . . except this one. Recently married, and exceedingly happy, the horse breeder didn't leave the country . . . and he decidedly did not come to scandalous clubs. "Jonas," he greeted. Having suffered a broken heart when the woman he'd loved wed his brother, Jonas had ultimately found a deserved happiness. Though never one to visit London, he was even scarcer now since his joyous nuptials.

"I'm in London for business," he explained. "Discussing the sale of a mare for Lord Drake's young daughter." Jonas gestured to the vacant seat. "May I?"

Robert tipped his chin toward the chair. He'd suffered through a parade of gentlemen asking after his father, making it a point to not invite any of them to sit. This was a friend he'd never turn away. And with all he'd learned today, Robert was welcoming of the company.

"Your sister paid a visit to Gemma a short while ago."

Robert frowned. That was hardly news. The two young women, who'd somehow found themselves wallflowers, had also found themselves as thick as thieves in the Dials. "Did she?"

"Your sister is worried," Jonas said, knocking Robert into apprehensive silence.

Had Bea gathered their family was in dun territory? "Worried?" he repeated, flatly.

Jonas glanced pointedly about the room. "About the clubs you are visiting."

Relief rippled through him. "Hardly anything to worry after," he assured. That was the least of the Denningtons' trials. In a bid to turn the discussion to topics that did not involve him accounting for his presence here, Robert asked, "How is the lovely Mrs. Jonas?"

His friend drew out the opposite chair and slid into its folds.

"She is well." In a whirlwind romance, Jonas had met, wooed, and won the uniquely interesting Gemma Reed. Which only recalled the bloody summer party and his father's machinations. He took another long swallow.

"It is the day, isn't it?" At the abrupt shift in discourse, Robert stiffened, remaining silent as his friend spoke. "You were never the same after Miss Whitman's betrayal." No, he wasn't.

Before he'd met his wife, Jonas had loved another, a woman who'd instead given her heart to Jonas's younger brother. As such, he knew better than most the pain of a broken heart. What he did not realize, could *never* realize, was that Robert didn't remember Lucy Whitman with any real affection. Rather, her memory served to remind him of all the mistakes he'd made. Of the folly in loving. Nor did Jonas know the details of just whom Robert had discovered his former love with. The other man gave his head a wry shake.

"It does eventually lessen," his friend murmured, cutting into his thoughts.

Robert blinked several times. Knowing Robert as he did, and what this day harkened back to, Jonas would surely expect him to be mourning his past.

"You think you'll never find love because, well, frankly you're certain your heart isn't capable of withstanding that kind of pain again." Jonas gave him a look. "What you'll come to learn is that there is another deserving of you, who will bring you happiness Lucy Whitman never could have."

"I assure you, my visiting my clubs has nothing to do with Lucy Whitman." And certainly not any broken heart. "It is my father," he clarified.

His friend alternated his gaze between the nearly empty bottle and Robert's face. "I am sorry. Of course. The papers have made . . . mention," Jonas settled for. "Of your father's deteriorating condition."

Robert mustered a wry grin. "He's not dying." Though if anything had given him the push to wed, his sire's impending death had been it.

Jonas cocked his head. "He's . . . ?"

"Not dying," Robert supplied. "He lied." Downing the remainder of his drink, he then set his glass aside. "He did a rather convincing job of it, too."

Confusion filled the other man's eyes. "Why would he do something such as that?"

Robert stole a glance around the nearby tables. What his father had shared today was the manner of gossip that would feed the fodders well into the next century. This man before him now was more brother than friend. He dragged his chair closer, and settled his elbows on the table. "My grandfather made risky business ventures, which my father has been unsuccessful in resolving these past years."

Jonas scratched at his brow. "What—?"

"Our pockets are nearly to let," he said in hushed tones; and speaking those words aloud for the first time lent an even greater sense of realness that sent panic spiraling.

The other man sank back in his chair. "My God."

With a wave of his hand, Robert said, "This is the reason my father wished to marry me off. *Not* because of his impending death." A rusty chuckle slipped out. "How singularly odd to be both relieved and infuriated at the same time." The shamefulness in his father's deception was particularly sharpened when presented with this man, whose own father had died not even two years earlier.

With quick, fluid movements, Jonas proceeded to pour himself a drink.

A companionable silence fell between them, two men who'd been friends since Eton and who'd once shared a bond built on loss, and as

Robert drank, Jonas remained steadfast keeping him company as the hours marched on. It was Jonas who broke the impasse.

"Is your father expecting you to marry a certain lady, then?"

"He would rather I marry for . . ." His lips pulled. "Love." A fortune hunter who found love. He snorted. *That* was the matter of rubbish better served on the pages of the romantic novels his sister favored. And apparently to Robert's father, a more realistic possibility than his son managing to somehow reverse their financial circumstances. "Ironic, isn't it?" he asked, wryly, taking another sip.

His friend furrowed his brow.

"A duke's son and daughter, and neither of us can manage a single match." Though, given the oath he'd taken, the matter was largely settled. Just not formally . . . given the rules of mourning.

Jonas frowned. "Well, that isn't altogether true. You've both been . . ." The man seemed to search his thoughts. "Selective," he opted for.

He snorted and said nothing else. Selective in the sense that Robert had been a rogue who'd lived for his own pleasures, and Bea . . . well, Bea was still a romantic hoping that some worthy sop would come to love her and not her birthright. Robert looped his ankle over his knee. "Regardless, the matter is largely settled." At least in his father's eyes. The expectation being when the Duke of Wilkinson's seventeen-year-old daughter arrived in London, the unspoken arrangement would at last settle the uncertain Somerset line.

"And the lady is . . . ?"

"The Duke of Wilkinson's daughter," he supplied.

"Ah," Jonas said, inclining his head.

Yes, well, really what else was there to say, other than that? He shifted in his seat. Lords made matches with younger ladies every day. It was expected and the norm, and yet . . . there was something . . . wholly distasteful in the prospect of wedding a woman more than fifteen years younger.

"Of all the families to merge the Denningtons with, the Verney line is an honorable one." And a wealthy one. That admission hung unspoken between them. He shifted in his seat. If he entered into a union to salvage his family's wealth, then he was no different than Lucy Whitman. He fisted his hands. He could not marry with those ugly intentions. Surely there was something—

"I am sorry," Jonas said quietly, bringing him back from his contemplation.

Robert forced a laugh. "So hopelessly in love are you that you'd bemoan my emotionless, though advantageous, match?"

His friend met his dry amusement with a sad, penetrating look. "I had hoped for more for you."

He turned his attention to his drink. He'd never been one of those lords who'd spouted sonnets with romantic expectations for himself. Having been groomed for the position of duke from the nursery, he'd learned early on the expectations and responsibilities that would belong to him. He lifted his shoulders in a shrug. "It is the way of our world," he said with a pragmatism that elicited another frown.

Rolling his shoulders, Robert glanced about the club once more when, from the corner of his eye, the peculiar woman from before recalled his attention.

Attired in a modest green satin gown, she did not wear the same outrageous, gauzy creations donned by the other women wandering the floor. Her scarred pale cheeks, absent of rouge, and her lips devoid of color also marked her as a further oddity, different than the other whores employed at the Hell and Sin. As she darted her gaze about, Robert's intrigue doubled. A small frown pulled at her lips and she again ducked further behind the lone pillar, pressing herself against it as though she wished to become one with the towering white structure.

Since he'd begun patronizing the Hell and Sin Club he'd never before spied the tall, lean creature. He finished his brandy. He would have remembered one such as her. She was not in possession of the beauty to match the voluptuous, blousy creatures who were the Hell's regular girls, and yet the wistful gleam in her green eyes held him utterly captivated. Robert couldn't look away. Those eyes bespoke none of the jaded hardness that iced over most of the other employees. Perhaps that would come in time. For now, she'd somehow managed to retain the veneer of innocence amidst an opulent den of sinners.

His earlier desire to get well and truly soused lifted, instead replaced with curiosity for the compelling woman who peeked her head out occasionally from behind the column. Robert looked at his loyal friend. With his glass of brandy largely untouched, cradled between his fingers, he made clear by his presence that Robert had his unwavering support. "Go home to your wife," Robert said quietly. "You don't need to be here." At one time, after Jonas had suffered a broken heart, that hadn't been the case. Not any longer. And Robert may one day be a duke, but he'd never be one of those stodgy bastards who expected the world to wait and watch for him because of the title affixed to his name.

Jonas hesitated.

"Go," Robert insisted, again. He waggled his brows. "I'll finish my moping and then head back to my rooms no worse for the wear. No worries over me wandering the streets of St Giles."

His friend took a final sip of his drink and set it down. "Don't do anything reckless here," he said dryly. "We're well past our days of impetuous behaviors."

Robert drew an X on his chest. "I give you my word," his mock solemnity earning a laugh from Jonas. Smoothing his earlier amusement, he looked the other man in the eye. "Thank you," he said simply, the words enough, the meaning clear in the slight nod Jonas had given. No thanks were needed. During Jonas's darkest days, Robert had been steadfast beside him, sitting in other disreputable halls, allowing the man to drown his sorrows in spirits. "Give my best to Mrs. Jonas," he added.

"If there is anything I can do to help," his friend offered. "Anything at all . . ." His meaning clear. Robert need but ask.

"Thank you," he said again. No one but a master of numbers could salvage his family, now.

Jonas nodded, and then with a short bow took his leave.

Robert stared after him as he wound his way through the club until he reached the front doors, and then with a servant drawing them open, Jonas took his leave. Despite what his friend had hoped for or wished for Robert's own marital state, the reality had always been, and always would be, the responsibility that went with the ducal line. As a second son of a viscount, Jonas had been granted freedoms and luxuries not allowed a duke. It was simply, as Robert had said prior, the way of their world.

Shoving aside thoughts of future brides and ducal responsibilities, Robert returned to his drink.

A short while later . . . or mayhap a long while, time had all blurred together, Robert shoved away from the gaming table. The room dipped and swayed. Then righted itself. He gripped the sides of the table and moved with slow, deliberate steps through the Hell.

The greetings shouted his way came as if down a long hall.

There seemed to be a good deal of buzz? At the hazard table about the Marquess of Westfield's inebriated state. He blinked. Wait. *I am the Marquess of Westfield.*

He frowned, rather resenting the inaccuracy. He didn't get soused. Well, this night he'd *intended* to but he'd only drunk one . . . or had it been two? Mayhap three glasses . . . ? He spun back around and glanced at the empty tumbler on his table. A lone amber drop stuck on the rim of the glass. Or was it four? Surely he'd not had four?

He gave his head a shake, and then spun around so quickly all that kept him from toppling over was the edge of a faro table. The stone-faced dealer immediately dealt him in the hand.

"Thank yooou," he slurred.

The cards blurred before his eyes. He threw down his hand. Someone slapped him on the back and a round of cheers went up at the table.

He winced. Why in hell were they cheering? The dealer shoved a pile of winnings in Robert's direction. He blinked, bleary-eyed, at another winning hand of faro and collected his coins, stuffing them into his pocket.

The din of the gaming hell blared in his skull until his gut roiled with nausea.

Or mayhap that was too much drink.

As he wound his way through the Hell and Sin Club, he struggled to see his way through the dimly lit hall filled with the plumes of cheroot smoke. He wanted to clamp his hands over his blasted ears to blot out the raucous laughter and excited calls from around the lively tables.

He exited the gaming hell through the door leading to a winding staircase, and then up to the private suites rented out by gentlemen.

Robert swiped a hand across his eye wishing he'd stopped at half the bottle of brandy. A *whole* bottle was entirely too much. At least to then be expected to climb . . . he squinted . . . one, two, three, four—

Had he counted stair four already.

He cursed.

He jabbed his finger at the stairs lined in a thin, blood-red carpet. "One-twoo-threeee . . ." Oh, hell, this really wasn't working.

Perhaps it would be easier to climb the bloody thing and count steps that way.

Robert scratched at his brow. Only . . . *Why in hell am I counting stairs?*

The stairway pitched and he grabbed the rail to steady himself.

Ah, right, the whole treachery business. After all, everyone eventually manipulated.

He shied away from the truth of his own flawed judgment, even all these years later, and instead fixed his attention on more pressing matters: climbing the stairs without toppling over and breaking his fool neck.

Where had he been before the whole maudlin reminiscences of Lucy Whitman?

Ah, yes . . . counting the stairs to his private rooms. He'd been counting stairs for reasons he still couldn't recall. Robert drew in a long, slow breath and placed his foot on the first step, beginning the long, arduous ascent upwards.

Halfway up, he pitched against the wall. He clenched his eyes and willed the staircase to remain still. "Mmusnn't realize ahm a marquess," he scolded the steps. They shifted at his pronouncement. Yes, rather pompous of him. Nor would it do to offend those stairs any further.

He reached the main level and swayed unsteadily.

Robert cursed, throwing his arms wide to balance himself.

Then took several steps down the long, narrow corridor lit with alternating sconces at each door. He stumbled against a door.

A woman wearing a dowdy nightshift appeared at the end of the long hall. A *familiar* woman. Robert squinted as a memory slid through his liquor-induced haze of the Spartan-like creature at the edge of the gaming hell floor. The *same* Spartan-like creature who now held up her arm and—a flash of silver glittered in the dark.

He scratched his brow. Perhaps the club members below had the right of it and he'd indulged in too much drink. The woman hadn't *seemed* a cutthroat earlier that night. "Are you brandishing a knife?" He winced as his voice boomed off the corridor walls.

The fiery-eyed woman narrowed on him, and then like Wellington's men set on the charge, the slim-waisted hellion flew down the hall so quickly her nightshift and wrapper danced and flapped wildly about her slender ankles.

"Indeed," he muttered to himself. It appeared he'd not overindulged quite as much as he'd thought a moment ago. She did, in fact, have a blade in her hand. A vicious-looking dagger that she wielded like a warrior princess.

"You there!" She stuck her blade out and wagged it in his direction. "What are you doing on this floor? These are Mr. Black's private apartments!"

Suddenly more clearheaded than he'd been all night, Robert took a moment to evaluate the spirited tigress. With her pale, sharp features she'd never be considered a beauty. The modest nightshift accentuated the narrowness of her hips and the trimness of her waist. Yet for the otherwise drabness of the woman, a fire danced in her green eyes, lending interest to her; that shade heightened by the tight, no doubt painful, chignon at the base of her skull. Though . . . he scratched at his brow. What was the exact shade of her hair? "Neither red nor brown," he murmured. Streaks of red in brown. Surely there was a name for such a—

The woman narrowed her eyes into thin slits. "What are you on about?" she barked, again wagging her knife.

Robert held a staying hand up. He could name all manner of wicked deeds he'd rather do with the virago than be stabbed by her. The scandal sheets would have quite a bit to say about the future Duke of Somerset being slain in the infamous club. The too-much-drink business would seem rather secondary to such a juicy morsel.

"I'm in need of my rooms." He gestured down the hall, past her shoulder.

The abrupt movement unsteadied him further. He grabbed a nearby doorjamb to keep from toppling over but slid past it. Or did the door move? How would the owners manage such a feat . . . His hand collided with a door handle, and he pitched forward into the darkened chambers.

Robert grunted, and shot his arms out to brace his fall. He landed hard on his palms and sent pain radiating up his arms. With a groan, he rolled onto his back . . . and snagged his gaze on a naughty mural of smiling, buxom ladies twined in one another's naked embraces.

He groaned as the tall, decidedly *un*smiling woman leaned over him, obliterating that delicious view. "I asked, what are you doing here?" she demanded, running a cursory glance over his person. Robert opened his mouth to speak when she buried the tip of her foot in his side, ringing a groan from him.

"Did you kick me?" he said, his words slurring together. Blasted brandy. If ever there was a moment for a proper ducal tone then this was it.

"Yes."

Quite the curt creature. With a long, painful groan that echoed around his throbbing head, he shot a hand over his eyes. "Couldn't find the sweet-mouthed beauty," he muttered.

"What was that?" The sharp sting of metal biting into the fabric of his jacket brought his eyes flying open, and he dropped his arm to his side. Robert stilled. The woman gripped a vicious dagger with unwavering strength. He swallowed back a curse, suddenly sober. Then, the threat of death had that effect. One quick movement on her part, and one flawed on his, would see him with a gleaming blade buried in his flesh. Mind muddled from too much drink, he struggled for the charming words that had served him well through the years with widows, dowagers, and debutantes alike. It really wouldn't do to insult the woman with a vicious weapon in her fingers now pointed at him. "Uh . . ." That was the best response he could muster. He shook his head on the floor. *I am never touching a bloody drink, again.*

The woman narrowed her eyes all the more. "Never mind," she muttered. "You need to go."

Some of the tension left him. Well, they appeared to agree on that score. He . . . His gaze caught the naughty scene of luscious creatures with wings. Robert squinted. Did they have wings? Like voluptuous angels. A rather ridiculous . . .

His nearly six-foot-tall assailant buried her foot in his side, once more ringing another pained groan from him. "Did you kick me again?"

"I did." She spoke between gritted teeth. "Get. Up."

Robert levered himself up with his elbows and struggled to stand.

At last, she lowered that wicked blade. "Oh, for Joan of Arc and all her army," she said, exasperation coating her tone as she offered him her free hand.

He eyed her again. Even with her five feet six or seven inches, the woman was so slender, a strong wind could knock her down. He grinned and placed his hand in hers if for no other reason than to feel the heat of her delicate palm folded inside his much larger one.

She tugged.

To no avail.

The nameless stranger grunted and gave another tug.

She pulled once more and she flew backwards, landing hard on her buttocks. Her knife clattered to the floor, the clank of it muted by the thin carpet. She sat sprawled in the midst of the hall, her skirts rucked up about her knees. The severe chignon that held her brownish-red locks at the base of her neck tumbled free and her hair cascaded down about her shoulders and trim waist.

He blinked several times. "By God." *She really is rather . . . pretty.* In an odd, too-tall, sharp-featured way. In a way he'd never genuinely preferred.

The tall woman blew back the strand that fell across her eyes. "What is it?" Even drunk as he was, he'd have to be deaf to fail and hear the hesitancy in that query, so at odds with a hellcat who'd put a blade to his person.

Given their exchange thus far, compliments would only be wasted on her. Ignoring her question, he attempted to rise.

The woman hopped to her feet and hurriedly retrieved her knife. A moment later, she returned with a hand extended, once more.

This time, he allowed her to help him to his feet. "I need my rooms, and a warm bath and food." *Otherwise, I'm going to wake devilishly ill.*

An inelegant snort escaped her pouty lips. "I'd wager you'll wake devilishly ill regardless of what you eat this late hour, sir."

Sir?

He scratched at his brow and looked about for this sir-fellow she referred to.

She sighed. "You must go that way, sir."

Oh, *he* was the sir she spoke of. Not: my lord. Not: Lord Westfield. He found he preferred the anonymity of a simple "sir."

Displeasure snapped in her expressive eyes, and she wagged her hand. Shaking his head, Robert followed her pointed finger and the room lurched. He managed a jerky nod.

The woman peered down her nose at him. He frowned. As the future Duke of Somerset, he was sought after by young ladies, his presence desired by the most distinguished hostesses, and yet, not once had anyone ever condescended to look at him like this fiery-eyed woman whose sneer penetrated even his drunken stupor. Did she see him as the same reckless, witless dandies who wagered away their fortunes and drowned themselves in spirits nightly? "I'll have you know, I do not drink in excess," he slurred. For, somehow, being viewed in that same, unfavorable light, grated.

She snorted.

He bristled. "I don't."

"No matter," she said with a flick of her luxuriant tresses. She pointed behind her once more. "You need to walk down the corridor, past the long-case clock . . ." Her words droned on and on. The husky, almost musical quality to her contralto lulled him to distraction . . .

The earth swayed under his feet yet again and he tumbled into an ignoble heap at the feet of his dagger-wielding, blood-thirsty hellion.

She cursed roundly, the words vulgar enough to make a guard at Newgate's cheeks burn.

How very refreshing that with all the practiced words and false smiles around him, her response should be so honest. He grinned.

The woman planted her arms akimbo. "Do you find this amusing?"

"Er . . ." Her glare killed the admission on his lips. Either way, he would have chosen entertaining and diverting, and yes, he supposed amusing. Given the turn of events, he did find this whole exchange amusing. Listening to a tart-mouthed, fiery-eyed stranger and her inventive curses was vastly preferable to the thoughts that had driven him to the club.

She nudged him with the tip of her foot and as he tipped his head sideways, his gaze caught on dainty toes. Odd, he'd never before appreciated just how enticing a pair of feet happened to be. He fixed his tired stare on her right foot and the slightly crooked littlest toe. How very *endearing* . . . that slight imperfection on an otherwise perfect foot.

His eyes grew heavy, even as her melodic words washed over him, lulling him to sleep.

Chapter 4

Rule 4
Never approach a drunken man.

With the exception of her brother, Ryker, his partners, and Clara, the woman responsible for the prostitutes, no one entered the main living quarters of the hall.

Many, nay, nearly *all* women would have dissolved into a fit of tears or given over to the vapors at coming upon a strange gentleman in her home, but it would take more than a drunken gentleman to rouse fear in Helena Banbury's breast.

Standing in the main corridor of the Hell and Sin Club's owner suite, with a too-tall, well-muscled stranger, Ryker's fourth rule blared around her brain.

Never approach a drunken man.

How many times had those words been impressed into her? If her brother knew she'd been so foolhardy as to investigate the commotion instead of turning the lock and ringing for a servant, he'd build a keep and lock her away in it as he always threatened to do when she was a girl.

Except, Ryker really should have amended the rule to include, "Never approach a well-muscled gentleman more than half a foot taller than oneself." It put one at an extreme disadvantage.

A bleating snore escaped the same gentleman she'd been studying earlier on the gaming floor. Now thoroughly foxed and graceless, he bore no hint of the commanding, slightly sad figure seated alone at his table. She leaned over, her knife extended out toward him, and then waved the blade in front of his harshly beautiful face. Why . . . why . . . he'd gone and fallen asleep! *Here.* With the tip of her foot, Helena nudged him in the leg. She frowned when her ineffectual efforts were met with another broken snore. Some of the anxiety slid from her taut frame, as the earlier threat of a drunk, unpredictable stranger lifted. Helena fisted her blade, her gaze inextricably drawn to him. Over the years she'd made it a point to never look at noblemen visiting the clubs, either from her window or the floors when she was permitted to walk about during the day. Those men were treacherous fiends with but one thing on their minds where a woman of her station was concerned.

In the countless rules Ryker had heaped upon her shoulders, most had pertained to the unreliability and depravity of noblemen who believed women existed as nothing more than as diversions from their staid, proper lives. Avoid their attention at all costs. The lesson she'd learned at her brokenhearted mother's side had been lesson enough.

Or apparently not, given her unwitting fascination with this particular stranger. It was just . . . She chewed the inside of her cheek.

She stole a nervous glance about. There was no harm in simply *looking* at the lofty lord. Especially if that same lofty lord in his passed-out, inebriated state remained wholly unaware. She took a step closer to study him.

This stranger, however, in his immaculate black coat and crisp white cravat had the mesmerizing look of no other man she'd ever before seen.

Granted, her exposure to the world was rather limited, but this inexplicable pull held her enthralled. Perhaps it was the halo of unfashionably long, golden strands or the firm, unyielding jaw gentled just the slightest bit by a faint cleft at the center of his chin.

Blade held protectively close, Helena carefully lowered herself to the floor, and continued her examination. With his blond, golden lashes and the sculpted quality of his sharp features, he was far more beautiful than any man had a right to be.

She swallowed hard, and stole another look about. If she were discovered, her brothers would commit her to Bedlam for her folly in remaining at a drunken nobleman's side. Except she was riveted, transfixed by the glorious golden perfection of him. Her heart hammering wildly, she returned her attention to the stranger and gasped as his eyes flew open, and he smiled.

Butterflies danced riotously inside her stomach. Where was the proper fear and wariness? She'd long prided herself on being logical and practical in all matters.

For . . . with the previous distance between them in the darkened room, their color had eluded her. Endless blue. The color she imagined a countryside summer sky to be. Not that she'd ever been outside the dark, grimy streets of London. Nor likely would ever be, to verify such ponderings. But in her mind, she imagined the country to be different . . . and have the look of . . . this stranger's eyes.

Even drunk, there was an intelligence in his gaze, an intensity, as though he could see every foolish yearning she'd hidden from even herself.

Eyes that also suggested he knew he'd been the object of her scrutiny. A devilish half grin tugged at his lips, jerking her back from the momentary insanity that had clouded her senses.

Her skin awash with humiliated heat, Helena hopped to her feet. "You need to leave." She jabbed her finger toward the long-case clock. "Now." Squaring her shoulders, she stood with her feet spread, hands on her hips, until the intruder stood up and stumbled down the opposite direction. He turned the corner, and some of the tension left her. From down the length of the hall, a loud thump, followed by some inventive curses, reached her ears. Then silence, as he took his leave altogether.

She gave her head a disgusted shake, starting for her rooms once more. These were sad days indeed, when an exchange with a drunken stranger should highlight her otherwise tedious existence here.

She reached her chambers and pressed the handle.

Tension twisting inside, Helena began to pace. The *audacity* of him. To enter the private suites and collapse into his drunken stupor no less. She tapped the hilt of her knife against her palm. It would have served the scoundrel right if she'd summoned one of the men and had him physically removed.

So why didn't you?

The strategically stationed guards alternated shifts throughout the day but someone was assigned to those positions at all times. Only her own earlier foray onto the gaming floor, the crowded tables and crush of patrons, merited one of the guards stepping away from his post.

Ryker would have bloodied senseless the employee who'd abandoned his post, and then tossed the careless man into the street for his failings. Having lived with the uncertainty of nothing but fear and hunger for company, she'd not risk another's security in that way . . . even if he'd demonstrated an egregious lack of judgment.

But that is not the only reason, a voice needled at the back of her head. For if she were being honest, with at least herself . . . her reasons for not summoning Ryker moved beyond a noble reason to protect a guard from a beating and firing.

Had she raised an alarm, her brother's men would have broken more than the stranger's nose for having even walked the same halls as Helena's chambers—and such an elegant, aquiline nose deserved far more than that ignoble fate.

Filled with restive energy, she strode over to the rose-inlaid secretaire stacked with ledgers. Since her brother had hired her the best tutors, and she'd discovered a calming peace in the constancy of those numbers, they alone made sense. They could be understood and explained. And more . . . they posed a distraction from the hellish memories that could only come from living on the streets, at the mercy of a ruthless gang. Helena tossed her knife atop the leather book containing last year's numbers for the club and pressed her fingertips against her temples. In this instance, her mind was too muddled to work through the numbers Ryker expected of her tomorrow.

Restless, she peeled back the edge of the thick, sapphire-blue curtain and gazed down into the dangerous streets of St Giles. Even with the distance between her and the ground, the clatter of carriage wheels passing and raucous shouts from the streets carried up to her lone room. She rested her brow against the window and studied two dandies who stumbled out of the club and spilled into the streets, a bright splash of garish color in a dark night. How very small her world was. Envy twisted inside at the power granted and permitted men and gentlemen alike. In the company of a drunken stranger, all her deepest, long-buried yearnings to know a world beyond these walls reared once more. Oh, she didn't desire the company of a drunkard. She'd dealt with enough beatings and lashings at the hands of one of those unpredictable bastards: the man her mother had married after her protector had turned her out.

But did she truly wish to remain an accountant and nothing more? A woman not many years off from her thirtieth year, she'd never left London or interacted with anyone beyond a handful of de facto family inside the Hell and Sin. Was it a wonder she was more comfortable with numbers than people?

With a sigh she let the curtain go and rescued the ledger at the top of the pile, along with one of the many pairs of spectacles that littered the club. She studied her glasses, fiddling with the wire frames. She'd been so content with managing the books that she'd not given true thought to what she wanted her future to be. With the increasing limits placed on her movements inside and outside the club, she'd begun to chafe at those boundaries imposed. For the vital role she contributed to the success of the club, she was still largely . . . powerless. With that absolute lack of control, she'd come to appreciate everything she did hunger for: the ability to go where she wished, the freedom to speak to whomever she wanted, and the right to play a public role in the running of the club, not play in the carefully guarded secret it had been.

Shoving aside the brewing frustration, Helena put her spectacles on, collected the ledger, and made her way across the room. There was no room or place for woolgathering at the Hell and Sin, and most especially not when her reports were still unfinished.

Helena climbed into the massive four-poster bed and in the dim light cast by the fire in the hearth, reviewed the previous year's liquor expenses. The faint ticking of the porcelain clock at the side of her bed marked the passing moments in a grating, staccato rhythm, cutting across her efforts.

Unbidden, her gaze drifted from the page over to the door, as the stranger's visage wandered through her thoughts once more. Who was he, the late-night wanderer with his sad eyes who'd buried that misery in drink?

For the course of her life, with her brother's tutelage, she'd been trained to see noblemen as emotionless, unfeeling bastards. It had been a lesson already learned through her own experience on the streets as a child, begging for a coin at the hands of those lords and ladies, only to be invisible in her struggles.

Yet, the depth of emotion she'd spied in the blond stranger's agonized gaze contradicted those long-held truths. What pain should *he* know that he'd imbibe to the point of falling all over himself in such a disreputable gaming hell? Oh, yes, her brother said all men imbibed, but when she'd spied him in the club, there had been a wealth of emotion in his eyes. An intelligence and somberness absent in most of the men she observed from her lonely window abovestairs.

All that emotion had been lost to the effects of alcohol, but so remained the questions about what had driven him to lose himself in that bottle. "Enough," she muttered, and abandoning all hope of work, she slammed the ledger shut with a comforting thump. She tossed it onto her nightstand.

It spoke volumes to her predictable existence that she should allow one chance meeting with a drunken stranger to shape her thoughts and wonderings. She yanked off her spectacles, and dropped them atop the leather book.

Helena burrowed into the downy-soft feather mattress . . . and stared unblinking at the ceiling above. She frowned, and wiggled in her spot. Too many nights she'd lain awake, dreading the nightmares that came when she drifted off to sleep. With an aggravated sigh, she flipped onto her side . . . and looked at the opposite wall. Tonight's restlessness had nothing to do with the demons that lurked from her past.

Rather, the wicked grin of a powerfully built gentleman haunted her waking thoughts.

Firm lips found the sensitive spot along her neck, where her pulse fluttered. With a shameful moan, Helena turned into that sweet caress. In response, the stranger ran a large, strong hand over her back, lower, ever lower. He tugged at the hem of her nightgown. His fingers danced along her skin, and she arched, a breathless cry escaping her. His lips moved from the sweet spot he loved on her neck and she moaned in protest, but he merely shifted his attention to the peak of one breast. Her hips shot off the bed as she begged for more. Not knowing in her innocence what more was, but knowing he would show her.

And he did.

Another groan escaped her as he shoved her modest nightshift higher still. He searched his palms over the curve of her hips, and pulled her buttocks close against the vee of his hard thighs.

Heat, the kind rained down by a stream of sunlight, bathed Helena from within. The sensation filled every corner of her once-chilled body—

Helena jerked upright. Her chest moved quickly from the force of her dream. Not the nightmares which so often plagued her but rather a dream which a virgin, still at four and twenty, had no business having. With the clock ticktocking a grating staccato beat in the silence, Helena pressed her palms to her flaming cheeks, and concentrated on drawing in slow, even breaths. It was all manner of things improper and scandalous, and yet . . . Helena closed her eyes and fought to draw forth the memory of the faceless stranger who'd come to her. His unidentifiable features shifted in and out of focus, until he was transformed into a bold, midnight visitor with the face and physique of a Greek god carved in stone, so vastly preferable to the horrors that often dogged her sleep.

"Enough," she mumbled. There was business to attend. There was *always* business to attend. She glanced to the slight crack in the brocade curtains and choked. Sunlight filtered through that narrow opening. *Daylight?* Surely not. She shot her gaze to the clock. Ten minutes past nine? A groan spilled from her lips and she covered her face with her hands.

Making it a point to rise just before the sun peeked over the horizon, she never slept in. Laziness and sloth were unpardonable sins in the Hell and Sin Club, and she held herself to the same high standard Ryker expected of all his employees. She'd worked to build her position as one to command respect for what she *did* for the club and not her relationship to the owner of it.

Helena flopped back, her head colliding with the soft, still-warm pillow, and closing her eyes she ran anxiously through her daily tasks. The books needed tending. She still had to prepare the liquor reports for Ryker, and with the mess they were in, and her lolling about in bed, she'd be behind in her work. She was never, *ever* late in completing a—

A loud snore penetrated the quiet and she froze.

Tick-tock-tick-tock.

Helena whipped her head to the right, and her gaze landed on the same golden stranger who'd slipped into her dreams. All air left her on a swift exhale, as the wicked memories of her dream came rushing forward.

It had been a dream. Mayhap it still was a dream.

She quickly yanked her attention upwards, concentrating on the faint crack in the plaster, on the tick of the clock, on anything other than the panic roiling in her breast.

Angling her head ever so slightly, she stole a sideways peek. *Oh, bloody hell!*

The aquiline nose and high, proud cheekbones lent the midnight wanderer an aura of strength and confidence, even in sleep. Her breath came in quick, panicked spurts and she promptly pressed her eyes closed. Unleashing a silent stream of vicious curses, she forced herself to look at the man lying beside her. In her bed. Her redundant, panicked thoughts rolled over each other and she attempted to slow them as they rapidly careened out of control. Her lips still burned from the memory of . . .

She pressed her fingers to her swollen mouth, tamping down a groan. He'd kissed her. Helena slapped her palms over her face. How had she failed to lock her door? That rule had been the simplest of all the bloody rules laid out by Ryker. Pressure built behind her eyes as she tried to dredge up details of what had transpired after she'd finally managed to find sleep. She'd been so distracted by her encounter with the tall, golden-haired devil in the corridor, she'd not taken all of the one second it would have required to lock the door. She rubbed the points at her temples in a vain attempt to wake from this horrific nightmare.

To no avail. Sickening waves of nausea slammed into her as she tried to sort out that which had been a dream and what was, in fact, her reality.

And if he'd kissed her . . . Her jumbled thoughts skidded to a stop, and then picked up at a frantic pace. Oh, God. Her body still burned with the memory of the handsome stranger's touch. What if she'd wantonly turned over her virginity to the golden-haired lord? What if in her slumber, somewhere between dream and fantasy, she'd made love with him?

Helena set her teeth hard in her lower lip. Having guarded her virtue when most children and women in the streets were robbed early on of that gift, surely she'd know if she was now *without*? One of the girls employed by Ryker had taken the liberty of answering the questions Helena once had about what occurred in the rooms rented by the powerful peers. Determined to maintain her freedom and safety, Helena had resolved to never marry. As such, she had not really given much thought on that long-ago lesson. Now she wished she had. She quickly ran through all the words imparted that day. There had been talk of pain and discomfort and bleeding, even during that first encounter. She shifted her buttocks, moving her legs experimentally. There was no pain.

Lifting the sheet ever so slightly, she glanced about for any hint of crimson stains. Instead . . . she gulped, her eyes landing on the broad, naked chest of her bed-partner. Coils of golden hair upon a muscular canvas. Her mouth went dry and she searched desperately for the far safer panic and fury. Instead, her curious eyes wandered downward.

He still wore breeches.

Grateful for small measures, Helena cast a prayer skyward.

The gentleman at her side let out another bleating snore and she jumped. He flung an arm across her stomach, effectively trapping her. His touch penetrated the thin fabric of her nightshift.

With panic wildly spiraling, she tried to lift his muscled arm from her person, but he may as well have been carved of iron.

If she could manage to quickly dress and escape, then none would be the wiser to the fact that she'd spent the night with this man. With her parentage and upbringing, she would never be a respected lady, but she had her virtue and that meant something in her world, where girls tossed away their virginity for some coin and a hot meal. She pressed the backs of her hands against her eyes. Or she had, until last evening. Panic grew in her breast, suffocating.

Renewing her wiggling, Helena managed to scoot out from under his arm. Free of his hold, she stopped. Holding her breath, she stole another glance at the stranger.

His thick, blond lashes fluttered, lashes that no man should have the good fortune to possess. He turned his head on the pillow and their gazes collided.

A lazy grin played on his firm lips. "You," he said, his voice hoarse, and then he promptly winced.

No doubt alcohol had left him with the deuced awful headache. *Good, the bloody bugger.*

And because he had a grin as wide as the cat who'd caught the kitchen mouse, she hissed, "You bastard." How dare he look so . . . so . . . pleased with himself.

His grin fell, and he blinked several times.

Helena snapped her eyebrows into a line. Did he believe she would be thrilled by his presence in her bed? The arrogance of these nobles. She opened her mouth to blister his ears.

"What are you doing in my rooms?" he asked, his voice gravelly. "Not that I'm complaining or ungrateful." He winked.

Winked.

Winked?

As though she were some kind of Covent Garden doxy. "Did you *wink* at me?" Her hushed whisper shook with fury.

"I—"

Not wanting another one of his smug words or smiles, she used the full force of her body to shove him over the side of the bed. She panted heavily, out of breath from her exertions, rewarded a moment later as he landed with a loud thump.

He grunted, and then fell silent.

Gripping the edge of the mattress, she pulled herself over to glance down. Not taking her gaze from him, she fished around the edge of her bed for the handle of her dagger. Relief surged through her as her fingers met the reassuring cool of the steel blade.

"You certainly didn't need to enter my rooms if you didn't desire my attentions," he drawled in that gruff, lazy baritone that ran warm over her.

"Your rooms?" she squawked. With stiff, jerky movements, she leapt off the bed and kicked him in the shins. "You, sir, entered *mine*." She should have called for the guards last evening. Foolishly she'd believed the problem of the wandering stranger ended when she'd pointed him on his way, and then disappeared down the opposite hall.

So many mistakes. Too many of them.

The gentleman swiped his hands over his eyes. "Impossible," he muttered, those clipped, precise tones, a testament to his birth, sending outrage spiraling all the more.

In a world where you possessed nothing more valuable than your word, this man would throw into question her honor? "I am not a liar," she bit out, and kicked him again, this time in the lower portion of his well-muscled stomach. Who knew noblemen were so expertly sculpted in that region?

Fury flashed in his eyes, and he grunted. "If you are wise, madam, you will refrain from kicking me."

Helena spoke through gritted teeth. "I've faced far more threatening creatures in my life," unarmed no less, "than one inert, pompous toff."

He tightened his mouth. "I must say I've never received quite a reaction after spending the night in a woman's b—"

Helena buried her foot in his hip. "The insolence of you," she whispered furiously. As though she'd ever bed such an insufferable, overbearing lout. She studied him a moment: tall, elegant, graceful, refined. Everything she would never have. Everything she should never want. He remained seated with his knees drawn up, sinfully beautiful even in repose.

She swallowed hard. *Rule fifty-seven . . . do not desire insufferable, overbearing noblemen.* She brought her foot back. In one swift movement, he caught her ankle and yanked hard.

Helena gasped, and teetered precariously. She shot her arms out, righted herself, and brought her heel down hard on the inset of his palm, satisfaction surging through her at the hiss of pain to slip past his lips.

"Bloody hell," he barked.

Again, he tugged at her ankle.

She toppled forward. Her blade flew over his shoulder and fell uselessly to the carpet. Sprawled upon his naked chest, she forlornly eyed her weapon. Disarmed by a fancy lord. Whatever would her brother say?

Helena stiffened as the man settled his hands loosely about her waist, hovering a moment, and then traveled higher, almost searching, exploring her. He rolled her onto the carpet and came up over her. He propped himself upon his elbows and effectively blocked escape.

Trapped in the frame of his powerful arms, she swallowed hard. Weren't lords supposed to be well-padded, well-rounded figures? This gentleman was chiseled in muscle to rival a stone statue she'd once seen at the British Museum she'd insisted Ryker take her to one birthday. They two had earned disapproving glances and condescending sneers from the other visitors that day. It had been the last time she'd ever wanted to enter the glittering world of the haute ton.

"My name is Robert."

She gritted her teeth. "I don't care if you are a duke or prince or the King of England." The ghost of a smile played on his lips, and he palmed her cheek, quelling the vitriolic curses she'd been about to heap on his arrogant head. Her breath caught at his gentle caress. Never in the course of her life had a man put his hands upon her in anything other than violence. As a young woman and now a woman, her brother would maim or kill the man who dared to touch her as this man now did. For a heady moment borne of madness, she closed her eyes and accepted the gentle ministrations of even this stranger. "After our meeting in the corridor, I do not remember last evening," he said quietly. He brushed the pad of his thumb over her lower lip and her mouth trembled.

Was there regret in his admission?

She bit the inside of her cheek to keep silent.

"What is your name?" he pressed.

She shot a longing glance over to the door and a brownish-red tress fell over her eye. She blew it back. When it became apparent he had no intention of relinquishing his strong hold on her, she capitulated. "Helena."

"Helena," he repeated, as though testing it. He brushed the stubborn lock back. "It rather suits you."

Perhaps noblemen were sorcerers after all. For instead of the appropriate reservations, the hard wall of his body flush against hers stirred a shameful wanton heat at her core. "Why?" The breathy utterance tumbled from her lips.

Robert brought the strand to his nose and breathed in. "Whimsical, fanciful, bold. There is nothing common about you, Helena."

She curled her toes into the soles of her feet. A bastard daughter raised in the streets by a violent gang of warring young men, there was *everything* common about her.

Which only stirred the long-carried hatred and fury for all men of his ilk, who'd failed to see lesser people like her around, and killed the hypnotic hold he'd woven. "How fancy you are with your words," she spat. "I'm not so foolish that I'd be swayed by your glib tongue." Deep inside, where truth lived, she recognized the lie there. "But then a man who'd force himself inside a woman's room and steal into her bed would hardly care." She renewed her struggles, twisting and gyrating under him, ringing an agonized groan from Lord Robert With-No-Surname.

"Will you stop moving?" There was a pleading quality to those words, as if he were in pain.

Then against her belly, his manhood prodded her and she froze. She was a virgin still, but she was not so much an innocent that she didn't understand the significance of that hardness. Heat scorched a path up her body.

With his thumb, the stranger continued that distracting little movement that sent the oddest flurry of sensation throughout her being. He went on, his tone far gentler than she'd expect from one such as him. "I'd not ever force myself on a woman."

No, with a face and frame to rival the archangel Gabriel, he wouldn't need to. She clamped her lips tight.

"Nor do I normally make it a habit of getting soused . . ." A mottled flush stained his cheeks as though he were embarrassed by his actions last evening. Which was preposterous.

Noblemen were overindulgent, self-serving cads who placed their material comforts above all else. "I do not normally imbibe as I did," he finished quietly.

She pressed her lips into a firm line, stoically silent. All gentlemen indulged as he had. The dwindling week's supply of spirits was testament of that.

"You need to leave," she said quietly, as reason righted her world. It mattered not the mistakes that had found him in her chambers, or her outraged fury. Now, all that mattered was getting rid of him before—

Footsteps sounded in the corridor, and then someone rapped on her door. Helena's heart caught and she swung her gaze to the front of the room. "Are you awake?" Clara asked through the wood panel.

"Ryker wants you in his office," Clara called. Helena's mind raced. She wasn't scheduled to meet with Ryker. Why would he . . . ?

The ticking of the clock thundered in her chambers. Of its own volition, her gaze went to the intruder. She needed to get Robert out *now*!

Another knock split the quiet. "Helena?" Concern laced the other woman's tone. Well, mayhap not *this* exact moment.

"I believe she requires an—"

At that mellifluous whisper, Helena wiggled her hand free and slammed her palm over the man's lips. "Er . . . j-just a moment," she called out, glaring him into silence.

"Did you say something?"

"No!" she called.

Clara jiggled the door handle. "Is everything all right? Should I get Ryk—"

"Fine! I'm fine," she said, steadying her voice. "Tell him I'll be but a moment."

With the woman's retreating footsteps, Helena swung her gaze back to the stranger who'd stolen into her bedsheets and dragged her fingers through her tangled hair. Oh, God. What if Clara had gone to fetch Ryker? If he discovered this stranger in her chambers, Ryker would bloody him within an inch of his life, and then her judgment would forever be questioned in sleeping with a nobleman, and then who knew what he'd do. She closed her eyes once more, frozen.

Tick-tock-tick-tock-tick-tock.

Oh, bloody hell. This was bad.

Very bad, indeed.

Chapter 5

Rule 5
Always be prepared to properly defend yourself.

Robert should release the fiery vixen. It was, after all, the gentlemanly thing to do, and no one in the realm would dare accuse Robert of anything but being a gentleman. Well, a rogue, mayhap . . . but never a scoundrel who'd prey on a woman who did not desire his intentions.

When he'd brought the then-nameless Spartan warrioress down beneath him, his original intention had merely been to put a quick end to her assault. Now, with the dagger gone from her hands and her feet clearly contained, he paid attention to far more pleasurable details. Her small breasts pressed against his naked chest, the nipples pebbling against his skin. Desire surged through him, momentarily blotting out logic and all earlier threats from this woman's mouth.

Robert lowered his brow to hers.

She flared her eyes. "Wh-what are you d-doing?" she whispered, that faint, husky tremor hinting at her desire.

"Kissing you." For even as she'd never possess the beauty to inspire sonnets or poets, there was something captivating about her.

She squeaked. "You most certainly aren't. Not unless you wish to feel the wrath of Ryker." Except instead of turning away, she closed her eyes and angled her head up ever so slightly to receive his kiss.

He smiled. The spirited vixen was a riddle wrapped in a puzzle.

"Very well," he drawled, and Helena's eyes flew open.

"Who is Ryker?" He settled his hands on her waist to still her enticing movements.

Her eyes formed round circles. "Uh . . . *Mr.* Black. The proprietor of the club." Ah, the infamous owner of the Hell, known only as Black. "He wouldn't tolerate anyone wandering his apartments or touching me."

She was Black's mistress, then. A rush of disappointment followed that revelation. With her spirit and passion, she would prove an enthusiastic lover. The notoriously ruthless owner would no doubt take apart the man who'd dared put his lips and hands upon her person. "He expects loyalty then."

Helena jutted her chin up a notch. "He *commands* loyalty with his actions."

A surge of jealousy potent and powerful ran through him at the sign of her faithfulness. As the recipient of nothing but treachery and deceit, he'd long ago accepted no woman's intentions were truly honorable, but rather always self-serving. With her defense, this woman contradicted all he'd long accepted as truth.

"Mayhap," he whispered against her ear, deliberately baiting. "But your breathlessness hints at your desire for me." Robert brushed his mouth over hers, in a fleeting kiss, allowing her to pull away. But she leaned into his embrace, returning his kiss. Robert drew back and she blinked rapidly.

A gasp spilled from her lips and she wiggled her knee. "Bastard," she gritted as he shifted, narrowly missing her blow. "I want you gone and if you're wise, you'll not come back." No doubt those were the truest words ever spoken in this club. And yet . . . With a grunt, he rolled to his side and in one fluid movement, drew her back against him. The minx wiggled her rounded buttocks and his shaft jumped. With a groan, he closed his eyes, and counted to ten. Then prayed for patience and when both proved ineffective, he laid her down upon the floor once more.

He searched his gaze over her face. "Do you want me to release you?" he whispered against the corner of her mouth.

Her long brown lashes fluttered wildly and she leaned into him. She gave her head the slightest shake.

After Lucy's treachery he'd come to appreciate that the safest, truest connection with a woman was the pleasure to be found in her arms. Robert rolled to his side and pulled her close, so quickly their bodies never broke contact.

"What are you d-doing?" Her breathless question enflamed his senses.

He touched the tip of his finger to her lower lip. Even in his drunken stupor the previous evening, her spirit had beckoned. Though she'd never be considered any beauty in any sense of the word, there was a raw realness to the woman that set her apart from any of the respectable ladies or less respectable courtesans he'd ever met. "Kissing you again."

He braced for the flash of spirit in her expressive eyes. Instead, a breathy sigh escaped her, the faint stirring of air brushing against his skin, and she tipped her head back.

Desire pulsing through him, Robert slowly lowered his mouth close to hers. If she pulled away, if she rejected him in the slightest, he'd set her free. "I do not remember how I came to be in your bed, only that I did. My only regret is that I was too bloody soused to remember the feel of you in my arms."

Her breath caught on an audible intake.

This woman in his arms would forever remind him of the perils of drink. To not recall what had transpired, if anything at all, was the greatest of tragedies. "And if I let you go now, if I let you flee without kissing you, I shall forever regret it."

Only, he suspected that after feeling her lush hips in his hand, the swell of her buttocks, that a mere kiss would never be enough.

He trailed the tip of his tongue over the seam of her lips.

Her breath caressed his lips. "Y-you shouldn't," she said, the protest halfhearted.

He touched his lips to the corner of her mouth. "I should," he whispered. "May I kiss you?"

Surprise glinted in her eyes, but she said nothing and with a groan he took her lips under his. Slanting his mouth over hers again and again. The seductive scent of lavender and lemon that clung to her skin invaded his senses, more intoxicating than all of the spirits he'd consumed last evening, and he deepened his kiss.

With a moan she slipped her arms from between their bodies, and twined them about his neck. Encouraged, he took her hips firmly in hand and anchored her to the center of his thighs.

A low, strangled groan spilled from her lips and he swallowed the sound. Robert found her tongue with his, tasting, exploring, branding her as his.

He worked the edge of her skirts up and her thighs fell open in invitation.

Robert wedged his knee between her slender legs and pressed hard against her hot center. He rocked his leg against her in a slow, undulating movement. "Please," she moaned, arching against him. He worked his hand between them and brushed the wisp of curls that shielded her womanhood.

A keening little cry escaped her and he again consumed that heady sound. He shifted his lips away from hers and trailed a path of kisses along her jaw, down her neck, lower to the soft swell of her cream-white breasts, and then closed his mouth around her nipple and she gripped his head, anchoring him close. Desire surged through him and he worked her nightshift up. "Helena," he breathed against her skin.

Her eyes flew open on a gasp. Horror etched her features and in one swift movement, she brought her knee up quick between his legs.

With a hiss of pain, he rolled away, clutching himself.

In a brilliant blaze of shock and fury, Helena leapt to her feet. "Don't you ever . . . how dare . . ."

"Words, princess," he rasped, and through the tortured agony of movement rose unsteadily to his feet.

She clasped hands at the bodice of her nightshift, clenching and unclenching her fingers. "How dare you." Her eyes formed round circles. She searched around, and he followed her gaze to the flash of silver on the floor. The muscles of his body went taut and he dove for the knife before the harpy took it to her head to bury her blade in his heart. Or worse . . .

Helena stumbled back. "Hand me my weapon, sir." And if she hadn't nearly unmanned him moments ago, he'd have felt like the worst sort of bounder for the high-pitch panic in her demand.

Robert held the dagger above her reach. If she believed for one moment he intended to hand a dagger over to a woman spitting mad with fury—a fury directed at him—she was madder than old King George himself. He stuck the blade between his teeth. "Do you know?" he bit around the edge of the blade. "I don't believe I will."

As he retrieved his rumpled shirt and pulled it over his head, a stream of inventive curses filtered about the room. Taking a perverse delight in ignoring the woman's clear outrage, he next stuffed his arms into the sleeves of his coat.

"Did you hear me?" she demanded, her chest rising and falling.

He sat at the edge of the bed, with the sheets still wrinkled from their night together, and tugged on a boot. "Which part?" he drawled.

"Your question about my paternity?" Robert paused midreach for the other boot to lift a brow. "Or your accusation of my possible proclivity for carnal activities with a female dog?"

She gritted her teeth so hard, the sound of it reached past the space separating them.

"I said I want my—"

"You'll have your knife. As soon as I'm ready to take my leave. I'd be mad to trust you won't stick your wicked blade in my belly."

If looks could kill, he'd be a smote pile of ash at the foot of her rumpled bed. "I wouldn't stick it in your *belly.*"

As he'd suspected. He waggled his eyebrows. "That hardly inspires the level of confidence that merits returning a weapon to your possession," he said, removing the knife from between his clamped teeth. Robert waved it and the woman followed those deliberately casual movements with her furious gaze. "But at least be honest, princess. For all your indignation, I gave you leave to rebuff my kiss." He tucked the knife between his teeth once more so he might pull up his other boot. "I don't make a habit of drinking or forcing my attention on uninterested women," Robert said around the blade. He winged an eyebrow up. "Nor did I imagine your moans and the warmth betwixt your beautiful thighs."

Color flamed her cheeks, a reaction at odds with the experienced women who lived in this den of sin. "By God, when you hand over my bloody knife I will bury it in your heart, you son of a bastard."

Now, *that* vitriolic diatribe was what one would expect of an experienced woman living in a den of sin.

He had been going to return the weapon to her care. Now he'd be a bloody fool to trust any weapon to this one's hands. At last managing to yank his boot up, Robert leapt to a stand. Removing the knife from between his teeth, he strode to the door.

The spitfire's gasp echoed around the room. "What are you doing?" she called as his fingers collided with the door handle.

Robert paused, and tossed a glance over his shoulder. "This is what one calls *leaving*, madam." He opened the door just as her quiet cry went up.

"Sir, my knife!"

He closed the door between them with a soft, decisive click. He'd wait a moment until the woman was calmed and then he'd leave the blade to her care. Robert reached for the handle.

A soft thump hit the paneled door and he'd wager the rumpled clothes he now wore that the little shrew had tossed her boot at the door. Another thump followed.

He sheathed the blade in his boot. Mayhap, he'd return the weapon at a later date. Which would require again seeing the prickly miss. Robert grinned. Yes, perhaps he'd wait after all.

The distant rumble of male voices sounded from around the hall and Robert started in the opposite direction. He quickened his stride, making for a staircase. No doubt, title of marquess be damned, the whispered-about owner would take umbrage with a patron infiltrating his private quarters. The harshly guttural voices became increasingly clear and Robert ducked down the servant's stairway. He paused, giving his eyes a moment to adjust to the dimly lit space. And he'd even *less* doubt that the ruthless king of the gaming world would remove the entrails of any man who'd dared touch his mistress.

Something dark and niggling, something that felt very much like *jealousy* slithered around inside. He scoffed. Why should the idea of the hellion, who'd threatened to split him open, with Black grate? And yet—it did. As the heir to a dukedom, he'd grown accustomed to all manner of ladies clamoring for a place in his bed: the unhappily wed ones, the recent widows, the not-so-recent widows. For all those women, however, there had never been a spirited woman such as Helena, so uncowed by status or title—and she belonged to Black.

He walked down the hard wood stairs, careful with his footfalls. After a lifetime of fawning and preening, the realness of her response, that total disregard of status or birthright was . . . refreshing. Since he'd been in the cradle, all anyone had ever seen was a future duke. He'd worn his rank the way a person did a head of hair or birthmark upon his skin. A small grin hovered on his lips.

And he'd wager all his unentailed property that if the woman learned he possessed one of the oldest titles in the kingdom, her reactions and actions would have remained the same.

Robert reached the bottom of the stairwell. For her breathtaking fury and claims of indifference, her body had burned hot with the proof of her desire. His body stirred in remembrance of their encounter: the swollen tips of her pert breasts, the heat radiating from her hot center. Yes, she might have wanted to gut him, but she'd also wanted *him* . . . even as she'd denied it to herself.

He stepped out into the corridor and froze.

From down the length of the hall, a great big hulking bear of a man stopped and Robert swallowed a black curse at his carelessness. With an incredible ease for someone of the man's bulky frame, the scarred figure set the bucket of water in his hands down on the floor and rushed forward. "Wot ye be doin 'ere?" he barked.

Feigning nonchalance, Robert tugged on his lapels. "I seem to be lost." The lie slipped out with effortless ease. "Would you be so kind as to direct me to the exit."

The pit-faced, nearly bald brute stared boldly at him with blatant suspicion. Then, he grunted. "Ye'll follow me, guvnor," he grunted. "Black don't loike fancy toffs runnin' about 'is 'alls."

Robert fell into step beside the man, who continued to cast sideways glances in his direction as they walked down a long hall. The sconces lit with candles cast eerie shadows about the crimson-red painted walls.

"'Ere ye go, Yer Lordship," the man mumbled and nodded toward a door. He jerked open the thick oak panel and blinding light from the well-lit chandeliers of the main floor of the hell spilled through the opening. The rightfully suspicious man crossed his arms, and stood in wait as Robert stepped back out onto the empty gaming floor.

He kept his gaze directed forward. With each step he took, the skin at the back of his neck pricked with awareness.

A broad, towering, loudly, if elegantly, clad man stepped into his path. Though they'd never spoken, he recognized him as Niall Marksman, one of the club's owners who regularly walked the floors of the club.

Suspicion flared in the blue-nearly-black irises of his eyes. "Might oi be of assistance, my lord?" The hint of cockney to the man's words contradicted the gentlemanly façade his attire inspired.

The ruthless underbelly of London was one he'd only casually and infrequently visited. He had appreciation enough for life that he'd been content with the mundane crowd and pleasures of the respectable White's and Brooke's. Still, he'd not be intimidated by these men who ruled their powerfully built gaming empire. Robert flicked a cold stare over the man still intently scrutinizing him. "I am leaving," he said.

"Ye'll find your carriage waiting for ye." A muscle jumped at the corner of Marksman's left eye and he folded his arms across his broad chest in a menacing fashion.

Inclining his head, Robert continued walking. He reached the front of the club and a liveried servant pulled the door open and Robert stepped out into the morning light. He scanned the quiet streets. His driver hopped down from the perch atop his box and pulled the door of his carriage open. Robert strode over to the conveyance. "Oxford Street," Robert instructed, as he climbed inside.

The riveting Helena had proven a much welcome distraction from his current circumstances, but with his departure from the club, reality now intruded. There was his father's man-of-affairs to meet with so Robert could know the full extent of his family's finances. As his carriage rattled on through the streets of London, taking Robert away from the seedy, dirtied streets of St Giles, he forced away thoughts of the spirited beauty who with her outrage toward him had proven herself more honest than any woman he'd ever known.

Chapter 6

Rule 6
Never be caught without your weapon.

He'd stolen her knife.

As Helena rushed through her morning ablutions, she yanked a brush through her tangled curls; with each tug of the strands, she took a perverse delight in the distraction. Though robbing her really wasn't the worst of the crimes committed by Lord Robert No-Surname. Her nipples tightened with the thrill of his remembered caress. His expert caress. With a growl, she gave one final yank of the brush and set to work braiding her hair. She was no weak ninny to go and moon over a man who'd taken liberties . . . even if his kiss did sear her soul.

All she needed to do was go through the records and search all the patrons named Robert . . . and then, what?

She grabbed a gown from her armoire. "Search each guest suite?" she muttered. And risk being discovered, which would cause all different manner of problems . . . for the club . . . and with Ryker. Which only reminded her that even now her brother, who waited for no one, expected her nearly a half hour ago. Her panic mounted.

Another knock sounded at the front of her room.

Stepping into her dress, Helena hopped across the room and yanked the door open.

Clara spilled in. "What is keeping you?"

"Help," she pleaded, deliberately ignoring the question.

The other woman's gaze went to where Helena clutched her gown at her front.

With military precision, Clara spun her around and began fastening the dress. When she'd been a girl, Helena had taken pains to hide the puckered scars crisscrossing her back until Ryker had seen the marks. In curt, gruff tones he'd called them her badges of strength and courage and ordered her to find pride in them. From that moment, she'd seen them as more than angry, ugly stains upon her person, but rather as a reminder of the perils that awaited a woman alone, with no skill to recommend her beyond her *talents* in the bedrooms.

"There you are." Clara fastened the last pearl button. "Your brother is *not* happy," the other woman said as Helena proceeded to fetch her serviceable boots.

She plopped on the edge of her mattress and took her time tugging them on and lacing them up. Her braid flopped over her shoulder. "I expect he's not." The man fueled by his power and success would find equal displeasure in her unfavorable liquor reports as he would in being kept waiting.

Helena hurriedly collected her spectacles and settled them on her nose. Welcoming the diversion that would keep her from thinking about the golden-haired nobleman and his wicked grin, an unholy anticipation filled her to go toe-to-toe with her obstinate brother. "Thank you, Clara." Placing a kiss on the other woman's cheek, Helena collected her ledgers and strode over to the door.

Clara quickly pulled it open. "Good luck."

Helena stepped out into the hall. Yes, she should really be focused on her upcoming meeting, especially given the financial update she brought to Ryker. As she stomped through the empty corridors, she lamented her lack of a boot with a thick heel, and that her brother hadn't bothered to lay carpet upon the hardwood floors.

Then she might feel some satisfaction and not this delicate tread of a young woman who'd been effectively disarmed, by a gentleman no less, and who'd then had her weapon stolen.

Stolen.

Whatever would her brother and the others say about that indignity?

She reached Ryker's office, dreaded by most, and shifting the burden in her arms, pressed the handle and entered. Helena did a quick sweep for the displeased brother.

Standing beside the sideboard, Calum poured himself a brandy. "Adair called him to the floors," he said, following her searching gaze.

With a nod, she carried her ledgers over to the foot of the broad, mahogany desk littered with papers and leather folios. She made to sit.

"Where were you?"

Helena froze, and then settled into the unupholstered wood chair. By rule, furniture in Ryker's office was hard and darkly austere. But for a single, eerie reproduction of Bosch's *Death and the Miser* that hung above his desk, not a single artifact served anything beyond a functional purpose here. She'd long suspected it was a way to keep his employees and visitors from being too comfortable around him. In a deliberately dismissive move, she dropped her ledgers on the edge of Ryker's desk, grabbed the book on top, and opened it. "I slept later than usual," she said, dryly. "Given it was the first time in the ten years I've been keeping books, I expect it's forgivable."

What was decidedly not forgivable was moaning for the kiss of a powerful nobleman patronizing the club. Heat scorched her cheeks. What manner of man could manage to set her blood aboil with fury and her body ablaze with desire? She tamped down a groan. And a pompous nobleman, no less.

"Why are you doing that?" Calum pressed.

She kept her attention on the rows of numbers detailing last autumn's liquor expenses. "It is my *job* to look at the books." And she'd always done an admirable job of focusing all her efforts and attentions on nothing other than the finances of the Hell and Sin. Only recently had the constraints thrust upon her, in the name of safety, stirred restlessness inside. A hungering for more.

Calum took a sip and studied her over the rim of his glass. "I meant blushing." His suspicious tone only sent further warmth coursing up her neck. She gripped the edges of the book in her hand. Did she wear Robert's kiss upon her lips, still? "Why are you blushing?" Tall, dark, threatening to most, terrifying to all, men quaked in his presence as she'd witnessed from the secret observatory at the top of the gaming hell floors and on the streets of London.

Not her. To her, he'd always be the serious young boy who'd let her curl in his lap when the nightmares came. It was hard to fear him, even when he'd become one of the most notorious gaming hell owners in all of London. "Oh, I don't know. Because I'm fair? Because I'm annoyed? It's no doubt a combination of the two." As such, it was easy to return her attention to her books. She picked up her head, and quirked a brow. "Though if you are requesting a scientific explanation for it, then I'm afraid I can't help you."

He lowered his brows.

Digging deep for the proper nonchalance, she drummed her fingertips on the open ledger.

"You never sleep late," he stated bluntly.

She ceased midtap. His persistence spoke of his suspicion. Pale skin be damned, she'd learned to prevaricate as well as every other member of the Hell and Sin Club. "I was more tired than usual." Which wasn't altogether untrue. Confronting a stranger in the middle of your home in the dead of night and waking up to that same man's kiss had that effect.

Calum carried his partially drunk brandy over to the desk and perched on the edge. "Niall said he heard noise on the main apartments last evening." He continued to scrutinize her through hooded lashes.

Helena stilled. The club had eyes and ears in every room and hall. She carefully picked through her thoughts. If she mentioned the golden-haired gentleman who'd found himself not only on the main floors, but in her bed, Calum, Ryker, and the other men who'd fashioned themselves as her defenders would find him, hunt him down, and remove his entrails. "Is that a question?"

Calum's brows dipped. "Helena?"

. . . Nor did I imagine your moans and the warmth betwixt your beautiful thighs . . . Her skin pricked under Calum's focus and she schooled her features. "I didn't hear anything." The lie slipped out easily. Too easily.

He leaned forward, relentless. "Diggory's been spotted outside the club. Ryker suspects he's infiltrated the inside."

Oh, God. And just like that, all memory of her arrogant nighttime visitor faded. *Diggory.* The hated name of an even more hated man. A monster who roused terror and fury with equal measure. Unwittingly, her gaze strayed to the nub of the candle on the edge of her brother's desk. Her heart thumped loudly in her ears. *Please, please, stop. Please . . .* She closed her eyes as her screams from long ago pealed around her mind.

"Did you hear me?" Calum's concerned voice drew her back from the brink, and she clawed her way from the never-absent horror. "I said, your brother believes Diggory has penetrated the Hell."

She managed an uneven nod. "I heard you," she said, despising the faint quality of her reply. Nearly twenty years later and the man's name alone could reduce her to the blubbering, begging girl she'd been. "It wasn't Dig—*him*," she said blankly.

He studied her the same way he eyed the patrons on the gaming hell floor, and she went still under that scrutiny. "You don't see the threat he poses." His was a statement of fact, and the tight frown on his lips hinted at his displeasure.

They couldn't see her as anything more than a girl who still battled nightmares of her past. Yet, *they* were the ones who saw demons in the dark. This talk of Diggory, the threat he posed *now*, so vastly different from when she'd been a child, this she could handle with a woman's strength. "I see the threat, Calum. To the *club*," she elucidated. "Not to me."

For a long while, Calum stared incredulously back. She remained still under his perusal. "Do you truly believe that?" he asked at last. His probing manner better fit a Bow Street Runner than a protective brother.

Where her brothers believed some twisted game of revenge drove the bastard and that he intended her harm, Helena was rational enough to see she no longer served a purpose for Diggory. "I've no doubt he's responsible for the damaged shipments," she said, pragmatically. "But that is all. He doesn't know I keep books here." If he did, then he'd have tried to off her already. As such what use would he have with her?

Calum scoffed. "If you believe that, then you're a fool."

The faint click of the door killed all further debate on Diggory and his plans. Their gazes went as one to the front of the room.

Ryker filled the doorway. Five or so inches past six feet with thick muscles and a crooked nose from too many London street fights, he possessed midnight-black hair that lent an ominous quality to a man already feared by all. And most of the time, Helena did not exclude herself entirely from that company. The only brother she shared any blood with flicked a harsh, unforgiving stare between Calum and Helena. Unflinching under his fierce scrutiny, Helena sat motionless. Ultimately Ryker settled his focus on her. "What is this about?" A lethal edge of steel underscored his demand.

Snapping the ledger closed, Helena shoved to her feet. "Ryker."

Calum jerked his chin. "Your sister slept late."

This again?

Her brother closed the door behind him. His ice-blue eyes seemed to take inventory of her person. "Why?" he asked, his voice harsh and guttural as one who said few words and valued silence.

She despised the heat rushing to her cheeks. "I was more tired than usual."

Ryker folded his arms across his broad, muscled chest. "Why?" He was relentless.

Because I was dragging a man from the main floor of our apartments. Because I was desperately kissing a too-handsome nobleman. A nobleman whose full name she'd not even bothered to learn.

Helena pointed her eyes to the ceiling. "Because I was tired. Because I—"

"The nightmares?" he supplied for her.

Ryker and his crew had lamented her as being the worst liar of their small street-made family. They'd done their best to school her on the art of prevarication; after all lies often saved lives.

"Yes," she lied.

Some lies came far easier than others.

He rolled his shoulders. "You're certain?"

The glint in his eyes indicated he knew she withheld from him. After all, you didn't carve out an empire built on faro tables and roulette wheels if you hadn't perfected the ability to perfectly read others. But to tell all about the man named Robert was the manner of crime Ryker would never forgive. "I'm certain."

"She's certain, then," he said to Calum. And just like that, the matter was over.

Once again, frustration gripped her. Though she appreciated the support and security they'd provided her through the years, she was now a woman, and yet she was treated with the same hovering overprotectiveness befitting a small child. "I believed I'd been summoned to discuss the liquor accounts," she said, proud of the evenly modulated tones. "Or am I really here to be questioned about my sleep habits?" Tossing aside the ledger, she stuck her leg out and tapped her foot in an agitated staccato.

Ryker said nothing. Instead, he assessed her with that impenetrable stare that saw all and knew even more. Then, he strode over to his desk with the ease of a man who ruled the world. She stiffened at his approach, but he continued past her. "As you are in an answering frame of mind, I'll have you also answer for the nearly depleted brandy stock," he said in cool, emotionless tones as he settled into the high leather wingback chair behind his desk.

At the abrupt turn in questioning, Helena blinked and struggled to readjust.

He leveled her with a look, and she sprung to motion. "I spoke to you last month about the increasing expenditures for spirits." She claimed the chair opposite him. "At this precise time, last year, the club membership and attendance were seven percent less." Helena turned the book for his perusal.

He didn't so much as shift his gaze from hers. She jabbed a finger at the column. "And yet, you've only increased the budget for spirits by five percent." Helena shook her head. "Even as skilled as I am with the accounting, I can never make those numbers work."

"I don't," *like excuses,* "tolerate excuses." Close enough. "In anything."

"It isn't an excuse," she said, equally pragmatic. Her spectacles slipped and Helena shoved them back into place. "It is a fact." And time had proven facts were what governed every aspect of Ryker Black's life. "In your bid to compete with Forbidden Pleasures—" Her brother's gaze darkened, but he otherwise gave no indication of her mention of Diggory's club. She continued, ignoring the warning look Calum shot her. "You are determined to provide the greatest quality—"

"Would you have me compromise the reputation I've established?" That hushed, gravelly whisper barely reached her ears.

Ryker took great pride in the empire he'd built. As he should. No one, not even her, his only sister, knew the details of how he'd amassed his wealth. But for all his success, it was clear to those closest to him that he lived with nightmares that came from how he'd had to scrape together some of those funds in the early days. She shoved her braid behind her shoulder. "I am telling you to be wise in the suppliers you use," she said with a bluntness she'd learned at this man's hand. "The delivery that comes to the club has consistently yielded, on average, four to six broken bottles each month, and each case." The detail oddly suspicious enough in itself. It was too mathematically precise. It had also been quickly discounted by Ryker and the others.

Alas, battling the nightmares of her past as she still did, they erroneously questioned her rightfully suspicious spirit, in matters of business.

Ryker didn't miss a beat in his relentless questioning. "How many cases do we require to sufficiently stock the club through the month?"

"Ten cases of brandy, seven cases of whiskey, and six of sherry," she said unhesitantly. For as they'd long jested, Helena knew little about people, but she indisputably knew her figures.

"And what percentage increase has the club seen in membership since last month?" he shot back.

Helena clenched the arms of her chair, as guilt assailed her. She gathered up her ledgers, organizing them into a neat pile. "I have not finished the calculations." Never in the course of her time as bookkeeper had she ever failed to complete an assigned job.

Her brother tightened his mouth, that faint hint of his displeasure more glaring than if he had verbally condemned her. She curled her toes into the soles of her serviceable boots. What would he say to the fact that she'd been otherwise occupied with one of his lofty patrons? "I will see to it by the end of the day," she promised.

Ryker glanced past her, and she followed his stare to Calum who stood at her shoulder. "Place the order."

The other man nodded.

Helena folded her hands together and rested them on her lap. "I would like to handle the negotiations."

Two pairs of eyes swiveled in her direction.

Ryker reclined in his chair and steepled his fingers before him. "What?" That harsh, emotionless whisper would have terrified most.

She jutted her chin up a notch. She'd never been one of those women to favor fancy garments and baubles. She'd long appreciated the uselessness of those fripperies. Thin slips of soft satin did little to protect one from the harsh elements of a cold London winter. What she'd long found pleasure in were numbers and negotiations. "I want to speak to our liquor distributor." She may as well have asked them to slay the monarch and name Helena queen for the peculiar looks she earned. She didn't ask for much. Largely because she needn't ask for much. Through her handling of the finances and the hard work of her brothers, the club ran like a well-oiled machine.

This request, however, was about more than a practical purchase . . . it was about stepping outside these walls and having a say in the blade she'd carry to protect herself.

Calum took a sip of his brandy and continued to study her with that indecipherable expression. He was the first to break the silence. "Niall handles those discussions," he supplied for her brother.

Ignoring the other man's logical determination, she looked to Ryker. "Yes, but he's not been effective."

Another look passed between them. Calum whistled between his teeth, and stepped back, motioning for Ryker. For the same way they'd not let her set foot outside, was the same way they'd not cede over this important responsibility. "I'm in need of a new weapon," she continued. "And thought when I went to market I could also—"

"You already have a weapon," Ryker interjected with a frown.

It came as no shock he'd be distracted by that particular piece, and not the request she'd put to him. "I've had the same one for nearly twenty years." And in a matter of seconds a fancy lord nicked it. Self-disgust tasted bitter in her mouth.

He peered at her with that dark, unflinching stare and she resisted the urge to shift. No person should have the power to disarm a person with a single look. "Very well. Tell Adair." Tell Adair. Because Ryker was entirely too busy to see to such mundane matters as "another" blade for Helena, and she was, by their thinking, unable to care for herself should the situation merit.

"As for the liquor distributor," she began, neatly steering the discussion to the original point of request.

"No," Ryker said in final tones.

"But . . ."

He fixed a glower on her that withered the protest on her lips. Shoving to her feet with stiff movements, Helena gathered her folios and, just like that, she was dismissed. Again. Odd that she, who was singlehandedly responsible for the finances of the club, should somehow still be treated like a small child who didn't know her own head. It was a good deal better than the fate of most women. But she didn't want "a good deal better." She wanted her deserved control. Helena started for the door.

She frowned at having been so easily dismissed. That was Ryker. She didn't doubt his love. She didn't even doubt he'd lay down his life to save hers if the situation warranted. But neither would he ever be the affectionate, warm brother who'd comfort.

Perhaps life as a pickpocket, and then whatever other dark secrets he kept, had forever frozen his heart.

Helena marched over to the door.

"Oh, Helena?"

She paused, her fingers on the handle.

"Niall discovered a patron leaving the club earlier this morning."

Bloody hell. Blasted Niall whose job it was to walk the gaming floors missed nothing. *Just tell Ryker.* If she mentioned the whole of the events and how she'd handled it, then the matter would be between them and they could hate her handling of it, but at least she'd own it and harbor no secrets. Except something stayed the words on her lips. Where did the urge to protect this stranger come from?

"Did you hear me?" Ryker, who never repeated anything, asked the question a second time.

If he learned of what had transpired last evening and . . . her skin burned all the hotter . . . this morning, he'd lop the other man's hands off. She quirked a brow. "Is that a question?"

He folded his arms. "Do you know anything of it?" he asked bluntly.

One could never out-question Ryker. She shook her head. "No. Nothing." She wet her lips. "Why do you expect I would know . . . ?" Her nervous ramblings trailed off at the slight narrowing of his gaze. "No." She tipped her chin up defiantly. "I don't know anything about any gentleman in the private suites."

Ryker said nothing for a long while, continuing to study her with the same unrelenting, fierce stare that had earned him the reputation as one of the most ruthless men in the streets of St Giles.

"Is that all?" she asked, commandeering his inquiry.

He gave a brusque nod, and again she reached for the handle.

"Helena?"

She stiffened.

"I didn't mention anything about a gentleman in the private suites." Her stomach dropped, and she cursed her loose tongue. "There were rules."

Were rules?

No word master, she still picked up on that defining term. Fear blotted out coherent thought.

"You ask for more control in the running of the club, and yet . . ." He arced a single black eyebrow up. "It was reported that you had one of the guests in your chambers."

The world came to an abrupt screeching halt. *He knows.* Panic slapped at her. Of course he knew. He knew everything. His summons had nothing to do with her accounting. His earlier inquiries about the books all had been nothing more than a bit to cleverly test her loyalty and word. How neatly she'd walked into his trap. "It was a mistake."

He tightened his mouth. "Yes, it was."

Silence descended, and she shifted back and forth on her feet. Surely that was not all he'd say on it? Surely, there would be some charged response beyond "Yes, it was." Helena hugged her books close. "Is there anything else you require?" How was her voice so calm?

"That is all."

Helena nodded. Perhaps she was more a coward than she'd ever believed. Abandoning her previous fight, she jerked the door open and raced from Ryker's and Calum's knowing eyes. She sprinted down the halls, her breath coming fast from her exertions. Skidding to a halt outside her office, she threw the door open. As soon as she was safely inside, she closed the door and let fly a string of curses.

There had been little reason for her to withhold anything of what had transpired last evening between her and the nameless gentleman. So why had she not shared the truth of it?

Helena slowly banged the back of her head against the door. How could she have been so foolish as to leave her door open? As it was, her brothers had questioned her judgment and ability to care for herself. Inevitably, they would have learned of the nobleman who'd found his way to the private suites.

Leaning against the door, she borrowed support from the oak surface. Even with her brother's stern-faced disapproval, there was certainly a deficit in her character. For in this moment, she was not thinking about the inevitable ramifications of lying not once, but twice to Ryker . . . but the stranger in all his golden perfection. Her breath quickened.

And brother's disapproval be damned, she'd not trade that night— or Robert's kiss—for anything.

Chapter 7

Rule 7
The club, and those who live in it, come before anyone else. Always.

The following morning, in order to get a grasp on the midweek floor activity, Helena abandoned her usual bookkeeping work in favor of the observatory that overlooked the gaming floor.

Nay, her scan of the Hell had *nothing* to do with the golden-haired gentleman who'd made her blood race, and her skin tingle. Nothing at all.

Liar.

Thrusting aside thoughts of Lord Robert With-No-Surname from where she now stood, Helena continued her sweep of the gaming floor.

The roulette tables were full.

The faro tables were not.

Ten partially empty tables in total, three less than the previous week.

She froze. Those mundane details and her midnight visitor now forgotten, she took a step closer to the glass window and peered down. Mayhap she needed spectacles for more than reading and her calculations now, because it looked a good deal like . . . it looked very much like Ryker was speaking to someone.

Nay . . . a gentleman. She briefly rubbed her eyes. Surely not. But the sight remained.

Ryker didn't speak to anyone. Niall, Calum, and Adair, they often did. Ryker, never. He generally moved as a specter among the gaming floors, avoiding gazes, and assessing his empire, and that was all. She scrabbled with her skirts. *What if he's replacing me because of my folly . . . ?*

Helena registered the door opening, and then closing. "Helena," Calum said with a heavy amount of surprise. "What are you doing here?"

She lifted her hand in an absent greeting, but remained fixed on the teaming on the floor below. "I'm assessing the tables," she explained, vaguely.

For a solitary figure like Ryker to suddenly form a pair, with a stranger, was reason to give one pause, indeed. All the more peculiar when Ryker, coldly emotionless and reserved, engaged a portly, smiling, and wildly gesticulating man in discourse.

Helena leaned closer, and squinted. Her breath fogged the glass, but she quickly brushed it back, leaving a palm-print stain. The discourse between those two men was not what she should be attending. Particularly with the still-incomplete reports for Ryker. There was something vaguely familiar about the bewhiskered man with his balding pate. Just then the man thumped Ryker on the back.

She furrowed her brow.

Thumped him on the back . . . ? Even with the distance from the window and the floor, Helena detected Ryker's body jerk at that physical touch.

"What has you so engrossed?"

Startled into movement, she spun around. "The tables," she dissembled.

Calum gave an absent nod. "Ryker was looking for you earlier," he muttered.

Looking for her? Ryker had just been conversing with a patron on the gaming floor. A sense of foreboding held her suspended, motionless.

The only people Ryker actively looked for were men and women he intended to sack. Otherwise, you saw Ryker only at the times he carved out for you in his schedule . . . and that rule extended to family.

She was being irrational. Ryker wouldn't sack her. Not simply because she was his sister, but because he needed her. The club's success was owed in large part to her expert handling of the books. *But you were caught in a bald-faced lie . . . one that potentially put every member of the family at risk.* And there was the gentleman whom Ryker had been walking the floors with. "He is looking for me?" she managed to squeeze out.

"You weren't in your office." She'd been here. "You know your brother doesn't tell me everything," Calum said, not meeting her gaze.

The pebble grew to the size of a boulder. *Why is he not meeting my eyes?*

"He certainly tells you more than he tells me." Bitterness won out in her failed bid for humor.

Calum came over to where she stood at the window, and stopped beside her. A sad glimmer flecked in his eyes, as he searched her face, escalating her growing disquiet. "Your brother loves you," he said unexpectedly, in those soft tones she'd only heard from him after she'd awakened from the nightmares. "Everything he has ever done has been with you in mind." He paused. "All of us."

His words rang eerily of goodbye. She thrust off the silly thought. He'd never send her away . . . *But he would if he found a larger reason you should not be here . . .* And she'd certainly given him reason enough. Any other worker would have been summarily dismissed and tossed out for her crimes yesterday.

"Yes, well, I'm working now." Unless she was specifically summoned, she was wise enough to not go looking for her brother. As a man so single-mindedly driven by his gaming empire, he'd at the very least respect her devotion to her responsibilities. Helena shot another glance over her shoulder, searching for her brother. Ryker and the jolly, fat nobleman had since gone. Tired of Calum's cryptic words and glances, she coughed into her hand. "If you'll excuse me? I've the liquor accounts to see to."

Calum gave her a long lingering look, and regret flashed in his eyes. He stepped out of her way.

Helena curled her hands into tight fists, and made her way past him.

Once gone from the observatory, she drew in a slow breath, and started for her office. Although Ryker's looking for her roused nervousness, for its unpredictability in a man committed to sameness, she'd not quake and tremble. It was not as though he'd specifically summoned her. Now if he'd made it a bid to see her called to his office . . . well, then she'd be suitably terrified.

She reached the end of the hall when the quick tread of boot steps sounded down the opposite corridor.

"He's in my office?" Ryker's gravelly voice echoed in the quiet.

". . . I just escorted him there. He asked when he might see . . ." The remainder of Niall's response to Ryker's terse question was lost. "You do not have to do this." Niall's murmur reached around the hall. "Helena has not been . . ."

Heart thudding painfully, Helena quickly ducked into a nearby storage room, and drew the door closed. *Helena has not been what . . . ?* Her mind screamed. She left a small crack in the heavy panel and squinted.

". . . There is no other choice." There was a finality to Ryker's harsh pronouncement.

No other choice? The cryptic quality of that, linked with Niall's earlier use of her name, sent fear racing. *He is going to sack me.* She tightened her grip on the door handle, and pressed her ear against the wood.

". . . Do you truly believe we cannot protect . . ."

Helena's grip slipped on the door handle, and she stumbled into the door with such force, she knocked it open and landed hard on her knees. She grunted as pain radiated up her legs.

Bloody hell on Sunday.

Ryker and Niall paused at the end of the hall and in unison turned around.

Mustering a smile, she climbed to her feet as though they'd met on the gaming floors and not as though she'd been blatantly discovered listening in on their discourse. "I was inventorying the linens," she lied. Their matching, piercing expressions said they knew it, too. Helena shoved herself to a stand, while embarrassed heat flooded her cheeks.

Niall rushed over. "Are you—?"

"I am fine," she assured him. How protective they'd always been. As a girl and young woman she'd appreciated it. As a woman grown, it threatened to suffocate her.

Ryker, however, remained where he stood. "I was looking for you earlier. Niall, escort her to my office." His was a command more than anything else.

She stared, perplexed, at his retreating back. Helena pasted a wry smile on her lips and looked to Niall, who at six feet tall nearly met her gaze squarely. "I expect this is important for him to call me away from my daily responsibilities."

"You know your brother." Niall gave her a gentle smile, and she bit her cheek. Calum, Niall, they each wore the same regretful look. Of all her brothers, however, Niall had always been the one easiest with his grins, and freer with his words.

"Why is he looking for me?" she asked bluntly, as they fell into step.

"It's not my place to say." Which meant he knew.

Very well. He'd be stingy with his words this time. "But he could not be bothered to wait for me?" she shot back.

Niall lifted one shoulder in a shrug. "He has someone waiting for him in his office, and you know Ryker and punctuality."

Yes, it was why she'd known when she'd overslept, with Robert in her bed, that questions would ensue. Dread mingled with panic. "Who is he meeting with?" *It is the man he's hired in my stead.* She battled down the fear of that possibility.

"You'll find out, Helena," he said, bringing them to a stop outside Ryker's office. Mayhap he feared any further questions, because as she opened her mouth with another, he shoved the door.

Helena stepped inside.

Her gaze went first to Ryker, seated behind his desk, his hard face a deadened mask. But that impenetrable, coldly emotional person he'd always proven to be was not who called her attention. Rather, it was the smiling, portly, vaguely familiar gentleman seated in the too-small chair across from Ryker. She searched his heavily jowled face for a hint of knowing.

The man's smile widened on her, and she shifted her gaze away, unnerved by the stranger's scrutiny. Who was this man that Ryker would call her here even now? *He is your replacement . . .* What was she without her numbers? She fought to order her thoughts.

Wordlessly, Ryker motioned to the vacant seat.

With wooden steps, Helena walked to the chair and perched on the edge. She stared expectantly.

And in this parallel universe where Ryker went looking for her and commanded control of all situations, the stranger spoke. "You have the look of your mother."

Helena stiffened. Well, that had not been what she'd expected from this man. She flicked a frigid stare over the insolent stranger. "Then, you did not know my mother, sir," she said in frosty tones. Just a couple of inches over five feet, with pale blonde tresses, the only hint of similarity between mother and daughter was their green eyes. All traces stopped there. How dare this nobleman enter her brother's office and spout his flawed likenings?

A twinkle lit his eyes.

The man was a bloody lackwit, and if Ryker hired him in her stead, he was an equal fool.

"You've her spirit and courage."

Heat rushed to her cheeks and she turned, angling her shoulder in a deliberately dismissive movement. "You were looking for me, Ryker," she snapped.

Ryker peered at her through dark lashes. "You've given me reason to question your safety here."

Robert. She cast a pointed look at the toff beside her. "I hardly think this merits discussion in front of a stranger," she said, proud of the even deliverance.

Ryker leaned back in his high-backed chair and laid his palms on the arms of his seat. "I've allowed you to remain here . . ." *Allowed me to remain here?* ". . . confident that you will be safe." From Diggory. The name hung on the air between them.

"Oh." She stretched out that single syllable. "Here I thought I remained because I managed your books so flawlessly." *And because I'm your bloody sister.* Her nails dug vicious crescents into her palms. Damn her brother for being the cold, emotionless bastard he was.

"You have become increasingly frustrated with your circumstances here."

How could she not? She gritted her teeth. Clara. Calum. Adair. In their broken confidences, they'd all betrayed her. Where were the codes of honor they'd discovered in the streets? But then, you're just Helena Banbury to them. Ryker is master, not to be crossed. "I am not having this discussion with a stranger present." He'd question *her* judgment? She looked to the now solemn stranger.

The older man made to rise but her brother waved him back to his chair.

"Your lapse in judgment has proven your weakness." She jerked, feeling as though he'd slapped her. The marks on her back, face, and hands were testament of her strength. A woman never forgot the hell that shaped her. "That weakness would be your end, Helena. Given your error—"

"It was a single mistake," she snapped. A large, horrible mistake.

"And the increased risk you face," he continued as though she'd not spoken. "I've come to a decision." A decision. His decision. Not hers. Not anything she'd been consulted on.

Her mind skidded away from the finality in his statement, clinging instead to something safer. "The increased risk I face? Is this about Diggory?" she asked, damning the slight quaver to that name which only strengthened her brother's argument.

"Given all that," he said over her. "I found this is the ideal time for you to determine precisely what you want," Ryker said in his gravelly tones, bringing her back from her musings.

"Do you know what I want?" She sat forward in her seat. "I want freedom on the floors, just like every other club proprietor. I wish to have full freedom to go outside as I wish, when I wish," without goddamn permission from every brother here. "And now, now I want to return to my books."

"You are not keeping books."

It did not escape her how neatly he'd sidestepped her other statements preceding that particular one. "No, no I am not," she said with a nod. "I'm sitting here speaking to you about my actions as though I'm a child and not a woman of nearly five and twenty years." She climbed to her feet.

"Sit down, Helena." That low, dangerous whisper brought her back to a slow sit. As long as she'd known her brother, he'd taken care to avoid the use of names. When she'd been a girl, she'd tried to understand why. Now, she wagered it was his successful bid to keep people at bay.

"You wish to know what life is like outside these clubs."

She flattened her mouth. Where was the crime in wanting to see more than the walls of this club?

"You've to determine which life you wish to live." Not taking his icy gaze from Helena, he motioned to the still-quiet lord at her side. "This is the Duke of Wilkinson." She swung her gaze around and took in the details to previously escape her. The colorful attire. Those chocolate-brown eyes. Five or six stones heavier, he was still the same man—her father. *Oh, God.* A faint humming filled her ears and she was grateful for the sturdy chair under her.

"The duke has agreed to take you in. You'll be safe there."

She'd be safe there? Away from her family? "Take me in?" she parroted, her words coming as if down a distant hall. All the while panic crested in a wave that threatened to drag her under.

"For the Season," the duke piped in, resting his hands on his large paunch. "You'll quite enjoy it. There's the theatre and balls and the park . . ." As he continued prattling on, Helena whipped her gaze back to Ryker.

"You are mad," she rasped. "Corked in the brain."

He narrowed his eyes. Anyone else would have surely felt the wrath of his fist for such a charge, and in this moment she wished she'd been born a male of equal strength so she could bloody his face for this betrayal.

"I do not wish to go. I wish to remain here."

"You've been asking to go out," he shot back quietly.

She blinked rapidly. How did he know that? Because this was the life she wanted. The only one she knew. "How do you know you wish to be here and not in London?" she returned, when she at last found words.

The ghost of a smile hovered on his scarred lips in a fleeting expression of . . . pride? Amusement? From a man who took care to show nothing to the world. "Four months. The remainder of the Season," he said, and gone was all hint of mirth.

Her breath came in loud, noisy spurts. "The books," she rasped. She clearly did not matter to him. Given the ease with which he'd send her away, she never had. But he at least loved the club. Surely he could not send her away so easily, not with all the ways in which he relied on her efforts?

"Adair will see to them."

Helena fell back in her chair. For just like that, with five words, he'd dismissed her worth at this club. "I h-have put this club first before a-anyone and anything," she whispered, hating the quaver to her voice.

Gaze trained on Helena, Ryker ordered the duke to wait outside.

She stared incredulously as the corpulent lord ambled to his feet. "Of course, of course," he said obligingly, and took his leave.

As soon as the door closed with a faint click, Helena launched into Ryker. "I have been nothing but loyal and for all my work, you'd repay me with *this*?"

Ryker sent a single eyebrow arcing up. "Ah, but that isn't altogether true, is it?" The dangerous steel underscoring could cut as surely as the dagger that bastard had nicked from her. "You put Lord Westfield first."

She shook her head uncomprehendingly. Who in blazes . . . ?

"Lord *Robert* Westfield."

Robert.

The bloody bastard.

Her brother peeled his lip back in a faint sneer. "You'd place a gentleman whose identity you did not even know before the people in this hell."

"He entered my chambers," she gritted out between tightly clenched teeth.

"And spent the night," Ryker said, glancing at the clock beyond her shoulder.

He is going to end this discussion, which isn't really a discussion. He is going to run me off so he can return to his very important business. Her fury rose, with her brother, with the family who'd betrayed her, with the bastard who'd stumbled inside her rooms, and with herself for having blundered the whole bloody situation.

"You'd send me away because of him, then?" she snapped. Ryker, who hated the whole of the peerage more than anyone or anything, would force her to go live with the duke who'd abandoned them.

"Yes," he said with a bluntness that drained the blood from her cheeks. "You wish to know what life is like outside these walls, then you shall. You have four months. If in four months you wish your post back, then it is yours." With finality ringing in that pronouncement, Helena's breathing increased.

She surged to her feet. "Do not do this," she pleaded, and held her hands up imploringly. "I beg you." Tears filled her eyes and she hated that with her words and actions she was this weak, pathetic creature.

If he was at all affected, Ryker gave no outward reaction. "It is settled. Your belongings have been packed. His Grace is waiting." With that, Ryker looked again to the clock. "I've business to see to."

Business.

And she was just family. Not so very important, after all. The club came first. She'd always known that, but she'd in a night full of folly allowed Lord Robert Westfield to dismantle her world.

Four months. She'd but four months to endure the haute ton.

A dark fury threatened to overtake her, as she damned the day she'd ever had the misfortune of meeting Lord Robert Westfield.

St Giles, England
Spring 1821

Chapter 8

Rule 8
Be wary of rakes and rogues.

Anyone who believed Helena Banbury, girl of the streets, would ever find a husband was as corked in the head as a Bedlamite.

When she'd been shipped off to the Mayfair district of London, Helena had realized it.

The duke's wife had taken one look at Helena and known precisely what she was, and had *also* realized it.

And most importantly, all respectable members of the peerage realized it.

Women such as Helena would never, ever make a respectable match. Ever.

Not that she wished to *make* a respectable match.

Or to be specific . . . *any* match. The whole idea of legally binding herself to any man who could put his hands on her in violence, and his prick inside her with lust . . . well, yes . . . she was better off without all worry of a husband.

She stood at the back of the modiste's shop while the duchess spoke with Madame Bisset, who was no more French than Helena was a lady born and bred. Periodically the women would glance in her direction and shake their heads in that deploring way. The way governesses employed by her brother had when she'd shown a greater proclivity to numbers than she had any ladylike endeavor.

Her skin pricked with the familiar stares trained on her person, and she stiffened. A pair of flawlessly beautiful brunette twin ladies pointed and whispered. Bitterness twinged in her breast. Then it was not every day a genuine lady had opportunity to stare at a duke's scarred by-blow. What those ladies failed to know was she'd suffered far greater cruelties than any they could ever inflict. She turned her attention to the arrangement of bows, and to give her hands something to do, she trailed her fingertips over each silly scrap, silently counting each blue ribbon as she moved down the narrow aisle.

One.

Two.

Three.

Four.

How many times as a child had she hovered outside shop windows much like this one, hungering to step inside and trail her coarse, dirtied fingers over those satin and silk fabrics?

She paused, staring blankly down at the fifth blue ribbon in the pile. She'd spent so many days yearning to know how the other half lived, casting wishes up at the dirty star-studded London sky for a chance to dance just once outside the streets of the Dials and inside the ballrooms of the elegant lords and ladies who'd failed to so much as see a small starving child.

Now Helena looked about the oblivious ladies in the shop, so casually throwing away their wealth, the same way their husbands, brothers, and fathers tossed coins upon the gaming tables. How much that love of frivolities and waste said of the people her brother had sent her to live amongst.

"They are lovely, aren't they?" A voice sounded just at her shoulder. "I think with your coloring you'd look magnificent in a shade of green, but alas Mother insists you don pale yellows and beiges."

That prattling pulled Helena from her own musings. She shifted her attention from the assorted bows to the fresh-faced, oft-smiling daughter of the Duke of Wilkinson. His only *legitimate* daughter. At seventeen, and only just having made her Come Out, Lady Diana was either hopelessly naïve or incredibly generous of heart to not mind that her Season had been crowded by her father's by-blow.

"Hmm?" Lady Diana urged, holding up two ribbons: a striped mint-and-white scrap and a sage-green bow. "Which would you choose?"

As much as she despised the world she'd been thrust into by Ryker, she could never muster a hint of meanness for the always-kind half sister who'd been far more tolerant than any other lady surely would have ever been.

Absently, Helena touched the ribbon in Diana's right hand.

"Lovely choice." The girl beamed. "I shall tell Mother . . ."

"No," Helena said, her high-pitched request bringing the young lady to an abrupt halt. At the questioning look shot her way, she mustered a smile. "Her Grace has already been generous enough." Which was not untrue. The woman had proven magnanimous with the garments and fripperies that filled Helena's once-drab wardrobe. Just not with any true kindness. From the front of the shop, the blonde duchess, with her pinched mouth, glanced at Helena.

She made little attempt to stifle the loathing teeming from her gaze.

"Oh, do not be silly," Diana protested. "Papa would wish you to have it. You are, after all, their daughter."

Helena choked on her swallow, that sound lost to the smattering of giggles from the twin beauties, who whispered and gestured all the more. She would never be a daughter to the hateful Duchess of Wilkinson, and she would only be a child to the duke in the strictest sense of blood. Through the hint of the other girls' meanness, Diana chatted on, as she always did, hopelessly oblivious. The girl gathered her ribbons and carried them to one of Madame Bisset's girls.

A rush of energy surged through Helena; her feet twitched involuntarily with her need to flee this stifling world to which she'd never belong. The scar down the side of her right cheek throbbed, a kind of mocking reminder of just how out of place she was.

The stinging fury, the blinding sense of betrayal burned now as strong as the day she'd left. Not for the first time since she'd been scuttled off by Ryker and sent away to the man who'd never been any real kind of father, beyond the seed he'd planted in Helena's fool mother, a healthy fury and rage gripped her for that stranger who'd entered her rooms and ripped her life asunder.

Lord Robert Westfield. She'd read enough of his name in the papers to know he was a rogue, and future duke. Beyond that, there was nothing to recommend the man. In short, there was really nothing to recommend him, then.

What if I'd locked the door? Then he would have never entered my rooms. I would have continued sleeping. He would have continued walking. And even now, she'd have been closeted away in her office at the Hell and Sin Club, where no one gave a jot about the scar down the right portion of her face, or the marks on her arms and back, because they were the manner of people who saw a person's worth.

Her throat worked spasmodically under the force of her hungering to return to the Hell and Sin Club, to a gaming hell that had been more home than any other she'd before known.

She pressed her eyes closed. Had she truly longed to step outside those comfortable walls? Because now, dwelling in this cold, purposeless world where she was prodded and fitted like a child's doll, with no true role, she ached to have control restored.

But it was not to be.

Not until the end of the Season, at which time there was the foolish expectation that she'd make a match . . . and if she did not . . . Helena drew in a quavering breath. Then freedom.

Having long found solace in numbers and calculations, she found a new solace in the three remaining months, ninety days, two thousand one hundred and sixty hours and . . . Helena frowned. Breaking the days into hours and seconds made the time she would be here husband hunting interminable.

Regardless, she'd been in London a month, and had not had to deal with a single suitor. Where other ladies would lament, well . . . she celebrated. For when her time here was up, and no match made, she would be free to return to the world in which she fit. Her gaze wandered to the door of Madame Bisset's, and she stared blankly at it. For happiness hadn't truly belonged to her at Ryker's establishment either. In the Hell and Sin she'd been trapped behind the club walls in different ways, all the while working, but also longing for freedom and control that had forever been withheld. Oh, she'd had purpose in her role, a role she'd enjoyed. But no one had listened to her. Not truly. Her brothers had been so bent on protecting her from Diggory, and the success of the Hell, that they'd stifled her voice . . . and in that, her happiness.

"Miss Banbury," the duchess snapped from across the shop. "We are leaving."

A surge of relief gripped her and she took great lurching steps to the front of the room, earning another round of giggling from the mean girls. Head held high, Helena continued marching proudly past. Having had a switch applied to her back and a candle touched to her face, any cruelties she'd known at the members of the *ton* paled.

As a young servant rushed to open the door for the duchess, the regal woman filed out, not pausing to verify whether Helena followed. She hesitated and briefly contemplated slipping from this shop and taking off running in the opposite direction until the fashionable streets gave way to dirty, muddied roads, and danger lurked at every corner.

Three months. She'd but three months left.

With the words a litany, echoing around her mind, she started after the duchess and her daughter. Helena stepped outside and sunlight slapped her face. She lifted her hand, momentarily shielding her eyes from the blinding rays. Searching her gaze about, she found the duke's liveried driver handing Her Grace into the elegant black barouche. Lady Diana followed close behind.

Quickening her step, Helena made her way to the carriage, and allowed the servant to help her up. Murmuring her thanks, she climbed inside and settled onto the bench alongside her half sister.

"You've lessons this afternoon with a dance instructor." The duchess directed those words at the top of Helena's head. "Then watercolors immediately following." She flicked an icy glance up and down Helena's form. "But the duke has requested to speak with you first."

Her heart sank. All the efforts of instructors hired by her brother had proven a lesson in extreme waste. "There is really no need for all the lessons, Your Grace," she murmured. "Although I am . . ." She searched her mind. "*Grateful*, for the efforts, I'll not be here long."

"No, you won't," the duchess concurred, her lips tightening. "Regardless, while you are here you'll not be an embarrassment to His Grace."

From the corner of her eye, Diana flashed her a sympathetic look. In her eyes was a glint of knowing that came from a young woman who had long ago come to expect disapproving words from her mother. Dismissing the duchess, Helena peeled back the curtain and stared at the passing streets. As a child she'd envied girls born to those vaunted families. What struggle could they possibly know? In the short month Helena had been immersed in the glittering world of polite Society she'd found even ladies of the *ton* knew struggle.

Life had proven that unkindness was not reserved to a station. Men, in general, had proven themselves wholly selfish, putting their needs before anyone else's. Once again, the memory of the golden-haired lord who'd stumbled into her chambers and upended her world slid into her thoughts and a growl worked its way up her throat.

"It is impolite to make noises like a street animal," the duchess snapped, cutting into her thoughts.

Heat stained Helena's cheeks, and not for the first time she cursed Lord Robert Westfield, rogue without a care. This time for earning her further censure at the Duchess of Wilkinson's.

A short while later, the carriage rumbled to a stop beside the white stucco façade of the duke's elegant Mayfair townhouse. Servants rushed forward, drawing the door open, and setting down a step for the duchess. All the pomp and circumstance of such a mundane activity again so at odds with the straightforward life Helena had known—until now.

Helena waited for Diana to exit, but the girl hesitated. Fiddling with her muslin cloak, she worried her lower lip. "If you would like to practice our watercolors together, I might be able to help." She opened her mouth, but Diana rushed to speak. "I do not presume to be any manner of teacher." She dipped her head. "I just thought it might be . . . fun," she finished softly.

Helena tried to imagine what the days must be for this girl who had no hope of change from this staid, stilted lifestyle that she'd welcome even a change that came in the form of a bastard child of her faithless father. "That would be lovely," she said softly, and the girl beamed.

"Splendid!" With more of a spring in her step, Diana hurried from the carriage.

Bracing for a day of tedium in the form of more lessons and lectures, Helena followed with far greater reluctance. She smiled at the servant, who averted his gaze. Even as Helena felt more comfortable around those in the duke's employ, amongst the peerage, servants were largely invisible.

Marching up the handful of steps, her skin pricked once again at the stares fixed on her by passersby. Then, it wasn't every day a duke found a long-lost daughter and brought her to Town for a Season. It was quite the juicy on-dit for people who really didn't know anything of import outside the cut of their garments.

As Helena stepped inside the foyer, she shrugged out of her cloak and a servant rushed forward to claim the garment. She smoothed her palm over the muslin fabric, her fingers aching for the coarse, familiar brown wool she'd always donned.

The footman waited patiently, and she blinked. Then she opened her fingers with alacrity, the cloak slipping from her hands into his waiting ones.

"Miss Banbury, His Grace is waiting for you in his office," the duchess snapped, with her hands on her hips. As much as Helena despised this woman for her coldness, there was at least an honesty to the furious wife's anger that she could appreciate.

Helena dropped a stiff curtsy, and started from the cavernous foyer done in white Italian marble. The tread of her slippers was silent as she made her way through the carpeted corridors. After all, how horrid it must be for a woman so proud to have her husband's infidelity paraded before the *ton*. Except that unkindness was not reserved for Helena, but rather bestowed upon her own daughter.

Helena continued striding through the halls, glancing at the hanging portraits of the duke's relations.

When she'd first arrived, she'd believed she would never learn her way about the more-mausoleum-than-home residence inhabited by the duke and his family. Alas, the only way she'd managed to put some semblance into the lavish townhouse was by assigning portraits specific numbers.

Helena stopped beside portrait twenty-six, and rapped once on the duke's door. Periodically, she was summoned for the express purpose of assuring the duke that she was, in fact, well.

Which she was. Because with each day she was one day closer to returning home.

"Enter," the owner of that ever-cheerful voice called out.

Helena pressed the handle and stepped inside. "Your Grace," she murmured, closing the door behind her. She dropped a curtsy for the portly, bewhiskered gentleman.

Oftentimes when she met him, she searched for some hint of herself in the white-haired, fleshy-cheeked duke. But for his pale skin, she couldn't see any evidence that she was, in fact, his daughter.

"Helena, Helena, do come in, girl," he called in his usual jovial tones. He came to his feet, and moved around the desk with his hands outstretched.

Having lived amongst elder brothers who by rule had shared no affection, for the ways in which it weakened you to your enemies, Helena still didn't know what to make of this man's warm greetings. So at odds with his frigid wife. Mayhap that coldness was what had driven him to Helena's kindhearted mother. "Your Grace," she said quietly.

"None of that, now," he said guiding her to the chair across from his desk. Instead of claiming the commanding position behind the broad, mahogany piece, he sat in the leather seat closest to Helena. "You are adjusting well?" he asked, tugging his chair closer.

She hesitated, and then nodded. "Quite," she lied, easily. After all, for all those she held to blame for her being here, Ryker, herself, and that rogue, Lord Robert Westfield, she could never fault or blame this man. He'd attempted to at least do right by her when most powerful peers would have been quite content to leave their by-blow buried in the underbelly of London.

"Good, that is good," he said, his smile widening, as he leaned back in his chair. He hooked his ankle across his knee.

Shifting in her seat, Helena glanced about. She'd never been one of those women full of words. Unlike the duke's legitimate daughter, who was always ready with a word and story, Helena was often left searching.

"You've not had any suitors, yet," he said gently, as though he were imparting some recent information.

"No," she said. After all, what really was there to say? She'd not bother telling him that she was quite content free of those self-centered, pompous lords who sought to marry, and then carry on at those same gaming hells Helena called home.

"Humph," the duke grunted, and settled back in his chair. "There is no accounting for taste."

She bit the inside of her cheek. How many times had she uttered that about her mother's dreadful proclivity for attaching herself to the worst possible men?

"But then, all gentlemen require a little help, eh?" A little twinkle lit his kind brown eyes.

She furrowed her brow. "Your Grace?" she asked hesitantly, while distant warning bells went off at the back of her mind.

"All gentlemen expect a bride with a dowry."

Helena froze. For the course of a month, but for the snide whispers and cruel stares, she'd remained largely invisible to the *ton*. There had been no friends outside of Lady Diana. There had been even fewer suitors, and she'd relished the absence of those pompous prigs. *Oh, God, no.* She shook her head, but he continued over her rapid-growing hysteria.

"I am attaching a ten-thousand-pound dowry to you."

"Ten thousand," she repeated back dumbly, as a buzzing filled her ears and blotted out the duke's happy ramblings.

When she'd been a small girl saddled with governesses, Helena had hated all aspects not mathematical of the miserable women's teachings. One afternoon, laboring through a tedious reading about ancient Greek battles Helena had stumbled upon the legend of the Ten Thousand, that great, feared, and revered mercenary unit who'd attempted to wrest power from the Persian Empire. That tale of ten thousand ruthless warriors had resonated with a girl raised on violent streets.

And now, in a great twist of irony, her father had turned her into one of those creatures who'd sell themselves for someone else's gains. He'd steal her anonymity and mark her worth in coin, so that was all anyone would ever see. Fortune hunters who'd seek to trap her and confine her to a new cage—a gilded one. Helena covered her face with her hands.

"No need for that, gel," he said, incorrectly interpreting the reason for her response. He patted her on the knee. "I would have done more for you and your mother . . ." His voice broke, and she dropped her hands to her lap.

Oh, how she wanted to hate this man. *Had* spent years despising him. Every switch that Diggory had rained down on her back. Every tear her mother had shed. Through all of it, she'd found solace in her hatred. *I don't want to feel pity for him . . . I don't want to feel anything . . .* "You have been so very generous, Your Grace," she said quietly. "Please, I ask you. Do not do this." *Please.*

"Do not give it another thought, gel," he said, shoving to his feet. "It is done." He ruffled the top of her head the way he might a child of five and not a woman of almost five and twenty. "Now, I believe you have dance lessons?"

She forced a smile, and thought her cheeks would shatter from the expression of falsity she plastered on her face. "Indeed. Thank you." Helena dropped another curtsy.

As she took her leave of the duke, her mind turned over the sudden complication of remaining invisible for another three months without the constant barrage of suitors. If she'd been born a male she'd not even now be in this predicament. Her brothers . . . Lord Robert Westfield . . . they, by nature of their birth, could command at will. Where society sought to stifle females, they'd not dare do so to gentlemen. Particularly a marquess, and eventual duke. No, with men such as the Marquess of Westfield came even greater power and control.

Helena slowed her steps, as a niggling of an idea took root.

Chapter 9

Rule 9
Be sure to evade notice.

As Robert Dennington, the Marquess of Westfield, slipped outside the Earl of Sinclair's ballroom, he came to a realization—someone was staring at him.

Not that it was *un*common for him to be stared at. Matrons and misses, widows and ladies, there were always glances cast for a future duke. As such, it was not ego with which he thought, as much, but rather an understanding those ladies placed on his eventual rank.

It was *also* deuced inconvenient. Given his arrangement to meet Baroness Danvers in the last room in the Earl of Sinclair's townhouse, it wouldn't do to be seen leaving for an assignation.

A confirmed bachelor and rogue three years past his thirtieth, the *ton* had well come to accept, and expect, he enjoyed the wiles of a widow.

As Robert strode purposefully through his host's home, a grin pulled at his lips. In this instance, there was a particular widow whose wiles he intended to shortly enjoy.

Except, while he walked, the sense of being watched increased and mayhap it was the midnight quiet or an overactive imagination, but there was something decidedly, well, *unfriendly* about the heat on his neck.

Floorboards creaked, and he froze, glancing about. Shadows cast by the lit sconces flickered off the walls in an ominous dance. He skimmed his gaze up and down the earl's corridors. When a distant footfall reached his ear, decidedly not of the female persuasion, Robert silently cursed, and hurried inside the nearest room, closing the door quickly and quietly behind him.

Silence hummed loudly in the empty parlor and he stared at the wood panel of the oak door until the heavy footsteps passed. Then continued waiting, unmoving, even longer.

A frown pulled at his lips. After his near wedding to Lucy Whitman and her betrayal at his grandfather's hands, Robert had committed himself to a carefree, roguish existence. One in which he'd quite taken his pleasure. There were no risks of entangled hearts or too-powerful emotion. His heart was safe and his mind clear in terms of his expectations for and of all women.

Still, hiding behind a parlor door the way he had so many times over the past twelve years, a certain restlessness surged through him. Ennui and frustration rolled together at the remarkable sameness of that existence. On the heel of that came his father's admonishment from months ago, chiding Robert for being like every other lord. At the time, he'd been filled with a seething resentment for his father having lied about his impending death, all with the purpose of forcing Robert's proverbial hand.

Now, perhaps it was the quiet of the empty room, with the near-discovery moments earlier, but there was something so very . . . hollow about these clandestine meetings. He slowly grinned. Not that he would be in the habit of failing to honor *said* clandestine meetings. He was bored by life but he still rather enjoyed the pleasure of a woman in his arms. And women had proven with their breathless cries and soft, pliant bodies that they were just as eager.

Consulting his timepiece, Robert squinted, bringing the numbers into focus. He was late. Quickly stuffing the gold watch fob inside his jacket, he slowly opened the door and stepped outside. A cursory search revealed nothing but empty halls and still-dancing shadows. Quickening his step, Robert turned on his heel and continued on.

It was preposterous to believe an unkind stare could be fixed on him. He didn't have an enemy in the world. He frowned. At least, not one he could identify on his fingers, or in any other sense. Nor did he have to worry about an irate husband. The doddering letch Baroness Danvers had the ill fortune of marrying some years ago had made her a widow in short order.

A memory trickled in of a cursing, furious bed-partner whose room he'd unwittingly stumbled into. His grin widened. Given his near-discovery by the ruthless club owners, he'd taken care to avoid that particular hell. There was still the matter of the knife in his possession belonging to that enchantress, but Robert's affinity for his neck, and the whole living business, far exceeded any sense of honor for a woman who'd threatened to spill his guts.

Yes, he far preferred his women pliant, welcoming, and not at all shrewish. As such, the baroness made the perfect lover.

Reaching the end of the corridor, Robert came to a stop at the last door and pushed it open.

"You are late, Lord Westfield." The baroness's seductive purr sounded from deep inside the room. The lady moved in a noisy whir of satin skirts, stopping at the center of the room.

With a lazy grin, Robert shoved the door closed behind him and turned the lock. "Baroness," he greeted. With a lush décolletage spilling indecently over the scandalous neckline, she had the look of a fertility goddess. He ran his gaze over her dampened gold skirts. Generous hips and equally generous buttocks, she, with her midnight curls and rouged red lips, fit within all the desirous musings of a healthy gentleman. So, why in this instance, did he feel this . . . ennui?

The small, well-rounded widow sauntered forward. "Do you like what you see?" Her sultry whisper wrapped around him.

Battling down his restlessness, he forced himself to look her over appreciatively. "Indeed," he drawled, and a teasing smile played on her lips as she stopped before him.

"Are you bored, perhaps?" The promise in her words traveled to his ears.

"And if I said yes?" He brushed his hand over the generous swell of flesh spilling out of her gown, and the lady's lids fluttered as she swayed closer.

"Then I would say I can think of all number of amusements to help with that, my lord." She layered herself against him and twined her hands like ivy about his neck, bringing his mouth down to hers.

By the force of her kiss, and the fingers she roved along his back, the lady was an inventive piece who commanded his attention. Or she should. Yet, as he returned her embrace, the sense of being watched froze him.

As he distractedly trailed his lips down her neck, Robert opened his eyes and looked about the room for . . .

From within the thick, gold brocade curtains, a pair of furious, and most decidedly unfriendly, eyes met his.

Robert stiffened. Long ago he'd enjoyed the thrill of performing for wicked voyeurs. He'd not for some many years now. Even so . . . the faint flesh of pale fabric and the lady's flared eyes hinted at an innocent, and the distance between them did little to conceal the spark of antipathy that lit her eyes. Then she disappeared behind the thick curtains.

All desire died a rapid death. Robert drew back.

"My lord?" the baroness whispered, blinking wildly at the sudden loss of his attentions.

"There is . . . business I've only just until now recalled." Which was not untrue. One thing was certain; he'd little intention of being trapped by an innocent hiding in the curtains. And the sooner he had the identity of the little schemer, the safer he'd be from being trapped by that one.

The widow opened and closed her mouth, and then a full-sounding laugh spilled past her lips. "You jest." She shot her fingers out, and rubbed him through the front of his breeches. "I have even more important business to discuss." Lady Danvers dropped to her knees, all the while toying with the placket at the front of his pants.

A sound that had the hint of disgust emerged from within those curtains and Robert shot his gaze across the room. And he, who'd believed himself long past blushing, felt a dull flush climb his neck. He staggered back a step, removing the baroness's determined hands from his person, and jerked the lady to her feet. "I am afraid our meeting will have to wait until another time, Baroness."

His almost lover pursed her lips and in that moment there was nothing remotely pretty or pleasing about her pinched features. "You might find I'm a good deal less obliging after this, my lord," she snapped.

"My apologies," he murmured, and on a huff, the baroness sailed to the front of the room, and took her leave in a magnificent show of fury. She slammed the door in her wake with such force it shook the foundations.

Robert took three long strides, and again turned the lock. With a healthy dose of aggravation, he turned around and folded his arms. "You may come out, my lady."

For a long moment, the curtains remained still. He peered for the interloper who'd gone and ruined his bloody enjoyment. Another wave of frustration stirred. "Or . . ." He stretched that one word out in slow, lazy tones. "Are you waiting until your mama arrives before flinging yourself into my arms? I am afraid if those are your intentions, my lady, then your efforts are wasted." Though in fairness, a prickle of apprehension burned his neck. For in his bid to gather her identity, he may very well have stepped neatly into her trap.

The young lady shoved aside the gold brocade and stepped out. Robert squinted in the dark, as something pulled at the edge of his thoughts. There was something familiar about the figure who stood, partially cloaked in shadows. *Who is she?* "I assure you, my lord," she said sardonically, "the last thing I wish, want, or would ever do is bind myself to one such as you."

Robert blinked, her voice hauntingly familiar. And the stranger's spirited reaction brought him back to another woman. Another night. Inside a gaming hell. *I don't care if you are a duke or prince or the King of England* . . . He gave his head a hard shake. Impossible. He'd apparently had more champagne than he recalled. It was the only thing to account for seeing the minx who'd captivated him inside a gaming hell . . . inside an earl's parlor. Suddenly, tired of being toyed with like a mouse caught between the cat's paws, his patience snapped. "Madam, have I done something to offend you?" he demanded tightly.

"Indeed, you've done far more than that," she bit out as she strode forward, and with each step that brought her closer, the sense of familiarity strengthened, until she stood before him. Taller than most, clad in pale yellow satin, the woman had the look and tones of a lady. However, with the space now gone between them, he took in the detail that had escaped him—the large scar down the right corner of her cheek. The air left him on a whoosh. "*You.*" How had Ryker Black's mistress come to be here now? Questions spun wildly inside his mind.

"I see you at last have placed me," she said dryly. "I must say, I am impressed, my lord. I expected you'd less familiarity with scarred ladies." Her lip peeled back in a sneer. "Or mayhap it was me whom you forgot, altogether?" Had those words been uttered by any other woman, there would have been a coy search for platitudes and assurances. From this one, there was nothing but an admonishment, lined with disgust.

"I did not forget you," he said, a muscle jumping at the corner of his eye. No sane man would ever lose the memory of her lips, and the satiny softness of her skin. Desire slammed into him.

"It matters not," she said with a cool indifference that effectively doused his ardor. "Though I don't expect one who ruins women, and meets married ladies in his host's home, has much honor. I expect you have, at the very least, *some*."

Fury ran through him, and he compressed his lips into a hard line. "Are you calling into question my honor, ma'am?" he demanded in terse ducal tones his grandfather would have been impressed by.

The woman snorted. "I expect if you cannot tell that I am, then I should also call into question your intelligence."

"Furthermore," he bit out. "She was a widow." Vastly different than a married woman, whom Robert decidedly did not dally with.

"Ah, that makes your clandestine meeting here all the more . . . *honorable?*" she sneered.

Robert narrowed his eyes when the woman tugged off her white gloves and beat them together, bringing his eyes to her long fingers and the marks at the top of her hands. The stinging rebuke died on his lips as he fixed on those scars.

Following his gaze, she colored and hurriedly yanked on her gloves, concealing her hands once more.

"Helena from the club," he said, with wry disbelief, still marveling through her sudden reentrance in his life.

She pursed her lips, and said nothing.

Arms still folded, Robert drummed his fingertips on his sleeve. How did one of the whores at the Hell and Sin Club come to be here in the Earl of Sinclair's ballroom? The man must be dafter than the late King George himself to have let a woman with Helena's spirit go.

"I'm not a whore," she snapped.

"I did not say you were," he said in lazy tones, even as his neck went hot. He'd merely *thought* she was.

"You didn't need to," she shot back.

Fair enough.

Wise to not continue this odd discourse along that decidedly unfavorable, never-to-end-well path, he turned a question on her. "What do you want?" For inevitably, all women wanted something. And Lucy Whitman had taught him a healthy dose of circumspection for women of her station. Inevitably that something was invariably marriage and money. Though the two went hand in hand.

The young woman jutted her chin up. "For you to do right by me."

Ah, so there it was. As it always was. A hard, humorless grin pulled at his lips. "Ah, you expect marriage, then?"

"Marriage to you?" She snorted. "I'd sooner dig Boney's dead body from the grave and drag him down the aisle than tie myself to one such as you."

One such as him? He should be equal parts offended and horrified. Except . . .

It was hardly every day that he, the future Duke of Somerset, received *that* manner of response to the prospect of marriage to him.

The lady narrowed lethal eyes on him. "Are you smiling?"

Distantly, he recalled the impressive fury of her feet as she'd buried them in his side. "Not at all," he said, smoothing his features.

She leaned forward and peered at his mouth. If he hadn't effectively disarmed her, and claimed possession of her knife, he'd be worried about another attack.

Robert raked his gaze over her person. "Is this about your blade?" he asked, when she still said nothing. "If so, you needn't have gone to the trouble to don that dress." A rather hideous gown, too. "And steal into the earl's home."

Mimicking his movements, the young woman folded her arms at her flat chest. "Is that why you believe I'm here? To retrieve my knife?" A knife which he really should have found a way to return. "A weapon you really should have returned," she said in an eerie echo of his very thoughts.

"I will see it done," he said, in the tone he used to settle his fractious mount.

The woman studied him, tapping her slipper in a distracted staccato on the hardwood floor. Then she narrowed her eyes all the more. "Why, you've no idea what I am doing here?" She uttered that accusation as though he should know. The vixen made a sound of disgust. "Then, why should you?" She scraped another disgusted glance up and down his person. "You hardly would know what transpired when you left."

His stomach tightened. *What transpired when I left?* In a display of total self-absorption he'd not given another thought of the woman at the Hell and Sin beyond the fleeting moments that trickled in of her memory. "What happened?" he asked quietly. "Have you become a gentleman's mistress?" If so, surely that was a station a good deal safer and preferable than that of whore in a notorious gaming hell?

She snorted. "And I'd sooner wed you than become a gentleman's plaything."

Which given her earlier desire to drag Boney's bones up and march him down the aisle was indeed saying much about her views on being a man's mistress.

"I am here because of you," she said, at last shedding some still-vague light on her presence here. "After you left the Hell and Sin, it was . . ." She grimaced. "Discovered that I'd been concealing your presence in the club."

He stilled. "You were sent away for it," he said quietly.

She gave a terse nod.

Once again guilt assailed him at his own total self-absorption. He'd not given another real thought to the woman beyond curiosity at her spirited reaction.

"I was sent to live with my . . ." Splotches of color suffused her cheek. "F-father." She stumbled over that last part, and then glowered at him, daring with her eyes for him to say a word about that particular detail.

He took in the fine quality of her garments and her reluctant admission. She was a by-blow. That was how she'd come to be here.

Fire lit the green of her eyes. "I expect you to do right by me."

All previous guilt immediately died. A wry smile formed on his lips. Inevitably they all came round to the matter of marriage. It would seem even this feisty woman.

The lady pointed her eyes to the ceiling. "I've already said I'd—"

"Sooner wed Boney's dead bones," he interrupted dryly with a wave of his hand. "Yes, I remember all that." Frustration again gripped him. "Why do you not say what it is you've come to say, Miss . . . ?"

"Black. *Helena Banbury*," she supplied, and by the ice in her gaze, this was not the first time he'd been in possession of that particular detail.

"Given your appearance here," in the midst of his assignation, "you've gone to a good deal of trouble to discover my whereabouts and follow me here."

She sighed. "How arrogant you noblemen are," she spoke, more to herself.

He chafed at being lumped into the rather unimpressive category where she'd filed away all other men. Then, given his deplorable indifference toward her thus far, he'd no doubt, in her estimation, rightly earned that less-than-distinguished place.

"I overheard you speaking to your lover," she said, still tapping her foot in a grating rhythm.

"Overheard me?" He'd been at the back of the ballroom, away from prying eyes, and the baroness's invitation had been a barely there whisper. If he were of a mind, he'd correct her on the matter of his being any lover, past or present, to the baroness. Thanks to this one's poorly timed interruption.

"You nobles do not know the meaning of the word quiet," she explained. He let his arms fall to his sides. By her tone she intended to deliver a lecture on subterfuge. Hardly surprising given a *lady* who called the Hell and Sin home and carried a knife on her person.

Robert hitched his hip on the back of a nearby leather button sofa. "Given your sentiments on marriage to me, I suggest you get on with what's brought you here, before we're discovered, and you're ruined." *Again.* That word hung silent, unspoken between them.

Guilt dug at him.

Helena nodded. "I am to spend the entire Season here." She wrinkled her nose. "If I do not make a match, in three months' time, then I am free to return to the club."

"And you prefer that?"

She must have heard something in his question that she didn't like for she shot her gaze to his. Robert braced for another stern dressing down from the tart-mouthed woman. "I do," she said tersely, and proceeded to pace. "I've three months and I've no desire to make a match."

Given her nasty temperament and unconventionality that should not prove difficult. Members of the peerage often proved themselves remarkable dolts, incapable of seeing past the surface of a person. "It's but three months," he pointed out, swinging his leg back and forth.

The lady stopped abruptly and glowered.

He abruptly ceased that distracted movement. Once again, he'd clearly demonstrated a lack of understanding for the lady's plight. "Have you . . ." He searched his mind. "Been heavily courted?" Robert concealed all hint of surprise from that inquiry.

Another inelegant snort escaped Helena. She motioned to herself. "Do I strike you as one who has had to deal with too many suitors?"

The lady no doubt referred to her marked face and hands. He'd not bother to point out that it was her shrewish temperament more than anything that surely deterred gentlemen. And her status as by-blow. Most lords would not look past that lowly birthright.

"Or I didn't have to worry after suitors," she mumbled, and resumed her pacing. "My father settled a dowry on me." Helena paused, and looked up at him.

By her pointed stare, she expected something from him. He lifted an eyebrow.

"Ten thousand pounds," she said bluntly.

Robert widened his eyes. Well, yes, that would certainly land the lady all number of suitors. Most of them with pockets to the let and in need of a fat dowry. All manner of gentlemen a lady would take care to avoid. He tightened his mouth. Men whose company he had the ignoble fortune of now keeping.

She stopped her distracted movements, and came over to Robert. "I want you to court me," she said so unexpectedly he cocked his head.

He didn't *believe* he'd misheard her. Though three and thirty he was not an aged lord, hard of hearing. "Beg pardon?"

"Court me," she repeated. "You're a future duke, no?" With the way she peeled her lip back in a sneer, that question was spoken as an indictment more than anything.

Her disdain for his title was at odds with everything he'd come to know of all women. Feeling like a player thrust on a stage without the benefit of his lines, Robert nodded.

"I expect you're accustomed to having what you want, when you want it?" she continued. "Ladies no doubt fawn over you." This woman represented the exception. "Gentlemen would never do anything to offend you."

And when having his life painted with such accurate strokes and so very . . . coldly, there was something rather humbling. "And you wish me to court you? To what end?" he asked, his tone deliberately, coolly unaffected. He'd not allow her the pleasure of knowing her words had needled.

She sighed, and then in tones better reserved for a slow-to-grasp student in the nursery, she said, "No one would dare step on the toes of a future duke. I'll just have to suffer through your occasional visits and company, and then I'll be free to return."

"This is your plan?" he asked, incredulity creeping into his tone, earning another frown. "You expect me to court you . . ."

"For three months," she interrupted. "Yes. At which point, I will return to the Hell and Sin and you . . ." She waved her hand up and down his person. "Will be free to do whatever it is you do."

With her stinging words and sharp commands, he was close to sending her to the Devil and marching onward.

Yet, something froze him.

Mayhap it was the realization that in this, in her being thrust into polite Society, he was, in fact, in the wrong.

Mayhap, it was a sense of guilt for not having given proper thought to what might happen to the woman after he'd left the Hell and Sin.

Or mayhap it was the recent reminder of his own, until recently, obliviousness of his family's circumstances.

"Well?"

"I am thinking," he said absently.

His father believed the only way Robert could help set the family's finances to right was by marrying a lady plump in the pockets. As such, he was expecting Robert to make an advantageous union. If he *courted* Miss Helena Banbury, he'd be spared from most matchmaking mamas' efforts and free to work on restoring their once-prosperous estates.

Yet his willingness moved beyond his own personal gain. After having his life manipulated by others, he'd be affording this woman some control that had been, until now, wrested from her. "Very well," he said at last. "I will help . . ." She narrowed her eyes. "Do it," he amended. The woman possessed more pride than any of the gentlemen he'd known thrown together.

At his capitulation, most women would have shown gratitude, or surprise.

Miss Helena Banbury gave a pleased nod. With that, she started for the door.

That was it?

"And just what do you expect this courtship should entail, Miss Banbury?" he called out, staying her with his words.

She paused at the doorway, and shot a look over her shoulder. "Lord Westfield, I'm as much a member of the peerage as you are a thief from the Dials," she drawled. "I expect you know a good deal more about the matters of courting." Her lips twitched. "Even if you are one of those rogues." With a dismissive snap of her skirts, Helena unlocked the door.

"I daresay I should know where I'm to pay call?"

"The Duke of Wilkinson's," she said, not bothering to turn around.

He went still, as shock slammed into him. "The Duke of Wilkinson?" he called after her.

Yes, mayhap his ears were, in fact, failing him . . .

Helena Banbury cast another glance in his direction. "I assure you, there is nothing wrong with your hearing, my lord. If you'd paid closer attention to *ton* news, you'd have read of the duke's bastard daughter come to Town." With that, she sailed from the room.

And Robert, who'd never before paid any attention to gossip columns or whispers, wished he'd paid just a single jot. He dragged a hand over his face.

Of all the blasted women whose chambers he could have entered, who'd then in turn propositioned him, it could not be . . . whom he'd agreed to help. A garbled laugh escaped him. For tart-mouthed Helena Banbury proved to be the daughter of his father's closest friend, the Duke of Wilkinson. Given his father's romantic spirit, and peculiar thoughts on class differences, he'd applaud Robert's sudden devoted interests in the recently appeared, suspiciously long-lost, Helena.

Robert rolled his shoulders, dispelling some of the tension. It was but three months. What harm could come in this pretend courtship with a woman so wholly out of her element in glittering Society?

Chapter 10

Rule 10
Never be seduced by pretty words.
Especially from a nobleman.

The following morning, with the house quiet, Helena scribbled furiously on the page before her. Chewing her lip, she skimmed the handful of sentences. Squaring her jaw, Helena shoved back her desk chair, and rushed to ring for her maid.

A moment later the young woman opened the door. "Miss Banbury?"

"Will you see a footman delivers this to the Hell and Sin Club?" she instructed, handing over the note. *It matters not. They'll not respond . . .*

With a nod, her maid accepted the missive, curtsied, and rushed off.

Having been awake now for two hours, Helena arched her lower back and then started from her temporary chambers, proceeding to the Blue Parlor. Where was the sense of purpose in this trivial world? A lady sat around and waited . . . for balls and soirees and all things that didn't matter.

As she found a spot at the window seat, Helena stared out the floor-length windows that overlooked the London streets. Her entire life had been devoted to her work. Given her grasp of numbers and effective accounting, she'd foolishly believed her role in the running of that club had made her invaluable to them. Now, for all the notes she sent round pleading for them to take her back that they'd not even deigned to reply to, they'd proved how little she'd truly mattered.

How easily they'd cut her from the equation. Seated in the window seat, with her legs drawn to her chest, Helena set her copy on Jean-Robert Argand's life on her knees. Removing the spectacles from her nose, she perched them at a precarious angle atop the open book, and shifted her attention to the fine streets she had no place walking, let alone living near. In the welcome silence of her solitary company, she accepted the feelings of resentment and hurt, taking those emotions in and giving them life.

Where so many women hungered for fripperies and useless baubles, Helena never had. She'd longed to be heard, a woman with worthy thoughts and opinions, opinions that were listened to and, through that, validated. She'd wanted to be seen as a capable woman, wholly trusted with responsibilities beyond her ledgers. Yes, her brothers had trusted her skill with the books, but they'd never let her speak to their distributors or patrons. Instead, those tasks had belonged to the *male* proprietors. And when she returned, would any of that have changed?

A carriage rattled by, pulling her from her maudlin thoughts, and she turned her efforts on a matter she had proven some surprising control over—the Marquess of Westfield's pretend courtship.

Their meeting had proven far more agreeable than she could have ever hoped. Or expected.

Yet . . . She chewed at her lip. As a future duke, she expected a man of his lofty status would have bristled at the charges and requests she'd put to him. He had blood bluer than a sapphire running through his veins, and as such hardly needed to answer to or accommodate a bastard woman. Even if she was a duke's illegitimate offspring, her life and entrance into Society would never merit respect from the peerage.

After she'd returned from Lord and Lady Sinclair's ball, she'd lain abed, tossing and turning on her unfamiliar mattress. Life on the streets had also taught her to be wary of anything that was too easy. And though the tight lines at the corners of full, perfect lips and snapping eyes hinted at the marquess's fury, he'd still listened . . . and agreed to help her.

"Why would he do that?" she whispered to herself. Plucking her spectacles from the top of her book, she popped them open and placed them on her nose. She continued to trouble her lower lip. Or mayhap, he'd been so eager to be rid of her that he would have agreed to overthrow the king if it would have seen her gone. All the while, he'd no intention of helping her.

Helena grabbed the small tome and fanned the pages. Having witnessed her mother's broken heart after the duke's abandonment, and then Diggory's manipulation of her only real parent, Helena had the benefit of a daily lesson on all the ways in which to be wary of men . . . of all stations. Then having spent the better part of her life inside a gaming hell, well, her appreciation for treachery and deceit had only been further cemented. What grounds did the marquess have to aid her? She mattered to Ryker and her other de facto brothers, and they'd snipped her from their lives. She was even less to Lord Westfield. He was . . .

Here.

Helena furrowed her brow. Now? He'd come? Book in hands, she pressed her forehead against the window in a display of boldness that would have earned a stern lecture from the Duchess of Wilkinson. From the crystal windowpane overlooking the streets, she studied the marquess as he dismounted from a magnificent black horse. A street urchin rushed forward to collect the reins of his mount and a sad smile pulled at her lips. Then, men such as he had people rushing forward to his aid and assistance, when women such as she remained largely invisible. The marquess handed the boy several coins and said something that earned an emphatic nod.

She used the moment to study him. In her chambers, garments rumpled and a day's worth of growth on his face, he'd still possessed a masculine beauty that gave a woman pause. The shadows of the earl's parlor had only lent an air of mystery to the marquess. In the light of day, with his face clean-shaven, and his aquiline cheeks and strong, square jaw on display, she appreciated his as the kind of beauty that made fools of other women.

Not that she was one of those foolish sorts. She wasn't. She was coolly practical. And logical and would never make a cake of herself for any fancy toff. He started for the front of the duke's house. As he reached the top step, he removed his hat. The morning sun cast an ethereal glow off his golden tresses.

Breath quickening, she briefly closed her eyes as memories came rushing forward. Of his kiss. Of his gentle caress. The forbidden thrill of his lips on her person. She steeled her jaw. For as masterful as his touch had been, it was nothing for which a woman would ever throw away her future, freedom, and security. Which is invariably what she'd done—through a mistake that was largely his, and partly hers. After all, she'd not bothered to lock that blasted door.

A few moments later, footsteps sounded outside the room, and she swung her legs over the side, climbing to her feet, just as the duke's butler, Scott, stepped into the threshold. "Miss Banbury," he said in ancient tones, a familiar smile on his weathered cheeks that contradicted everything one would expect of a duke's butler. "His Lordship, the Marquess of Westfield, to see you."

With murmured thanks, she returned the old servant's smile. Other than the duke and his young daughter, old Scott with his kind eyes often seemed as though he were genuinely pleased with her presence here. He tipped his chin.

Helena gave a vague shake of her head. *What is he trying to tell me?* Scott coughed and stared from the corner of his eye at the marquess. There was something she was missing. Her mind raced. Every aspect from their balls and soirees to something as simple as a morning visit was beyond her realm of comfort and familiarity.

The servant took mercy . . . or mayhap he just despaired of her gathering the proper protocol for receiving a marquess. "I will bring refreshments, Miss Banbury."

"Uh . . . yes . . . thank you," she murmured as Scott flashed her another smile and a look of support, and then took his leave.

At last alone, the marquess sketched a bow. "Miss Banbury," he greeted in that slow, mellifluous baritone that caused a round of delicious shivers.

"My lord," she motioned him in.

He stalked forward with slow, predatory steps a panther would have envied. Helena held her ground. She'd faced and defeated far greater dangers than this man. Although, at this man's hands, she was only coming to find there was sometimes greater peril than the violence she'd endured.

As fate's mocking proof, Lord Westfield flashed a devastating half grin. "May I?" No gentleman had a right to be so gloriously perfect. Particularly when a woman herself was so horribly scarred.

Helena ran the tip of her tongue along her lips. "May you what?" She followed his pointed gaze to a nearby seat. "Oh . . . uh . . . yes," she said, so wholly out of her element, and plopped into the closest chair.

Instead of doing the same, the marquess came closer, and Helena's chest tightened as he slid into the red upholstered King Louis XIV chair closest to hers. As he settled his tall, well-muscled frame into those folds, he easily shrank the space between them and she swallowed hard.

Perched on the edge of her chair, Helena clenched her fingers reflexively around her book. In her plan that required this man's constant presence for the next three months, she'd not thought through the obvious detail that she'd actually have to speak with him.

The marquess laid his forearms over the sides of his chair and cast his glance about the room, as though seeing it for the first time. He drummed his fingertips on the mahogany arms. "Given the time we intend to spend together, I expect we may as well find common ground with which to speak on."

Where most ladies would most assuredly be offended by that directness, and the absolute lack of pretense at a courtship, Helena appreciated it. Welcomed it. In fact, that directness was not what she'd expect from a man dripping with charm, and in possession of a glib tongue, and it momentarily unsettled her. "There is hardly a need for such pretense," she said, proud of that smooth delivery.

He chuckled, and removed his gloves. "Isn't that the point?" he asked, stuffing them into his jacket.

Yes, well, there was truth there. Though she'd sooner slice off her littlest fingers than admit as much.

Lord Westfield leaned forward in his seat, shrinking the space between them, and freezing her thoughts. "Nor would it be wise to discuss any talk of pretense, given that we nobles know nothing about the word quiet."

At having her words from last evening turned on her, a wave of heat scorched her face. "Very well," she conceded, despising that he was right. It was far preferable to see him as a sloppy drunkard who wandered into her rooms and upended her existence.

He lifted an eyebrow. "Do you read?"

She blinked, and followed his pointed stare to the forgotten book in her hands. "No." Helena warmed. "Yes."

The ghost of a smile hovered on his lips. Odd, not even a month prior, those lips had been on her mouth and person, teaching her in ways no man would ever have the right. Her skin tingled. "Well, which is it?"

Helena held her book up, turning the title toward him.

He wrinkled his brow. Did he fail to recognize Argand's name? Or was it her reading selection he found exception with? "Are you familiar with Argand's work, my lord?" she asked, opting for the former.

"I am not." He settled back in his chair, eying her through those splendidly thick golden lashes.

"He is a mathematician," she said and warmed to a topic that she could actually speak with some familiarity and comfort on. "He is responsible for the geometrical interpretation of complex numbers."

The marquess flared his eyes wide. "You are a bluestocking."

She jutted her chin up at a mutinous angle. "Do you disapprove of a woman of knowledge?"

"Why do I expect you already believe you know the answer?" he returned, waggling his eyebrows.

Because she already did know the answer. Men of all stations and classes had but one desire in a woman, and beyond her face and body, those men saw little use or purpose. "Do you know?" he murmured, leaning forward in his chair so their knees brushed. "I believed it was just me whom you'd taken umbrage with." He lowered his voice to a hushed whisper. "But I am finding you are suspicious of everyone's motives, Helena."

She angled her chin up another notch. What did he know of it? "I've been given good reason to be suspect," she said, boldly meeting his gaze.

He held her stare for a long while, and lingered his gaze on her scarred cheek. Helena curled her toes into the soles of her slippers. Long ago she'd ceased to care about the marks on her body. She'd come to accept them, celebrate them as badges of courage and strength as her brothers had called them. How humbling to be proven a liar before this man's intense scrutiny. She did care about those jagged white marks and what they said about her story. Wordlessly, he sank back in his chair. "I too have been given," he lifted an eyebrow, "how did you say it? 'Good reason to be suspect'?"

Questions spilled to the surface, killing her momentary descent into self-pity. He had reasons to be suspicious? She scoffed. "Fortune-hunting ladies?" she put forth.

His gaze darkened, and the scornful words on her lips died a swift death. The dark emotion glinting in his cerulean-blue eyes, she'd seen too many times reflected back in her own mirrors. "I said we'd speak of our interests, Helena, not our pasts." His warning meant to deter only cast a lure of further questions about the demons he himself battled.

Helena gave her head a slight shake. It hardly mattered what he'd known in his life. Having been born the son of a duke, destined to a title just a step below royalty, he could never have known the pain and suffering faced by people who dwelled in the streets. "I enjoy mathematics," she conceded, swiftly diverting their discussion to far safer, far more courting-couple, discourse than any mention of his or her pasts.

"Do you ride?"

"No." First there had been no funds, and then there had never been a need.

"Do you paint?"

"Poorly."

He grinned, and that honest turn of his lips was so vastly different than that practiced grin, and somehow more potent. Her heart tripped several beats.

"Do you enjoy the theatre?"

"I have never been." Life had ceased to exist outside the walls of the Hell and Sin Club.

"Never?" he repeated with some surprise.

Helena shook her head. Never inside. As a young girl, begging the lords and ladies entering those splendorous buildings, she'd hovered at the steps with her hands outstretched.

"You've systematically eliminated riding in the park, visits to museums, and trips to the theatre."

Ah, so that was the purpose of his questioning. "Just because I do not paint or know how to ride doesn't mean I would not enjoy a trip to a museum or a stroll in Hyde Park."

With the piercing intensity of his eyes, she stilled, alarmed he might see through her to all the secrets she carried and the hopes she'd once had.

"Fair enough. We shall begin with a trip to Hyde Park tomorrow afternoon," he said, climbing to his feet.

An inexplicable rush of disappointment filled her as she quickly stood. "You are leaving." It should hardly matter if he left. His presence here was a mere façade meant to trick and deceive potential suitors desiring of her company and dowry. Still how to account for this . . . regret?

As if on cue, a servant entered bearing a silver tray. Helena's personal maid trailed in quickly behind. Eyes lowered, the young servant found a chair in the corner of the room.

Robert rescued her gloveless fingers and Helena had an urge to yank her scarred hand from his flawless, olive-hued ones. As she made to draw back, he retained his grip and drew her wrist to his mouth. His breath fanned her flesh as he placed a fleeting kiss upon her skin. "It was a pleasure, Helena." He dipped his voice to a conspiratorial whisper. "Given the nature of our . . . relationship, I expect you should call me, Robert," he said, running the pad of his thumb over the sensitive flesh of her inner wrist.

Forbidden shivers radiated from the point of his touch, racing along her arm, and sending heat unfurling through her entire body. Helena managed a jerky nod, and tugged her fingers once more. This time, he allowed her that freedom. Which felt like the very hollowest of victories. "Robert," she said, hating the breathless quality of that word, his name.

That faint, triumphant smile on his lips hinted at his knowing. "And Helena?"

Flutters danced within her belly.

"You were wrong. I do not."

She cocked her head.

"Disapprove of a woman with knowledge. Quite the contrary." Then with an infuriating calm, he dropped a bow, and took his leave.

Helena closed her eyes, never needing the calming effect of numbers more than she did in this moment. She fixed on the ticking porcelain clock atop the mantel, concentrating on those rhythmic beats marking the passing moments. Anything but her muddied thoughts from the faintest touch. A touch that had conjured a long-ago morning in her bedchamber.

Frenzied footsteps sounded in the hall and she looked up at once as the duchess stepped into the entrance of the room. "Lord West . . ." The duchess's words trailed off and the false smile on her lips withered into a scowl. She cast a furious glance about the room. "Where is His Lordship?"

Helena went still. "He left a moment ago, Your Grace," she murmured.

The woman tightened her mouth, contorting her pretty features into something quite ugly. "But . . . where is Diana? Has His Lordship escorted her to the park?"

Fiddling with her skirts, Helena at last looked at this particular meeting the way the Duchess of Wilkinson would. Her seventeen-year-old daughter, the model of English ladylike perfection: there would be no more ideal a candidate for the role of future duchess. Oh, bloody hell. Helena picked carefully around her thoughts. "Lord Westfield was . . . paying me a visit," she said, as the other woman turned to go.

Mayhap she'd let the matter rest.

Mayhap . . .

In an uncharacteristic display of spirit, Her Grace spun about. "Wh-what?" she sputtered. She glanced at Helena, peering down the length of her nose at the by-blow in her residence. "Surely you jest?"

Helena looked to the maid in the corner, who pressed herself against the back of her chair. Did she wish to make herself invisible? In this particular moment of cowardice, Helena well identified with that sentiment. "I do not jest." The detail she would omit about the marquess's shocking suit was the whole bit about it being nothing more than a put-on, concocted by Helena, that Lord Westfield—Robert— had agreed to help her in.

If looks could kill, Helena would be the charred ash of tinder at this woman's noble feet. Then . . . the duchess tossed her head back with a humorless laugh.

Helena stiffened under that condescension. Pretend courtship be damned along with rank and title, she'd not be mocked by this woman, or anyone.

"The marquess wouldn't pay a visit to you out of anything beyond politeness. There is no secret in Society about the eventual connections between the Wilkinson line and the Somerset one. My husband," *not* your father, "and the current duke have been friends since Oxford."

Two ducal families, uniting kingdoms and empires. Since she'd developed her scheme to avoid suitors with the marquess's partnership, hesitation stirred. The gentleman had made no mention of Diana. With the families' connection going so far back, what if there were feelings on her sister's part?

"Is Diana . . . in love with the duke?" If she were, Helena would swiftly end her plan, cut the marquess free, and deal with the suitors hunting her dowry in some other way.

"Love." The woman all but spat that word. "You plebeian." She scraped her gaze over Helena's too-tall form. "We do not deal in matters of love. We deal in the practical. Wealth. Power. Prestige." Those callous words turned Helena's blood cold. Many times, she'd lamented her brothers' inability to show feeling, but there had never been the emotional deadness that marred this woman's black soul. "Furthermore," the duchess went on, "it matters not whether—"

"What are you two ladies so passionately discussing?" A voice sounded at the front of the room, filled with amusement. They looked to the doorway where the portly duke stood, smiling his ever-present smile. "Hmm?" he asked, coming forward. "Could it be a certain marquess?" He waggled his bushy eyebrows. "Paying you court is he, Helena?"

When she'd concocted her scheme and enlisted Robert's support, she'd seen only the deterrent he'd pose for interested fortune hunters. Not being part of this world, she'd failed to properly consider the enemies she'd earn herself by gaining the attention of a future duke . . . *Always think a plan fully through* . . . Her skin burning under the force of the other woman's glare, Helena gave a slight nod.

How many times had that rule been hammered home by Ryker? She'd made the misstep in forgetting those rules applied to all, but the perils in being trapped by a fortune hunter were far greater than a duchess's displeasure.

The duke settled his hands on his pea-green jacket, smoothing his paunch. "Westfield has always been a good boy." Despite the thick undercurrent of tension blanketing the parlor, Helena smiled. With the marquess's powerful physique and command of a room, there was nothing boy-like about him. "He'd make an excellent match, wouldn't he, Nerissa?"

The duchess flushed.

"And I always thought to see my family tied to Dennington's."

A strangled choking sound escaped the duchess, and without a word, she spun on her heel and stormed from the room.

My family.

This man who'd chosen another over Helena's mother, and failed to acknowledge his by-blow's existence, saw her as . . . *family?* Helena stared bewildered at the man whose blood she shared.

The duke patted her on the arm. "Never mind her. She's merely overcome with joy at the prospect of you marrying Westfield."

And if her situation hadn't become incredibly muddied by the connections shared by these two powerful ducal families, Helena would have laughed.

As it was, she'd seen the hatred glinting in the duchess's eyes and knew she'd found an even greater enemy in the woman.

Three months.

She'd but three months, and then she'd be free of it all.

Chapter 11

Rule 11
Never be lured by a pretty face.

Arriving at his father's townhouse a short while after his first meeting with the spitfire Helena Banbury, Robert dismounted his horse. As he dismounted, and turned the reins of his mount over to a waiting servant, a shiver of apprehension brought his shoulders back. With a frown, he looked about his father's fashionable Mayfair Street home. Brushing back the irrational response, he strode up the steps.

The butler pulled the door open and Robert shrugged out of his cloak.

A footman rushed over to collect the garment.

With murmured thanks, Robert looked to Davidson. "Davidson, my father . . . ?" he asked, tossing over his hat.

"Is in his office, my lord," the man said, easily catching the article in his fingers.

Inclining his head, Robert started down the hall. The sting of visiting that loathsome office to see his fiancée rutting with his grandfather still burned. This dreaded march reconjured the evil of that day. It had driven him to seek out a bachelor's residence, and set himself up away from the pain of it. With time, the pain of Lucy's treachery had faded from these walls. Instead it lived deep inside, in a place borne of caution. As the late duke had correctly proclaimed, Robert hated the bastard still, but he was grateful for the lesson imparted.

It was why he didn't know what to make of Helena Banbury with her palpable hatred for his title, and, if his ego would allow—for him.

Then given the state she now found herself in, hating polite Society and missing the previous life she'd lived before his interference, it certainly explained away her sentiments. A smile pulled at his lips. Nevertheless, her faint, breathless words had hinted at a woman not wholly unaffected by him.

Robert reached his father's door, and not bothering to knock, pressed the handle and stepped inside. "Father."

The duke glanced up from his ledgers, heavy surprise coating the older man's features. "Robert," he greeted, his pen frozen over his books.

Following their exchange a month ago, after his discovery that his father had tried to manipulate him into marriage, they'd settled into an uneasy existence. Assured his father was, in fact, very much alive and well, Robert had sought out his bachelor's residence once more.

"I am surprised to see you," he said quietly when his son still said nothing.

Yes, Robert had quite carefully avoided his father following his charged statements about Robert's worth a month prior.

"You are well?" the duke gently prodded. He searched his stare over his son's face. Did he think to find the answers to the questions of what brought Robert here?

"I am," he said tersely. "And you are also well?"

Something flashed in his father's eye. There one instant, and gone the next, so Robert thought it was merely a trick of the light.

"Aren't I always," his father said in amused tones. White lines of strain formed at the corners of his mouth.

Perhaps there was guilt there after all for the older man's attempt to manipulate Robert into marriage. There was no solace in that. All his life, he'd been at the clever machinations of others: Lucy, his grandfather, his father. It made a man wary.

"What brings you round?" his father asked, setting aside his pen and sitting back in his chair.

Robert claimed a spot at the foot of the broad mahogany surface. His gaze snagged on that piece of furniture that had carved an indelible imprint in every aspect of Robert's life. Involuntarily, he curled his hands over the arms of his chair.

His father followed his stare, and a wistful look stole over his sharp features. "I should have seen to the commission of another desk," he said quietly.

Robert tensed his mouth. The day he was in possession of that desk, he'd have it carved up and burned as firewood. Even from the grave, the late duke still retained a hold on this household, and his son. How peculiar. The *ton* saw in the current Duke of Somerset a powerful, indomitable nobleman who proudly carried on the legacy of his esteemed sire. They did not see the unshakeable grip that bastard had exerted—a man who'd cut out his own daughter. "What do you know of Wilkinson's daughter?" he said, shifting the discussion away from talks of the dead duke.

"Lady Diana?" His father steepled his hands before him. "She is seventeen, nearly eighteen. Wilkinson said she is quite a skilled artist."

. . . *Just because I do not paint or know how to ride doesn't mean I would not enjoy a trip to a museum or a stroll in Hyde Park . . .*

"His illegitimate daughter," he said impatiently cutting across a cataloging of the young woman his father had been neatly trying to steer him toward since the summer.

"Ah." The duke tapped his fingertips together. "After the girl and her mother went missing, Wilkinson believed both had perished." He turned his palms up. "At his last visit, he was quite . . . effusive in his happiness at Helena's reemergence."

Yes, animated, garrulous, and quite surprisingly free in sharing his emotions, the Duke of Wilkinson would never fit with anyone's expectations of a staid, proper duke. "Is it possible she is an impostor?" he asked with a blunt jadedness that came from life. Given her presence at the Hell and Sin Club, there was reason to be wary.

Only the woman who'd ordered him about, and spoken of hating polite Society, was clearly one who wanted no part of the *ton*.

"An impostor?" his father repeated back with surprise. He scratched his head. "I expect not," he said with far too much trust. "Wilkinson knew Helen when—"

"Helena," he amended.

"Yes, yes. Helena . . . Her mother was his mistress and he knew the girl for . . . Oh," he waved his hand. "Five or six years, I believe. He kept them in a townhouse." His expression darkened. "Then she disappeared, and Wilkinson was deeply . . . affected," he settled for. "He loved her," he said simply.

Having loved his late wife, and then supported his sister after she'd been exiled for her disadvantageous match, the current Duke of Somerset had proven himself romantic in ways that men of his stature generally were not. That generosity of spirit and sentiment had then extended to his niece, whom he'd taken in to his home when she'd fled scandal years back. Still for that defining part of the duke's character, he spoke of the sentiment as though it were the single-most defining marker.

Had the lady by chance found another protector who'd promised her more, but had left her with an uncertain future, and little security for her daughter? "He loved her so much and yet she simply . . . vanished?" Robert couldn't keep the cynicism from creeping into his tone.

Women had proven themselves remarkably inconstant with their affections, driven by a hungering for wealth.

His father gave him a sad look. "It is not my place to cast questions or suspicions on Wilkinson or Miss Banbury's mother." He leaned forward, holding his son's gaze. "I expect the young lady has the answers you seek."

Helena's visage flickered in his mind: her scarred cheek, her hands. All marks that spoke of a hellish existence.

With a grimace, his father shifted.

Robert frowned. "Father?"

"I am fine," the duke said gruffly. "We are not discussing me." He leaned his weight back in his chair and it groaned in protest. "Why the questions about Miss Banbury?" Curiosity glinted in the older man's eyes.

The question gave him pause and in a bid for nonchalance, Robert lifted his shoulders in a faint shrug, carefully weighing his words. "I met the young woman at the Earl of Sinclair's ball." He settled for the vaguest, truest admission. After all, he could not readily come and ask questions, and not expect the same in return. Yet, with his delving, Robert had expanded beyond a faint curiosity over the woman whom he'd, in a moment of madness, agreed to assist.

"Her mother was lovely," the duke murmured. He captured his chin between his thumb and forefinger, and rubbed. "I believe her name was Dahlia or Delia. I expect her daughter is a like beauty."

Robert made a noncommittal sound. Since his first meeting with the young woman at the Hell and Sin Club, he'd not seen any stretch of beauty that fit within his and Society's constraints. Taller than most men, and so slender it looked as though a strong wind might knock her over, she'd proven herself . . . interesting in other ways that defied expectations of beauty.

"She is not lovely, then?" his father prodded. The creases on his forehead hinted at his befuddlement.

"She is . . . *interesting*," he settled for.

"Yes, well there is something to be said for interesting, too."

The duke rightfully assumed Robert's questions came from a gentleman who'd found himself captivated by a lady. Never would Robert make that same fatal mistake. Not again. His father could not know as much given his failure to know about the late duke's actions in this very room. Neither refuting nor accepting his father's supposition, Robert shifted in his chair. "You know nothing else about the lady?" he pressed. Surely a man who'd been friends with Wilkinson since their university days had some information about the lady beyond those small scraps?

His father shrugged. "I do not." A twinkle lit his eye. "I'm afraid you will have to find out the answers to your questions about the lady."

The duke no doubt believed he saw much with Robert's questioning. What he could not know was the scheme Robert had agreed to help the lady with, all in the hopes of keeping at bay dishonorable suitors.

. . . I'd sooner dig Boney's dead body from the grave and drag him down the aisle than tie myself to one such as you . . .

He chuckled. It would seem there existed one lady in the whole of the kingdom, wholly uninterested in him and the title attached to his name.

Footsteps sounded in the hall, and then the door opened. Beatrice stood at the front. "Robert," she said with a surprise to rival their father's earlier reaction. At the faintly accusatory glimmer in her eyes, a sliver of guilt stabbed at him.

At three and twenty, she should have a husband and a passel of babes at her feet. The fact that she couldn't find a single gentleman to properly court her spoke volumes of the lack of worthy nobles in the kingdom. "Bea," he said, climbing to his feet.

Beatrice pointed her eyes to the ceiling, and strolled forward. "Bah, do not waste your attempts at gentlemanly bows on me. You've not come round." She fell into the seat next to him and motioned to the chair he'd just vacated. "Well?" she prodded.

From the corner of his eye, he detected the smile on their father's lips. "Well?" Robert repeated. With her worrying and questioning, she'd become more like a concerned mama than the younger sister who'd dogged his shadows when he'd been visiting from college.

"Is this about your morning visit to a certain duke's daughter?"

Ah, so gossips had begun the furious whispers, and by his sister's knowledge they'd already found their way here. Which would mean the papers, by tomorrow, would be well documenting his sudden fascination with the duke's illegitimate daughter. "Paying attention to the gossips now, are you, Bea?" He made a tsking sound.

"Do not try and change the subject," she scolded. "She's too young and innocent for you, Robert. Do you not agree, Papa?"

Brother and sister looked to the surviving patriarch and he held his hands up. "It is not my place to interfere in matters of the heart."

With the exception of cleverly thrown-together summer parties. Robert smiled wryly and his father had the decency to flush.

"I thank you for your concern, Bea," Robert said, shoving to his feet. "I assure you I know what I am doing where the lady is concerned." And as she opened her mouth to either protest or press him for further details, he dropped a bow.

The meeting to obtain information about Helena Banbury had proven less successful than he'd hoped.

Though, it hardly mattered. Given the fool plan he'd agreed to last evening, he would assuredly find out all there was to know of Helena Banbury.

And somehow, as he took his leave of his father's office, the ennui to dog him last evening, remarkably, was absent.

Chapter 12

Rule 12
Never show weakness.

Helena really *should* have stipulated that Lord Robert be in attendance at any of the balls she'd the ill fortune of having to accept an invitation to.

That realization came entirely too late and she now found herself sandwiched between the Duke and Duchess of Wilkinson. She'd taken refuge between them after she'd noticed some such gentlemen eying her the same way a starving child coveted a slice of bread. She sank back in a bid to make herself as small as possible. A rather impossible feat for a woman nearly six feet in height.

While the duke and duchess conversed, Helena searched her gaze quickly about Lord and Lady Drake's ballroom, peering around the crush of guests for a certain gentleman, a gentleman who represented her only hope of escape from the grasping attentions of men determined to corner her, ruin her, and be off with her ten thousand pounds.

Though, it wasn't truly her ten thousand pounds. When she left in three months (two months, twenty-eight days if one wished to be truly precise), then those funds would remain in the duke's care. Her gaze landed on the neck of a lady across the room. Draped about her neck were enough diamonds and sapphires to have fed Helena's family for years. During those darkest days, as she'd come to think of them, when she'd suffered at Diggory's hands, she would have easily sold her soul for a single pound, let alone a thousand of them. Now she'd gleefully burn the thousands of pounds settled on her . . .

She curled her fingers into tight balls. She'd be damned if she accepted a single farthing from the Duke of Wilkinson. Since she'd been delivered to his Mayfair residence, he'd proven himself kind, ready with a smile. But those showings of kindness could never, would never, erase the hell she and her mother had endured.

Helena drew in a slow, calming breath. Alas, she'd slipped the door open and Diggory had stepped inside.

Not here. Not now. These were the moments of madness that saw women carted off to Bedlam. That truth increased the rapid-growing panic.

Around the chambers of her mind echoed her screams and cries until the memories merged with the uproarious laughter of Lady Drake's guests, forming a cacophony of distorted sound. Her chest moved fast, and she concentrated on the task of drawing in slow, even breaths. *Do not look at the light. Do not look at the light* . . . Except, like a child too innocent to know not to play with fire, she lifted her gaze to the crystal chandeliers aglow and her stomach lurched.

Helena pressed her eyes tightly closed as the acrid burning of flesh filled her nostrils. Her own flesh melting . . . dying . . . pain. So much of it . . .

You are stronger than those memories . . . Fight those thoughts, Helena . . .

"Helena?" The Duke of Wilkinson's booming voice cut across her tortured memories, and sucked her back from the abyss.

She blinked rapidly, dimly registering the benevolently smiling duke, his glowering duchess, and . . .

Helena tipped her head, taking in the gentleman who'd, at some point, joined their trio.

Robert. Here. Flawlessly attired in midnight breeches and jacket, the expert tie of his stark white cravat accentuated the olive hue of skin that hinted at old Roman roots. Her stomach sank. How long had he been standing here? Too many times when the nightmares took hold she became lost in them, and when she came to, time and details had all blurred together. The marquess stood, a model of cool elegance, appraising her through thick, blond lashes and she stood there—well, *Helena.*

His lips turned up in a slow, knowing smile that sent heat coursing through her.

At being caught gawking, she wanted the marble floor to open and absorb her. She was not a weak ninny who'd ooh and aah over a fancy lord. *Isn't that what you've done so many times with this man . . .*

She gritted her teeth at that taunting reminder rolling through her mind.

Never more grateful for the duke's garrulous self, Helena sank back a step. "Westfield, my dear boy," the duke was saying. He thumped Robert hard on the back. "A pleasure, as always."

The duchess turned her lips in the semblance of a smile. "Do say you intend to come to my ball?" Another bloody ball. At the very least it was in the duke and duchess's home and it would be vastly easier to escape the ballroom during the infernal affair.

From over the couple's heads, Robert locked his gaze on Helena. "I would not dream of missing it for the world," he murmured, his blue eyes radiating a powerful heat and intensity that sent butterflies dancing within.

His words and presence here now were merely a façade at her bequest. How very easy it was with Robert's enigmatic pull to believe in a sliver of a moment that there was truth to his look.

She studied him as the duke commanded his notice.

"How is my friend, the old duke, doing, eh?" The older man chortled as though he'd delivered the cleverest of quips. "Always jested about that, you know."

Helena hovered, an outsider to their exchange. What was the jest between those old dukes? For that matter, were peers even *capable* of humor?

From over the duke's much shorter frame, Robert caught her eye. "Yes, he's older by an entire day, isn't he," he said, explaining for Helena's benefit.

And a flicker of warmth fanned inside her at his concerted effort to include her.

Unnerved by that gesture from a man she once believed incapable of anything but his own self-absorption, Helena looked away. For in two days, Robert Dennington, the Marquess of Westfield, had not only agreed to assist her in her efforts, but he'd also shown this additional thoughtfulness. That man did not fit with everything she'd witnessed and heard about members of the peerage, and she didn't know what to do with this unsettling discovery.

"Indeed, Your Grace. I trust your old injury is not paining you?"

As the duke replied, Helena caught the inside of her cheek between her teeth. With that handful of sentences, and the ease of familiarity between these two men, she had a glimpse into a world she'd never before known existed. Members of the peerage were incapable of warmth and affection. They didn't speak with any real sincerity, or make inquiries into past injuries. Yet, these two men—Robert and the man who'd sired her—in fact, did. And she didn't know what to make of it. It unsettled the previously stable foundation upon which she'd built her well-ordered existence.

While the two noblemen conversed, the duchess glared at Helena in a very unduchesslike display of volatile emotion. Fortunately, the duke said something requiring his wife's attention. At being spared that woman's open apathy, Helena relaxed her shoulders. She'd faced thieves in the Dials who inspired less evil than the duke's wife. Not for the first time, the duke's one-time affection for Helena's effervescent mother made sense.

Mayhap this was how the other half lived. With men marrying where they had to, but living a life of some happiness outside those respectable unions.

"Miss Banbury?" The duchess's sharp tone brought Helena's head swiveling back to the group. Again, her skin tingled with the force of Robert's gaze. "His Lordship is speaking to you," the duchess said between tight lips.

A surge of color rushed to her cheeks. "My lord," she said quickly.

He inclined his head, and took a step closer, effectively angling the duchess out of Helena's line of vision. Were his movements a deliberate bid to divert that vitriol away from Helena's notice? "May I?" he asked quietly, that grin the Devil would have traded him for on his lips.

"May you what?" she blurted.

Robert indicated the bloody card dangling from her wrist, and Helena followed his gaze. She snapped her other hand over the offensive piece.

"Dance with you, Miss Banbury," he said smoothly, and reached for her card.

Helena gulped. "No." That terse exclamation froze him midmovement. Head bent over her card, he lifted his gaze.

The duke and duchess alternated their stares between Helena and Robert like spectators at a tennis court.

Then, in the show of arrogance she'd come to expect of him, the marquess collected her wrist, and skimmed the empty card.

She tugged. "I don't."

He returned his attention to her face. "You do not what, Miss Banbury?"

As though to accentuate the full extent of how ill suited she was to this world, a strand escaped her chignon and fell over her brow. "Dance." Of all the tutors and instructors Ryker had hired her through the years, there had never been a need for a dance master.

"You do not . . . ?"

Nor had she seen the need or benefit of wasting funds on such a frivolous activity—until now. "Dance," she again supplied, waving to the couples completing the intricate steps of some set or another. "I do not dance." Now this inability only accentuated further her oddness amongst this world.

A frown hovered on Robert's lips. What accounted for that faint expression? Was it disapproval for the woman he'd agreed to help? A pang struck in her chest.

"A stroll about the dance floor, then?" He held his elbow out.

"Go along, Helena," the duke urged. "Lord Westfield is one of the good ones."

One of the good ones who'd entered her rooms, kissed her senseless, and then shattered her world. One of the good ones, indeed. Helena tamped down a private smile, and reluctantly placed her fingertips on his sleeve.

Grateful to be free of the duchess's constant glowering, she kept her gaze trained forward. Again, years away from company, with only her laconic brothers for companionship, she'd little practice with matters of discourse.

Ever the proper nobleman, Robert broke the silence. "You do not dance," he whispered, that obvious fact coming from the corner of his mouth. "That is a detail you may have mentioned, yesterday."

"You did not ask," she returned, eyes trained forward.

He continued in hushed tones. "You are making the whole manner of your courtship—"

"Our courtship," she interrupted.

"Vastly more challenging."

She wrinkled her nose. "I expect strolling about the dance floor is statement enough for the guests present."

He brought them to a stop beside a tall Doric column, shifting his body so he placed himself between her and the gazes of the other lords and ladies present. "Ah, but strolling around the ballroom is markedly different than dancing, Helena." His breath fanned the shell of her ear, and her eyelashes fluttered wildly.

"I-Is it?" she managed, hating that faint quality of her tone.

"Oh, yes," he whispered, dipping his head lower still, and the male scent of him, brandy, blended with mint, cast a quixotic spell.

She'd long despised spirits, but on this man, it was more intoxicating than any potent brew. She closed her eyes and drew in a deep, heady breath.

"All it will take is my hand over the small of your lower back as I draw you close to make it very clear that my attentions are not to be challenged."

Helena could make right and reason out of any set of numbers with barely any effort. That comforting order had been her lifeline when so much of her life had been ugly and unclear. But there was no order to the way this made her feel. There was no way she could neatly reason out what she felt in his presence. This man had a mastery of words that had the power to weaken. *Pull yourself together, girl.* Helena forced away the seductively thick haze he'd thrown over her and she blinked back that fog. His efforts here were nothing more than a bid to present the very façade she'd asked of him a day earlier.

And for some inexplicable reason, she hated that his was nothing more than an expert show put on by a rogue.

"You are indeed, correct," she said quietly, and he went still. "Given our . . ." She searched her gaze about, but Robert's positioning continued to shield her from Society's view. "Relationship, it would certainly be beneficial that I take part in certain activities that ladies partake in." Grateful to have logic restored, she gave a decisive nod. "It is settled."

Robert angled his head. "Settled?"

"Why, you'll need to instruct me."

. . . You'll need to instruct me . . .

For the scheme Helena had enlisted his aid in, he didn't give a bloody jot that she couldn't paint or ride. He did, however, for entirely selfish, roguish reasons, ones that had absolutely nothing to do with said scheme, very well care that the lady could not dance.

Robert's body immediately hardened with her barely there utterance, conjuring all manner of wicked deeds he'd delight in teaching the lady.

Her breathy utterance raised remembrances of the feel of her body flush to his, the crimson hew of her nipples. The breathy moans of her desire.

A groan escaped him.

"Are you all right?" She creased her brow.

No. "Yes," he managed, his voice garbled. "Surely the duke has hired private dance masters."

"Three."

He cocked his head.

She held up three fingers. "He's hired three of them. In a month's time. They've proven remarkably . . . unhelpful."

In an attempt to not smile, Robert schooled his features. "And you expect I should have the skill to . . ." He lowered his head closer to her ear. "Teach you?"

Helena snorted. "No. I *do* think given the need to put your hands on my body in a specific way that I'd be better served by your instruction."

Robert tamped down a groan as the sound of her hushed contralto unwittingly drew forth wicked images of her on her back, arms extended up toward him, while he worshiped her generous mouth. He shook his head. What a sin that he'd not recalled that night with her in the Hell and Sin Club. With fate mocking him all the more for that failing, the lady folded her arms before her, plumping her small breasts, and bringing his gaze to her modest décolletage as another hot wave of desire filled him. Had he truly found her . . . less than pretty? How, when she was . . . ? He gave his head another hard shake.

The lady made an impatient sound, and tapped her slipper on the marble floor, that gesture faintly muted by the strands of the orchestra. "You won't, then?"

What in blazes was she running on about? Given the hard look she leveled on him, she expected some response.

"Teach me?" she said slowly, as though instructing a slow-to-comprehend child.

How had the tables been so flipped that she should be perfectly composed while he lusted over her less-than-abundant décolletage? "You wish me to provide dance lessons?" he asked gruffly.

The lady was safer with a knife in her hands than she was with seductive words on her lips. Understanding lit her eyes. "Ah, I see." Apparently she'd little need for his involvement in the discussion.

"Just what do you see, Miss Banbury?" he said, his voice garbled. The roguish part of him longed to know precisely what wicked suggestions would tumble forth from her lips.

"Is it that you have a problem being alone with me?" Given their first two encounters, when she'd first tried to gut him, and then unman him with her foot, followed by their third encounter, where she'd called into question his honor, he really should have all number of reservations in being alone with this woman from the Hell and Sin Club.

"I assure you, I've no worry over being alone with you." He infused as much sardonicism into that handful of words as he was able.

Her eyebrows dipped, as she took a pugnacious step closer. "Then I expect a rogue such as you can bring himself around to touch me enough for your sufficient lesson." She wrinkled her nose. "Particularly as you were able to bring yourself to do so in my chambers. Then there was the fact that you were foxed, so perhaps it was that, hmm?"

Understanding dawned.

The lady believed he didn't wish to dance with her. He ran his gaze over her sharp features, and the mark upon her cheek. The world was on the whole a merciless place. What was that world to a woman who wore scars upon her skin, and called a gaming hell home? "You misunderstand, Helena."

He may as well have presented her an unsolvable word riddle for the befuddlement in her expression. "I do?"

Something tugged at his heart, an organ he'd long believed incapable of feeling anything for anyone beyond his family. "Quite the opposite, love," he murmured. "I am looking forward to the opportunity to properly . . . touch you."

As her eyes formed round moons, and her breath hitched noisily, another surge of masculine triumph gripped him. For her flippant words, desire fairly seeped from her tall, lithe frame. Then all hint of passion receded. She squinted up at him. "Are you making light of me?" she demanded.

"I've well learned the perils in crossing you, madam," he assured her with a dry twist of his lips. Some of the tautness left her narrow shoulders and as she held his gaze, something passed between them. Something indefinable. Some peculiar connection that came in mention of that first exchange that had temporarily changed the course of her life.

God help him, with a sea of the *ton*'s leading lords and ladies, he was going to kiss her. In a rash moment of madness, he didn't give a bloody hell who saw it . . .

"Robert, there you are!"

Robert silently cursed as fate tested the veracity of that previous silent thought. He spun toward that excited voice belonging to his sister. He quickly positioned himself between Beatrice and Helena.

Tamping down frustration at having his interlude with Miss Helena Banbury interrupted, Robert greeted his ever-smiling sister. "Beatrice."

She took his hands, and leaning up on tiptoe kissed his cheek. "Since you've left for your bachelor residence, I've not had an opportunity to speak to you." There was a faintly accusatory edge there that fanned his guilt.

"I've been otherwise . . . occupied," he said, mindful of the woman at his back. Helena's gaze bore into him.

His sister snorted. "Occupied."

Yes, given the dissolute lifestyle he'd led, why should his sister believe he'd in fact committed himself to daily meetings with their father's man-of-affairs? Regardless, he'd not have the discussion in front of Helena. He yanked one of her blonde curls. "What do you require, scamp?"

She grinned. "I wish to visit a bookshop on St Giles Cir . . ." Her words trailed off, as past his shoulder, her gaze bumped into Helena. Interest filled her expressive eyes. "Oh, hello."

Robert quickly shifted so he no longer obstructed the crowd, or his sister's view of the young woman.

"Hello," Helena murmured, and dropped a hasty, if less than pretty, curtsy.

He opened his mouth to make the proper introductions, but Beatrice reached past him. "Forgive me, I did not see you there. I am Lady Beatrice Dennington." She gestured to him. "Robert's sister."

Helena hesitated, and then placed her gloved fingers in his sister's, returning that slight shake. "Helena Banbury. The . . ." Color suffused her cheeks. "Duke of Wilkinson's daughter."

A gasp exploded from his sister's lips and she swung her gaze from Helena up to Robert. Understanding filled her eyes. "*You* are the duke's daughter."

Helena stiffened. "I am."

He'd known Helena Banbury for only a handful of exchanges but had come to appreciate the way in which she brought her shoulders back, and tipped her chin up with those expressions of pride and defensiveness. What whispers she must have endured in her short time here to account for the reservation there, and how he despised every bloody bastard to put that guarded look in her eyes. She made to draw back her fingers, but his sister retained her hold.

A small, clear laugh escaped Beatrice. "Oh, I am so very glad."

Helena furrowed her brow and looked blankly at Robert.

He gave his head a shake. It was hardly the place to explain that his sister had drawn the erroneous assumption that he'd launched an official courtship of the duke's barely out of the schoolroom daughter. Even with Helena's elevated status as a duke's daughter, Beatrice would never disdain a person because of their station.

"May I pay you a visit, Miss Banbury?"

Helena tilted her head at an endearing angle. "Visit?" she parroted back.

His sister's smile dipped. "Unless, you'd rather I did not?"

Wary caution blared in her eyes. "N-no," she stammered. How much unkindness had she known that she'd built up these guarded walls about herself? "I would . . ." A hesitant smile quivered on her lips. "Like that very much." And more, why should it matter to him? He was aiding her for the remainder of the Season out of a sense of honor to make right a wrong he'd done. Robert fisted his hands. So why this need to know the stories and secrets that had turned her into this guarded creature?

Beatrice clapped her hands. "Splendid. I shall call tomorrow afternoon."

That snapped him back from his tumultuous musings. "No," he exclaimed, earning the attention of both young women. "Miss Banbury was explaining that she has lessons with a very skilled dance master on the morrow."

A charged look passed between Helena and Robert, and by the rapid rise and fall of her chest, she too was now thinking of all talk of his hands on her and the lesson she expected.

"Oh, drat," his sister said and patted Helena on the hand regretfully. "They are rather tedious, are they not? Another time, then?"

Helena nodded. "That would be lovely, my lady." She glanced across the ballroom, and then smoothed her palms down the front of her skirts. "I see the duchess motioning to me. If you'll excuse me?" She stole another glance at Robert.

He swiftly captured her fingers and raised them to his mouth, damning the fabric between them that denied him the feel of her skin against his. "Miss Banbury," he said quietly, in even, modulated tones.

"L-Lord Westfield."

And as Helena turned on her heel and marched away, and his sister prattled on, he conceded that, for the first time in the course of his life, he was rather looking forward to a dance lesson.

Chapter 13

Rule 13
No friends.

Perched in her familiar spot in the window seat, Helena and Diana sat in a companionable silence.

While Helena read, the duke's daughter, proper in all ways, bent her head over her embroidery, attending that task the way a military general attended his battle plans.

The young woman's faint humming filled the otherwise quiet of the room. Using her sister's distraction, Helena contemplated Lord and Lady Drake's ball. More specifically, she thought to the tender exchange she'd witnessed between Robert and his sister. Lady Beatrice was just one young woman, amongst a sea of so many . . . and yet, early on Helena had come to appreciate all a person could learn from the number one. Beatrice was a single person, a loving sister to Robert, who believed the sun set and rose for him. And that spoke volumes more than the years' worth of preconceived notions Helena had carried about members of the peerage.

Not everyone was as she seemed. Wasn't Helena herself—and her brothers—proof of that?

She returned her study to Diana. And here was another young woman who threw into question everything Helena had long ago accepted as empirical fact.

When she had entered this household, she'd been determined to hate anything and everything here, for they were extensions of the man who'd abandoned Helena and her mother, whose defection had seen them in the clutches of a man who would make Satan cower in dread.

With the emerald pendant she always wore and her expensive white satin gowns, Diana represented all Helena had hated through the years. As a child begging and thieving in the streets, she'd seen the Lady Dianas of the world, flawless and perfect, and oblivious . . . with nothing but a look of disdain for the Helena Banburys and developed an easy loathing for all of them.

Or she thought she had.

Every day spent in this rapidly confusing Society, everything she'd believed to be fact proved just as murky and muddled as those early days when her mother had taken up with Mac Diggory.

Helena looked to where the young girl sat, drawing her needle through the fabric stretched out in the embroidery frame. Yes, she wanted to hate her.

Except Diana, with her innocent smile and even more innocent acceptance of Helena, had made it impossible *to* hate her. There was a greater likelihood of hating spun sugar and rainbows than this girl.

She was the sunny, joyful woman who gentlemen wed. Men like Robert. Men who had titles and wealth and who kept mistresses on the side, and visited scandalous gaming hells.

The duchess's seething pronouncement from days earlier slipped into her thoughts. These two powerful ducal families who'd been so closely connected, and the expectation of at least the duchess that her daughter would one day wed Robert.

At the time, she'd not truly given the thought consideration. That when she left, Robert would find his proper, perfect bride, and why should that bride not be Diana? They would be the model of a flawless, golden English couple matched in their lineal connections and wealth. Unlike Helena, who would always be, no matter the Duke of Wilkinson's futile efforts, the daughter of a whore who'd spent more years on the streets than in the comfort the duke had afforded his mistress.

The book trembled in Helena's hands, bringing her attention to the jagged, scarred flesh.

She stared blankly down at those marks.

Badges of honor, Ryker had called them.

Helena smiled sadly. What rot. What utter and absolute rubbish. They were hideous. They were the hands of a common street urchin and not the manner of smooth, soft hands that managed ladylike skills such as embroidering.

A maid appeared at the entrance of the room. She dropped a curtsy. "My lady, your mother has asked you join her in the foyer."

Diana paused midhum, and looked up from her work. "Oh, splendid. I'll be but a moment," she said, and the young maid rushed off. And the peculiarity of it all was that given those happy tones, the girl rather meant that. She caught Helena staring, and smiled. "Mother and I are to visit the modiste," she said happily. Happy. She was always happy. Even at the prospect of an outing alone with her shrewish, always scolding mother. "I am to be fitted for a new bonnet," Diana said, with an ever-widening smile. It was the duke's smile, just another gift he'd passed down to one of his offspring. "You will come, yes?"

Retaining the book in her hands, Helena swung her legs over the side of her seat, and her skirts settled noisily at her ankles. "No." She gentled that rejection, by lifting up her book. "I am," waiting for a scandalous dance lesson. Or she had been. "I am going to remain behind and read."

Diana made to rise, but Helena placed a staying hand on her knee. "Before you go, I would speak to you on . . . something," she began slowly. A tight ball of dread curled in her belly.

Diana stared patiently back. "Yes?"

Searching her mind, Helena slid into the chair closest to the duke's true daughter. She set Argand's work on complex numbers down on the rose-inlaid side table. How she wished for the skilled ability to converse with anyone, about anything. Including this matter. She'd not known this particular issue could be a problem until the duchess's furious words, yesterday afternoon. "The Marquess of Westfield," she began.

And then she had nothing. Secretly she prayed the other young woman was capable enough with discourse to handle this entire discussion for the both of them. For what if Diana expressed that her heart was in some way engaged? A deep, dark, ugly sentiment that felt very much like jealousy slithered and twisted around inside.

Diana continued to blink like a confused pup. "What of him?"

"Your families are . . . quite close," she settled for, recalling the easy familiarity between the Duke of Wilkinson and Robert in the midst of the Lord and Lady Drake's ball.

"Our families."

Helena looked blankly at her.

"Well, it is just, you said 'your' families, and this is your family too, Helena. So 'our' families."

At that beautiful gesture, tears misted her vision. She blinked them back. Why could all these people not be the same nasty beasts as the Duchess of Wilkinson?

"You were asking?" Diana steered her back to the reason of her questioning.

"Uh, yes." She drew in a steadying breath, and then spoke on a rush. "Are there feelings on your part?"

Please say no. Say no. Because if she said yes, that rapidly growing envy inside would consume her.

Diana lowered her embroidery frame. "Feelings for . . . ?" Then she rounded her eyes. "Do you mean the marquess?" A little giggle escaped her. "Oh, Helena, surely you jest. Lord Westfield is *old*." Then with a surprising maturity, all hint of her amusement died, and she scooted closer to Helena. "Is this about your feelings for the marquess?"

Helena sat immobile. Feelings for the marquess? She did not have feelings for him . . . beyond annoyance and frustration. He vexed her. He teased her. How could she possibly come to care for a man who'd so shattered her existence by inadvertently thrusting her into the glittering world of polite Society?

He's also helping you to put it to rights . . . Helping her when he really had no need to.

"I overheard Father discussing it with Mother," Diana was saying. She lowered her voice to a conspiratorial whisper. "Papa is quite elated at the prospect of your uniting the two lines. He's long been friends with the Duke of Somerset. Papa sees him as a brother." Diana dropped her chin atop her hand. "Not that I knew anything of that level of friendship." She brightened. "Until you."

At that inherent goodness, Helena felt . . . *shame*. She'd been steadfast in her love and loyalty to Ryker, Calum, Adair, and Niall . . . and yet, having been taken into the fold of this new family, she'd not had that same level of devotion to this earnest, young woman. "If there are feelings on your part," Helena said hesitantly. "I will . . ." free Robert of his pledge to help. Something sharp and painful twisted at her heart.

The clear bell-like tinkling of Diana's laughter filtered between them. "Do not be silly. Lord Westfield is nice enough, but he is also old enough to be my father." Helena released an audible breath she'd not realized she was holding.

Perfectly unaware, Diana hopped to her feet. "I mustn't keep Mother waiting." She gave Helena another hopeful look. "You're certain you do not wish to join us?"

Helena smiled. Her first true smile that day. In many days, she thought. In fact, when had she found joy in anything beyond her book-keeping at the clubs? How peculiar to realize happiness existed—outside the club, even. "I am certain," she said, and returned Diana's wave.

Oh how she envied the girl that uncomplicated joy. With her sister gone, and left alone with her own musings, Helena carried her book over to the window seat and skimmed her chipped fingernails over the gold lettering of Jean-Robert Argand's name. Helena's life was so much more like this man's, a self-taught mathematician who'd managed the accounts of a bookshop, than the one she awaited.

A man she'd been waiting on for several hours.

Though, as it did involve numbers and she was everything precise where those digits were concerned, she'd counted seven *waking* hours. Or four hundred and twenty minutes. Or if one wished to be most accurate, twenty-five thousand, two hundred seconds.

That was how long she'd been waiting for Robert's visit.

Which was . . . peculiar. She didn't even like the gentleman. He was the man who'd gotten her sent off to the fancy side of London, and he was part of her plan to evade suitors for the remainder of the Season.

Yet . . . Helena drummed her fingertips on the top of her book. If that were the case, why was she, in fact, sitting here waiting . . . for him? *Why did you feel this great relief at Diana's earlier words about the marquess?* It didn't make sense and she was, if anything, sensible.

Only, you've never been truly sensible around this gentleman . . .

From the night he'd stumbled into the private halls of the Hell and Sin Club, she'd broken one of the most important rules in approaching the drunken stranger. Then she'd returned his kiss and hungered for his embrace.

Filled with a murky confusion, Helena returned her attention to the small leather tome. He was just a man. A man, who with his clever tongue, and even more clever lips, had proven himself the wicked sort she'd been warned away from. She firmed her resolve.

And she would do well to remember as much when he came and delivered a hopeless dance lesson—all with the purpose of putting his hands on her body.

If he came.

Seated in her familiar window seat, Helena looked outside at the busy London streets. Her heart tripped a beat. As though she'd conjured him, Robert drew his powerful black mount to a stop. In a near repeat of yesterday's visit, a young boy came forward, and he turned the reins over to the child.

Swiftly lowering her feet to the floor, Helena jumped up. She ran her fingers down the front of her soft yellow skirts. Hideous color. Even she who didn't know a jot about fashion knew that women with deathly white skin should never, ever wear those pale hues. Then, mayhap, that had been the duchess's intentions?

Not that it mattered. She began to pace. It hardly mattered what she wore in Robert's presence. Theirs was an act. An adult charade, and nothing more.

"His Lordship, the Marquess of Westfield," Scott intoned from the doorway.

Helena emitted a startled shriek, and knocked against the table, sending her copy of Argand tumbling to the floor.

"My lord."

The butler gave her a pointed look and she flared her eyes. "Refreshments."

The old man gave a pleased smile. "As you wish, Miss Banbury." His rheumy eyes sparkled with approval.

Again, that sense of . . . belonging filled her. Sentiments she'd only known amongst her brothers. Feelings she'd thought she'd never know outside of the comfort and safety of her world.

What is happening to me?

Robert had bedded countless numbers of skilled widows and clever courtesans. Sometimes together. But never had he lain awake, hungering for something as innocent as a dance with the spirited Helena Banbury. That anticipation had only grown in his short ride over this afternoon.

And by the lady's flushed cheeks and parted lips, she was not wholly immune to him.

"Shall we?" He held out a hand, and she darted her tongue out and ran it over the seam of her lips.

"I-I do not think with the furniture there is space enough for a lesson." He smiled at the regret in those words.

"Indeed, there is not," he concurred, and her expression fell. He offered her his elbow.

She eyed his elbow a moment, and then looked to him. "What are you doing?"

Robert brushed his knuckles along her sharp jawline. "Evading your maid, who is no doubt already being fetched."

The lady pressed her mouth into a flat line. "And I take it you are proficient in avoiding being discovered with women?" A slight edge underscored that supposition, telling all the same.

The actuality of it was, he, in fact, was skilled in carrying out clandestine meetings and wicked assignations behind his host's parlor doors. After the night he'd bore witness to Lucy's treachery, he'd found a safe pleasure in all those meaningless entanglements. "I wish to dance with you," he said quietly, and with no small amount of shock he realized his words did not come from the easy store of pretty comments and praise he had on the ready.

Helena peered at him. Did she seek the veracity of his profession? He went still under her scrutiny, and then the lady rolled her eyes. "You needn't play the rogue for my benefit. Where are we to dance?"

It was perfectly reasonable for her to see falsity in his claims, and yet disappointment tightened his belly. Disappointment that, for the first time in twelve years he'd spoken without the intent of seduction, and Helena had seen nothing more. Plastering on a perfectly practiced grin, Robert slid her fingers into his sleeve. "Having hidden in these halls as a child, I've the benefit of knowing my way around with some familiarity."

Her lips twitched. "I expect you were troublesome."

"Oh, most," he easily concurred, ringing a laugh from her, and he missed a step. Her face wreathed in a smile, and cheeks flushed from her contagious joy, she was a siren.

Helena lifted her sparkling gaze, and some of the light dimmed. "What is it?"

Unnerved, Robert forced a grin. "I was simply thinking of all my outrageous antics." He neatly steered her down the hall, leading her on a twisting and turning path through the mammoth residence. Yes, the lady's poor maid would need a map to locate her mistress. Robert grinned.

"Tell me."

How direct she was. Where ladies prevaricated and spoke with deliberate words, she commanded.

"Well, there was the summer party, I gathered sheets from all the guest chambers, knotted them together, and made a makeshift rope." As a boy of eight, he'd believed his parents would, if not be pleased, at least appreciate that he'd not touched the linens on any of the beds occupied by their family.

"For what purpose?"

He grinned at her. "Why, I, at the ripe age of eight, I fashioned myself an explorer." She giggled and again he tripped over his thoughts. Those carefree, innocent expressions of mirth, so common and practiced in other women, were as rare as a fire rainbow with this woman. Lest he kill that fleeting joy, Robert rushed the remainder of the story out. "I tied the sheets together and knotted one end around the balustrade that overlooked the foyer with the express intention of climbing down." Robert spread his hands wide.

She widened her eyes. "Surely it was not as high as—"

"The duke's foyer?" he neatly interrupted. "Higher." His lips quirked. "I made it nearly three quarters of the way down." Before his weight had pulled free the less than impressive knot he'd worked around the balustrade. "I suffered nothing more than a sprained arm, and a month's long loss of dessert following evening meals."

Helena slapped a hand over her mouth, stymieing the amusement on her full lips. Her shoulders shook with the force of her laughter, and her mirth contagious, Robert joined in. He didn't speak about his past, any part of it, with anyone. What was it about her that had called forth this particular memory?

Unease rolled through him. This off-kilter effect Helena Banbury had on him was a sentiment he'd believed himself immune to after Lucy's betrayal, and yet how easily she threw his thoughts and emotion into tumult? Eager to divert the discourse to safer grounds, Robert steered her to the back of the duke's townhouse and brought them to a stop beside the doorway that emptied out into the duchess's prized gardens. An image flitted in his mind of who she would have been as a child of eight, a gangly girl, in all manner of mischief. "What of you, Helena, what were you like as child?" he asked as he pushed the door open. He took several steps before he realized Helena remained in the doorway.

Gone were all hints of mirth. In its place was a dark somberness that sent a chill skittering along his spine. She forced a smile that stretched her cheeks. "I thought we were not to speak of the past." There was an underlying thread of desperation that hung on that reminder, and a vise squeezed about his lungs.

He'd no right to her secrets. But he wanted them all the same.

"Come, your lesson, then," he urged gruffly, and without hesitation, she drew the door closed, and stepped into his arms.

"We'll not bother with anything beyond a waltz," he said quietly, angling her in his arms, and guiding her hand up to his sleeve. "This is most conducive." He settled his hand on the small of her back, bringing her body closer. A hungering to cup her buttocks and drag her closer filled him.

"Most conducive to what?" Her tremulous question hinted at her also weakening control.

Robert lowered his mouth to hers so only a hairsbreadth separated them. "Why, for touching you," he breathed. Her lashes fluttered and he guided her into movement.

Her eyes shot open, and she stumbled against him.

"You enjoy mathematics," he said matter-of-factly, and Helena stared unblinking at him, promptly missing another step. "Think of dancing in terms of your calculations. Concentrate on the numbers." He hummed a discordant tone that earned another of her elusive smiles. "Pay attention," he rebuked. "It is a one-two-three—one-two-three," he murmured. "Remember all the beats of the waltz are equal." He guided her back. "You start with the right foot and you go back on the first step with the right foot." He dipped his brow to hers. "Then side with the left and close right foot to left." Angling her body closer still, he led her through the rhythmic movements.

Cheeks flushed, Helena chewed at her lower lip, and missed a step. "Concentrate," he whispered. "Think of the numbers, Helena. Think of the steady one-two-three." They continued through the first stilted, then gradually smooth, movements, as their bodies together found the rhythm. "One-two-three," he murmured, waltzing her around the duchess's prize rose bushes.

As the moments fell away, he moved his hand lower, to the small of her back, just above her buttocks, and her breath caught. "This is the touch," he continued in low tones. "This is the one that any gentleman will see and know."

Her lips parted as she drew in a shuddery breath. "Know what?"

"That you are mine." In this game of pretend that suddenly felt all too real.

The back of Helena's legs knocked against a stone bench, forcing them to a jerky stop. They stood, bodies flush, their chests rising and falling in a matched, heavy rhythm. Robert moved his hand up, folding his palm about her nape, and angled her head up.

Their lips met in a fiery explosion and on a low moan, Helena twined her fingers about his neck, meeting his kiss. He slanted his mouth over hers again and again, working his hands over her body, exploring the curve of her hips, and the small swells of her breasts.

He dragged his lips away from hers and she cried out, searching for his mouth, but Robert continued his quest. With his lips, he explored the long arch of her neck, sucking at the soft skin where her pulse pounded, and then lower. He quickly worked the fabric of her décolletage lower, and worshiped the satiny expanse of flesh with his lips. "So beautiful," he whispered. How had he failed to see it before, this beauty that would make sailors flail themselves against the rocks at sea. Her legs weakened, and he collected her to him, cupping his hands about her buttocks and dragging her close to his jutting shaft.

"Robert," she rasped, his name emerging as a keening moan. She parted her legs.

Sitting on the stone bench, Robert settled Helena on his lap, and worked his hand up her skirt. "I've hungered for this since I awakened in your bed," he growled, hating that even now, he didn't recall the moments they'd shared because of his drunken state that night. He again claimed her mouth and slid his tongue inside.

She boldly met that thrust and parry, matching the intensity of his kiss. His breath came heavily and he found the slick folds of her womanhood.

Robert swallowed her sharp cry with his mouth, and proceeded to work her with his fingers, toying with her nub, exploring her. He slid a finger inside her channel and she stiffened about him. Then, with a long, agonized groan, she grinded into him, thrusting rapidly against his palm with her body, urging him to finish her.

"Please," she begged against his mouth, and that entreaty from this bold, commanding woman, drove him mad with desire. Increasing the pace of his strokes, he pressed the heel of his palm against the silky curls shielding her womanhood, and Helena's body jerked. Then in a glorious display of sensual abandon, she tossed her head back and cried out, thrusting and gyrating, coming in long-rippling waves, and he rang every drop from her, until she collapsed against him, breathless and sweaty. Never more had he wished he were a rogue in the truest sense, because then this blasted sense of honor would not keep him from lying himself between her thighs and thrusting himself deep inside her hot, welcoming heat.

Robert folded his arms around her, holding her against his chest until his heart slowed to a normal cadence. As they silently stood, and he righted her garments, a sense of panic pulled at the corner of his senses. Not since Lucy Whitman had a woman held this pull over him. And if he were not careful, with her candidness and bold ways, Helena had the power to shatter those well-constructed defenses he'd built in years past.

Which would be folly, indeed, especially in a woman so determined to cloak herself in the shrouded mystery of her past.

Not for the first time, questions about Helena Banbury whispered around his mind.

Chapter 14

Rule 14
Never bind yourself to a man.

For ten years of her life, Helena would awake, visit her office, open her books, and work through the accountings of her brother's club.

In the whole of those ten years, with the exception of that morning of madness with Robert's invasion of her chambers, she'd never deviated from her safe, predictable routine.

How vastly different one's life could become in a handful of quick moments. Her mother going from beloved mistress of a duke to lover of a violent gang leader in London had been proof of that.

And sitting here, on the stone bench in the Duchess of Wilkinson's walled-in gardens, with her head tipped up toward the sun, after years of her safe morning routine, was now proof.

It was not that she didn't miss her work. She did. It was just . . . this new sense of discovering life beyond the Hell and Sin Club. In the immediacy of Ryker's sending her away, she'd not seen past her own sense of hurt betrayal. How dare he simply turn her out? Not only because in doing so he'd devalued her role with the Hell, but also because it had proven his inconstancy in a sea of already faithless men.

Helena angled her head back and the sun's rays bathed her face in a warm, soothing heat.

Mayhap this is why Ryker sent her here. Mayhap, he'd known that she needed to confront the life she could belong to outside of the Hell and determine where her place truly was. She absently skimmed her fingers over the puckered flesh on her opposite hand. The nicked skin, brutally and meticulously carved away, a testament to the truth that she could never truly belong here.

She'd long ago pledged to never bind herself to a man the way her mother had, not with her flesh, nor her heart, and certainly not her name. Now she appreciated how very easy it was to make those very mistakes.

"The marquess is waiting for you."

The Duchess of Wilkinson's sharp tone brought Helena's head around. *Robert.*

The harsh glint in the woman's eyes quelled Helena's initial rush of pleasure and she slowly came to her feet, warily eying the other woman. For her brothers' ribbing about her inability to accurately read a person's character, they'd proven wholly wrong. The unrestrained hatred in the duchess's gaze contained a level of evil to rival the darkest soul in the Dials. Apparently that emotion knew no regard for rank or title. Nor would it send a woman of the duchess's station all the way to the gardens to announce Robert's arrival. Such a task would be reserved for a servant.

"Your Grace," she greeted, and started toward the doorway. A frown formed on Helena's lips as the duchess pulled the door closed.

The woman flicked a glacial stare up and down Helena. Peeling her lip back in a sneer, she said more powerfully than any words could her every thought on her duke's by-blow.

Helena didn't care if the woman was a duchess, queen, or princess, she'd not be browbeaten. "If you'll excuse me? Lord Westfield, as you indicated, is waiting." She squared her shoulders, and used the additional four inches she had over the duchess to look down at the woman.

"I do not want you here, Miss Banbury."

She stiffened.

Well, that made two of them. *Or it had . . .* Four days ago . . .

The duchess dusted her palms together. "Your mother was a whore," the woman spoke with the same casualness she'd use if she'd remarked upon the weather. Helena schooled her features, while all the while rage slithered around. In living in the streets, you learned quickly that your enemies sought to uncover and exploit your weakness. If you revealed a crack, they'd slip in and destroy you. The older woman's eyes disappeared within thin, narrow slits. "And with your wiles, you've stolen the attention of the marquess away from Diana. He'll bed you, but he will *never* wed you." Her voice shook with the force of her loathing.

At Helena's continued silence, the duchess snapped. "Do you have nothing to say to that?"

Helena turned her lips in a slow, hard smile. "About my wiles? This is the first I've ever been credited with such."

"Because of your scars?" The sharp, piercing, shriek-like quality of those hateful words hinted at a woman with a thin grasp on her control.

Helena nodded. "Yes. Because of my scars." Those intersecting marks upon her person, as clear as numbers, that stood as testament to her origins and her very existence. If the duchess thought to use those old wounds to break her, she'd be very disappointed. She took a step around the duchess, when the woman shot a hand around her forearm, gripping her hard enough to raise bruises.

"The marquess will find out about you. He will find you are not one of us. Trash from the streets like your brother."

Helena stared blankly down at those fingers upon her, crushing the flesh in a painful grip. It had been nearly nineteen years since she'd had a hand raised to her in violence. Distant cries from long ago echoed around her mind, stealing her breath . . . *Ye brat* . . . *Oi should kill ye* . . . Ryker's enraged face, as a boy in the streets bloodying Diggory within an inch of his life, drove back the remembered horror. Then, that had been the man Ryker was. Fearless. Undaunted. The memory of that long-ago day brought Helena's shoulders back. "My brother has more honor and worth in his smallest finger than you have in your entire person." She leveled her with a look. "Now, unhand me, madam."

The duchess released her suddenly. "My daughter was born to be a duchess, and you've inserted yourself in this family," she seethed. "Just as your mother inserted herself in my husband's life. So you may bed Lord Westfield, but he will belong to Diana. Is that clear?"

"She doesn't want to wed him," she shot back.

"It matters not what she wants. It matters what she was born to." Just as it hadn't mattered to Ryker what Helena wished. Regardless of birthright, decisions were made for women. Robert belonged with a woman of his station, and when he should wed, Diana, in her kindness and properness, would make him an ideal bride. Even with the girl's protestations, she would be no match for her parents' desires for her. Those two families would one day unite, and Robert would no doubt see himself to Diana. A dagger-like pain stabbed at her chest.

"I see you understand," the duchess said, searching her gaze over her face, and Helena hated being exposed before this ruthless woman. "I've no problem if you bed him," she said, the way she might offer a guest the last pastry on a refreshment tray. "As long as you do not think to make yourself a duchess. You are not one of us, Miss Banbury. It is important you remember that."

How could she ever forget such a detail when Society had ingrained that lesson into her since the moment she'd come wailing into the world? Still knowing it, accepting it, that savage blade turned all the more. "You may go to hell," she bit out, ringing a gasp from the other woman.

Helena yanked the door open and strode the same halls she'd wandered yesterday when Robert had led her to the gardens and awakened her body to a dangerous desire. The duchess's unneeded reminder only heightened the truth of that great divide between Robert and her. From their births, they'd been each set upon a different course. Even his talk of his childhood had marked that gulf. He, a child who'd had guest chambers and soaring foyers and played, and Helena, who'd . . .

There were bannisters. She jerked to a stop and stared unblinkingly at the end of the long corridor.

I slid down the bannisters whenever the duke came to call . . . and he would laugh and capture me in his arms . . .

Her lower lip quivered, and she pressed her eyes firmly shut against the force of that long-buried memory, unleashed by Robert's laughing revelation yesterday afternoon. Helena fisted her hands in her skirts. She did not want those memories. She did not want to think of life as it had been in those short five years before her world had been filled with violence and evil.

Coming to the moment, Helena continued onward to the foyer.

Robert stood, head bent as he consulted his timepiece. At the sight of him, not even a day after he'd strummed her body with his skilled touch, heat exploded in her cheeks. By his actions yesterday, and the duchess's accusations a short while ago, they no doubt expected her to be a skilled whore long past shame.

At the sound of her approach, he glanced up and she braced for the leers she'd observed on the faces of too many gentlemen inside the Hell and Sin. He smiled. "Helena," he greeted, dropping a short bow.

Blast him. Emotion lodged in her throat. Why must he continue to unsettle her world by contradicting everything she expected where powerful peers were concerned? "My lord," she said softly, as he took her gloved fingers in his. He bowed over her hand, and then made to pick his head up—and froze.

A hard, lethal sheen iced his eyes, and she staggered back under the force of that emotion. He held tight, and she followed his brutal stare to the finger marks on her forearm. No one except her family at the Hell and Sin had ever radiated such palpable rage over the marks left by another on Helena's skin. She captured the inside of her lip between her teeth, hating that his volatile reaction should so matter.

Quickly disentangling her hand from his, Helena accepted the cloak from a footman with a word of thanks, eternally grateful as those bright red marks were concealed. Next, she collected her bonnet, placed it on her head, and neatly tied the ribbons under her chin.

The butler drew the door open and she hurried outside.

Wordlessly, Robert handed her up into the curricle, and climbed in behind her. A moment later, he snapped the reins and the carriage lurched forward. She closed her eyes and welcomed the gentle spring breeze slapping at her face. Mayhap he'd let the matter rest.

His gaze trained on the busy streets ahead, Robert asked in crisp tones, "Who put their hands on you?"

She sighed. "No one." The lie formed easily. She didn't care to speak about the duchess or her dark words.

"Helena," he growled, and his knuckles whitened over the reins.

"I slid down a bannister."

He briefly shifted his attention from the road to Helena, and then retrained his attention forward.

Helena plucked at the fabric of her skirt. "You asked if I was a mischievous child. Whenever my . . . the duke," she quickly amended. She'd ceased seeing the Duke of Wilkinson as her father long, long ago. "Came to visit, I would straddle the bannister and shimmy down, and he would capture me in a hug and swing me about." Not the actions of a man who'd then easily cut his mistress and child from his fold, and yet . . . that is what had happened. "I forgot that until now," she murmured. "Until you shared your story."

Someone had put their hands on her.

And Robert wanted the name of the person so he could take them apart with his bare hands, and stuff his limbs into his bloody mouth. From the corner of his eye, Robert evaluated Helena. She leaned against the seat, her eyes closed. Her face relaxed, showing no hint of the guardedness that she cloaked herself in. Using her distraction, he fixed on the rippled flesh of her right cheek.

Until now, he'd not allowed himself to think about how a young woman came by those marks. Coward as he was, he wished to believe they were marks of her birth.

He was a nobleman; however, he was no fool. Someone had hurt her—and badly. The kind of hurt that moved beyond the physical and stretched into every aspect of a person's existence.

Twelve years ago, inside his grandfather's office, he'd bore witness to depravity and ugliness. But he'd wager his very soul on Sunday that what someone had done to Helena was the level of evil that indelibly marked a person.

Robert fisted the reins.

Only, it hadn't been any person—it had been Helena Banbury with her bold and unflagging spirit.

Even though in just three months' time she would leave, return to the Hell and Sin, and he'd never again see her but for, perhaps, maybe a glimpse if he visited the club, he wanted to know—about her and the secrets she carried.

They arrived at Hyde Park, and Robert shifted the reins, guiding the curricle through the quiet path, onward.

"You do not say much do you, Helena Banbury?"

She opened her eyes. "No."

They shared a smile.

"My brothers often teased that I was far more comfortable with numbers than people."

He started. "You have brothers." Of course she'd just indicated as much. But how odd he'd not known that particular detail.

Helena nodded. "One brother and . . ." She scrunched her mouth. "Three who, though I don't share blood with them, are more family than my actual father."

How casually she spoke of three men who were not related to her by blood. That piece she shared would have shocked any member of polite Society. In what capacity had she known those men? Questions tumbled around his mind. She'd called them brothers, but had there been one of those men who'd, in fact, been more to her? Had one been a lover with whom she'd resided at the Hell and Sin? Robert gripped the reins hard as a seething jealousy worked its way through him like a slow-moving cancer.

"You are shocked," she observed when he still said nothing.

"I shock far less easily than you believe." In a bid to conceal the volatile emotion thrumming through him, he winked.

They reached Kensington Gardens and Robert brought the curricle to a stop. Birds happily chirped their morning songs, while the thin branches of nearby elms danced gently in the spring breeze.

"They are beautiful."

The soft, wistful quality of Helena's voice carried to his ears.

Robert followed her gaze to the floral gateway that spilled into Kensington Gardens. Colorful blooms lined each side of the graveled path.

"The flowers," she clarified.

"Do you know, in all my rides through Hyde Park, I've never much noticed them?" he admitted. When in London, he rode through Hyde Park nearly every morning. Yet, he'd never looked about him. Not truly. Not in the way she now gazed almost longingly at those blooms.

Her startled gaze shot to his. "Surely not."

"Surely," he said, hating the flash of disappointment in her eyes. She'd found him wanting. The death of her smile and glimmer in her eyes said as much.

She stared out at the blanket of purple flowers with their yellow centers. "I've never left London."

He blinked at that sudden change in conversation.

"I have always lived here," she continued, a faraway quality to her husky contralto. "First, in a townhouse rented by the duke and then . . ." She breathed slowly through her lips. "Then, we lived in a small room in St Giles." His heart hitched. St Giles was a place safe for no man, woman, or beast, and certainly not a child. He struggled to draw breath. What hell must she have known? "I always wanted to go to the country." She may as well have spoken of her preference of milk and sugar with tea. "My mother grew up in Kent and she spoke of the blue skies and fields of wildflowers, and I could not believe there was a place where flowers just . . . grew. How could that be?" she asked softly, a faint smile on her lips. "How when there are only grounds of stone and dirt?"

A weight pressed on his chest.

"There were many days we didn't have food." She motioned to the purple flowers. "I was in the streets where shopkeepers would empty the refuse and one day I saw this . . . blanket of purple lying upon the streets." A soft laugh escaped her, and she gave her head a wistful shake. "I raced over believing I'd found the flowers my mother spoke of." She paused. "They weren't."

"What were they?" he managed; all the while shame ate away at him, and he hated a world in which a small Helena Banbury had foraged for food like a starving pup, just as much as he hated himself for a self-absorption that had prevented him from truly seeing those children about him.

Flecks of silver danced in her eyes, as she leaned up toward him. "They were red cabbage leaves," she whispered. "I'd found something more magnificent than even flowers. I would pretend I was in a meadow, collecting flowers, but then we could cook those leaves and eat them, too."

A groan lodged in his chest. "Helena . . ." He was useless. Utterly useless, incapable of any words that could or would ever be able to erase the suffering she'd known.

Then, in the midst of the darkness of her story, she did something he suspected, even when he was one of those old, doddering dukes with a cane and monocle, he would forever recall—she smiled. Such joy lit her face that a powerful warmth exploded inside him. Something intangible and terrifying that he could not sort out in this moment.

"There was a time I could not speak of those days. I called them my 'dark days.' You never forget what it is to have a hungry belly, wondering and worrying about where your next meal will come from, but as time passes, and you have food, and a home, and safety, you begin to appreciate all you had to do in order to survive." She again tipped her face up toward the sun. "And there is something very wonderful about surviving."

Oh God, with her every unwitting admission, agony tore at Robert's heart, threatening to cleave him open. While he'd been a boy tying together his mother's fine linens and learning to ride his first mount, she'd been a girl who'd hunted flowers in the stone, and pillaged for food. Emotion wadded in his throat, and he struggled to get words past it.

She was far braver than he ever had been, or ever would be. Selfishly he'd come without a servant so he could be alone with her. Now with that faraway glimmer in her eyes, he wished he'd brought someone to attend his bloody carriage. So he could escort her down, and lead her through those gardens he'd never before noticed, never would have noticed, until her.

Relinquishing his death grip on the reins, he claimed her left hand. Slowly, he pulled off one of her gloves.

She made a sound of protest, but he continued on to the next so that her palms lay bare between them. "What happened?" he asked quietly, stroking his thumb over the scars on the top of her hand.

A sheen of tears filled Helena's eyes, and she averted her gaze. When she looked back, the familiar strength radiated in the depths of her green eyes so that those fleeting mementos of sadness may as well have been imagined. "I prefer to think about bouquets of red cabbage, Robert." He wished to press her for everything she withheld. Wished to know everything when he had no right. But somewhere, in the course of four days and a chance meeting at gaming hell a month earlier, this fiery woman who'd openly challenged him in Lord Sinclair's parlor had slipped past his defenses.

And for the first time since Lucy's betrayal, Robert wished his heart were intact . . . because Helena Banbury would have been a woman worthy of it.

Another quiet laugh spilled past her lips, rusty as though from ill use. "I suspect we've been here a sufficient amount of time? We've been seen?"

The pretend courtship. Her fleeting time here. And her eventual return to the Hell and Sin Club. He imagined her reentering that world, amongst lascivious lords and powerful proprietors of that hell . . . and something dark, and primitive, roared to life.

Robert gave thanks for the years of practice he had of false smiles, for he forced his lips upwards in a half grin. "Indeed, Miss Banbury. Shall we return?"

"I'll . . . see you tomorrow then?" Was there truly a hopeful quality to that hesitant question, or did he simply wish there to be?

He tweaked her nose. "I am afraid tomorrow, I've a previous engagement."

This time, there was no imagining the crestfallen expression that fell over her face and a lightness filled him.

"Of course," she said quickly. "I was just wondering. Curious. Given the true nature of our . . . our arrangement; however, we do not need to see one another *every* day."

"What if I say I want to?" The hushed question left his lips before he could recall it.

And just like that, their world was restored. Helena rolled her eyes to the sky. "I'm not one of your conquests you need to waste your words on, Robert. It is not my intention to take you away from your . . . pleasures."

He flexed his jaw. Long ago he'd earned the status of rogue and it had been one he relished. Never more had he despised that reputation than with her flippant charge. For the time they'd spent together, short though it was, did she still only see him as a lord living for nothing but his own pleasures?

"My family is in deep," he said in solemn tones.

Her gaze shot to his. Then, like a fish plucked from the sea, she opened and closed her mouth. "What?" Consternation weighted that word.

Robert expected there should be suitable reservations in confiding this secret. If it were discovered, it would open his sister and father up to nasty gossip, and where he didn't give a jot about what they said of him, there was Bea to protect. But he'd no doubt in trusting Helena with this.

"My grandfather made some substantial investments," he said finally, keeping his stare forward. "And our pockets are nearly to let for it."

"What type of investments?"

Once again, she held him frozen in awe for how unique she was to all other ladies he'd ever known. With his revelation, any other woman would have been slack-jawed with shock or disdain, and yet Helena spoke with a rational precision better suited to a skilled man-of-affairs.

"Steam," he said.

"You are certain it is so very . . ." Her eyes raced quickly over his face. "Dire."

He gave a rusty chuckle. "Oh, quite. I've been in frequent meetings and short of letting go the whole of our servants, selling off unentailed properties, and abandoning those steam ventures, there are few options, except . . ." He grimaced, and promptly firmed his mouth.

"What?" she asked, too clever to ever miss that telling word.

A muscle jumped at the corner of his eye. "My father would tell you the only option is for me to marry an heiress." As soon as that admission left his mouth, he cursed.

Helena swiveled her gaze up to his.

And he, long jaded by life, found his neck going hot with embarrassment . . . and shame. He forced another laugh, and it emerged sharp with enmity. "He wished it so much that he'd even faked he was dying and staged a summer party to marry me off, all with the purpose of salvaging our depleting coffers." Once again, the still-fresh resentment brewed under the surface, and threatened to spill over.

"Oh, Robert." Helena covered his hand with hers, pulling him from the brink of bitterness. "And you do not wish to save your family's fortune that way." As hers was more statement than anything, he remained silent. Helena caught her jaw between her thumb and forefinger and tapped. "You're certain there are no other ways. That the man-of-affairs is competent?"

Actually, for his father's faith in the man, Robert wasn't entirely certain of the aging man's skills. With Stonely's disdain for investments, he very much harkened back to rigid strictures on nobles *dabbling* in trade. "I believe my family would do better with someone more capable," he settled for.

"Perhaps I can look at your—"

"Let us speak of something else," he said quietly. Shame needled at his insides. What a purposeless existence he'd lived for so long. All Helena had shared this day, and she would worry with her eyes and words about his family's finances. Finances he'd not given thought to in the course of his life. "Please," he added, when she made to speak. "I just wished you to know why I cannot visit on the morrow." *Even as I desire it more than anything. More than is wise.*

She gave a reluctant nod.

As he gathered the reins and guided the carriage from Hyde Park, he reflected on what an utter fool he'd been these years.

How much he'd failed to see. Not only his family's finances, but beyond that. To something so much more important—the suffering others had endured around him. And how much more he would have failed to see if he'd not stumbled into the wrong chambers in that forbidden hell.

Chapter 15

Rule 15
Always remember who you are.

The following morning, standing in front of the bevel mirror, Helena's pale cheeks stood in even greater contrast than usual. She stared unflinchingly at the puckered scars, seeing them, remembering: remembering when of late it had become so very easy to forget that this was not her world. To remember that she belonged elsewhere.

Helena touched trembling fingers to the scars left by Diggory's cruel enjoyments, a forever visual testimony of her place in the well-ordered world. She might don fancy skirts and learn the steps of a waltz, but she was, and would always and only be, Helena Banbury, the daughter of a whore.

And two days earlier she'd proven herself, very much, her mother's daughter. For she'd panted, pleaded, and writhed on Robert's lap like a common street doxy. She let her arm fall quavering to her side. If he'd continued, she would have given herself to him. There in the duchess's gardens, she would have parted her legs, and given him her virtue without a single stab of regret. Nor had it been strictly this physical hungering that only he'd ever roused in her.

. . . So beautiful . . .

Her eyes slid closed, and she drew in a slow, shaky breath. When he'd spoken that word, blanketed in a thick cloud of desire, she had actually believed it. Felt it. Felt she was more than Helena from the streets—all because of his skilled, seductive words.

Only yesterday, something far more dangerous than any forbidden touch had happened. She'd shared stories of her girlhood days, stories she'd shared with no one. Parts of her life that not even her brothers spoke of. You let the past stay buried.

But she hadn't. She, who'd always been terse and silent, had talked. And talked. And continued talking, telling stories she'd not even remembered until they were spilling from her lips.

Helena jammed her fingertips against her temples and rubbed. This was all careening out of control. The scheme she'd concocted involving the marquess had been simple. Three months together, where he'd pretend to court her, until the end of the Season, when she was then free to go on her practical way back to the Hell and Sin.

What a mocking twist of fate or irony, or both, that in a mere four days, he'd upended her thoughts.

In all her calculations and practical deductions, she'd not accounted for the possibility of not only desiring Robert, but also . . . liking him. Of seeing a man who'd once been a boy who tied sheets together and dangled over ledges. A boy who'd become a man who spoke affectionately to old dukes. A man in need of a fortune, and who'd willingly helped her anyway and forsaken plans that could have saved his family's finances. She dragged her hands over her face. Those discoveries didn't fit with everything she'd come to know. With everything she'd been told or seen.

I am losing myself . . . After just over a month amongst the haute ton, she'd somehow forgotten all the rules ingrained into her by Ryker.

If he'd sent her here as some test or another, she'd failed abysmally. Her sole intention for enlisting Robert's assistance had been to avoid fortune hunters out to trap a duke's by-blow, so she might return to the life she'd quite contentedly lived. In doing so, she'd unwittingly endangered them both: he, with his inability to secure a proper, advantageous match . . . and she, with her weakening heart.

For, how often had she longed for her office? Or her books? Or the actual club itself? Not truly, she hadn't. Not beyond some amorphous thought of three months from now when she would return.

Panic churned inside, a need possessing her to rekindle that connection with the only life she'd truly known. For what if this was some kind of grander test conducted by Ryker? What if in her absence he discovered someone far more skilled and capable with the club's accounting? Then what purpose would she have?

She steeled her jaw, tamping down the worry wreaking havoc on her senses.

She may desire Lord Robert Westfield, even like him, but that did not mean she belonged here or wished to. What purpose was there for a woman who lived amongst polite Society? What kind of existence beyond a fat dowry for an impoverished husband who wagered too much and kept just as many whores?

Robert is not that man . . .

Helena froze. Just four days ago she would have scoffed at that defense of him. Given his actions in the Earl of Sinclair's parlor with that stunning beauty, he'd quite neatly fit within her expectations for him and all nobles.

No longer. She gripped her hands against the fabric of her skirts. Neither did this new appreciation for Robert, as a man and person, matter. There was no place for them together in any sense of the word. She'd no doubt he'd make her his mistress, scars and all . . . but never his wife.

"Not that I want that position," she muttered under her breath.

Why did that ring hollow?

Striding over to her armoire, she threw the doors open and fished around the far back. Her fingers brushed a coarse, familiar fabric, and she froze. This brown cloak was her world. This was the harsh, but safe existence. Not satins or silks or muslins.

With slow, regretful fingers, she let the garment fall back into place and collected a soft muslin cloak.

Yanking it on, she drew the deep hood up, and sprinted over to the side of her bed. With quick movements, she dropped to her knees and fished under the soft feather mattress. Of course, theft within the duke's home was as likely as a snowstorm in summer, yet life had ingrained the perils of leaving your monies about; that was why she'd hidden those funds the moment she stepped inside this temporary home.

Jumping to her feet, Helena stuffed the handful of coins into the front of her cloak and strode purposefully across the room. If she stayed here, in this room, in this home, with these turbulent thoughts about Robert and her place in Society swirling around her mind, she'd go mad.

Almost instantly, her maid, Meredith, entered the room. The girl, with heavily freckled cheeks and jutting front teeth, smiled. "You rang, Miss Banbury?"

Helena nodded. "Will you see the duke's carriage readied? I'd have you accompany . . . shopping." Isn't that how everyone expected a young lady to spend her days? Bitterness soured her mouth.

The young woman nodded, promptly closed the door, and hurried to do Helena's bidding.

A short while later, in the duke's comfortable carriage, with her maid on the opposite bench, Helena made her way to Lambeth. As she settled back in the comfortable squabs, an invigorating thrill coursed through her. Hers was a small show of control, but there was a heady sense of power in stepping outside those suddenly suffocating walls. How many years had she still been viewed as nothing more than the snarling, spitting child of eight, dependent on her brothers to go anywhere or do anything? She'd been that same closed-away person since she'd arrived in Mayfair, dutifully tucked away in the duke's townhouse like a wounded bird in a gilded cage.

As the carriage drew her farther and farther away, she drew the curtain back more and stared boldly out. Still quiet at the early morning hour, vendors pushed their carts into place, preparing for a day of hawking their wares.

Even the vendors and streets of the nobility were cleaner. As opposed to the crass men and women who'd sell their teeth, soul, and body against a crumbling building for coin, if it were offered. Then, that was the world to which they were born. The *ton* . . . and everyone else. Nor would Helena trade the freedom and power she had to be one of those purposeless ladies. She'd carved out a world where she'd never be dependent upon a man, not the way her own mother had.

First a powerful lord, who'd chosen a proper lady as his wife, and then the protector her mother had found in Mac Diggory.

An icy dread froze her, and she pressed her eyes closed. Hatred, potent and tangible, all these years gripped her in its familiar grasp. Helena curled her fingers about the edge of her seat. How many switches had he taken to her and her mother's backs? How many scars did she now wear because of his drunken rages? How many times had he sold his wife to a fancy gent, all for some coin that he only wasted on more drink?

The agonized cries of her long-dead mother echoed around her mind, and Helena pressed her eyes closed, willing them gone. Nothing could come from those remembrances. Pain brought weakness. There was no healing or happiness that could ever come from thoughts of the life they'd lived.

The only good that had come of those dark days, as she'd come to call them, had been the invaluable lesson—men were not to be trusted. Neither gentlemen nor men in the streets. Even as Robert had demonstrated that he was unlike so many of those cruel lords, he'd proven himself far more dangerous in other ways. His touch, heady and hypnotic, had the power to weaken . . . it was the gentle, seductive caress that a weaker woman would have traded her virtue over for.

The carriage slowed to a stop, and she pitched forward at the sudden, jarring halt.

Meredith looked expectantly at her. "Miss Banbury, we've arrived." The girl with her frizzy carrot-red hair pulled back the curtain and stared with a dubious expression out the window.

Yes, ladies did not come shopping in Lambeth, and certainly not in these streets.

"You remain here," she ordered. "I'll be a short while."

The young maid gave her head a hard shake. "Oh, no, Miss Banbury. His Grace would not allow that."

She bit the inside of her cheek to keep from pointing out that His Grace had, in fact, allowed it for nearly twenty years. Helena gave a firm look, gentling it with a smile. "I'll be but a short while," she pledged, drawing her hood up.

Before the young woman could issue further protest, Helena shoved the door open and jumped down without assistance. She shot her arms out to steady herself, and then pulling her hood further over her eyes, she started down the streets. As she wound her way through the throng of wooden carts, and coarse-looking men and women, Helena glanced at this end of London. Women and children held their hands outstretched, begging for coin. From her.

A wall of emotion, shame, shock, and remembrance, all slammed into her with the force of a fast-moving carriage. After she and her brothers had escaped the streets, what had they done for those who were not so fortunate, those people whose bellies were still empty and those children collecting cabbage leaves? Helena struggled to swallow past the wave of guilt choking her.

Fishing out a handful of coins, she pressed them into outstretched hands as she walked. How had she, Ryker, Calum, Adair, or Niall been any different than the lords and ladies they'd so disdained? Because they'd provided employment at the Hell and Sin? Robert, the duke, all of the nobility, they too provided work for men, women, and children. Yet, she'd never seen those as magnanimous gestures.

By the time she reached her destination, her breath came hard and ragged in her ears, deafening.

She looked up at the crooked wooden sign hanging above: In the Spirit.

She pressed the handle and, pulling the door open, stepped inside.

A wall of dust slapped her face, and she promptly sneezed. Shoving back her hood, she perused the small shop. But for a table and a counter, covered in books and *more* dust, the small space remained devoid of anything else.

Footsteps sounded from within a doorway draped with a black cloth. A corpulent man with greying hair, and spectacles on his nose, stepped inside. "Hullo, how may I . . . ?" His polite greeting died. No doubt it was not every day a young woman set foot inside his *shop*.

Helena tugged off her white gloves and strode forward. "You supply the Hell and Sin Club with their alcohol," she said without preamble. Even saying the name of her club, and speaking on a matter of business, brought a calming sense of ease. This she was comfortable with. This she understood. Not goldenly glorious gentlemen who spoke about her past, and caressed her scars with tenderness.

The man frowned, all earlier hint of warmth gone. "It is not my place to discuss Ryker Black's business with anyone." Then, he stole a look about and spoke in hushed tones. "Unless ye had some coin to pay. Then I might have details."

She sneered. Quality spirits be damned, how did her brothers do business with a man such as this one? With that a familiar wave went through her, at the lot she had the sense to see through when her brothers, so confident in their judgments, failed to do so. "Your deliveries are coming through with nearly ten percent broken in transit. Is that also a product of what someone is paying you?" she asked, settling her palms on the counter.

The man's fleshy cheeks turned a mottled shade of red. "How dare you . . . ?" he sputtered.

She jabbed a finger at him, striking him in the chest. "I dare because I'm the one who has to answer for the erroneous liquor accounts." *Or I did, until my brothers ceased to see my value.* Resentment breathed to life again, as powerful now as it had been the day she'd been summoned to Ryker's office to find the duke waiting.

"You?"

"Yes, me."

His eyes disappeared into thin slits as he leaned forward, peering at her. "If you're working for Ryker Black, why haven't I seen you before?"

Because they kept me sheltered away. Because I was too much a fool to challenge that and not demand visibility in the world.

She continued, deliberately ignoring his question. "If I have my way, Mr. Black will have a new supplier of his liquor." All the color leached from his face, leaving a pale white pallor. "I expect your next shipment will arrive flawlessly." With deliberate movements, Helena drew on her leather gloves. "That is, unless Sam Davies at Forbidden Pleasures does not pay you a greater purse to see them ruined?" She winged an eyebrow up.

The man coughed spasmodically. "H-How dare you?"

Her brothers may say she was a rotten read on people. However, this man rung his hands together and rapidly shifted his eyes about, avoiding her gaze, the way any criminal at Newgate did.

"I dare because I'm Ryker Black's bookkeeper." *Or I was.* She'd just omit that particular detail. "And his sister," she added. Helena peered down her nose at him. "Do we have an understanding then, sir?"

"W-we do," he continued to sputter.

"Very good." Helena dusted her gloved palms together. "I expect this meeting will remain between us?" The forgotten satisfaction that came from actually doing something that was not buying bonnets and fancy dresses, but rather something that required intellect and finesse, filled her with a heady sensation.

He gave a jerky nod, and as Helena drew her hood back into place and took her leave, she cast a final look back at the establishment. This is why she'd never belong in polite Society, no matter how much the duke wished it. The Helena Banburys of the world were not meant to sit politely with their heads bent over embroidery frames, discussing balls and soirees. She was meant to do something more.

This fleeting visit had been reminder enough. She may enjoy Robert's company, and smile and laugh more than she ever did in his presence, but she could never have anything more with him, not simply because of the station divide between them, but because of her own need for purpose.

Why, gentlemen such as him, they didn't even know these parts of London existed, no doubt.

Giving her head a clearing shake, Helena turned to go.

When a sharp cry went up.

Always run from a cry . . .

She momentarily squeezed her eyes shut. *Never toward it, Helena. Never toward it . . .*

Another wail split the buzz of activity.

She opened her eyes just as a small child's exclamation echoed somewhere in the distance.

Bloody hell.

And Helena started toward that plaintive cry.

Chapter 16

Rule 16
Never venture into the Dials or St Giles alone. Ever.

"Can you not find a perfectly fashionable bookshop to attend?" Robert muttered, escorting his sister through the bustling, dirty streets of St Giles Circus. The Temple of the Muses. The Corner Bookshop. As it was, leaving his sister in the company of a maid *and* a footman while Robert went on to see his man-of-affairs gave him sufficient pause—pause enough to personally accompany her to the establishment.

"You are becoming stuffy in your advancing years," Beatrice scolded. "Furthermore, what business do you have here?" she asked, too cleverly turning the tables on him.

He silently cursed. Of course Bea, who missed nothing, wouldn't be content to let the question about his trips to Oxford Street be.

"I'm meeting with Father's man-of-affairs," he settled for. There, truth. Certainly enough to silence any further—

"To what end?" she pounced. Then she slowed her steps, paling. "I believed you said Father was merely pretending to be ill."

He fell back a step. "Father is fine," he said in calming tones, while passersby bustled on noisily about them. She studied him a long moment, and then they resumed walking.

Feeling her gaze on his face, he kept his stare trained forward. "Is it so very shocking that I at my . . . How did you refer to them?" he asked, winging a brow up. "My advancing years? That I should take some interest in the family's estates."

Bea turned a suspicious look up at him. "Why?"

Ballocks, was there anything she did not see? "Because I've failed to do right by my responsibilities before now," he said quietly, the words spoken with the ease that truth gave them.

Except, he'd almost abandoned his meeting altogether this morn. He'd almost been the self-absorbed bastard he'd been all these years. He'd almost said no. He'd almost begged off, saying he had other plans, because in a sense he did. With Helena Banbury and their pretend courtship. Now, as they resumed walking and he skimmed his gaze over the rough streets on the fringe of London, he gave thanks that he hadn't been so selfish in his intentions, because he'd no doubt, knowing Beatrice as he did, she'd have found a way here, herself.

"Quite sad, isn't it?" His sister's quiet inquiry recalled his attention.

He didn't pretend to misunderstand; instead, he looked about the dirtied streets where Charing Cross intersected with St Giles Circus.

They were red cabbage leaves . . . I'd found something more magnificent than even flowers . . .

That familiar pressure squeezed about his lungs. This was Helena's life. One of dark, dank streets and hungry beggars. Robert swallowed hard. Nay, hers had been far worse. Hers had been the streets of St Giles, where the only thing between living and dying in that area was good fortune. And the brothers she'd spoken of yesterday.

"I expect you hardly think there is anything interesting in visiting a bookshop, Robert."

Walking alongside his sister through the growing crowds about Westminster Bridge, with a maid traveling close on their heels, Robert smiled. "Do you think I'm one of those illiterate lords?"

His sister shot him a look. "Hardly," she scoffed. "But if you are the rogue the papers purport you to be . . ." By the pregnant pause and long look, she was expecting an answer. Which he assuredly would not oblige her on. "Well, then you do tend to find your enjoyments at your clubs and scandalous events."

Robert choked. "What do you know about scandalous events?" He tugged at his cravat. When he'd agreed to accompany Beatrice several days ago, he'd hardly anticipated a discussion with his innocent sister about how he chose to spend his nights.

"Not enough," Beatrice muttered under her breath, casting a look about at the lords and ladies picking their way among wagons and shops. She gestured furiously to the small corner shop in the distance. He squinted, reading the crooked wooden sign. Ye Olde Bookshop. "After all, this is my idea of great fun."

He made a noncommittal sound. After all, that was quite how a gentleman preferred his sister's interests to be—wholly unscandalous.

"What are your clubs like?"

Robert blinked, as Beatrice's innocent query cut into his musings. "What are my . . . ?"

"Clubs like," she finished. "I confess, I'm quite bored with all the same, tedious events of the *ton*. I'm conducting research."

A memory trickled in of a full, tempting mouth as the spirited nameless vixen had brandished her knife about. Then her words registered. "Conducting research?" he choked. "For what purpose?" Now, this is how a gentleman did *not* prefer his sister to be.

"Do not be prudish and straitlaced," his sister scolded.

Prudish and straitlaced, he mouthed. Those were assuredly the first time such accusations had ever been leveled at him.

A frown formed on his lips. So *this* was why his sister had been seeking him out. A desire for . . . information. Information he'd sooner carve his tongue out than utter for her innocent ears. Yet, it was still safer than speaking to her of the family's finances. "I am afraid you'll require research material that is decidedly not from your brother," he said dryly, ruffling the top of her head.

Beatrice pursed her lips. "I'm not a child, Robert. Nor do I have the same luxury as a gentleman."

"Luxury?" he repeated with a wry twist that only deepened her frown. Were they truly different in the expectations Society had of them? His actions, though freer, were still closely scrutinized and whispered about by gossips and recorded in column sheets.

"I cannot go about and spread my proverbial wings," she said, throwing her arms wide. "Not without absolute ruin."

The solemnity in her tones elicited another frown. His sister spoke with the same frustration of a lady who'd tired of her lot and station. There was a faint desperation there that could only come after four unsuccessful Seasons. Where most gentlemen relished their unwedded state, ladies largely lived with the hope and expectation of a match.

He picked around his thoughts, searching for something, anything slightly scandalous but still safe to feed her proverbial interests. "There is a thrill at the wagering tables," he said at last. Or there had been. Now, more than ever, those once-thrilling enjoyments had begun to grow tiresome.

Beatrice's eyes lit, and she leaned close, urging him with her gaze to share more. "Do you play whist or faro or hazard? I suspect you are more of the hazard-playing type," she prattled, as they continued walking, making their way through the largely empty streets. She cast a look upwards.

"Hazard," he supplied.

She gave a pleased nod. "As I suspected. I overheard Papa speaking to his man-of-affairs about those clubs you visit."

He gnashed his teeth. His father was speaking to old Stonely about Robert's habits. It apparently mattered not at all to either man that Robert had committed himself these weeks now to poring over ledgers and cutting expenditures where he could. Fortunately they reached the small establishment, sparing Robert from answering. He removed his hat and beat it against his leg. His sister paused on the stoop, and cast a questioning look back.

Robert motioned to her and the lingering servants. "I will allow you the privacy of your research," he said with a wink. "While I see to my busi—"

A cry went up somewhere ahead, cutting into his parting.

He and Beatrice swung their heads as one toward the sound. "What is it?" She stretched her neck about, straining to see.

He took her by the arm. "It is nothing for a lady's eyes to see," he said tightly, neatly steering her toward the entrance of the shop. Never again was she coming here. Ever. Even if he had to assign a bloody guard to her.

His words earned a deeper frown, as his sister dug in her heels.

Another muffled shout carried the length of the busy street. He searched his gaze ahead and then swallowed a curse as a colorfully clad dandy brandished his walking cane while a street urchin cowered at his feet. A surge of fury went through Robert. The wind carried over a boy's sharp cry, as the gentleman brought his cane back and—

Robert's blood iced cold as a tall, cloaked figure shoved herself in front of the boy. His insides twisted. "Get inside," he gritted out, and knowing his sister's penchant for exploration, he turned to the footman. "See her inside."

"Robert?" Beatrice's concerned voice followed after him.

He quickened his stride. Mayhap he was seeing the woman everywhere. Mayhap that was all that accounted for his conjuring her here, throwing herself in front of a stranger's raised cane. Because no woman in her right mind would ever dare risk coming here to these streets and putting herself before harm . . .

Helena would.

Bloody hell.

The knots tightened and with his breath rasping in his ears, Robert broke into a run, shoving through the throng of coarse street folk.

"You bloody cork-brained bastard," Helena shouted, glorious in her crimson-cheeked fury, as she shook her fist at the young earl. "What manner of brute are you that you'd put your hands on a child?"

Lord Whitby, one of the *ton*'s notorious dandies, stood, mouth agape. Of course, with her elegant muslin cloak and cultured tones, he couldn't know what to make of being challenged by a lady. "Madam," he at last sputtered. "This thief lifted my timepiece."

Fire flashed in Helena's eyes, and she put her arms behind her, protectively touching the child. Robert narrowed his eyes as with the faintest flick of her hand, she slipped the timepiece from the boy's hand. She marched so close to Whitby that their noses nearly touched. "I'm sure you are mistaken." And had Robert not been studying her movements so closely, he'd have failed to see the flash of gold before it disappeared.

Whitby scowled. "I assure you I'm not."

She placed her hands on her hips. "Check your pockets."

His eyes bulged. "How dare you—?"

"I demand you check your pockets, sir." Her sharp cry shook with fury. "I am a *lord*."

"I do not care if you're God in Heaven come to call—" At her escalating pitch, Robert stepped forward.

"Whitby," he drawled, even as tension thrummed through him. What in blazes was she thinking risking her safety in this way?

Because that is the manner of woman she is . . .

The cluster of people assembled swiveled their gazes to Robert.

A gasp rang from Helena's lips and she touched her hand to her breast. "Rob—*my lord*," she whispered. Was it shock that filled her expressive eyes? Guilt? What should she have to be guilty of? Did she think he'd condemn her for her intervention? Or did something else bring her here this day . . . ? All number of inquiries tumbled forward, and he thrust them aside. For now. There would be time enough later to put his questions to Helena Banbury.

The child, with his dirt-stained cheeks, alternated his attention between Helena and Whitby and backed slowly away. Robert rested his hand on the lad's small, narrow shoulders. "Miss Banbury, a pleasure, as always," he greeted.

The Earl of Whitby opened and closed his mouth. He scratched at his head. "You know this chit?"

The lady darted her eyes about, giving her the look of a doe caught in the hunter's snare. He positioned himself between her and a path of escape, and then turned his attention to the dandy in his yellow satin knee breeches. "Indeed. My family is quite closely connected with her father's." He gave the other man a hard look. "The Duke of Wilkinson."

Whitby emitted a strangled cough. He offered a belated bow. Then: "She's come between me and my timepiece," the man said in a remarkably brave display. Or stupid.

"The lady said to check your pocket," Robert said coolly.

"The boy lifted . . ." At the hard look Robert fixed on him, the man gulped audibly, and patted his jacket.

"See? It is as I—?" The man froze, and shook his head. "I don't . . . ?" He scratched at his puzzled brow. "I didn't have it a moment ago," he mumbled, his cheeks flushed, as the small crowd dispersed.

"I take it the matter is settled?" he drawled, winging an eyebrow up. The street urchin wiggled, and he tightened his grip.

"The apology," Helena piped in. They looked to her. "He owes the boy an apology." She tipped her chin up a notch.

"Wait, just a moment," Whitby began, the color heightening in his cheeks. "I do not apologize to street—"

Robert glowered him into silence. Granted, with her sleight of hand, she'd maneuvered the stolen timepiece back onto the man's person, but what manner of life had she known, as a lady outside of the peerage?

"What is your name?" he gently asked the boy, aching inside for all Helena had known, and now this boy.

The boy, with his gaunt cheeks and tired eyes, jutted his chin at a mutinous angle, and Robert's heart pulled. That defensive, proud gesture so very much Helena's. "James," he said, reluctance drawing out that utterance.

"An apology for James," Robert said tersely.

Some emotion flared powerful in Helena's eyes, and then she dropped her gaze to the boy's head.

"I apologize," Whitby bit out.

Robert inclined his head. "Oh, and Whitby?" he halted, as the dandy turned to go. "If you raise that cane or a single hand to another man, woman, or child, I'll beat you with it. Are we clear?"

The earl emitted a strangled choke and with his cheeks flushed, he gave a jerky nod.

"That will be all, Whitby," Robert said in austere tones.

Dropping a tight bow, the other man wheeled on his heel and sprinted down the street.

Robert fished out a fat purse and handed it to James. "You are, of course, free to continue picking pockets until you find yourself swinging from a hangman's noose." He paused. "Or you can use that coin and have a hack deliver you to the Marquess of Westfield's residence in Mayfair." Robert fished around for a card and finding one, he held it out.

The child jerked away from his hand, and eyed Robert with thick suspicion in his jaded eyes. "Who is the Marquess of Westfield?"

"*He* is," Helena said softly, and the boy jerked his angry gaze to her.

"It is your choice," Robert said, motioning to the coin in his scarred hands. Helena's hands. Nausea roiled in his belly. *What suffering had she known . . . ?*

"It's fair work?" the child demanded. "Ye ain't one of those fancy lords lookin' te bugger a boy?"

His gut clenched. Is this the hell endured by children on the streets? Never more did he feel the sting of deserved shame greater than this moment.

Helena spoke in affirmative tones. "His Lordship is not one of those lords."

"Wot do ye know of it?"

Yes, what did she know of it? Robert fisted his hands, hating a world in which Helena knew the extent of ugliness that existed.

The proud young woman fell to a knee, and said something close to the boy's ear. His eyes went wide in his dirt-stained face, and then slowly, he took the card.

The other man gone, Robert turned his attention back to a pale Helena. Since the moment he'd stumbled into her hallway at the club, the lady had always met his eyes with a bold, unwavering strength. Until now. Now she looked up at the sky, the ground. "Miss Banbury, you are incapable of doing anything without drama," he said with forced levity. All the while the terror that had threatened his sanity the moment she'd stepped between the child and Whitby's cane slowly receded. "Do you know," he said, and shrinking the space between them, he spoke in a hushed whisper. "If you'd wished to see me this day, you needn't have gone through all the difficulty. I would have gladly obliged." He held his arm out.

Helena opened and closed her mouth several times, staring at his fingers as though she'd never before seen a hand. "Why did you do that?" she asked softly.

Annoyance stirred. Did she believe him to be one of those self-important bastards who'd simply ignore the plight of a child on the street? *Then, would you have truly seen the world around you if it hadn't been for her . . . ?*

Robert leaned down, and put his mouth close to her ear. "Should I have called the constable on the boy for lifting that timepiece?"

She flared her eyes.

He captured her hand in his, raising her knuckle to his lips. "You are quite deft with your fingers, Helena," he murmured, brushing a kiss over them.

Some of the tension left her narrow shoulders and she faintly smiled. "Thank you," she said, "for helping me and the child."

He lifted his lips in a cynical smile. "There is no thanks necessary." Was her opinion of him so low that she believed he'd have ever stood, a silent observer to the plight of a defenseless woman and child? "Despite what you may believe, madam, I am not a monster."

There was a stricken look in her eyes. "I do not believe you are a monster." And he'd wager his future ducal title that that was the closest Helena Banbury had ever managed in terms of a compliment for any man. She gave a wave of her hand. "But you did not just help the boy."

"James," he amended.

"You did not just help *James*." She paused and looked up. "You offered him employment."

"I did." They continued to make their way through the streets, onward to Ye Olde Bookshop.

"Why send him in a hired hack with a purse?" Far greater wariness than any young woman her age should possess filled her tone.

"I expect if the boy truly wishes to begin a new life of honorable employment, he will think on it, and ultimately take the steps. I've merely given him the means to do so," he said, keeping his gaze ahead. "The decision is his."

As they continued down the street, silence fell between them. When it became apparent Helena had little intention of speaking to the very obvious question, he said, "Well?"

A puzzled expression marring her sharp features, she looked up at him.

"Do you truly think I'll not wonder about the coincidence in meeting you here this morning, madam?"

Her cheeks pinkened as they stopped before the shop where he'd left Beatrice and her maid. Then her eyes flew to the sign dangling above their heads. "The bookshop," she blurted. "I was here for . . . a book." She narrowed her eyes into thin slits. "And what are you doing here, my lord?"

Ah, so he was "my lord" again, was he?

Robert reached past her and pressed the door handle. "I was escorting my sister here." He paused. "And then seeing to business with my man-of-affairs." A flash of understanding brightened her eyes, which she quickly concealed. He motioned her inside. "After you, Miss Banbury." She'd had as much intention of visiting this bookshop than he had of attending Almack's that night. His suspicion roiled all the more.

She cocked her head, and looked at the open doorway to Robert, and then wetting her lips, she stepped inside.

"There you are, Robert." His sister, a book in hand, came skidding to a stop before them. Surprise marred her face. "Miss Banbury! Hello," she said with a widening smile.

Helena sank into a curtsy. "My lady."

Beatrice tucked the small leather volume under her arm, and held out her opposite hand for Helena's. "Oh, please, you must call me Beatrice. Would you care to join me?" Before Helena could formulate a reply, his sister gathered her hand and placed it on her arm, leading them away.

Helena cast an almost desperate glance over her shoulder, and he winked.

Mayhap, the lady would think twice with dissembling. His lips twitched.

Just then, Beatrice said something commanding the other woman's notice, leaving Robert alone . . . to consider, just what business Miss Helena Banbury, daughter of a duke, former worker at the Hell and Sin Club, had in this end of London.

As his sister's laugh rumbled from somewhere within the shop, he folded his arms.

Helena had her secrets, that much was clear.

And Robert was determined to figure out just what those secrets were . . . whether the lady wished to share them, or not.

Of all the rules ingrained into her, she'd been schooled on evading notice from the moment Ryker had rescued her. Not only had she been discovered today, Robert also knew she was lying.

And *Helena* only knew because she'd spent so much of her life with liars and thieves, and suspicious stares, that she'd recognized her paltry attempt at prevarication, and the glint of suspicion in Robert's usually warm gaze.

If she were wise, she'd be focusing on the fact that he'd caught her red-handed. So why could she not rid her mind of his efforts on behalf of a common street thief? Warmth spilled into her heart and she closed her eyes. A boy whose name he'd taken time to learn, and whom he'd given a choice to, in a world where those of her station had few.

"Have you been here before, Miss Banbury?"

Heart hammering, Helena's eyes flew open. Robert's sister stared patiently at her. Her mind raced as she tried to drag forth the young woman's question. "Please, call me Helena," she insisted. "And no, I've not." As soon as the truth slid out, she silently cursed and stole a glance over her shoulder for Robert. He remained at the front of the shop, arms folded, staring boldly.

"Come along." Beatrice guided her farther down the aisle until Robert was no longer in sight. "He is a wonderful brother," she said as she skimmed the dusty titles on the floor-length shelf. "But he is ever so protective. Even now he should be at his meeting, but he remains here." She lowered her voice to a soft whisper. "Though I suspect your unexpected appearance has just as much to do with his decision to stay."

Cheeks heating, Helena managed a smile, and opted to speak to the lady's former remark. "I well know about overprotective brothers." Men who'd trust her with the finances of their successful gaming establishment but also believed her undeserving of any real control in her future.

"Do you?" Beatrice looked up from her perusal. There was curiosity in her gaze.

Unnerved by the ease with which this woman spoke, Helena glanced down at the tips of her slippers. The only ladies she'd ever had any dealings with had been in the streets, and those women had yanked their fine cloaks and gowns away as Helena had woven herself between them. "I do," she said at last.

"Are you close with them?" The young lady's gentle probing brought a lump of emotion to Helena's throat.

Since Ryker had sent her away, she'd spent so much time angry and bitterly aggrieved over his interference in her life. She'd embraced the betrayal from each of them, because it was far easier to fuel her anger and resentment than to think about how desperately she missed them. "I am," she said softly.

"Do you see them often?"

At the relentless questioning, Helena hugged her arms to her stomach, and glanced wildly about. Peers didn't probe. They saw on the surface, and never bothered to learn anything more about a person, and yet Robert, and now his sister, did in ways that exposed Helena, and brought down years' worth of walls she'd built up. "I did." Before they sent me away. "We are." *Were.* "As I said, close." She drew in a shuddery breath. "Very close." Though could they ever be again, when she returned in three months' time?

Which only raised the reminder that her time would soon end here; and there would be no more Diana or Beatrice, and more . . . there would be no more Robert. Agony pulled at her heart. Oh, God, how to account for this vicious blade twisting in her chest? "They are protective," she supplied, feeling the other woman's stare on her.

"Aren't all elder brothers?" Wry amusement underscored that handful of words.

They shared a look, as a kindred connection was born.

"It doesn't matter that you are three and twenty." Or in Helena's case, four and twenty. "Or that you know your mind." The lady gave her head a rueful shake. "Nothing matters beyond a lady's marriage, does it?" That soft, faintly spoken question barely reached Helena's ears. "Gentlemen wouldn't expect a lady to be anything *but* a lady."

She'd spent her life believing herself so very different than all these flawless ladies, only to find amidst a dusty row of books that they were more alike than she could have ever believed. "Not to Society," Helena said quietly. When the woman lifted a confused gaze, she clarified. "To Society, they expect you . . . *women*, to wed, to be a husband's property, even as you do not want to cede every part of yourself over to a man."

Beatrice's eyes lit and she nodded enthusiastically. "Yes." That single word emerged as a kind of prayer.

"It is why it is important to hold on to *you*." For Helena, the sense of control she'd found in a world so wholly lacking in it for women had been numbers.

Beatrice stole a glance about, and then moved closer to Helena. "I write." Then her cheeks pinkened. She pulled a book from the shelf and turned it over to Helena.

Accepting the small tome, she skimmed the gold embossed title. *Rogues, Rakes, Rapscallions, and Other Wicked Gentlemen . . .*

"It is for my . . . work," Robert's sister explained. "You see, I am conducting research and . . ." She peeked about. "And I wish to use my knowledge to help other ladies." By the flat set to her pretty, bow-shaped lips, Beatrice Dennington intended to say nothing further on her pursuits.

Helena turned the book over and the young woman hurriedly accepted it. "I expect I might be able to provide additional . . . *research* should you ever require it." Given all she'd witnessed at the Hell and Sin Club, she herself could write a book, if she could properly assemble those words into a semblance of anything someone wished to read.

"Truly?" Beatrice asked on a reverent whisper.

Guilt needled at her. Given the other woman's kindness and willingness to share with Helena, she at least owed Robert's sister the truth of her background. "I spent the last ten years in a gaming hell, my lady."

A brassy bell chimed at the front of the shop, indicating someone had entered. Otherwise, silence stretched on, and heat stained Helena's neck and bathed her cheeks. She'd always found pride in that part of her existence. So why this sudden awkwardness in sharing that piece? *Because ladies don't know anything of those hells.* It was one thing to read a book about rakes and libertines. Quite another to actually witness those men visiting their clubs and visiting with whores.

"Do you know, Helena," Beatrice said at long last. "I think we are going to be very good friends. Very good friends, indeed." And a spirited glimmer she'd only seen in her own eyes lit Beatrice's. "I can certainly see why Robert's fallen in love with you."

Helena stilled. She shook her head.

Beatrice nodded.

Helena gave another shake.

Beatrice nodded once more. "Yes."

Her heart gave a funny little leap. "Oh, no. No," she said, turning her palms up. "You are mistaken. He does not. It is . . ." *Pretend.* She stopped from speaking that truth. Apparently they'd both delivered a convincing performance. As much as she liked Robert's sister, she didn't know her enough to share the details of what had brought her into the marquess's life.

"It is . . . ?" Beatrice gently prodded.

"It is . . ." Furthermore, anything real between them was impossible. Men such as Robert didn't fall in love with women like her, and when they did, they only made those women their mistresses, while binding themselves to cold, unfeeling ladies like the duchess.

"Do you not love him?" Four creases lined the lady's noble brow.

"*Do I love him?*" she choked.

Robert's sister stared expectantly back.

Of course she didn't love him. She'd known him but a handful of days. Footsteps sounded at the end of the aisle and she looked up, saved from formulating a response. Robert stopped and leaned against the bookshelf, and grinned. His lazy half grin was the kind of smile belonging to a man who well knew he was being discussed. With a wink, he continued strolling. Only as he disappeared around the next shelf, the panicky pressure weighting on her chest deepened.

How could she possibly love him? She'd not even liked him. He'd been arrogant and he'd stolen her knife, (a knife he still had) and her heart and . . . Helena shot a hand out, grasping the edge of the nearest shelf. *Oh, God, I love him.* Loving Robert was madness. There could never be a future between them. *Why, not . . . ? Why can't you have a life with him . . . ?* Because he would be a duke and she was a bookkeeper, and more, she would always be a bastard. Neither suitable duchess material. Nor did she even *want* to be a duchess . . . Oh, God. Her breath came ragged in her own ears.

His sister cut across her rapidly careening out-of-control thoughts and patted her hand. "Is it as difficult as I've read in books?"

"My lady?" she managed, scrabbling at the fabric of her gown, as she tried to muddle through her emotion.

Beatrice clarified. "Being in love?"

She closed her eyes for a long moment, and then gave a jerky nod. *It is worse.*

The longer she was here in this world, the more she lost of herself. "If you'll excuse me?" she asked, her voice emerging on a high-pitched tenor that earned a concerned look from Robert's sister. "I must return home."

The lady's pretty features fell. "Do say we'll meet again?"

Helena nodded. She'd promise the woman anything to be free of this place and her careening thoughts.

"Another trip to St Giles Circus?" She was relentless. "Shall we say Saturday, then?" She peered around Helena's shoulder. "Did you hear that, Robert? Will you be so good as to escort Miss Banbury and me back on Saturday morn?"

Helena whipped her head around. Robert stood, arms folded at his chest. "Of course." Why must he be so stealthy?

"Splendid," Beatrice said with a clap of her hands. "It is decided."

Helena swallowed hard. Indeed, it was. "I-If you'll excuse me?" She stammered over her words in her bid to make a quick retreat. Then, spinning on her heel, she rushed past Robert, and darted from the shop.

She'd never survive three months more here. Not without losing her heart and her sanity.

She needed to go home.

Chapter 17

Rule 17
Nobles can never be trusted.

Shortly after Helena fled Ye Olde Bookshop, Robert had continued on to Oxford Street for his appointment. The reports remained as grim as they'd been since his first meeting with the aged man-of-affairs a month prior. The man, Stonely, was so mired in the past that despite Robert's arguments to the contrary, he believed selling off all those late-made advancements of his grandfather was the only solution for the Dennington family.

Hours later, with his head bent over the ledgers, Robert squinted at the damned numbers. Except no matter how long he looked, not a blasted thing changed.

With a black curse, he dug his fingers into his temples and sat back in his chair.

Given the dire appointment with old Stonely, Robert ought to be attending the ledgers before him with far greater care.

Instead, Helena fully laid siege to his every thought. With their every meeting, his well-ordered world was becoming more and more muddied.

By God in hell—

He liked Helena Banbury.

Nay. He'd always liked her. Desired her. Admired her.

This discovery, however, was vastly different.

Robert stared absently down at the neat columns of grim numbers. He cared for her—*a lot*. His mind shied away from anything further. After all, his heart was incapable of more. He absently drummed the back of his pen on the open page. Particularly given that it had been just a week since the hellion who'd interrupted a tryst with Baroness Danvers had crashed into his world. The same vixen who'd threatened to gut him with a knife, and called into question his honor and his intelligence.

His lips twitched. And not only once.

Yes, for all that—he cared for her.

Are you familiar with Argand's work, my lord? . . . He is responsible for the geometrical interpretation of complex numbers . . .

She enjoyed mathematics and fashioned herself as something of a bluestocking. She didn't give a jot that he would one day be a duke. And she placed the safety of a child's life on the street before her own.

With a groan, he tossed his pen down. It landed on the desk with a soft thunk. In truth, how could one not like Helena Banbury? She was refreshingly honest amidst a sea of falsity, and more . . . she was a woman of strength who'd shown more courage defending a boy in the streets than the combined strength of an entire regiment in the King's army. He pulled open his center desk drawer and withdrew a heavy dagger, crusted with rubies, turning it over in his hands.

It had been far easier when he didn't like her, and simply felt a sense of obligation to right the wrong that he'd inadvertently done that drunken night at the Hell and Sin. He touched the tip of his finger to the sharp blade and a single drop of blood pebbled. Staring at the fleck of crimson, his mind raced.

He'd resolved to never be a fool again where a young woman was concerned. Lucy's treachery had made him wary of the motives of all. Robert wiped the blood from his finger, then scrubbed his hands over his face. When he was with Helena Banbury, however, he didn't think of Lucy and the bitterness of her betrayal . . . or his grandfather's hand in that awakening. He simply thought—of her. Helena Banbury with her reddish-brown hair and blunt honesty.

How could he possibly forget twelve years of bitterness after knowing a lady but a week? Because she'd forced him to see aspects of who *he* was, and how other people lived, in ways that he'd selfishly failed to note. He'd spent years despising his grandfather and Lucy Whitman for the ugliness in their souls, but what about who Robert had been?

I'm not reckless . . . I wager no more than most gentlemen . . . I keep one mistress and I'm careful to never beget a bastard on those women . . .

Those words he'd tossed at his father now floated back, words he'd uttered as a statement of his character.

Filled with a restlessness, Robert tossed Helena's dagger down and strode over to the sideboard. Grabbing the nearest decanter and snifter, he proceeded to pour himself a glass and then took a long, slow swallow, welcoming the warm trail it blazed.

He'd always known precisely what his responsibilities were as future duke—those realities never more clear with all his father had imparted. Though he was unwed still at three and thirty, he'd every intention of doing right by the line . . . just not to save the family from financial ruin. To do so would be bartering his own self-worth when he'd long condemned Lucy Whitman for that same ruthlessness.

I'm not worried about you being the same as other noblemen . . . I worry about you setting yourself apart from them . . .

Those words once tossed at him by his father were now sharpened with an acuity he'd previously lacked—*because of Helena.* He stared down into his drink. Years ago, he'd determined the exact manner of woman he would wed. She would be a lady of the *ton*, whose open desire of his title would be the only honesty he'd come to hope for.

Now there was Helena, a woman who, even if he wished to make her his future duchess, would sooner return to that notorious club than be married to him. He frowned into the contents of his drink. Not that he wished to wed her. He didn't.

There were too many reasons not to. Her disdain for polite Society, a sentiment he could, on most days, easily share. But more importantly, there was the life she wished for. Robert swirled the contents of his drink in a circle.

What if you do offer her marriage . . . ?

His hand shook, and liquid splashed over the rim, hitting his fingers.

A knock sounded at the door, and he looked up quickly, grateful for the interruption. "Enter," he boomed.

His butler, Fuller, opened the door. "My lord, the Duchess of Wilkinson has arrived to see you."

The duchess? He shot his gaze to the long case clock and frowned. Twenty minutes past ten. What matter of urgency would have the always-proper duchess here, now? Nervousness pulled at the edge of his consciousness. "Show her in," he said, and the greying man took his leave.

A short while later, Fuller was escorting the poised duchess in. "The Duchess of Wilkinson."

Robert swiftly set his glass down and quickly came over to greet one of his family's oldest friends. "Your Grace."

"Lord Westfield," she greeted, the corners of her mouth pinched, her eyes haggard. "I hope you can forgive my impoliteness in arriving so and at this unfashionable hour." She paused. "There is a matter of some urgency I would speak with you on," she said, fanning his apprehension.

Robert motioned her in. "Please." He gestured to the leather button sofa, and with the regal elegance of a queen, she swept over to the chair with the possession of one who owned this very room. "Is the duke—?"

"He is well." She sat, and then for the first time he could ever recall, the duchess wrung her hands. "I am not here about the duke."

He took in that telling gesture that spoke volumes of a woman who'd chided her daughter for laughing too loudly as a child.

Following his gaze, the duchess stopped abruptly, and then primly folded her hands in her lap. "I am here about Miss Banbury."

Her words held him momentarily immobile. "Miss Banbury?" he repeated slowly, and claimed the leather chair across from the duchess.

The older woman gave a brusque nod, and pulled off her gloves. "I hesitated in coming tonight, my lord. But given our families' connections, I knew I could trust your discretion." She laid the elegant pair of gloves on her lap.

He balled and unballed his hands to keep from shaking answers from her. "Of course," he said quietly, while his disquiet grew.

"As you no doubt know, my husband was . . ." High color flooded her unwrinkled cheeks. "In love with his mistress." Through that admission, Robert remained silent. What was there to say to a proud woman on the matter of her husband's fidelity—or in this case, *infidelity*? "It is that love that has so blinded him to Miss Banbury's true character. I have reason to believe she is stealing from His Grace."

Robert stilled. The lady the Duchess of Wilkinson spoke of was incapable of treachery. *Did you not believe that about another . . . ?* How long had he truly known Helena to reject the duchess's accusations?

As soon as the sliver of doubt entered, he quashed it. What need did Helena have to steal from the duke? The man had attached a ten-thousand-pound dowry to her, and would no doubt grab her the moon should she request it.

"I know it is no doubt difficult for you to hear this, given your budding affection for the lady," she said. "And she . . ." The duchess cast a glance about, and then looked to him once more. "Her maid reports that she takes the duke's carriage to unfashionable ends of London to meet someone with those stolen items. The young woman reported that Miss Banbury forces her to stay in the carriage while she conducts her activities."

He stitched his brow into a line. Those actions were not consistent with a woman who'd throw herself before a child.

"I worry for my husband, Lord Westfield," she said with a strident edge in her tone.

Robert sat back in his chair. "I do not—"

"Miss Banbury's left for St Giles Street."

The muscles of his stomach knotted. "Left?" he parroted like a bloody lackwit. Where would she go at this hour . . . and with whom? The doubt and indecision grew as his past merged with his present. What lady with honorable intentions would be found in the streets of Lambeth and St Giles . . . and at this hour, no less? "When?" he demanded tersely.

"This evening. Not even thirty minutes prior. I had a servant follow her *hack*." Her lip peeled back. "To the Hell and Sin Club."

The earth hung suspended and then resumed whirring at a too-fast rate. Helena was in the streets of St Giles at this hour. Terror consumed the fertile seeds of apprehension that had previously taken root. It mattered not that she was born to that world, and surely capable of handling herself amongst the seedy underbelly of London society. For her strength, she was not invincible against all manner of danger that existed for man, woman, or child in those streets.

Liar. Selfishly you're more worried about her leaving your world, and never coming back . . .

"I ask that you just be aware." The duchess interrupted his riotous thoughts. He fought down the urge to throw her out bodily so he could make for St Giles. "I ask that if you see anything suspicious with the young woman that you please speak to my husband."

"Of course," he said curtly. Bloody hell, be gone. Signaling an end to their meeting, Robert climbed to his feet.

Alas, she'd been bred to be a duchess.

Climbing to her feet with unhurried, graceful movements, the older woman firmed her mouth. "His Grace has a large heart, but flawed judgment where women are concerned." With meticulous movements, she pulled on her gloves and abruptly turned the discourse. "I can expect to see you at the ball tomorrow evening, my lord?" Was she mad? That she could so casually move from talk of Helena paying a night visit to the Hell and Sin, and then speak to him of her bloody ball?

Robert offered a deep bow. "Of course, Your Grace." He followed her to the door, and reached for the handle.

"Again, I thank you for your prudence with this matter. Given my relationship with your father and the late duchess, I would see you protected from Miss Banbury's machinations."

Smoothing her palms over her skirt, she gave a slight, dismissive, very duchess-like nod, and he drew the door open.

As she took her leave, he closed it, and stared at the wood panel. His mind spun with the charges and accusations leveled by the duchess. Charges and accusations that could never be true about Helena Banbury. *Except . . . what was she doing at Lambeth this morn, alone . . .*? With a curse, he stalked to the front of the room and yanked the door open, bellowing for his carriage.

The duchess's warnings harkened back to those issued by another. Warnings given twelve years ago by a hardened duke who'd seen the treachery in Lucy Whitman when Robert had been blinded.

Surely he'd not be a fool twice where young women were concerned?

He frowned as a wave of guilt assailed him at that willingness to believe ill of her. Helena did not even belong in the same category of a woman such as Lucy. Those two were nothing alike.

Except in his weakness for them.

Chapter 18

Rule 18
Danger comes in many shapes and forms.

A person could never forget the smells and sounds of St Giles. The dank scent of refuse and rot permeated the air, penetrating the carriage.

Seated as she'd been for the past thirty minutes, Helena sat on the uncomfortable bench of the hired hack, and closing her eyes, welcomed the familiarity of it all.

Here, in these rough, dark streets, life made sense in a way she understood.

She opened her eyes and stared out the ripped curtain.

Amidst a sea of dark, cracked, and crumbling buildings stood one impressive stucco structure. Awash in candlelight, it conveyed a sense of day amongst night. She touched her fingertips to the muddied windowpane. This hell represented an escape from her past, and a solid, certain future. Her ruthless brother had sent her away as a test of sorts.

After questioning her judgment from one chance encounter with a nobleman, Ryker singlehandedly decided her fate. He'd scuttled her off to Mayfair. For his ill opinion in her judgment, she was not her mother.

Or she'd told herself that for the course of her life. Several dandies crossed the street, climbing the steps of the Hell and Sin. The club doors opened, and the light cast by crystal chandeliers spilled onto the front stoop. And then closed once more.

Helena pressed her forehead against the warm windowpane. In the end, she'd proven Ryker correct in all his worst suppositions about her.

She had been weak. Only she had been seduced, not by fine fabrics and pretty baubles, but by kindness. She had entered the world of polite Society resolved to hating everything and everyone connected with that world. And here she sat, her heart hopelessly belonging to a future duke.

A broken laugh spilled past her lips, and she buried it in her hands. Oh, it was the manner of irony the Great Bard himself could not have crafted better. The bastard daughter of a duke, who'd judged her own mother, had committed the same folly.

She let her trembling hand fall to her lap. If she spent the remaining days and months with Robert, amongst the haute ton, she would lose every part of herself that she valued. She'd abandon every pledge she'd taken.

She needed to leave that world, and return here.

Letting the curtain fall into place, Helena drew her cloak hood up and reached for the handle.

Her fingers froze, and she stared blankly at her scarred hand.

For if she climbed those steps and disappeared inside, she would never, ever see Robert again, but for perhaps nights when he visited the hell. Time would pass, and she would continue tending her books, and he would carry on as he had before he'd agreed to her madcap scheme. Then he would marry and have perfect, flawless noble English babes. Vicious blades of jealousy ravaged her.

Helena dug her fingertips into her temples and rubbed. Indecision raged in her breast.

If she did step out of this carriage and demand to be seen, always unbending, would Ryker even take her back until the terms of the agreement he'd laid out had been met?

With quick movements Helena pressed the handle and stepped down from the carriage. She cast a look up at the driver perched atop the box. "Wait for me and there will be more," she pledged, handing over several coins. Standing in watch, as a pair of stumbling fops climbed the steps of the club, she waited until they'd entered the Hell and then gingerly picked her way across the street.

She'd grown up here. Had known no other way of living until just a month and a week ago, and yet dread raced along her spine. The sense of being watched. Inaction in the Dials often meant death, and yet she went still. Her gaze strayed to a solitary figure leaning against a dilapidated building. A cap pulled low over his eyes, the man remained with his arms folded. He shoved the hat back and grinned coldly. *Diggory.*

Oi'll beat ye until ye listen, girl . . .

She swayed dizzily, and wrapped her hand about a nearby lamppost to keep herself upright. A scream built inside and hovered on her lips.

Raucous laughter spilled into her whirring nightmare, and she opened her eyes. Blinking, Helena looked to that broken-down building for that hated figure.

Except for the dandies entering Ryker's club, not a soul lingered. Some of the tension left her. What weakness had overtaken her since she'd left this world that she'd made monsters out of shadows? It only affirmed how very desperately she needed to be back. Drawing the hood of her cloak further over her forehead, she burrowed inside, and quickened her stride.

Her bloody dagger. Robert still hadn't returned that precious piece, and lulled by the seeming safety in the duke's residence, she'd shamefully not given it a proper thought—until now.

A stranger stepped out of the alley between two buildings, and her heart quickened as the absolute folly in being here flooded her with a belated apprehension. She shot a quick glance back at the waiting hack, and then hurried forward. Helena reached the alley between the Hell and Sin and the next set of establishments.

Someone wrapped a hand around her forearm, and her pulse sped up. *Diggory!* She opened her mouth to tear down the streets of St Giles when the stranger clamped a large, gloved hand over her mouth. Helena bit hard, the taste and scent of fine leather flooding her nose, and a harsh, angry voice cursed against her ear.

A very familiar voice. Helena's shoulders sagged. "R-Robert?" How was he here?

"You are as bloodthirsty as the day I met you, Miss Banbury," Robert drawled.

Of course, he'd come to his clubs. She slid her eyes closed, and let her shoulders relax. Of all the bloody bad luck. Except . . . she squinted into the inky dark of night. A hardened suspicion glinted in his eyes.

"What are you doing, madam?" His terse, more duke-like command raised a frown on her lips.

He'd expect her to account for her whereabouts? Wasn't that the way of the world, then? Women were not afforded the luxury of going where they wished, when they wanted. Even with her role as bookkeeper that existential truth had held. Capable with numbers and charged with accounting, she'd been given explicit rules . . . for her protection.

Yet where had the ownership of her own self existed, even when she was employed at the Hell and Sin?

"What are *you* doing here?" she returned.

His eyebrows lowered. Then, as a lord, he'd certainly never been expected to account for his whereabouts.

Robert dipped his face close to hers, and with the space shrunk between them, the seething suspicion blared bright in his blue eyes. "I am here for you, madam."

She gulped, the menacing arrangement of his features at odds with the charming rogue she'd come to know these days. Swallowing hard, Helena glanced from her brother's gaming hell and then back to the hired conveyance. For a very brief, tiny moment, she considered darting across the street and fleeing so there were no questions to answer.

Robert wrapped his hand around her forearm, again.

She narrowed her eyes on his gentle hold, prepared to send him to the Devil for that dark suspicion. *What would you expect . . . ? Ladies do not visit St Giles . . . and certainly never alone . . .* Even with a justifiable reason for that suspicion, pain stabbed at her. Her chest heaving, she met his unflinching stare. "Did ye believe oi'm up to some havey-cavey activity, moi lord?" She tauntingly slipped into coarse street tongue.

Her annoyance swelled as he remained coolly unaffected, and silent. Staring at her in that piercing, searching manner.

Ribald laughter sounded from the opposite direction, and she stiffened.

Several gentlemen strolled in their direction, and Robert released her arm, his meaning clear. She was free to dictate the terms of their discussion. The trio of loud, stumbling men sprung her into action. Tamping down her frustration, Helena started back toward her hired hack, with Robert easily matching her steps. They reached the carriage and he pulled the door open.

Handing her inside, he followed; his tall, broad muscular form shrank the small quarters. He claimed the opposite bench and folded his arms. And said nothing.

Helena shoved back her hood, and glared. "You followed me." She hated that the sharp charge rang thick with hurt, preferring her fury.

"You were at Charing Cross Road and now here. Hardly fashionable ends of London for a lady to visit."

"I never professed to be a lady," she gritted out at his high-handedness.

"What are you doing here?" he pressed.

They remained seated, locked in a silent battle. Helena jutted her chin. If he thought to cow her into answers, he was to be sadly mistaken. She'd perfected the art of silence at the hands of men far crueler, far more terrifying than Robert, the Marquess of Westfield. Her cheek throbbed. How peculiar to actually be grateful for that painfully earned lesson.

Robert broke the impasse. "The duchess believes you are stealing from His Grace."

She narrowed her eyes, even as a sharp pang struck her heart. "Is that what you believe, my lord? That I'm a thief?" He gave no outward reaction to her volley. Instead, he sat in cold, unyielding silence. Emotion roiled in her breast: fury, pain, regret. She'd lost her heart to a man who'd question her honor. A fool. She'd been a bloody fool for having lost her heart to him. Unable to meet his eyes, Helena jerked her gaze to that slight crack in the curtains, and stared out to the dirtied London streets.

"No," he said quietly.

She stiffened, but did not take her attention from the front façade of the Hell and Sin.

"I do not believe her."

She didn't want it to matter, but his words did. And yet . . . "You are here though, aren't you?" she taunted, slipping a harsh, humorless smile at him.

He quirked a single golden eyebrow, and how she hated his cool. "Would you not have me find out what has you first at Charing Cross and now the Hell and Sin Club . . . in the dead of night, no less?"

After years of being expected to answer and account for her every action and movement, and the stifling oppressiveness of that, she boiled over. Her patience snapped. "Go to hell, Robert," she spat. Ryker, Robert, her other de facto brothers, they thought they were all deserving of explanations, as though she were a child. "You ask questions and demand answers." She raked her gaze over his elegant, flawless person.

From the top of his thick gold hair and his unblemished olive-hued skin to the tips of his shiny boots. "Do you know why I'm here?" She didn't allow him to reply. "I'm here because this is my home." She rested her palms on her knees and leaned across the space between them. "My brothers own the club."

Surprise flashed in his eyes.

The fight drained through her tautly coiled body, seeping through her feet, and she sank back in her seat. "I am their bookkeeper, Robert. This morning I was visiting their liquor supplier." Bitterness twisted her lips. Or she had been the bookkeeper until they'd decided it easy enough to cut her from the fabric of the club. She braced for the shock or condescension over that revelation. After all, *ladies* didn't oversee businesses.

Part of her wished for him to sneer at her revelation, for it would make it easy to despise him for his judgment. "I resulted in your loss of that position," he said quietly.

Helena remained close-lipped.

"Why are you here?"

Because I need to be. Because the longer I remain in your world, the more I lose pieces of my soul, so that nothing will remain but a weak woman like my mother . . .

She stiffened as he touched his knuckles to her jaw, gently bringing her gaze to his.

"You were leaving." Shock underscored those three words that were more statement than anything else.

Looking into his eyes, the flash of pain did not speak of a man indifferent to her.

And she didn't know what to do with that emotion.

He dragged his hand over his face.

"They sent me away," she said softly, and he dropped his arm to his side to look at her. She needed him to understand why she was here, and why she could never be part of his world.

Not that he asked you to even be part of it . . .

Helena glanced out that small crack in the ripped curtains. "It mattered not that I'm their sister. It mattered not that I've overseen the books since they opened the club." Her throat bobbed. "You give so much of yourself, and what do you receive for that loyalty?" She looked slowly back at him, a small, sad smile on her lips. A man just a step below royalty commanded that sentiment just by sheer birthright alone. In her world, it was earned and, often, all that mattered. "Though, I expect you know nothing of that."

"Because lords and ladies do not know hurt or betrayal?" He winged another eyebrow up.

She wrinkled her brow. She'd wager he'd never known the pain of a gnawing, growling belly or a fist being driven into your face.

Robert hooked his ankle over his knee, and rested his hand on the edge of his boot. "Do you believe members of your station hold dominion over those sentiments, Helena?"

She shifted, and her cheeks warmed. When he put that query to her in that manner, it made her sound self-important. "Do you?" she shot back. "Have you been betrayed by *your* family?"

"Yes," he said quietly.

His admission sucked the energy from the carriage. Of all the responses she'd expected, it had not been that gruff one-word utterance. Questions spilled to the tip of her tongue, but she bit the inside of her cheek to keep from probing. It was not her place to know. There was no need to know . . .

I want to, anyway . . .

"My grandfather," he explained. He grimaced. "And my fiancée."

His words sucked the air from her lungs. "You were betrothed," she said, her breath faint. Of course he'd been. He'd just said as much.

When he gave a curt nod of affirmation, a vise squeezed about her middle. He'd been betrothed. To a flawless English lady, and by the tension at the corners of his mouth, mourned the loss of her still. In

Helena's end of London one didn't probe a person about their past, present, or future. Particularly when futures were often bleak and doubtful. "What happened?"

He flicked a hand. "She was my sister's nursemaid."

"A nursemaid," she exclaimed. Future dukes did not marry nursemaids . . . they didn't marry any maids. Just as they didn't wed scarred by-blows who'd lived in the streets.

"It hardly mattered to me if she was a maid."

Oh, God. He'd loved her. So hopelessly that he would have defied Society's expectations for it. This was so much worse. A vicious, biting envy ate slowly away at her, threatening to consume her.

Robert held her gaze. "It mattered that she did not see my title." His eyes took on a distant quality and he was looking back into a world where she'd never been . . . but only that nursemaid who'd won his heart. "I loved her for her kindness and her ability to laugh. I loved that she was not a spoiled Society miss, and that she took pride in her work."

All this, when nobles failed to see those servants and people in the streets. Only . . . that wasn't really true. She'd only *believed* it to be so. This man had seen more. In another woman. "What happened to her?" Her whispered question floated between them.

"My grandfather, the then Duke of Somerset, didn't find her . . ." His lip peeled back. "*Suitable* material for a future duchess. I did not care. I would have married her anyway and to hell with him and Society. We planned to elope."

A knife-like pain shot through her. Unlike her father who'd made Helena's mother his mistress and nothing more, this was the manner of man Robert Dennington, the Marquess of Westfield, was, then and now. One who'd turn his finger up at the rules and do so for women such as a maid and a bookkeeper. To be the woman deserving of that devotion.

"My grandfather summoned me the day we were to wed. I went to his office." He cleared his throat. "He was . . ." Robert shook his head. "It is hardly fit for a lady's ears."

"I'm not a lady," she blurted.

Robert ran a tender gaze over her face. "You're more lady than most queens, Helena Banbury."

Warmth exploded in her heart. Not a single person, in the whole of her life, had treated her as anything more than a woman who'd climbed from the streets. Even her brothers had so clearly attached that part to each of their individual stories, it had become an inextricable fabric of who they were. Yet, this man before her saw more. "Tell me," she urged, wanting the details he withheld. Needing them.

He hesitated and for a long while she expected he'd say nothing. Then: "Lucy was there." *Lucy.* The woman had a name, which made her unknown-until-now rival all the more real and hated. "With my grandfather."

His words penetrated her blinding jealousy. Helena slowly blinked. Surely she'd misheard? Surely he'd not said . . . ?

"They were together," he confirmed with a curt nod.

Oh, God. Agony ran through her in sharp, torrential waves. At the hurt he'd known, and no doubt still did. Was it a wonder he was mistrustful of women of her station? "Oh, Robert," she said, softly covering his gloved hand with hers.

He glanced down at their connected hands. "My life is not yours, Helena," he said matter-of-factly. "I did not live in these dangerous streets and I've certainly not known the pain you have. But money and status does not make a person immune to emotion or life."

And yet, she'd gone through her own life naively believing that very thing. Believing that lords and ladies did not feel pain or hurt, and certainly not the treachery he'd spoken of.

His words hung in the air between them, and as they sat in silence for a long while, Helena wished she were one of those skilled with words and not her practical use of numbers, because then she'd have something to say to all Robert had shared.

He motioned to the door. "Would you have me escort you home?"

Her throat closed around the emotion stuck there. He would do that. He would guide her across the street so she might see her family and plead for the opportunity to return now. She should be touched by that gesture and yet . . . his gesture left her with a hollow emptiness. He'd let her go so easily. How to explain the part of her that wanted him to want her to be here . . . ?

I am not ready . . .

She shook her head. "I'd return to the duke's," she said quietly.

Robert rapped on the roof. Helena blinked. "What of your carriage?"

"Do you think I'd leave you alone?" he asked quietly. Oh, God. Her heart convulsed, making it impossible to drag forth a single breath. Why did he have to be so bloody caring? To the boy James. To her. It only confounded her already muddied thoughts. "I'll return for it after I've escorted you home."

A moment later, the hired hack lurched forward, with Helena's world all the more confused.

Later that night, Robert climbed the steps of his father's townhouse, this hated home he'd feared as a child and reviled as a young man betrayed by his grandfather.

Just as every loyal butler to ever serve these halls was trained to do, the door was promptly drawn open.

Davidson stepped out of the way, permitting him entry. "My lord," he greeted, accepting Robert's hat. It was a testament to the servant's reserve that he betrayed no surprise at Robert's late-night visit. "His Grace has retired for the evening. Should I—?"

"I do not require His Grace," he murmured, turning his cloak over.

The servant bowed and backed out of the foyer, his footsteps echoing in the nighttime quiet. Robert did a small turn about this hated foyer.

How many times as a child had he shifted in this very room, dreading those required visits with the great Dennington patriarch? Now he stood here a man still bound by the unrelenting grasp of the past on his present.

Robert started down the corridor, walking with purposeful strides toward one particular room. He came to a stop outside his father's office, the same space his grandfather had once held dominion over. Pressing the handle, Robert stepped inside.

It took his eyes a moment to adjust to the inky darkness. When it did, he closed the door behind him, and made his way to the broad, mahogany desk.

He stared emptily at the immaculate surface where the late duke had taken Lucy like a corner doxy. That had been the single most defining moment of Robert's life, the one in which he'd resurrected protective walls designed to keep all women out—even in the ways that most mattered. It had proven safer that way. Better to have nothing but meaningless exchanges than the jagged agony of betrayal and pain. He'd been moving along quite contentedly, too.

Until Helena.

Helena, who'd slipped past every defense and slid inside, properly turning his world on its ear.

And who in the span of the evening had proven how little he in fact mattered to her.

Robert drew his hand back and strolled behind the desk once occupied by the late duke, and now the current . . . a chair that would one day, hopefully not until the far-distant future, belong to him. He sank into the edges of the leather wingback seat, and glued his gaze to the place Lucy and his grandfather had fornicated all those years ago.

At the time, there had been no greater despair than witnessing a woman he'd trusted, and believed himself in love with, in the arms of another, his grandfather no less. It had cemented the reality that women, regardless of station or lot in life, would never see anything more than a future title in him.

Then, one drunken evening, he'd stumbled inside the wrong chambers, and now there was Helena Banbury, a woman who didn't give a bloody damn if he was duke, king, or pauper. Robert brushed his palm along the edge of the desk. And she had thrown into question everything he'd come to accept as fact where women were concerned.

Helena was a woman of strength and spirit who'd battered down every flimsy wall he'd constructed, and who'd in the span of this evening had proven, once again, how very little he mattered. She was the sister of gaming hell owners, men who'd no doubt built an empire in ways that would curdle a weaker man's blood . . . and knowing that, accepting that, it mattered not. She had mattered. Too much.

He swiped a wary hand over his face. Had the duchess not come to him with Helena's whereabouts, she'd have disappeared from his life for good. Those moments he'd built up as something so much more, something real and beautiful, she would have forsaken.

Nay, she would eventually forsake. Her words tonight could have not been clearer. She didn't wish to be part of his world . . . whether he was in it or not. Yet again proving that women ultimately did not choose him. They chose wealth or power, as Lucy had shown. Or, in Helena's case, chose a previous life and profession.

He let his hand fall back to the desk. He'd do well to remember the folly in caring too deeply. What existed had only been something he'd built to be more in his own mind.

There remained three additional months with her. Three months to retain his sanity and a hold on his heart. He'd been a rake for twelve years. How difficult could it be to retain that former way and wear the false, practiced smile and give Helena nothing more than charming words? To give her more was a peril he could never recover from.

Ultimately, women did not choose him. Lucy hadn't. Tonight, with the ease with which she'd nearly left his life, Helena had proven it, too.

He'd do well to not forget that again.

Chapter 19

Rule 19
Decide your own fate.

Helena stood on the fringe of the Duke and Duchess of Wilkinson's ballroom, distractedly eying the festivities.

Through the whole of the receiving line, with bated breath, she'd looked for a single guest . . . with an anticipation that had nothing to do with the ruse she'd asked him to be part of. She ran her gaze over the sea of guests twirling about the dance floor. Whispers and polite laughter filled the room in a cacophony of muted sound.

How very miserable she'd been when Ryker had first sent her to this place. She was as much an outsider here as a fish pulled ashore to live on land, with the breath being slowly choked from her. Until Robert. Until him, she'd not known she could smile or laugh or be happy in this place. Nor had she believed men of his station capable of being hurt or knowing suffering. Last night, he'd lifted the blinders from her eyes and she was shamed by her very narrow view on living and life.

Now that she did know it, she didn't know what to do with that discovery. For ultimately, it changed nothing. She was still who she was: a bookkeeper at the Hell and Sin Club who wished for control in her life when women were lacking in it. He was a marquess and future duke who'd been betrayed by a woman not far off from Helena's station. Why, no doubt when she took her leave in two months and three weeks' time, he'd forget her altogether. Helena caught her lower lip between her teeth, hating that. And hating herself for the vicious pain that truth caused.

There was a faint stir at the front of the ballroom, and she looked to the entrance.

Her breath caught.

Standing at the top of the white Italian marble staircase, Robert surveyed the ballroom with a lazy elegance. The chandelier's glow cast a soft light on his luxuriant, golden tresses and she ached with the need to run her fingers through those faintly curled strands.

As he made his descent, the flurry of whispers increased. Scandalously clad ladies with plunging décolletage touched their fingers to their chests as he moved past them. Debutantes fluttered their lashes. Never breaking his forward stride, he lifted his head in a vague politeness, revealing that lazy half grin that dulled the pain of rejection.

A rogue. He was a rogue in every sense of the word . . . and she'd fallen hopelessly under his spell. Helena momentarily closed her eyes. She'd entered polite Society with clear expectations of him . . . and for herself. She wasn't the weak ninny who'd ever fall as her mother had. Only heartbreak and heartache came in loving these men.

Yet, that is what I've done.

When she opened her eyes, she found his gaze on her, robbing her lungs of air. The veiled, potent stare that had the power to make her feel as though she were the only woman in the ballroom. Then he smiled, and her heart quickened for altogether different reasons. For this was not the false rogue's grin he donned for the peers, but rather that smile that reached his eyes.

She returned his grin, inclining her head.

The Duke and Duchess of Wilkinson stepped into their path, shattering that connection. As the trio exchanged polite greetings, the duchess's warnings and cruel taunts came rushing back.

As long as you do not think to make yourself a duchess. You are not one of us, Miss Banbury. It is important you remember that . . .

Helena fisted her scarred hands, those unwitting reminders standing as a mocking testament to the accuracy of the duchess's claims.

"I have been studying you for an hour now, Miss Banbury, and I cannot determine whether you are attempting to hide, or plotting your escape."

She gasped, and spun to face the owner of that unfamiliar, faintly amused voice.

The gentleman of a similar age to the Duke of Wilkinson stood, evaluating her in an appraising manner. Where the duke had let age soften his middle and round his cheeks, this man stood lean and powerful still, even with the cane in his hand. But for the drawn lines at the corners of his blue eyes, there wasn't a hint of weakness to the man.

"Perhaps a bit of both," she said at last.

The nameless stranger smiled.

Suspicion brought Helena's lashes sweeping down. Long ago she'd learned to be wary of the motives of gentlemen. Though she hadn't been born to this world, she well knew no respectable one would approach a lady so and speak with such familiarity. "Forgive me," she said between tight lips. "You have me at a disadvantage."

"Of course," he murmured. "I am the Duke of Somerset."

The Duke of Somerset. Robert's father. The man who by Robert's admission had sought to manipulate him into a proper match. Her skin pricked under his pointed stare. He'd surely read the papers linking her name to his son's and sought to assess her worth as a future duchess.

Alas, if he were hoping for a miss with all the proper responses, he was to be disappointed. Helena dropped a belated curtsy. "Your Grace," she murmured. She cast a look about for Robert. She'd no doubt this meeting was not coincidence, and given his station and connection to the Duke of Wilkinson, his was, even for the ghost of a smile, not a friendly chance exchange.

"So very dreadful," he murmured to himself, as he turned his attention out to the ballroom. The latest set just concluded, couples filed off the dance floor. Her gaze landed on Diana, being escorted over to her parents, by her respective partner . . . and Robert. A spasm wracked her heart.

"These affairs," the duke was saying.

Yanking her gaze away, Helena looked questioningly up. What was he on about?

The older man waved his cane over the crowded room. "I never liked them, you know."

Helena opened and closed her mouth several times. Actually, she didn't know. She'd simply believed attending these events was an additional function, like eating and breathing, to these people. How odd to know one of the most powerful peers in the realm should also despise them.

"What of you, Miss Banbury, do you enjoy the balls and soirees?"

"I . . ."

Robert's father settled his walking stick on the floor, and shifted his weight over it with a grimace.

She took in the strain in the older man's eyes. His ashen complexion. The white, drawn lines at the corners of his mouth. *He is ill . . .* Sympathy battered away the aloof demeanor she'd donned moments ago. By God, Robert didn't know the truth of his father's circumstances. He was so focused on his family's finances, he'd failed to see the truth right in front of him.

Her gaze locked with the Duke of Somerset's, and a silent understanding passed between them. His Grace flashed her a sad smile, an affirming smile that said with more than words that she'd correctly gauged his circumstances. "Well, Miss Banbury?"

"There are certainly other things I would prefer to be doing," she settled for.

He chuckled. "That is true. If you enjoyed it, you wouldn't even now be hiding in this corner talking to me."

"Oh, I'd vastly prefer to speak to you than . . ." most others. Heat exploded on her cheeks.

A knowing twinkle lit his eyes, momentarily dimming the strain in their blue depths. *Robert's eyes.* "What would you be doing?"

At the unexpected question, Helena cocked her head.

"Other than attending balls and soirees." He motioned once more with his cane.

I'd rather be alone with your son. Speaking freely and laughing when I'd forgotten how . . . She gave him a small smile. "I enjoy numbers, Your Grace."

"Numbers," he repeated with no small amount of surprise.

"I enjoy mathematics and learning new equations."

With his spare hand, he captured his chin in his hand and rubbed it contemplatively. "To what end?"

She tipped her head.

"A number is a number, isn't it? They are not words that can be shaped into different, poetic meanings."

Yes, that was how he must see it. To Helena, they'd long made sense, and revealed so much in an equally magnificent way that words did. "Ah, yes, but where would we be with only words and numbers?" she said, gesticulating with her hands. And perhaps if she were another woman she'd be properly shamed by the way the duke flared his eyebrows. "Before the sixteenth century, there was an addition and subtraction sign, but do you know how mathematics equations were once written?"

He gave his head a bemused shake.

"With words. Which given their nature, those equations should have been poetic, no?" she asked, taking a step closer. "But can you imagine keeping ledgers or recording accountings for your estates or business with only words? How much time that would take, and how much time you would lose from life for it." A flash of understanding lit his eyes. "Therefore, I would argue, even though each is uniquely different, there is a place for both, Your Grace."

The duke stared at her a long while in an appraising manner, and she shifted under that scrutiny. Then, he smiled, and that gentle mirth dulled the previous pain. "Indeed, you are correct, Miss Banbury. One would say, brought together, even vastly different, a beautiful harmony is found."

Did she imagine the veiled meaning of those words?

He leveled her with a stare that threatened to see inside her.

"Would you object if I steal Miss Banbury away for the next set?"

They swiveled their attention to Robert.

"Rob—My lord," she swiftly amended, her cheeks flaming.

He winked, and her heart tripped a beat. That fool woman who'd thrown away his love. And Helena must be in possession of the blackest soul, for in this selfish moment she was wholly glad there was no longer a Lucy.

"Of course, of course," the Duke of Somerset said, gesturing to Helena.

"I do not—"

Robert held out his hand. "Dance? This isn't a dance, Miss Banbury." He dropped his voice. "This is a waltz. I've it on authority that you've perfected the waltz."

And though dancing had quick become a lesson in humiliation during her time in London, the desire to be in his arms far outweighed her pride. Helena dropped a curtsy to the Duke of Somerset. "It was an honor, Your Grace," she murmured, and then allowed Robert to tuck her hand in his sleeve and lead her to the dance floor.

"We'd but one lesson," she said under her breath, as he positioned them at the edge of the dance floor.

"I'm offended, madam, that you'd question my skills as an instructor. Did you forget that day in the gardens so easily?" Desire glinted his eyes and heat sparked in her veins and spread in a slow conflagration that threatened to consume her under the memory he roused.

Helena managed a jerky nod. She swallowed a moan as he guided his hand lower on the small of her back, and then the orchestra proceeded to play. As their bodies moved in an easy harmony to the whine of the orchestra's violins, Helena was reduced to nothing but a bundle of sensation. Heat poured off Robert's broad chest, and her fingers tightened on his thickly muscled biceps.

He lowered his mouth close to her ear, and by God she would go with him now, wherever he'd lead. The promise in the gardens. The feel of his touch. She wanted it all before she left London, never to again see him. This magnetic pull he had over her was one that could not be repelled.

"Surely you've not forgotten, there is still the matter of demonstrating to those fortune-hunting swains, too, isn't there?"

Except that. That could shatter this haze. His words had the same effect as tossing a bucket of cold Thames water over her. Of course. This was all pretend. For him. That had only just ceased to be the case for her. The fake smile she donned strained her cheeks. "Of course, I've not forgotten." It was, after all, the whole reason she'd enlisted his aid.

Robert ran an uncharacteristically somber gaze over her face. "What is it?" He growled. "Did my father say something to you?"

"No," she said quickly. "He was quite kind." Her gaze found the duke on the fringe of the activity. It was hardly her place to interfere on a matter between Robert and his father. She was not long for this world with Robert, but before she left, she could open his eyes to the inevitable loss awaiting him. "Your father appears . . . strained."

Robert frowned, and followed her stare. "Are you being deliberately evasive?" He lowered his head so their brows touched. "Or are you so wholly unmoved by being in my arms?"

His arms were the only place she wished to be. *Forever.*

She missed a step, and he caught her against him, righting her.

"What is troubling you?" he asked again, running a sharp gaze over her face.

I love you . . . "It is nothing." *Everything.* "I am merely counting beats." Liar. Until her brief meeting with Robert's father, when had she last thought about anything mathematical? Or the club?

In a short time, this man had become everything to her.

"One-two-three. One-two-three," he whispered close to her ear, his mellifluous baritone a silken promise that had her wishing for all number of things that could never be.

Unable to meet his piercing stare, Helena looked around his shoulder to the sea of guests eying the Marquess of Westfield with his unlikely companion. The befuddlement in their expressions, and the condescending stares, spoke of people who judged and found her wanting.

"Do not look at them," Robert said quietly, jerking her attention up. In this moment, with the dark, nameless emotion in those eyes, she could almost believe he felt the same. "Look at me. Only me. No one else matters but me and you." Her heart faltered. And whatever piece of that rapidly pounding organ that hadn't previously belonged to him fell away and into his hands.

Helena closed her eyes, swaying against him, and allowed him to right them again.

The music drew to a stop, and as couples politely clapped and began to file from the dance floor, Helena stood, a bundle of throbbing nerves and feelings, wicked and wanton as her mother.

Only . . . frozen before Robert, with their chests moving in a quick rhythm, she understood. Understood what had driven her mother. She could no sooner stop loving this man than she could stop the earth from moving and send it spinning in the opposite direction. It was Robert who managed to pull her from the spell. Shifting her arm to his sleeve, he led her from the dance floor.

As he guided her to the edge of the room, the duchess, a determined glint in her eyes, stood in wait, with Diana at her side.

"Lord Westfield," the duchess said with forced cheer when Helena and Robert stopped before her. "As promised, Diana is free for the next set."

The charged energy between Helena and Robert on the dance floor may as well have been conjured by Helena's own yearnings. With his patent grin, Robert captured Diana's hand and raised it to his lips. "Lady Diana, it is a pleasure," he greeted her, and Helena curled her toes so tight her arches ached.

"Likewise," Diana said, blushing a delicate pink, and not the splotchy red Helena had always managed through the years.

Jealousy stabbed at Helena, vicious and ugly and dark. Her sister's giggling responses were lost to Helena. What would it be like when Helena left and he found another? How did one live with the jagged agony of wanting and love and loss?

Oh, God, this was the hell her mother had known. She'd spent her life hating Delia Banbury, who'd forsaken all to be a nobleman's pleasures. Loving Robert as she did, Helena saw how very easy it would be to throw away all for any fleeting joy to be had with Robert. So many years she'd judged her mother, had held her to blame for their circumstances. Now, with a woman's eyes, she saw that her mother's smile had been partly broken from the pain of that loss. More, Helena now knew that pain herself.

As Robert guided Diana upon the dance floor for a country reel, he cast a final look at Helena, his expression inscrutable, but then his partner said something requiring his attention.

As the orchestra struck up the lively set, Helena stood shoulder to shoulder alongside the duke's wife, immobile.

"They make a lovely couple, do they not?" the duchess murmured, not deigning to look at her husband's by-blow.

Helena kept her face deliberately blank. But then she caught sight of the rosy-cheeked Diana and smiling Robert as the steps brought them together again. The hell of it was, the Duchess of Wilkinson was correct. They did look splendid as a pair: he, tall, powerful, golden perfection and she, a dainty model of English femininity.

Then there was Helena, with her too-tall height and pale cheeks and scarred face and hands.

Never had she despised those marks more than in this moment.

"As I said, Miss Banbury," the other woman continued conversationally, with no apparent need for comment from Helena. "Lord Westfield will wed a lady, never one who was carved up quite handily by a street ruffian. What was it he did?" She flicked a bored look over Helena's cheek. The scar throbbed at the old memory and the woman's vitriol. "Burn you?" she guessed.

The air left Helena on a swift exhale as the duchess, with her casual, throw-away supposition, dragged Helena from the present to that dark, ugly past she'd spent years fighting down. She searched her hands about for the nearby column as memories crept in. The acrid smell of burning flesh. Her flesh. Diggory's cruel, maniacal laugh.

Spinning jerkily on her heel, Helena stalked off. Gaze trained forward, she eyed the back exit of the ballroom with a hungry desperation. *Not here . . . Not now . . .*

Please, don't . . . Don't . . .

Her own cries echoed around her mind and she sucked in a deep breath, unable to draw air past the pressure squeezing about her lungs. Helena knocked into someone and managed a murmured apology, but continued her lurching flight.

At last free of the ballroom, she tore down the hallway, sprinting through the corridors, onward. Escape. She needed it with the same desperation she'd needed it as a child in Diggory's clutches. When the nightmares came, there had been Ryker and Calum and Niall and Adair. They'd pulled her from the precipice of madness.

Quit yer croyin or oi'll give ye something to cry for . . .

She clamped her hands over her ears to blot out that coarse cockney. Helena's muffled sob filled the quiet halls, blending with her quick, panting breaths, and she quickened her pace. She reached the door to freedom and frantically shoved it open.

Warm air slapped her face, and she collapsed on the graveled path, sucking in with deep, gasping attempts to breathe, and retched.

Someone sank down beside her. Strong hands settled at her back, and crying out, Helena turned, and drew back her fist.

Robert easily caught her wrist in his hand, halting the blow.

She blinked wildly. Robert. Not Diggory. Helena slid her eyes closed. "Robert," she whispered, as the terror receded and she was left in the duchess's prized gardens with Robert at her side.

Emotion darkened his eyes, and he gently released her hand. "Did someone hurt you?" The lethal edge of steel underscoring that whisper promised death with it.

Through all the horror of remembered pain and the nightmares that would always be, tenderness unfurled within.

"Helena," he urged, his harsh, primitive growl rumbling around them.

She managed to nod. A sweat-dampened strand fell over her eye and with a tenderness that threatened to shatter her, he brushed it back.

Then he cupped her cheek.

That flawed, ugly, rippled part of her flesh. And for the first time since Diggory had silenced her tears, she let them fall freely and unchecked. She drew in a gasping breath, and she wept, dimly registering as Robert gathered her against his chest, holding her as though she were a cherished treasure. Her shoulders shook from the force of her sobs and she cried until her body ached with the force of her despair.

Robert cradled her close, his arms wrapped around her.

But he did not say anything. He did not whisper platitudes or ask questions or urge her to silence. And she took that offering. Crying for the child she'd never been. And for the torture she'd endured. She cried for the emptiness that had been her mother's existence. And she cried for everything she now wanted that could never be. Her tears dissolved into slow, shuddery hiccupping gasps, and she remained there clinging to Robert.

Robert settled onto the ground and shifted her in his arms, moving her closer, and she turned her scarred cheek against the place his heart pounded. Closing her eyes, she breathed in deep the sandalwood scent that clung to him. She closed her eyes. All these years she'd believed tears weakened a person. That had been a rule ingrained into her early on beside her brothers. Calm stole over her, despite the lessons about those salty mementos. Now she found how wrong her brothers had been. Those tears offered healing and peace. Robert rubbed smoothing circles over her back and she leaned into his caress.

During the course of her life, she'd moved from a townhouse to a one-room residence, to London streets, and eventually to one of the greatest gaming establishments to rise in England.

Never had she felt any of them was a home.

And in Robert's arms, she found that home was not walls and a roof after all.

It was a person.

Chapter 20

Rule 20
Never cry.

By his birthright, Robert was in possession of five unentailed properties and more than fifteen hundred acreages. He'd inherit seven entailed properties; a crumbling empire, rapidly bleeding money.

In this moment, with Helena in his arms, he'd have gladly turned over all his land holdings, including his life if asked for it, to spare her the pain that had sent her fleeing to the gardens.

Robert reached between them and fished a kerchief from his pocket. He handed it over to her.

Helena accepted it with a murmured thanks and then blew noisily into the fabric. She fiddled with the edges of the fabric, and then set it aside on the graveled path.

"You shouldn't be here." Her tear-roughened voice faintly reached his ears.

Attuned to this woman as he'd never been with another, Robert had spied Helena as she'd spun on her heel and fled the ballroom as though the hounds of hell were nipping at her heels. In that moment, the Devil himself could not have compelled him to remain dancing with Lady Diana or any other. "I should be where you are," he returned; placing his lips against her temple, he tucked another brown strand behind her ear.

She drew back. Her tear-reddened eyes scoured his face. "Because of the courtship." Her words emerged flat.

He swallowed around a ball of emotion. Last evening, he'd resolved to keep her out of his heart. What a fool he'd been. He was powerless to her hold.

How could she not know the hold she had on him? He gave her as much of the truth as he could manage in this jumbled moment. "Because I want to be where you are." Robert brushed his lips over her damp, satiny lashes, wanting the demons that haunted her so he could make them his own.

They sat, with birds chirping their night song overhead. He ran his hands in small circles over her back—

"I was quiet."

He paused midmovement, but did not release her from the strong, reassuring warmth of his embrace.

"You asked once what I was like as a child. I was quiet."

With those thirteen words, she'd let him in. And until she'd uttered them, he'd not appreciated how desperately he wanted to be here, knowing everything there was about Helena Banbury.

"I wasn't always," she said more to herself. "I used to chatter like a magpie, my mother said." A wistful smile pulled at her lips and he imagined a small Helena Banbury with questions and stories flowing from her lips. "I didn't even know what a magpie was." Then her smile slipped, and it had the same effect as the night driving back the day sky. "We were happy for five years, until a . . . gentleman arrived one day and told us the duke had tired of my mother. We were turned out. As a young girl, I could not understand how anyone could let her go." The duke had let both mother and daughter go that day. Did Helena see that? Or mayhap it was safer to ignore that very detail. "She was kind and beautiful." Had she been Aphrodite herself, the woman could not have eclipsed her daughter in every meaning of the word.

Helena went silent.

Did she not realize she needed to speak of those days after as much as he needed to hear of them? "What happened?" he asked, even as distant fear kicked up inside at the answers she would give.

For a long while she said nothing, and he thought she would skillfully shift them to a safer-for-her topic.

"We were in the streets, with nowhere to go," she said finally. "The duke's . . ." Hatred glinted in her eyes. "Man coordinated another protectorship, to a man who was . . ." She dug her nails into the fabric of his jacket, and even through the fabric, the bite of her fingers penetrated. "Cruel." She lifted her eyes to his. "I did horrible things because of him. I was a thief. I robbed from your kind."

His kind. The self-important bastards who'd been oblivious to a child's suffering. Shame cloyed at him. "You survived," he said gruffly. How easily she could have swung for her *crimes.* Acts of a hungry child she was forced to commit. Bile burned his throat.

"I set fires to establishments at his command. I am not a good person, Robert."

He choked. "Is that what you believe?" With every admission, a spear struck his heart. He would have been a boy of fourteen, at Eton, his life wholly uncomplicated and carefree—as hers should have been. "You were a child," he said, his voice a desperate entreaty. Surely she saw she was not to blame?

She lifted her shoulders in a slight shrug, and casually continued over his protestation. "My mother died within a year of us living with Diggory." Diggory. The monster had a name, which only made her horror all the more real. His fingers tightened reflexively. Helena winced, and he forced his hands open. "I could not stop crying." She caught her lower lip between her teeth and bit so hard, a drop of blood pebbled on the flesh. Robert brushed his thumb over the crimson dot. "He wished me to thieve for him the day she died, but I just sobbed and sobbed until he . . ." She pressed her eyes closed and at the darkness there in her whisper, a chill went through him.

"What did he do?" Did that hoarse, painful inquiry belong to him?

"He taught me to be s-silent." Her voice cracked, and the cold iced him from the inside out. "He held a candle's flame to my face so that I was no longer crying." *Oh, God.* Her body stiffened in his arms, and he drew her closer to him, wanting to absorb her pain, to make it his own, to take her suffering as his. "Whenever I cried, he'd touch the candle to me." Had she taken an old broadsword from his ancestral estates and laid him open, it could not have gutted him more. He groaned, the ragged sound befitting a tortured beast.

Her hands.

A dark, unholy rage roared to life. A savage, primitive fury at the man who'd put his hands on her. And if he were here, Robert would sever the bastard's limbs from his person and stuff them in his mouth.

"Oh, Helena." His voice broke.

"It was a short time," she said quickly.

She sought to reassure *him*? He sat, humbled by the depth of her strength and courage. With all she'd endured, she was far stronger than any man he'd known.

"My brother found me." That man who'd have Robert's eternal gratitude. "And we lived on the streets." Stealing. "Until we moved to the Hell and Sin Club." She shifted in his arms, and laid the back of her head against his chest.

Silence fell between them. Robert wound his arms around her, and cradled her to him. There were no pretty words or gentle teasing that could take away her suffering. It was, and would always be, a part of her, and he hated that he could not own all of it, sparing her that past.

"Thank you," she said quietly.

He rubbed his chin back and forth over her soft brown curls, which had escaped her neat chignon.

"I've not talked about that, ever. Not even with my brothers. You do not . . . talk of those moments."

Just as he'd not spoken of Lucy's betrayal until her. How very much alike they were. They'd both been indelibly marked by life and had allowed it to shape whom they'd become. She'd emerged triumphant, brave, bold, and powerful, where he'd simply moved along with a shift-less purpose—until her.

I love her . . .

He stilled, braced for the flood of terror. He'd resolved to never give his heart again. Yet, there was no fear. No trepidation. There was nothing more than an absolute sense of rightness. While his mind raced, Helena drew back and his arms went cold, empty at the loss of her. Except she shoved herself onto her knees, and framed his face between her hands.

"What—?"

Helena covered his mouth with hers, in a questing, searching meeting of their lips. The hint of lavender that clung to her satiny soft skin filled his senses, headier than any aphrodisiac, as it blended with the fragrant scent of flowers about them.

Helena would one day leave. In two months, three weeks, and a hand-ful of hours.

But before she did, she could not leave without knowing this man in every way.

She wanted him. In her arms and in her heart. Forever.

She wanted to sear her mind and body with the heat of his touch and the power of his kiss. This was the madness that had driven her mother to sacrifice all. At last, it made sense. And in a world where women were largely powerless, Helena would have this with Robert. This she had control over.

He parted her lips and slid his tongue inside and a low moan escaped her, as she met his strokes in a bold parry. A shuddery gasp exploded from her, that sound lost in his mouth, as he worked her décolletage down and freed her breasts to the warm spring night air. The air caressed her skin, and then he lowered his head, dragging his mouth over her breasts.

She cried out and lurched upwards. His mouth blazed a fiery trail over her skin, that tempting trail sending warm heat pooling at her center, so she was liquefied under the power of his touch. "So beautiful," he whispered, his breath fanning her skin.

Helena tossed her head back as he closed his lips around the tip of her right breast. He drew that sensitized bud into his mouth and sucked gently, then more incessantly. Her hips lifted in a desperate rhythm that came from wanting him and he worked the fabric of her gown up until he found her dripping center with his hands.

Robert swallowed her cry, and teased the nub of her femininity until she was incapable of anything but sensation. Her breath rasped sharply, and she closed her thighs tight around his hand, anchoring him close, needing so much more. She let her legs splay open, and with a pained groan, he drew away and rolled to his side.

Helena's body throbbed at the loss of him, and she hurried onto her knees beside him. "Why did you stop?"

"I cannot take you like this," he gritted out between great, rasping breaths. He flung an arm over his eyes.

Helena drew his arm back and lowered her face so their lips were a hairsbreadth apart. "I want this."

"You deserve marriage and a proper bed with satin sheets," he said gruffly. "You deserve—" She covered his mouth with hers, swallowing those words.

"I am tired of others telling me what I need or deserve," she whispered, slipping her hands inside to stroke him under his jacket. "I want you."

Robert hesitated, and then, in one smooth movement, stood, swept her into his arms, and carried her deeper into the gardens. He laid her down and she studied him through heavy lashes as he removed his jacket and laid it on the thick, green grass in this pretend Eden.

Helena shoved up on her elbows, and eyed him hungrily as he came down over her. His lips found hers once more, and she moaned and he slipped his tongue inside, tasting her, and the taste of him, brandy and mint, filled her senses.

"I have wanted you from the moment I first saw you, Helena Banbury," he said, between kisses. He dragged his mouth lower to worship her breasts once more, and she wound her fingers in his luxuriant silken tresses, holding him close.

Never stop. She bit her lip as he suckled and teased and tasted until she was a quivering bundle of desire. He dragged her skirts up and slipped his hand between them, finding her drenched center. Helena bucked against his hand, thrusting into his palm, needing him and only him.

Robert reached between them and freed himself from the confines of his breeches. The sight of his jutting shaft, tall, bold, proud, and stretched toward her, sent twin waves of heat spiraling and she reached out and wrapped him in her palm.

His eyes slid closed on a hiss, and he rocked into her hand. A thrilling sense of power at driving this strong, powerful man to desire surged through her, and she continued to stroke him in her palm. Up and down in slow, exploratory strokes until his hips were frantically pumping into her hold.

In a remarkable display of self-control, he pulled away, but he was only positioning himself between her legs. He slid his shaft inside her smoldering center, stretching her wider and wider, and she flailed her head back and forth on the earth, the throbbing ache at her center growing, the one only he could fill. Then he stopped, and she bit the inside of her cheek to keep from crying out.

Sweat beaded on his brow, and she reached up, brushing back a loose golden strand. "Please," she implored.

But he only lowered his head to her breast, suckling her until she was pulsating, a moment from shattering.

He thrust inside.

Bloody hell!

Robert swallowed her cry with his kiss, and she jerked as pain shot through her. He froze, allowing her body to adjust to his length filling her. She closed her eyes, and drew several deep, steadying breaths.

Robert touched his lips to her eyelids, her forehead, and then he again kissed her mouth. "So beautiful." And even with her scars and imperfections, in this moment, in his arms, she actually believed it.

Helena opened her eyes, and trailed her gaze over the chiseled planes of his face. And as he began to move, their gazes remained locked. The pain receded and with it came that slow, aching pleasure. She began to move, lifting to meet his thrusts, until their bodies met in a perfect harmony, until their hips rose and fell with a desperate urgency that drew Helena higher and higher to that maddening edge of ecstasy.

He pressed deep and she cried out, exploding into a sea of blinding white light and feeling. Robert shouted, and then poured himself deep, in great, rippling waves that filled her and left her replete.

With a great gasp, he collapsed atop her, careful to brace his weight on his elbows.

A dreamy smile pulled at Helena's lips as she stroked her fingers over his fine cambric shirt. There were so many reasons they could never be together. Not the least of which were his revelations last evening of Lucy Whitman and his broken heart. They came from different worlds, and she had the Hell and Sin . . . and he would one day be a duke.

All of those realities could intrude on the morrow.

Now, she'd have nothing but this.

"We have to return," he said, pressing a kiss to the sensitive spot where her ear met her neck.

Helena angled her head to better receive that gentle caress. For more than a month, she'd lamented the folly in leaving her door open at the Hell and Sin, only to find the greatest gift had come from it. She'd let Robert in and she'd have it no other way. "Must we?"

Passion clouded his eyes. "Marry me."

She blinked up at the twinkling night stars. Surely she'd merely imagined that hoarse half please, half command.

That dream he held forth tugged at her. A month ago, she'd have preferred death by quartering to marriage to a nobleman. Now she wanted all of what he offered . . . but selfishly she wanted more. "Oh, Robert," she said, flipping to her side so she could search his face. Uncaring that she was bastard born, he would marry her anyway. Tenderness pulled at her heart, as she fell in love with him all over again for defying every preconceived notion she had of noblemen and of women of her station. She stroked her palm over his cheek. "You don't have—"

"I want you." He captured her wrist in his hand, and dragging it to his mouth, he placed a kiss where her pulse pounded away.

Want.

Not love.

Helena studied him, the intensity pouring from his endless blue gaze. Since she'd been a girl she'd disavowed marriage. She had wanted nothing but the safety of her role at the Hell and Sin Club, and self-control of her life. If she wed him, she would be forfeiting that role. That self-control.

Robert removed a kerchief from inside the jacket on the ground and tenderly cleaned her. He shuttered his lashes but not before she detected the wounded spark there. His lips turned at the corner in his lazy half grin. "You're going to wound me with your silence, love."

Love. The single defining gift he'd not offered. *Because his heart was already given to another.*

With a sound of impatience, Helena sat up and set to work righting her dress. She'd never bind herself to a man out of his misbegotten sense of honor. She would not have Robert because of that. "I do not need you to marry me because of what we've done," she said, hurrying to adjust her wrinkled skirts and bodice. Honorable as he was, Robert would always wish to do the right thing . . . even by a duke's by-blow daughter. "You have to return to the ballroom."

As it was, her hasty flight would be noted. Had the guests present also spied the marquess's retreat? A laugh bubbled past her lips. Not that it mattered, either way. She was not long for here. Something stabbed at her heart.

"Is that what you believe?" he said quietly, as he gathered his jacket and stood. "That I'm offering for you because I feel a sense of obligation?"

"You are a gentleman, Robert," she said simply, as she attempted to shove her tresses into a semblance of an arrangement. Robert stuffed his arms into his sleeves, and then wordlessly turned her around, quickly setting her hair to rights. She glanced over her shoulder at him. "I do not doubt you'd marry me because—"

"I love you."

Her breath caught loudly. She shook her head.

He nodded.

She gave another shake.

"I love you," he said again, in quiet, solemn tones. He palmed her cheek with a tenderness that threatened to shatter. "I would marry you because I love you."

Her lower lip trembled. She'd thought taking Robert in her arms would be enough. *Only, three months would never be enough, and to marry him would mean abandoning her family, the club, and every pledge she'd taken.*

How had her life become so muddied in so short a time? Death by hot flame had always been preferable to life amongst the haute ton. Nor had there been a possibility of her sliding into this foreign world. Until she'd failed to lock her door and Robert had tripped into her life.

Is it truly abandoning a dream as much as embracing a new one? A dream she'd never allowed herself because of how unattainable it had been.

"Yes," she whispered, as he stroked the pad of his thumb over her lower lip.

He stilled. "Yes?"

With a smile, he held her close and she drew in the sandalwood scent of him. "I'll speak to Wilkinson on the morrow." Even that deliberate use of the duke's title, as opposed to the term "Father," spoke of Robert's awareness in ways that most nobles would never have.

There would be time enough for all that came with this in the morn. For now, she had this.

With reluctance, he set her away and consulted his timepiece. "I should return."

She managed a nod, and he hesitated.

Then, with several long strides, he reached the door and left.

As soon as it closed behind him, Helena buried her face in her hands. *How could she set aside the existence she'd made for herself as a woman with some control, for the life of a duchess?*

A faint click at the front of the gardens brought her head up, and her heart quickened. "Rob . . ."

The Duchess of Wilkinson closed the door behind her. Her astute gaze took in Helena's sloppy chignon and her wrinkled gown, and then settled on Helena's cheek. Vitriol poured from the woman. "You would not stay gone, Miss Banbury."

I was forced here . . . But how glad she was to be here . . .

The woman strolled over with the casualness of one walking in Hyde Park and as she came to a slow stop before Helena, Helena resisted the urge to break past her and flee. Alas, she'd endured far more evil than this angry duchess.

"I understand why you do not like me," she said softly.

"Do you?" the woman shot back in clipped tones.

Loving Robert as she did, Helena couldn't fathom the agony of marrying him and watching as his heart belonged to another. "I do." Helena turned her palms upward. "I am sorry you've known pain." And she was. Even as ugly as the duchess's soul was, life had turned it that way.

The duchess scoffed, that attempt at being dismissive ruined by the splotchy color in her cheeks. "You think this is about *love*? I do not love the duke." Yes, but Helena would wager at one time the woman had. "I do respect the distinctions of rank and birthright. You and your mother and brother inserted yourselves into my life." Hatred so strong brightened the crisp green of her eyes, and Helena took a step back. "She gave him a son, when I could not." The duchess closed that slight gap, taking a step forward. "And I will be damned if I see you take my daughter's right to rank by whoring yourself with Lord Westfield as you have." Her Grace flicked Helena's rumpled, limp cap sleeve. Then with smooth, expert duchess-like grace, the woman turned on her heel and walked away. She paused, and glanced back. "Oh, and Miss Banbury?" Helena stiffened. "I suggest you avoid returning to the ballroom. It would take but a single glance to know you were rutting in the gardens like your whore of a mother." With that, the duchess left, leaving Helena alone.

As soon as the lady left, Helena let loose a string of curses that would have only confirmed the woman's every last vile supposition about her.

For who could have ever believed that polite Society had evil greater than the beasts that lurked in the Dials?

Chapter 21

Rule 21
Do not let anyone inside your heart.

With her knees drawn to her chest, Helena sat at the window seat overlooking the London streets. Rain pinged off the crystal window-pane, and trailed a shimmery tear downward. Through the glass, she touched the tip of her index finger to one of those clear beads and followed its path until it converged with another drop and then they faded altogether.

Robert was set to arrive at thirty minutes past one o'clock to speak with the duke, and then their lives would be inextricably connected—forever. Her heart gave a funny leap.

Since she'd climbed abovestairs last evening, bathed, and sought out her bed, she'd lain awake, unable to sleep. This time it hadn't been the nightmares that kept rest at bay. It had been him. Helena rested her forehead against the cool window.

Since she'd been summoned to Ryker's office, he and her brothers had all believed Helena would choose the lavish life of polite Society.

For more than a month, she'd been filled with a bitter resentment. How dare they see her as different than them? They'd impugned her honor, when they'd long touted that there was nothing more important in the world.

But . . . she *was* different than them.

Ryker, Calum, Adair, Niall, any member of the Hell and Sin Club family would lay down their lives to save one of their own. That devotion was borne of a bond that went back to the darkest, most dangerous days in the streets when they'd clawed and scraped to survive. Yet, for that familial allegiance, they had each constructed protective walls to keep everyone out—including one another.

They'd not asked questions about their pasts, or shared in their pain. Why, they'd not even readily confessed to being capable of it.

And she'd not truly appreciated the solitariness of that existence— until Robert. He'd slipped inside, when she'd worked so hard to keep the world out. With him, she spoke about the hell of her past, but also the joy she'd known.

That was a life she would have . . . one of love, where you did not fear letting someone in, because love didn't weaken, it only made you stronger. Ryker and her brothers, shut away inside the Hell and Sin, would never know that.

Mayhap that is why they sent you away . . . ? Mayhap, Ryker saw what you yourself did not . . . That she'd wanted more of life, and she wanted all of it with Robert, but it could never be both.

In entering Robert's world, she would be leaving behind the only existence she'd truly known. She'd be abandoning Ryker, Calum, Adair, and Niall; and the family they'd carved out for one another. By his rank, Robert could visit the Hell and Sin Club, but those men she called brothers would never, ever leave St Giles to enter a world they so despised.

Their unwillingness to so much as respond to a single one of the many missives she'd sent this past month was evidence that as long as she dwelled amongst the *ton*, she was dead to them.

She bit her lower lip hard. How was it possible to have your heart filled with equal parts joy and despair? For there would have to be a goodbye. Only it was never the one she'd imagined making.

"Oh, dear, you are sad."

A soft voice sounded in the doorway. Helena twisted to face her sister. She hovered at the entrance with her arms hugged to her chest, uncertainty stamped in the delicate planes of her face.

"Oh, no. I'm not," she said softly, swinging her legs around. "I . . ."

Her sister quelled her with an uncharacteristically somber look. "I am not a child, Helena. Just as I've come to see how my mother feels about your presence here, I also see the sadness you so often wear."

Surprise brought her lips apart. Since she'd arrived she'd seen the always-optimistic Diana as an innocent, wholly incapable of seeing the world as it was around her. "I can be hopeful but also know what the world is truly like," the girl said gently, and pulled the door closed behind her.

"I am so sorry," Helena said quietly. Having been so judged through the years by her brothers, shame needled around her belly that she should have done the same to this young lady.

Diana drifted over, and hovered beside Helena's seat. Stealing another peek at the closed door, she slid into the spot beside Helena. "You were right," she said in a faint whisper.

Diana shook her head. "I didn't see what the world was like. Not truly. I believed my mother would be as happy to have you here, as I and Papa were." Her lips twisted with a new cynicism that struck sadness in Helena's breast. Inevitably all innocence was destroyed—even amongst polite Society. But how she hated that Diana should be so transformed. "Then I thought mayhap the longer you were here, she would appreciate that you had a good heart." The young lady hardened her mouth. "My mother is not a good woman, Helena."

Helena pressed her lips together. Mayhap if she were one of those masters with words, she'd be able to at least manage a halfhearted protestation to that, more statement than anything else, utterance.

Her sister stretched out her palm, and Helena glanced down at the neat stack tied with black velvet ribbons. Her breath caught, and she swiftly jerked her gaze to Diana's.

"I found these," Diana explained, turning them over to Helena's trembling fingers.

She yanked the ribbon free, and sifted through sealed note after sealed note addressed to Ryker. Oh, God. He'd not ignored her.

"My mother prevented them from being sent."

Helena shook her head. "Why would she do that?" she whispered. Had Ryker known how miserable Helena had been, and seen her pleadings, there would have at least been the *possibility* he might have accepted her back. Why would the duchess have interfered when she might have been free of her husband's bastard?

Diana lifted her shoulders in a small shrug. "I think she quite hates you," she said, and then slapped her palm over her mouth, as though she'd uttered a sailor's curse.

Helena gave the young woman a gentle smile. For everything she'd endured, at the hands of people far crueler, the duchess's hatred would never weaken her. "Yes, well for her hatred, there has always been you and the duke, kind and loving, and I focus on that good." Because the alternative was to be destroyed by the darkness.

Her sister made a sound of protest. "And why should I not be kind to you? Would you hate me for sharing the blood of my mother?"

"Never." Her answer was borne with the automaticity of truth. Diana had been as kind as if Helena had been a daughter gently bred and raised alongside her.

The young woman grunted. "Precisely."

Helena dropped her gaze to the stack in her hands. No, the duchess's hatred did not wound, but this betrayal . . . this gutted her. Helena's throat worked. The woman had singlehandedly cut off all hope of communication with the only family she'd known—out of nothing more than sheer malice.

"My mother saw that not a single one of your letters ever reached our brother."

Our brother. Helena startled. She'd not truly given thought to the fact that Ryker was as much Diana's brother as Helena's. He'd, of course, never recognize that familial connection. His heart was too hardened to ever set foot in this world, let alone see good in Lady Diana.

"Your maid is quite faithless, too, you know," the woman said with a sudden mature knowing.

Actually, she *didn't.* Helena frowned. How much else had escaped her notice that this young lady had seen?

Diana inched over on the seat, and lowered her voice to a soft whisper. "My maid, on the other hand, is not," she said, stealing another glance about, and then fishing around the front of her apron pocket. She held out a single note.

Helena's throat closed and she shook her head.

"I took the liberty of writing a letter on your behalf. Here," she said, pressing the thick ivory vellum into Helena's hands. "It is from Mr. Black."

With greedy fingers, Helena grabbed the note, that link to the family she'd missed these past weeks, the people she'd thought abandoned her, not even deigning to answer a note. She tore into the page and worked a hungry gaze over the handful of sentences in Niall's sloppy, ugly, smudged writing. Of course, Niall had long been the reasonable one of their family.

That familiar, inky mess raised a watery smile as she read.

> *Helena,*
> *Your home is always here.*
> *If you come, you will not be turned away.*

Your brother would see you this afternoon at fifteen
minutes past twelve.
    ~Niall

She slid her eyes closed, and folded the page. A tear squeezed out of the corner of her eye. Even that familiarity of Niall addressing all missives and written matters on behalf of Ryker filled her with that sense of being home.

Mayhap they'd not turn her away for marrying Robert. Mayhap they'd see what she herself had seen, a man who loved her, with all her flaws and imperfections.

"Thank you," she whispered. Diana had opened the door Helena thought forever closed.

Her sister beamed and patted her on the hand. "Do not thank me, silly. That is what sisters do."

Helena glanced over at the clock. Ryker was expecting her within the hour. He carved out his time with meticulous care and hers may as well have been a formal business meeting for the time he'd granted. She had but the brief meeting he'd allowed her to convince him of Robert's worth, and to carve out a permanent connection between her and her family at the club.

Nervousness churned in her belly.

"Do you know what else sisters do?" Diana asked. She leaned close and whispered against her ear. "They also accompany one another into dangerous parts of London so they are not alone."

Helena jerked her attention back. A mischievous sparkle lit Diana's pretty eyes.

She was already shaking her head. "No." Absolutely not.

The young woman surged forward. "Please, let me go with you." The faint entreaty in that handful of words tugged at Helena.

The underscoring of desperation in Diana's words spoke to a woman who chafed at the constraints where her capabilities were questioned, and she was expected to do whatever others thought was in her best interest, without allowing her the freedom of choice. Helena had battled a lifetime of frustration over it. She tamped down that weakening. "It is too dangerous," she repeated. Dangers that extended beyond the mortal kind and into the realm of her sister's reputation as a lady.

"Surely you do not think I'd allow you to go alone?" Diana pursed her lips.

Actually she did. Ladies didn't risk their reputations by entering the seedy parts of St Giles. "I've already said, it's not a place for you to be," Helena said, earning a frown. She'd grown up in those alleys and had knifed grown men who'd dared to harm her. She'd not expose Diana to even the hint of danger.

Her sister surged to her feet, and planted her arms akimbo. "If it is too dangerous then, you are not going either."

"I grew up there," she pointed out. As such, she was long past ruin or fear where those streets were concerned. "I'd not risk your reputation or your life." She loved her, this woman she'd been so determined to hate when she'd arrived.

"You think to protect me," she shot back with far more mature knowing than Helena had credited. "As you've been protected in being forced here?" A new, determined glint flecked her usually soft eyes. "He is my brother too, and I've not even met him."

Helena creased her brow. How had she failed to consider that familial bond shared by Ryker and Diana, one that would mean nothing to the man who despised all connections with their father? That truth alone would rock the trusting young lady. "You can't," she said at last. There were too many dangers and uncertainties.

"Very well." The young lady firmed her lips, the words ratcheting up Helena's apprehension. "Then I will make the journey myself."

She frowned. The determined set to the girl's narrow shoulders hinted at her resolve. If she didn't bring her along, Helena had no doubt her sister, in a bid to stretch her wings, would eventually find a way. She cursed. "You must change your gown. No finery and wear the plainest cloak you own. And you will stay close by me at all times," she ordered the beaming young woman. With each utterance, the folly in bringing this woman into the club sent warning bells blaring all the louder.

Diana nodded excitedly. "Then we must hurry," she said, and grabbing Helena by the hand, she tugged her along. "We have your meeting, and then the marquess comes to speak with Father, and I expect *he'll* expect to see you after that meeting."

Except, as she hurried abovestairs, she could not fight back her unease in leading the duke's legitimate daughter from the safety of her townhouse into a den of sin.

With an eerie similarity to his movements twelve years earlier, Robert climbed the steps of the Duke of Somerset's townhouse and rapped on the front door.

His father's loyal butler drew the door open almost instantly. "My father?" He turned over his hat and cloak.

There was no nervous swallowing or pale skin. There was no stammering or hastily averted eyes. "He is in his office, my lord," the servant said with a slight smile.

Yes, because, where the late duke's servants had been stone-faced and sacked for expressions of mirth, the new duke surrounded himself with a staff unafraid to show emotion.

"I will show myself in," he said, and he started down the familiar path, through the long-hated corridors. New carpets had since been laid, and the paint changed, but the same ancestral portraits hung along the corridors.

For years he'd kept his gaze trained forward on this walk, avoiding looking around at the home that contained so much evil and sin, and dark memories that had forever shaped him. Now as he walked, all that agony of betrayal was . . . gone. The bitter resentment that had shaped him into the careless, heartless rogue he'd been had lifted, driven back by a spirited minx who'd boldly challenged him at every turn.

Robert drew to a stop beside a familiar ducal portrait. His late grandfather's hateful visage stared back, commanding even in death. The hard set to his mouth, the coldness in his eyes, all expertly captured by the artist. Not a hint of frailty existed in the austere lines of those ducal features. He moved closer, peering into those eyes. He'd hated him when he'd been living, and hated him with an equal ferocity in death.

. . . you may have your tantrum and hate me for now, but someday you will thank me for this . . .

Robert would have wagered his very life that he'd never thank the bastard for his intervention. Shattered by Lucy's treachery and the late Duke of Somerset's machinations, Robert had been transformed into a coolly removed man who'd hardened his heart. Then Helena had stepped into his life and singlehandedly torn down every defensive wall he'd constructed, proving that his heart was still very much alive—and that it beat for her.

If not for the duke's lesson that day, Robert would even now be wed to Lucy Whitman, and there never would have been a Helena Banbury.

Holding the duke's gaze in the portrait, Robert gave a slight nod. *Thank you . . .*

As much as he'd hated his grandfather for his treachery, how could he not be grateful at having found the gift of Helena? Robert resumed his walk.

And for the first time since he'd strode this same path, he smiled.

He paused outside the heavy oak panel, and lifted his hand to knock when a strangled paroxysm penetrated the door. Robert shoved the door open, and paused. Seated behind his desk, his father held a kerchief to his mouth. His cheeks flushed red from the force of his coughing, and his frame shook.

Alarm skittered around Robert's insides as he closed the door and stalked forward. "Father?"

His father waved his hand, and continued choking until he drew a jerky, raspy breath. He brushed the back of his hand across his damp brow. "Robert," he said weakly, dabbing at his mouth with the white kerchief.

Robert's gaze went to that fabric and he stilled as Helena's observation crept into his mind. *Your father appears . . . strained . . .* He remained transfixed by the stark crimson stain upon that scrap. His father followed his stare, and gave him a long, sad look.

The energy went out of Robert's legs as he sank into the nearest seat. He tried to drag forth words, opening and closing his mouth several times. *No.* Robert shook his head. He'd faked his illness to see he and Beatrice found respectable matches. He wasn't truly ill.

The duke assembled his lips into the semblance of a smile. "Surely you know I'd never have the bad form to fake my own death?" he wheezed, and stuffed that bloodied cloth into the front of his jacket. "I am not my father, Robert." His father closed his eyes, drawing in slow and uneven breaths.

Agony spiraled through him, and Robert dragged a hand through his hair, searching about. Where in bloody blazes was Hanson. "Dr. C—?"

"Has gone for the day." Which implied the doctor attended his father daily.

He searched his gaze over his father. These past months he'd seen precisely what he wanted to see. Having been manipulated by so many before, he'd been blinded to the truth. Now he forced himself to look at that which he'd failed to note. The drawn lines at the corner of his father's mouth. His haggard eyes.

"No." That word rung deep from a place where in speaking it, he willed it to be.

His father nodded. "Yes." There was a gentle insistence that came from a man who'd come to accept his own eventual fate.

Robert gripped the arms of his chair. "I don't . . . I thought . . ." He curled his hands so tight he dug the flesh from them. *What a bloody fool I am.* Tears filled his eyes and he blinked back the useless sheen.

"You didn't do anything wrong, Robert," his father said softly.

"I did *everything* wrong," he said in harsh, guttural tones. He'd been precisely the self-centered, pompous bastard his father had all but pointedly accused him of being. And if it hadn't been for Helena, how blind he still would be to everything that mattered. Robert scrubbed his hands up and down his face.

"I spent months resenting you," he said, blankly. Shame, agony, and despair all twisted around his insides.

"And do you know why you did?"

A strangled sob worked its way up from a place where regret lived, and he shook his head.

"I was not the father you deserved, Robert."

An agonized protest formed on his lips. Where most lords had cold, pompous bastards as sires, Robert's father had loved his children. He'd not been driven by cold, powerful connections, but rather by the happiness of those children. And Robert had spent years secretly hating him, for allowing the late duke to control their family.

His father dissolved into another fit, and withdrew another kerchief. Robert surged out of his chair, but he waved him back to his seat. Closing his eyes, the duke laid his head along the back of his chair. "The thing about dying, Robert, is that you do not have time for lying to yourself or others. My father destroyed the happiness of so many. My sister and her husband." He opened his eyes. "*You.*" A sad smile formed on his lips. "That is my greatest regret, that I wasn't there more for you. I knew about Lucy Whitman."

He groaned, making a sound of protest. "Stop," he entreated.

"I knew you cared for her," his father continued, giving his head a regretful shake. "I also knew my father was aware. And given what he'd done to his own daughter predicted what he was capable of. Particularly when his grandson, a future duke, showed less than suitable attentions for a nursemaid." His last living parent leaned forward in his seat, and settled his arms on his desk. "I spoke to you recently about setting yourself apart, and not being like everyone else. I spoke from a place of knowing, Robert. I spoke to you as a man who never found the strength to defend his sister." He held Robert's gaze. "My son."

Robert shoved forward in his chair and matched his father's pose, leaning forward. "We are not responsible for the crimes of another. The duke was incapable of love and changing, and nothing you said or did would have ever swayed him. You were never to blame." He implored him with his eyes to see that truth.

His father leaned back in his chair, and closed his eyes. "Thank you."

At long last, the sharp, bitter divide, made by another, faded.

His father mopped his brow, and when he again looked at Robert, in this instance, the telltale marks of suffering lifted, and he was the robust, hearty father he'd always known. "So I take it you are here about your Miss Banbury."

"I am."

A pained smile pulled at his lips. "I like her a great deal." He waggled his eyebrows. "Something of a bluestocking."

Do you disapprove of a woman of knowledge . . . Robert managed his first real grin since he'd stepped inside this townhouse, that morn. "She is." He reached inside his jacket and withdrew the special license. Where the late duke had been driven by nothing more than the succession of the Somerset title and the noble bloodlines to connect the family to, his father had only wanted to see his children settled before he left this earth. "I intend to marry her."

His father gave an approving nod. "Smart boy," he said in the same proud tones he'd used when Robert had mastered his lessons as a child.

He folded his hands on his stomach. "Now, go along and speak to Wilkinson. I expect your Miss Banbury is waiting for you."

Robert lingered.

"Go, Robert. To your future."

And shoving back his chair, Robert took his leave of the townhouse that had contained so much sin and darkness, and made his way to the Duke of Wilkinson's.

A short while later, Robert was being shown into the older duke's office.

"Westfield, my boy," he boomed, shoving his large frame into a stand as the door closed behind him.

"Your Grace." Robert dropped a bow.

"Bah, no need for formality this day, eh?" he said, banging Robert on the back. "A glass of brandy?" Without awaiting a reply, he ambled over to the sideboard and proceeded to pour two snifters. He carried them over and motioned to the wingback chairs at the edge of the hearth.

Robert accepted the drink with a murmured thanks and slid into the comfortable folds. He opened his mouth to speak.

"You are here about my girl, I take it?" the duke supplied for him. "Helena," he clarified.

"I love her," he said, setting his brandy down on the table beside him.

The duke smiled over the rim of his snifter. "As I said, smart boy." Then his usual grin slipped, and he looked into the contents of his drink. "I've made many mistakes in my life, Westfield. I wasn't faithful to my wife. I failed Helena's mother. But for all the regrets I carry, I will never regret my daughter." He clutched his glass so tight, his knuckles whitened. "Her life has not been an easy one." The duke lifted his eyes, blinking slowly. "I do not even know what her life was like before Ryker rescued her." Ryker. The owner of the Hell, and Helena's savior.

The man would have Robert's eternal devotion for it. "But I know it wasn't a good one, just as I know you will bring her the happiness she deserves." He lifted his glass. "So before we discuss the terms of the contract, shall we toast?"

Robert reached for his glass just as a distant shrieking reached through the office door, followed by frantic footfalls.

The door burst open and an out-of-breath duchess stumbled into the room. Tears ravaged her unwrinkled cheeks.

Robert and Wilkinson shoved to their feet.

"They are gone," she cried, between her great gasping sobs.

Robert's heart thumped an extra beat, as a slow-building dread started in his belly and fanned out.

"Who . . . ?"

"I-I never thought D-Diana would go," the duchess sobbed into her hands, muffling her words. "It was just meant to be Miss Banbury."

The dread grew, licking at his senses, threatening to pull him under.

"What are you on about?" her husband barked, stalking forward.

She lowered her hands to her sides. "Th-they are going to that c-club to meet M-Mr. Diggory."

And Robert's heart stopped. The monster who'd burned her. The man who stalked her dreams and owned her nightmares. His hand shook, sending brandy spilling over the rim of his glass, and he set the glass down.

"Who is Mr. Diggory?" The duke furrowed his brow, and when his wife continued to blubber and stammer, he took her by the shoulders in an uncharacteristic display of strength.

His wife sobbed all the harder. "He is the m-man who I turned her and her mother o-over to. You have to believe I would have never orchestrated their meeting had I known Diana would have accompanied h-her." Then she launched into a new round of noisy tears. Wilkinson released her so quickly she stumbled backwards and caught herself against the side of the leather wingback chair. The man rushed across the room, and withdrew a case of dueling pistols.

A black sheen of rage descended over Robert's vision, momentarily blinding him. "Where is she?" he seethed. "Where is she?" he thundered when she continued weeping.

"A-At that club," she cried, as her husband handed one of his pistols over to Robert.

Wordlessly accepting the weapon, he leveled her with a frosty stare. This woman was responsible for the hell Helena had endured. She'd no doubt been the one to leave her fingerprints on her arms, and now she'd threatened her very life. Dread slithered around his belly. "By God, if anything happens to her, I will hold you personally accountable," he seethed. With the duke bellowing for his servants, Robert sprinted from the room.

He'd only just found Helena, and he would be goddamned if he lost her now.

Chapter 22

Rule 22
Remain silent on the streets.

With the reassuring, if slight, weight of her derringer tucked inside the clever pocket sewn on the front of her cloak, Helena made her way through the old familiar streets of St Giles. In this particular instance, she came to an unfortunate realization—Lady Diana Wilkinson would have made a rotten pickpocket.

"I am excited to meet him," Diana happily prattled at Helena's side, as they picked their way along St Giles Street.

"Shh," Helena hushed, casting a glance about. Alas, either the rumble of the carriages and the shouts of street vendors drowned out her urging, or her sister was too excited to work at subterfuge. Then when one was the proper daughter of a duchess there was no need for subterfuge. You didn't go sneaking off. You didn't know how to discreetly find a hired hack. And you most certainly did not ever visit these very streets where they found themselves now.

Yet through Helena's less-than-stellar influence, she'd brought her sister into the streets unfit for men, women, and children alike.

"Do you think he'll like me?" Diana asked at her side.

It was on the tip of her tongue to point out that Ryker Black didn't like anybody, but that would only fuel further questions from her loquacious sister. So instead she said nothing.

They reached the end of the street, and Helena put a staying hand on Diana's arm, bringing the girl to a stop. The younger woman pushed back her hood, and Helena cursed, promptly tugging the hood back into place. "You must leave your hood up," she scolded, stealing a look about. "You face ruin in being here." Not for the first time since she, in a moment of sisterly devotion and poor judgment, had agreed to let Diana accompany her, regret stabbed at her. In her innocence, Diana had no place being here.

"But *you* are here," Diana countered.

Helena closed her eyes and prayed for patience. How had she failed to realize how stubborn the young lady was? "I am a bastard."

"You are also a duke's daughter."

"It is different," she shot back. Was she truly debating the distinctions between a duke's offspring here, now, with some of the roughest, crudest men in London idling about?

"I don't see how . . ." the girl grumbled under her breath.

"And I am to be married," Helena added. That at the very least settled the discussion.

"Oh, you are?" Diana clapped her hands excitedly. "Splendid. Lord Westfield will make you a divine husband." She paused. "It is Lord Westfield, correct?" And even walking the streets of St Giles, attempting to evade discovery and ruin, a smile pulled at Helena's lips. The girl could have talked the late Boney into defeat with such skill.

"Yes. It is Lord Westfield."

"Lovely. Even if he is old," she rambled.

Helena took her by the hand and started across the street.

". . . after all, you are closer in age to the marquess. Not that you are old," Diana said on a rush. "You're only a little bit old. For a woman, that is."

Again, Helena's lips pulled in a grin. Mayhap it wouldn't be so very difficult to convince Ryker to accept Diana in this new world, after all. It would surely take one endless stream of conversation from this magpie to bring him round.

A tall figure stepped into her path, and she crashed into a hard, immovable wall, knocking her hood loose. Helena's hair tumbled about her shoulders as she was sent sprawling. She landed so hard on her buttocks pain radiated up her spine.

"Oh, dear," Diana cried, rushing over. "Are you all right?" She planted her hands on her hips, a little defender. "You, sir, should have a care," she chided.

Giving her dazed head a shake, Helena shoved herself onto her elbows and froze. Through the din of street noise and her sister's prattling, the world stopped. He, with his pockmarked face and gaunt features, came to her at the oddest times, haunting her sleeping and waking moments.

"'ello, Helena." Diggory grinned back.

The earth dipped and swayed. She closed her eyes hard and counted. One-two-three-wake-up. One-two-three-wake-up. She choked on bile. *He is not real. He is not real. He's merely the nightmare that's dogged you for nearly twenty years.*

She peeked under her lashes, and a wave of nausea assaulted her. Aged by time and life on the streets, the evil, cracked, yellow-toothed smile remained the same.

"Look at ye, all fancy now." That hated cockney sucked away rational thought, and she was once more that small, cowering girl with a flame touched to her skin. "Oi almost didn't recognize ye the other night in the street."

It had been him. She whimpered, and shook her head, inching away.

"Helena?"

She clamped her hands over her ears to blot out that hated sound. Only confusion raged inside her mind. For that sweetly spoken inquiry, laced with concern, did not belong to the demon in her dreams.

Diana.

She forced her eyes open, and looked blankly to her sister. Oh, God. Diana. "Run," she rasped.

Diana looked at her, opening and closing her mouth, and apparently there was more strength to the girl than she'd credited, for she flared her eyes and then, with a speed a wood sprite would have been impressed by, sprinted down the street.

Sending a silent prayer skywards to God, who did not exist, for the girl's escape, Helena pushed herself to a stand, and bolted.

Diggory easily overtook her. He wrapped his punishing hand about her forearm, and she bit her cheek to keep from crying out at the agony of his hold. She'd sooner die than cower before him again. "Black stole ye from me. Oi wasn't done with ye." He stuck his nose close to hers and she recoiled under the onion-and-garlic scent that slapped her face. "Oi promised the duchess to off ye when oi was through with ye. Oi never expected ye'd be the brilliant bookkeeper ye are or else I would have fought to keep ye."

Oh, God. He *did* know. Ryker's speculations had proven correct about just what Diggory had gleaned over the years. It had been Helena, however, who'd been lulled into a false sense of security. Then something he said registered . . .

The duchess? Helena's riotous mind spun under this demon's reappearance and the jumbled words he tossed at her. As he dragged her down the street, she glanced desperately about for anyone. Alas, this was not the respectable end of Mayfair, populated by fancy lords and ladies. These were the seedy streets of ill repute, where you took care to avoid the plight of others.

Jerking and pulling at her arm, Helena dug her heels in. She was no longer the frail girl of five.

"Enough of that, bitch," he hissed, wrenching her arm behind her with such force tears sprung to her eyes.

Fury raged through her, and she glared at him. She tossed her head back to let loose a scream when he jammed something hard and cold against her back. At the bite of metal penetrating the fabric of her coat, Helena froze.

"Oi'll end that bitch's life, too, if ye keep at it." A chill wracked her frame. Why had she agreed to bring Diana here? *Because you'd been gone from this so long, you'd been lulled into a dangerous sense of safety—a safety that didn't exist.* She wanted to toss her head back and howl with frustration. This is why Ryker had kept her shut away, because he'd correctly seen her weaknesses and known the eventual fate for those who proved incautious. "That's better," Diggory spat. "Now move." He jerked her forward, and she stumbled. "Oi can't do this 'ere."

Dread iced her veins. As a child, forced to thieve for him, she'd served a purpose. No longer. *He is going to kill me.* Fighting through the panic, she searched for the effortless words Robert had always proven so capable of, and found strength in the lessons he'd unwittingly shared. "Wait," she said coaxingly. "Surely you see I'm of far more value to you alive. The Duke of Wilkinson . . . my father will pay . . ."

He guffawed. "Do ye think a bluidy duke will give a rat's arse if oi gut ye in the street?"

A month ago she would have agreed. A month ago she'd believed she knew how the world was, and found the entire *ton* wanting. "My brother, Ryker Black, will pay you, as well."

He snorted. "Only after 'e gutted me fer this."

Relentless in her efforts, she angled her head back and gave him a meaningful look. "You forget . . ." She let the word linger between them.

His nostrils flared. "Wot did oi forget?"

"I can help you with the books at your club." She'd sooner sit down to dinner with the Devil. Nonetheless, the promise danced around the stale air. She could all but see the greedy wheels of his mind turning.

Then Diggory jammed the pistol deeper into the skin, and she bit her lip to keep from crying out. She'd not let him see another damned tear or hint of weakness. This man had already stolen so much.

She pressed her eyes closed, drawing forth Robert's visage, and struggled to breathe. This is how she would die. Here in the street like the guttersnipe she'd been. How bloody close she'd been to having everything she'd never known she wanted. She balled her hands as an unholy rage took root and spiraled like a slow-moving conflagration. *Stop, Helena. Think.* By God, she'd not die like a cowering child. Not at this man's hands. Helena panted. "P-Please," she rasped, as he pulled her farther into an alley. The moment he stopped at the end of the narrow passage, she'd be dead. With energy singing in her veins, Helena whimpered. "I-I can't breathe." Then she went limp.

Diggory's grip on her slackened, and he cursed.

Helena jammed her elbow hard into his stomach in three quick blows, and the air left him on a soft whoosh. The blood pounding in her ears, she shoved her heel against his kneecap, and he lost his hold on her. With his shout echoing after her footsteps, Helena fished inside her pocket and as she sprinted away from Diggory, her fingers brushed the reassuring cool steel.

She skidded to a stop.

A humming buzzed in her ears as she stared unblinkingly at the unlikely pairing at the end of the alley.

Surely this was another nightmare not borne of flame, but borne of the love she carried in her heart for him. "Robert," she whispered. One of Diggory's thugs stood with a knife at Robert's throat. Her stomach heaved. *What is he doing here?*

Robert worked a powerful stare quickly over her person. "Surely you didn't think I could ever leave you to go off alone?" he asked gruffly, following her unspoken thoughts. How harmonious they'd always been.

She wanted to toss her head back and rail at the fates, for in his eyes was love and an acceptance of his inevitable fate. No. This was not his world. He'd not die this way, in an alley like street trash, like Diggory and his gang. Gun in hand, she spun and pointed it at Diggory. "Stop," she called out, halting his stride. How was her voice so even? "Have him lower his weapon," she demanded, leveling her gun, while keeping Robert in her side vision. "Do it," she cried, when Diggory and his man exchanged a look.

The devil of her past cursed and waved his weapon about. "Wot are ye going to do, Helena? Kill me? Ye were never anything but a weak girl," he taunted, taking a step forward.

"Do not listen to him," Robert barked. "You were always stronger than him, Helena." A tortured shout burst from him.

Her hand quavered and she flicked a panicky gaze to Robert. Diggory's man dropped him to his knees with a swift punch to his kidneys.

"Stop," she cried out, her arm quaking uncontrollably.

"Yer shaking now just as ye were when I set ye on fire," Diggory taunted, as he took another step. "Ye cannot kill me." Triumph blazed across his harsh, ugly features as he turned his gun on Robert.

"No." The scream tore from her soul.

Three sharp reports, in staggering succession, rent the quiet.

Gunpowder clouded the air, and the derringer slipped from her fingers. Diggory's mouth formed a small moue, and then he collapsed facedown on the muddied ground. *Dead.*

"Helena!"

The faint clatter of another pistol hitting the ground penetrated the thick haze over her senses, and Helena spun around. Ryker stood beside Diggory's henchman, who now lay at his feet with a bullet in his head. Ignoring her brother, Helena raced down the alley. "Robert," she panted, and flung herself into his arms.

Robert folded his arms almost reflexively around her, and she burrowed against the hard wall of his chest, taking his strength. "How d-did you know I was here?" she choked out. He staggered under the weight of her embrace, and she stumbled into him, bringing them to their knees.

Something hot and sticky soaked the fabric of her gown, and she froze. *No.*

"I am fine," he said, his voice faint.

No. No. No. No. No.

Ignoring her brother who fell to a knee beside her, she worked her hand between them. "Robert," she rasped, and a low-pained moan strangled her, as blood coated her fingers. "No. No. No. What did you do?" she cried out, glancing up at the taut lines at the corner of his mouth, the wan hue of his skin, and the vague look in his eyes. A sob escaped her as she pressed her hands to his side to slow the ebb. So much blood. So much of it. His life's blood covered her palms, soaking her scarred fingers. Helena stared at those crimson stains as insanity licked at her senses, threatening to suck her away from right and reason. "Don't you dare leave me, Robert Dennington," she sobbed, tears streaking down her face, blurring her vision.

Wordlessly, Ryker guided Robert down on his back and shoved off the bloodstained black coat. He yanked off his own jacket and in one swift movement, shredded the fabric, and held it to that gaping wound.

Shouts and pounding footfalls sounded at the front of the alley, and her brothers burst forward, Robert's eyes slid closed, and Helena's world ceased to be.

Chapter 23

Rule 23
Run when you must.

The following morning, Helena's maid hurried about her chambers, gathering garments from the armoire and neatly folding them and placing them inside the open trunks.

Standing at the edge of the window, Helena stared blankly out into the quiet cobbled streets. Rain pinged the crystal windowpane, marking a fitting trail of sadness along the glass.

In the streets of St Giles, the slightest hesitation could prove costly. Deadly. It was a lesson ingrained into her since she'd been a small girl.

Of course, Robert would not have known that very rule. But she had. And she'd failed him, anyway. It was just one of the many reasons she'd no right to him.

Tears flooded her eyes, and she drew in a slow, shuddery breath. Oh, the bloody irony of it all. She'd raged at being sent here, and now she'd rather lop off a limb than be sent away.

Only she wasn't being sent away. She gripped the sides of her skirts. She was leaving.

She was leaving Robert.

A tear slid down her cheek, and she brushed the back of her hand over that useless remnant of her misery. She'd never been born for this world. Somewhere along the way she'd allowed herself to forget that she was the daughter of a whore, a child raised amidst such violence that it would forever be a stain upon her soul and her very life.

That was a darkness she'd not bring to Robert. Or Diana. Or Beatrice. Or her father.

None of them.

Yet, you already did . . .

No. She couldn't remain here. With her hand in murdering the ever-powerful Diggory, she'd only strengthened the feud between their warring factions. There would never be peace, and the threat of further bloodshed remained—stronger now than it ever had been.

Only, in leaving, she'd not take with her all the damage done that day. The pain and guilt of that stabbed her with an ever-familiar guilt. Diana, innocent and good, had been ruined the moment she'd stumbled into the Hell and Sin, crying for help. She'd forfeited her future to save Helena's life, and sacrificed herself in the process. Helena curled her arms close to her chest. Oh, the irony. To have judged these people wanting from the moment she'd arrived, only to learn how much better they were in their sacrifice and strength than Helena.

"Miss, your trunks are all packed," her faithless maid murmured at her back.

"That will be all," she said in curiously hollow tones. It was done.

From within the glass panel, she detected the quick nod, curtsy, and then the girl took her leave, closing the door quietly behind her.

At last alone, Helena let the tears fall freely, unchecked. Ryker had long proclaimed tears were a hint of weakness, and yet she didn't give a bloody damn about Ryker and his blasted rules. Or his curt, cold pronouncements about the nobility.

Nothing but a stinging, biting rage at him consumed her, so much healthier and safer than the despair tearing her apart.

He'd sent her to this place. He'd forced her into this world. And in it, she'd found Robert, a man who'd defied every last belief she'd believed about noblemen.

A man who'd treat her as a lady and offer her his name; the same man, who'd defend a common street thief, was a man so wholly worth loving. Her shoulders shook from the force of her tears. For he was deserving of a woman far more worthy than she.

She drew in a last, broken sob, and then dragged her hands down her damp cheeks.

The faint click of the bedroom door sounded in the quiet, and she stiffened.

Her sister called out quietly. "You are leaving, then?"

Helena gave a curt nod, incapable of speech. If she said a single word, she'd collapse into another blubbering mess.

"I don't want you to go," Diana said, coming to a stop at her shoulder.

"I have to," she said on a ragged whisper. She turned to face the young woman. In her sister's eyes was a new world wariness that came from one who'd been ruined by life. And guilt seized her chest once more. *I did this.* "I am so sorry." For everything.

A faint smile played on her bow-shaped lips. "Do you truly believe I'd ever regret stepping into that hell to save you? I love you, Helena."

Tears welled anew, and Helena smothered a sob with her hand.

Then, in the greatest of reversals, the younger girl drew her into her arms and gave a light squeeze. "Husbands are overrated anyway," Diana said with a dry humor. "Especially the noblemen type."

Oh, how I am going to miss you . . .

She was saved from responding by the opening of the door.

The duke's large form filled the entranceway. This man whom she'd spent her life hating.

Diana hurriedly took a step back. "I will come by before you leave," she murmured, and rushed from the room.

The Duke of Wilkinson closed the door. Father and daughter stood there, silent, studying one another. Gone was the ever-cheerful style. In its place were tight lines at the corner of his mouth, and a sadness in his eyes.

Another person forever changed by my presence. She swallowed past the swell of regret.

The duke came forward slowly, and as he stopped before her, she braced for his stinging vitriol. "Do you know the day you were born, you did not cry."

She cocked her head.

The duke's gaze took on a faraway quality. "I was not there the day Ryker was born. His delivery was long, and your mother and I were told he'd not survived." Coldness slithered around her insides. What evil that a newborn babe could have been stolen and given to another. He looked at Helena. "I was determined to sit outside your mother's rooms while she birthed you." Odd, she'd never given thought to that day, whether there had been joy or sadness or . . . *any* feelings about her birth. "The moment you entered the world, there was just this absolute *silence*."

She bit her lower lip hard. He'd have surely preferred his world that way, given the way she'd ripped it asunder.

"I ran into the room, and you just had this small smile on your lips."

The vise squeezed all the harder about her heart. His were not the words of a hateful beast or a vengeful duke. But rather, a man. How long had she seen nothing but the Duke of Wilkinson? Only to find he was, and always had been, her father.

"I am so very sorry for all the ways in which I failed you . . ." His voice cracked. "And your brother." Ryker Black, who'd hated his sire so much, he'd adopted a false surname that divorced himself from either of the parents who'd given him life.

Helena shook her head. "It is not your fault." Sometimes evil won out over good, as it had with the duchess.

He ran a hand over his balding head. "But you see, Helena. It was my fault. I didn't choose your mother." When he at last looked at her, regret bled from the depths of his eyes. "I chose responsibility, and she, and you, Ryker, you all paid the greatest price for my sins. I loved her," he whispered, and her heart spasmed at the grief which contorted his face.

Unable to witness that emotion there, Helena strolled over to her vanity. "Sometimes love is not enough." Her gaze caught the folded note and she skimmed her fingertips over the six letters marked on the vellum.

"You are wrong," he said, with only the optimism he could have, this man who'd failed to see the evil in his wife.

She shot a sad look back. "I'm not." If she was, she and Robert could be together. That day in the alley had proven the impossibility of them.

Her father fished around the front of his jacket, and withdrew a narrow box. He held a palm out. She started at the unexpectedness of that gesture and looked from him to that small package. He came forward. "Here," he said with a gruff tenderness.

Wordlessly, she accepted the modest package, and lifted the lid. She froze. Nestled amidst a small pillow of aged satin lay a gold necklace with a ruby rose pendant attached, and a memory whispered forth of a woman who'd worn this very piece. Long ago. For so many years she'd recalled nothing but the despair and horror of living on the streets with that broken woman and Diggory that she'd neatly forgotten all the cherished memories they'd once shared: tending gardens together, playing a pretend game of pirates, battling with imagined swords.

"It was your mother's," the duke murmured.

Helena managed a nod. "I know," she whispered. There wasn't a single item she had left of her mother. Every memory she had of Delia Banbury existed only in her mind, and with a young woman's bitter rancor, Helena had spent years hating her. Until now. Now she saw with mature eyes that her mother, who'd been hopelessly in love, was a far greater survivor than Helena could have ever been. For she'd endured the agony of losing the man she loved to another, and carved out an existence anyway.

Tears blurred her eyes. How very little Helena had truly known of the world, of love and joy and forgiveness . . . until Robert.

Something light and powerfully freeing blotted out all the long-held resentment. "Thank you," she squeezed out past a tight throat. The words for her mother, and the father who, in bringing Helena here, had helped repair that broken link between her and the woman who'd given her life.

"Stay."

The duke's words recalled her to the moment, and she lowered the gift to the smooth surface of the vanity. "I can't." *Even as I want to.*

"Is it because of what Diana did?" he pressed, and her teeth ravaged the skin of her inner cheek. No. It was because of what Helena had done, in bringing her there. "I'll not have her marry one of those arrogant pups who'd condemn her for her bravery," he said, demonstrating once more the manner of man and father he was.

She shook her head. "It is not Diana," she said quietly. What was another lie in the scheme of all the sins she was guilty of?

"Is it the duchess?" he asked, coming closer. "She will be going away. To . . . a hospital." He grimaced. For, of course, with her actions, the woman had demonstrated the level of her madness.

"It is because of *me*," she said at last. Picking up the note, she turned to face him. Desperate for this exchange to be at an end, she pressed it into his hands. "Will you see this delivered to Lord Westfield?"

He stared at the name a moment, and then gave a reluctant nod. "You are always welcome here, Helena," he said, his voice breaking.

All the years' worth of hatred lifted as Helena stepped into his arms and hugged him. "Thank you . . . Father."

In the week that followed, Robert had endured a parade of visitors to his room, from his family's doctor to Bea, to servants to his father.

When a future duke was shot, the world all but stopped.

Seated at the edge of his bed, Robert winced as Dr. Carlson probed the area he'd cleaned and stitched up in the immediacy of Diggory's shot.

"My apologies," Dr. Carlson murmured, not taking his attention from the pink flesh. "You are fortunate," the doctor said, and collected a set of fresh bandages. "Several inches closer and it would have pierced an organ."

Robert gritted out a smile. His side burned like he'd been set afire. Except with the doctor's words, it all came rushing back as vivid now as it had been in the moment. Helena. The bastard Diggory with a gun pointed at her chest. Her agonized cry. "But it did not, and I'm surely capable of leaving my chambers."

It had been an entire week since he'd seen Helena. Of course, given the impropriety of visiting his chambers she couldn't very well come here . . . and yet . . . disappointment assailed him. He'd wanted her here, anyway.

"Only if you care to risk reopening the wound and infection," Dr. Carlson said dryly, and Robert swallowed down another wave of frustration.

The door opened, and he looked to the entrance of the room, where his father stood framed in the doorway. "You are awake." Heavy lines marred his sharp features; his reddened eyes hinted at a restless night and the struggle of his own illness.

"And intending to go out," Dr. Carlson supplied unhelpfully.

The revelation earned a frown from the duke. Something sparked in his eyes, and he quickly averted his gaze.

Robert froze, as unease won out over pain. Nothing would keep Helena from him. A woman who'd face down a demon like Diggory wouldn't let propriety prevent her from visiting. "What is it?" he said tightly.

Taking his cue, Dr. Carlson hurriedly packed his equipment and made his leave. "It is Miss Banbury," his father said as soon as the door had closed.

Robert jerked and nausea roiled in his belly at the sudden movement. Had one of Diggory's henchmen punished her for that man's deserved death? "What happened to Helena?" Sweat beaded on his brow. *Oh, God, if she is dead, I am nothing . . .*

"She is all right. Miss Banbury is fine."

That gruff reassurance slowed his pulse rate, and Robert sent silent thanks skyward. He frowned. "What is it?" Then he registered the grim look in his father's eyes. Apprehension kicked the rhythm of his heartbeat into a frantic gallop.

"Tell me," he demanded, shoving to a stand. That subtle movement sent agony lancing through him once more.

"She is fine. I'd not lie to you. You need to rest, Robert," his father implored. "You risk reopening the wound stitched by Dr. Carlson. I no more wish to be coddled than you," he reasoned. "Given you're the one with the gunshot, and I'm merely the one dragging out his death day by day, I expect I win this argument." Robert's face contorted, and his father grimaced. "Poor jest?"

"Indeed," Robert said gruffly, and swung his legs back onto the bed. "*You* should be resting." *And I should be with Helena.*

"Bah," his father said, stretching his legs out and hooking them at the ankles. "I'll have all of eternity to rest but only a short while to reason with my son."

Though his mother had died far too young, Robert recalled the love his parents had. "Nothing could have kept you away from Mother," he pointed out.

Where all mention of the late duchess raised sadness in the duke's eyes, a smile pulled at his lips. "And soon I shall not have to." For all the agony that came with Robert confronting the eventual death of his father, the peace in his father's smile, and the happiness etched in his face, spoke of a man who'd been parted too long from his wife.

How had his father lived all these years without her? If Helena were gone from his life, what purpose would there be? What reason to smile? Or laugh? And yet, the duke had.

"I had you and your sister," his father said quietly, unerringly following the direction Robert's thoughts had wandered. "And though there was always a void in losing her, there was always a reason to find joy." He held his eyes. "I was blessed with two of them." His father reached inside his pocket and wordlessly turned a folded missive over.

Robert stared at it a moment, and furrowing his brow, accepted the ivory vellum.

With shaky fingers Robert unfolded the note.

> *Dearest Robert . . .*
> *We could not have been born to more different worlds. I allowed myself to believe I could live in yours . . . but the truth is, I cannot.*

He hurried his gaze over the page, his panic mounting.

With your convalescing, I've had ample time to think beyond the whirlwind week we knew together. In wedding you, I would be giving up all of who I am, just as you would be giving up who you are as a future duke. I am a bookkeeper. My life brings me peace, and though you brought me several very happy days, that can never be enough. Just as I can never be enough for you.

I pray for your quick recovery, and ask when you think of me, you do so with some fondness.

Ever Yours,

Helena

The crumpling of parchment filled the quiet, punctuated by Robert's rapidly drawn breaths. Surely he'd been mistaken. He unfolded the page and reread the words there. And reread them again. Yet, no matter how many times he worked his gaze over that bloody page, they remained the same. A practical, cool parting devoid of any true emotion. A vise squeezed about his heart and he shook his head, his raspy breath filling his ears. *No.*

"She left?" Stunned disbelief ripped those words from his chest.

His father hesitated. "The day after you were shot."

With another empty, black laugh, Robert scrubbed a hand over his face. *Is it really a surprise? Hadn't he found her in the streets of St Giles and Lambeth twice in just the short time he'd known her?* The sting of an all-too-familiar betrayal slashed across his muddied thoughts and he fed his slow-budding disgust for her for being fickle, and for himself for loving her, and for wanting her now, regardless.

She'd chosen a life without him, preferring her existence as it had been, where she saw to the bookkeeping at her brother's club. *But you never considered what she wished for . . . In your silence you expected her to give up her world—for you . . .*

An empty numbness seeped in and spread like a slow-moving poison, blotting out all warmth. He wrinkled the sheet in his hands, and collapsed against his pillows. Cold, empty mirth spilled past his lips.

"What is it?" his father asked quietly.

"At the bloody irony of it all." Closing his eyes, he shook his head back and forth. "I had one woman who would have sold her soul to be duchess, and another who," *I cannot live without.* "Who wants no part of it." And with that, wanted no part of him.

"She loves you, Robert."

A sound of bitter disgust spilled past his lips. Ever the optimist, even in the face of absolute darkness. "Just not enough," he spat. It had never been enough. Lucy had wanted a title. And Helena, she'd wanted her bloody books.

Had she asked, he would have promised her the role of bookkeeper of every goddamn hell in London if she'd wished. He would have simultaneously dragged down the sun and the moon, and handed them over to her had she but asked.

She shouldn't have had to ask . . . You should have known that love she had and honored it . . .

His face contorted in a spasm of grief and he wanted to toss his head back and rail.

A woman who'd long had more control than most any lady of the peerage, and who chafed at her brother's influence in her life, Helena would have never been one to simply toss aside that self-control. Even for his love.

"You love her," his father said simply.

It wasn't a question, and yet Robert nodded jerkily anyway. With all he was. Yet knowing the strength of her spirit, and her desire for more than a life as a leading societal matron, what had he offered her? *What can I offer her?*

"Go to her." The duke coughed into his handkerchief. "Just when you are able," he said weakly, and shoved slowly to his feet. A twinkle lit his pained eyes. "Something tells me you will need every strength to bring that lady to heel."

Only, Robert didn't want to bring her to heel. He wanted her to always be the strong, courageous, fearless woman who spat in the face of Society's strictures and took on the Diggorys and Whitbys of the world—he just wanted her to be that person, at his side.

Robert closed his eyes. Now how to convince the stubborn minx that she wanted to *be* at his side?

St Giles, England
One week later

Chapter 24

Rule 24
Never love.
All you need is love.

Thirty cases of brandy.

Twenty-one cases of sherry.

Twenty-two cases of whiskey.

Helena stared at the neat column of numbers.

Her calculations.

The very ones she'd insisted upon more than two months ago. Oh, of course those calculations had not taken into consideration the need to account for increased membership in that time, but still there was a remarkable significance in those numbers.

She touched her fingertips to the sloppy markings in Adair's hand. Her spectacles slipped over the bridge of her nose, and she shoved them back into place. For Ryker's frugality and his contradictions of increasing the liquor accounts, she'd fought his stubbornness, and, at last it would seem, in her absence, he'd adjusted the liquor accounts. A wistful smile pulled at her lips.

How very peculiar the turns life took. Had there not been a dwindling supply of spirits, would she have deliberately contradicted Ryker's rules and stepped out on that floor? Helena trailed her index finger over the top of the page, her gut clenching.

Yet, she had stepped onto those once-forbidden floors, and her life was irrevocably changed.

Or it had been.

A spasm gripped her heart, and she drew in a shaky breath. Giving her head a shake, Helena dipped her pen in the inkwell, and proceeded to tabulate the monthly living expenditures for the private apartments.

For now, her life was remarkably . . . the same. Just as it had been for the past ten years. Day in and day out she rose, visited her cramped offices, and managed the books.

Her mind hurried through the tabulations, and she marked the right column. Though it wasn't *entirely* the same—there was a single, and very important, difference. Upon her return, she'd been granted greater freedom to move about the club floors.

Mayhap in Ryker's shock that she'd chosen to return to the Hell and Sin, she'd at last earned respect from a man who despised any and every aspect of the *ton*.

Mayhap, in her absence, they'd come to appreciate the role she'd played, and she'd been granted greater freedom to successfully carry out that role.

Or mayhap, it was simply that in her absence, and with her return, they'd acknowledged the truth—she was no longer the six-year-old girl who'd been in need of protecting but was now a woman, just five and twenty and fully grown, and in possession of her own mind.

Through all of it, her additional responsibilities at the club, her freedom within these walls and halls, and her brother's admiration, she had everything she wanted.

So why was there this great, gaping hole of emptiness?

The pen in Helena's fingers trembled, and ink splotched the page. Setting the pen down, she slid her eyes closed.

Her entire life, she'd believed if she left the Hell and Sin Club she would be incomplete, that she would be forsaking years' worth of vows she'd taken, and all the self-control she so cherished.

I miss him. I miss his laughter and his smile. I miss speaking to him, and his touch and his teasing. She missed every part that made Robert Dennington, the Marquess of Westfield, who he was. He was a man who'd seen past her scars and not sneered at her love of mathematics.

And he'd nearly died because of her.

Helena opened her eyes and stared blankly down at the open ledger. In the end, by penning a note of lies and leaving, she'd set them both free.

Her throat worked, and though there would forever be this aching wound of loss, he was better for it. The damage Diggory had done was testament of that. She'd brought her world to Robert and his family, and that was a life she'd never have him be part of. It was a life she herself didn't truly want. Drunken gentlemen, tossing away coin while people starved in the street. Men who'd drink themselves to death and wager away their family's existence. That was the empire she'd lauded.

The door opened, and she quickly picked up her pen.

"I'm nearly finished," she said, not taking her gaze from the page.

"I didn't say anything," Calum drawled, closing the door behind him.

"You didn't need to," she muttered, grateful for the distraction. For the emptiness inside, there was also a balm in being with the familiarity of the brothers who'd always been there.

Calum perched his hip on the edge of her desk.

Helena glanced out the corner of her eye, and then continued working. "Is there something Ryker wished to speak with me on? Have I been summoned?" She lifted her eyes to his. "Again?"

He had the good grace to flush. "He'll never admit it but he did it to protect you. He knew Diggory couldn't reach you in polite Society."

Yes, because everyone had always done what was best for Helena Banbury, making decisions, setting rules. What she'd wanted or believed had never been considered—not truly. She'd been spoken *at*.

Only Robert had ever truly spoken *to* her.

"Nothing to say?" Calum's gruffly spoken question rumbled in the quiet, punctuated by the click of her pen striking parchment.

Surely they didn't expect that she could return the same woman who'd left? Particularly after having been forced out. "What is there to say?" She lifted her shoulders in a shrug. *But can you truly resent them that, when it brought you the most splendorous days you've known in the course of your five and twenty years?* "Ryker knows all. He knew what was best. I'd broken the rules, and I'm no different than any other employee." Disposable and replaceable.

"About what happened when you left," Calum said quietly.

She stiffened, and blinked down at the page. He wished her to speak about her time outside of these walls. A spasm wracked her heart. She didn't wish to relive those days and the regret she'd now carry in leaving Robert. "We don't—"

"Speak of personal matters," he cut in. "I know the rules."

Did her brother simply send Calum for further questioning to disprove her place here? Helena steeled her jaw. "You may assure Ryker that—"

"He did not send me to speak on it." At the wry twist of his words she looked up. "In fact, he asked I not put questions to you about it. He said to leave you to the books."

And they had. Every one of her brothers and the employees at the club had allowed her to seek out her office, and slip back into the old, familiar routine of bookkeeping. The task of going over reports and books had proven a distraction. A temporary one.

"Is this about Lord Westfield?" he asked bluntly.

Her eyes misted over and she blinked wildly at her page, willing the drops away, willing them gone so Calum wouldn't see those signs of her weakness and know that her heart had never been further from this club.

The floorboards groaned, and she stiffened as her brother sank to his haunches beside her chair.

"You love him."

She managed a jerky nod. With all she was, and all she would ever be. Unable to take his silence, Helena forced her blurry gaze to his. Even through the sheen, the bitter twist of her brother's lips shone bright. Of course, hardened and jaded as he'd always been, as they'd always been, he would never see love as anything but a mark against her character. A short while ago, she'd not been unlike them. "I thought I would be losing myself if I loved him," she said, willing him to see. "But I've found there is nothing weakening about loving someone. It does not make you frail, or incapable of successfully keeping books, or running a business. It makes you stronger."

Calum gave a discreet cough, and shifted. "Uh, yes." He patted her awkwardly on the back, and she sighed. Being with Robert, free in her thoughts and emotions, she'd forgotten the stifling oppressiveness of this constraint. "You should return to your books," he said gruffly, and she nodded. Once, she'd been like him and her other brothers, unwilling to talk of anything that truly mattered, beyond the clubs.

Helena returned her attention to her ledgers.

He started for the door, and then called her name.

She glanced questioningly over her shoulder.

"I am glad you are back," he said, with uncharacteristic emotion lighting his eyes.

Helena smiled, incapable of giving him that same lie. "Oh, Calum," she called when he pressed the handle. He stared quizzically back. "Someday, you are going to find yourself hopelessly in love, and not be able to tell up from down, and I'm quite going to revel in that moment, Calum Dabney."

He snorted. "There is no fear of that." His lips turned up at one corner, full of so much male arrogance, she rolled her eyes.

A moment later, he closed the door, and she looked back at her books. With a sigh, Helena pulled free her spectacles, folded them, and set them down on her ledger.

For the first time in the whole of her life, there was no calm in her numbers. Or peace. Or joy. Just this peculiar emptiness.

She rubbed at the sharp ache in her chest. When she had sat beside Robert in the street, as he was pale and drawn, feverish from a bullet he'd taken for her, small pieces of her soul had died, leaving in their place this jagged coldness, a forever reminder of what she'd brought to him.

In those moments, his ragged groans and moans had sucked at her sanity, and ultimately left in place a realization—she could not marry him.

She had no place being with a man such as him. Her world was one of violence and danger, and in simply being in it, he was at risk. As were his sister and his father. For even though there was no longer any threat of Diggory, there would always be rival club owners who knew the heart of Ryker's weakness—his family.

Helena clamped her lower lip between her teeth. The metallic taste of blood filled her mouth, and the horror trickled in.

Robert's blood staining her fingers, spilling onto the dirty London street, his raspy breath as his eyes rolled to the back of his head—

"The nightmare?"

The gravelly voice of Ryker Black cut across the terror and she spun about so quickly she wrenched the muscles of her neck. The nightmare—only this time, a new one that defied her own horrors at Mac Diggory's hands. "Ryker." She set the pen down and slowly stood.

Her brother stood several paces away, the harsh planes of his scarred face familiarly blank and unmoving.

They stood, their eyes locked in a silent battle.

"It isn't time for my weekly meeting," Helena said at last, shattering the tension.

Ryker folded his arms across his broad chest, and winged a frosty black eyebrow upwards. "I asked a question."

No, he'd stated two words. What accounted for his silence? What demons were his? She was his sister, and had known him the better part of her life, and still knew next to nothing about who he was. She tipped her chin up. "We do not speak about the past, Ryker. The rules." Those same ones that had gotten her sent away.

Then, when you were Ryker Black, you could break any rule, especially your own.

"Diggory's dead, and cannot harm you, ever again. You did that, Helena. You slayed that demon." That lethal whisper sent a chill rolling along her spine. How casually he spoke about her firing a bullet through Diggory's head in the alley that day.

"I am not worried about Diggory," she said quietly, and ran her fingers along the back of her shellback chair. It was the inevitable warfare that would come in taking down the leader of The Devil's Den.

He took a step closer, his eyes thin, impenetrable slits trained on her. "You wish to go back," he continued, not allowing her a chance to reply. "Even as Wilkinson's wife tried to off you, you'd return to that world." Wilkinson. Not "Father." Not "our father." That same man he so disdained, had, in committing his wife to Bedlam, ultimately chosen right over that noble tie.

Helena passed a sad gaze over her brother's face. "Oh, Ryker, you look to the nobility and see them as all the same." He saw the Duchess of Wilkinson's treachery and not the duke's kindness. Or Diana's bravery in running for help inside the Hell and Sin Club that day, and ultimately ruining her name and reputation. Guilt stabbed at her heart. "You judge me for *not* judging them?" A sharp laugh escaped her. "You are so consumed by your hatred of those people, that you have become blinded by it." Two months ago, she would have bit her cheek to keep from uttering words that would upset Ryker and her place in this universe. Not any longer. As much as she'd prided herself on her strength, she'd not truly been strong in asserting her place—inside this club, and inside her family.

A muscle ticced at the corner of his right eye, but he gave no other outward reaction to her charges. "I do hate them," he said in the most revealing words he'd shared with her, ever. "But with Westfield risking his own neck and coming for you, he has my respect." Which for a man who respected few, and liked even fewer, was saying much, indeed.

She shook her head sadly. Of course, Ryker would honor that ultimate act of bravery and foolhardy act of selflessness. But it would never blot out the years upon years of hatred he'd carried. Instead, he'd see her love of Robert, Diana, their father, as a testament of her weakness. "Is there anything else you require?" she asked tightly.

Ryker shook his head. Without another word, he turned on his heel and left.

She stared at the oak panel, and let the tension out of her shoulders. As a girl her life had existed with definable blacks and whites. There had been no confusion or questions about her place in the world. As a woman who was scarred and marked by the streets of London, that place could have never been clearer. Somewhere along the way, she'd begun to dwell in a netherworld of grey, where everything she'd believed had proven remarkably more complex.

Abandoning work for the day, Helena snapped her ledgers closed, and swiped her spectacles from the desk. Striding over to the door, she pulled it open and stepped out into the hall.

She started down the same familiar path she'd traveled so many times . . . and froze.

Her gaze caught and held upon the small scrap of purple. Unbidden, her legs carried her over to that leafy vegetable. Stealing a look about, she dropped to her haunches and picked up the cabbage leaf, holding it close to her eyes. Her heart pounded hard as she pushed to her feet and followed a trail of those purple scraps that abruptly ended outside her chambers.

Heart in her throat, Helena stood at the wood panel, and then pressed the handle.

She blinked, giving her eyes a moment to adjust to the darkened space, and stepped inside.

The air left her on a soft gasp.

Purple blooms blanketed her room, leaving a colorful trail to her empty bed, which was covered with flowers. Tears filled her eyes, and she searched for him. A thrill of knowing, a charged connection they'd always shared, went through her, and she slowly turned.

Robert stood framed in the doorway. "Helena," he murmured in that mellifluous baritone that had cracked her defenses from their first meeting.

"Robert," she whispered. What was he doing here?

Arms filled with several leather books, he stepped inside, and continued coming toward her, until his long-legged stride ate away the distance between them.

Her lashes drifted closed. Surely she'd conjured him with her need to see him.

"Do you know, Helena," he said with such soberness, her eyes popped open. "I thought a good deal about your leaving."

"D-Did you?" she managed, carefully watching as he settled his armful down on the purple irises littering her bed.

He inclined his head, and then retrieved something from his boot. "You forgot this."

She followed his movements and took in the ruby-studded dagger in his large hand. Helena wetted her lips, and alternated her gaze between that long-forgotten dagger and the flowers scattered about her rooms. "I-Is that why you've come?"

A wistful grin pulled at Robert's lips, as he drifted closer. He came to a stop, so only a hairsbreadth separated them. "Is that what you believe?" he asked, with a faint trace of amusement in his question. He palmed her cheek, and with that butterfly-soft caress, her lashes began fluttering.

She leaned into his touch. "I do not know why you are here." Or how he'd even gained entry. Again.

"Your brothers were more obliging of my presence on the floors when I expressed my intentions," he said, perfectly interpreting her thoughts.

Helena's eyes flew open. His intentions? Her heart skipped a beat.

"Surely you did not think I'd allow you to leave so easily?" he murmured, dropping his brow to hers. He rubbed back and forth. "Not without at least properly offering for you."

Helena leaned into him, taking in the warmth falling off his powerful, and very much alive, frame. She breathed in the sandalwood scent that was so very much Robert Dennington. "You already did." She'd accepted that gift, and then quickly abandoned it with reality's intrusion.

He made a tsking sound, and with his knuckles tipped her chin up, forcing their eyes to meet. "But I didn't. Not truly. I offered you marriage."

And how desperately she wanted that future with him, one of laughter and love and children . . .

"But I did not think of all you would be giving up." He spread his arms wide, motioning to her chambers, and she mourned the loss of his fleeting caress. Robert retrieved the leather books he'd deposited on her bed, and held them up. "You see, Helena, I can give you what every other woman has only wanted . . . a title." Fools all of them. "But with my crumbling estates, I can give you nothing more."

"I never cared about that, Robert," she managed to whisper.

He grinned. "Oh, I know that. You were quite clear when you stated your preference for binding yourself to Boney's dead bones."

A broken laugh bubbled forth. Had she truly said that?

"I assure you. You did." What a synchronic harmony there existed between them. "Then, as I lay in bed, which I did." He paused. "For a long while." The blade of guilt twisted all the deeper. *My fault. It was my fault.* He tapped a fingertip along his chin. "I considered what I could offer a woman who didn't have a desire for my title or a need for wealth."

Nothing. She'd needed nothing, but him . . .

He dumped his small stack of books into her arms. Furrowing her brow, Helena glanced at the burden.

"They are my family's ledgers," he went on. "I explained to my father that after a month of toiling over the numbers, we would no doubt remain in dun territory as long as Stonely handled our finances. I decided, and he agreed, only one person could make proper rights of our books." Her heart tripped a beat. "I would turn over the bookkeeping to you, should you desire it." He grimaced. "I've no doubt with your acumen, you can salvage my estates better than any man-of-affairs in the whole of the kingdom." Again, he glanced about her room. "Or if you prefer to remain on as bookkeeper here, then I would never stand in your way. Your dowry would remain in your hands, for our children." He held her gaze. "I would, however, ask that you allow me to live here with you."

Oh, God. How was it possible to fall even more in love with him? He would make that offering for her? He would trust his estates to her care? Her shuddery sob filtered about them, and she carefully set his books on her bed.

Robert held her gaze, continuing his relentless assault on her weakening defenses. "I love you, Helena Banbury," he said with such love radiating from his blue eyes, she sank to the edge of the bed. Helena hugged her arms to her waist and stared down at her feet, stiffening as Robert sank to a knee beside her. "If you left because you despise me and everything having to do with my title—"

"I no longer feel that way," she said on a tremulous whisper. Now, he was all her heart hungered for. Surely he knew that?

Robert caressed her face with his gaze. "I thought of what I would offer you," he continued in solemn tones that washed over her. "I'd offer you my heart, but you already know you have that, and it was not enough."

A teardrop squeezed from the corner of her eye and slid down her cheek. Followed by another. And another. "Is that what you believe?" Emotion hoarsened her voice.

He quirked an eyebrow. "Isn't it?"

How could he not know that her heart now beat for him, that he was her happiness and her light? Diggory's ugly laugh echoed around the chambers of her mind with the blare of a pistol's report. She jerked and with a sound of frustration, Helena shoved to her feet and began to pace. "You nearly died."

"And I'd do it again without hesitation," he said with such calm, her control snapped.

"But I do not want you to make that sacrifice for me," she cried. "I want you alive and happy and . . ." the fight went out of her. "Not dead." Helena shut her eyes, hating the weakness inside that made her want to selfishly take what he offered.

Warm, strong hands captured hers, bringing her eyes open. "Is that what this is about?" he asked, not relinquishing his hold on her. "Protecting me."

There was so much tenderness and love in that question that tears flooded her eyes. She nodded jerkily. "Diggory's men will not rest until he's avenged."

"Then we'll face it together."

A half laugh, half sob escaped her. How resolute he was. "I can't, R-Robert." Her voice cracked. How did he not yet see the peril that faced him in marrying her?

"Oh, Helena," he murmured, and with his thumb he captured a single teardrop as it trailed a path down her cheek. "You talk about wanting me alive and happy, and yet how can you not know?"

Her lower lip quivered. "Kn-know what?"

"That I've only ever been truly alive and happy with you in my life."

Oh, God.

"Marry me, Helena Banbury," he urged.

"But . . ."

He cradled her face between his hands, his eyes boring into hers. "Marry me knowing that there may be struggles and sadness, and that we, with each other's love, will find strength and joy in one another."

Helena leaned into him, and slid her eyes closed. *Take that gift he stretches out . . . Do not be afraid . . .*

And after a lifetime of living in the darkness, she opened her eyes, and the shadows lifted, replaced instead with the promise of love and forever in his eyes.

With a smile, Helena brushed a tremulous palm down his cheek. "I love you."

He ran his gaze over her face. "Is that a—?"

She leaned up and kissed him, silencing his question. Pulling back she said, "I spent so much of my life hating and fearing life outside these walls. I was so convinced that I did not need anyone but myself and my work." Her voice broke. "But needing you does not make me weak. Having you in my life only makes me stronger."

With a groan, Robert claimed her lips once more, and a lightness filled the darkness that had filled her for so long.

At last—she was home.

Acknowledgments

Being an author, you spend countless hours plotting and writing stories. If you are fortunate, you find friends along the way who share in the joy and excitement that goes into each book.

Eva Devon, I thank you for being one of those friends whom I was blessed to find!!

And for my husband, Doug . . . you may not be a romance writer, but you're always a sounding board . . . and I could not love you any more for it!

*A sneak peek
at the second
Sinful Brides novel,
coming soon.*

Editor's Note: This is an early excerpt and may not reflect the finished book.

Chapter 1

Dear Fezzimore,
      Mrs. Dundlebottom insists we remain silent through
her lessons on propriety and decorum. I tried, Fezzi. I truly
did. Alas, propriety and decorum are highly overrated.
      Penny, age 11

Somewhere between Ryker Black's rise from guttersnipe to ruthless owner of the Hell and Sin Club, the world had learned—you did not cross him, interrupt him, or interfere with his dealings.

Ever.

That rule went for the lords who tossed away fortunes at his tables, and the other proprietors of the club who'd proven more brother than had their blood been shared.

That also went for Calum Dabney, the second in command of the Hell and Sin, who stood at his shoulder now.

Standing on the fringe of the Hell and Sin, Ryker surveyed the club. Dandified fops and jaded lords in their bright silk fabrics flooded every corner like an overstuffed drawer. "Tell her to make an appointment," he ordered, in low tones. Raucous laughter and the sharp clink of coins filled the hell, nearly deafening in its volume.

"Your sister is here, at this hour, requesting a meeting, and you want me to tell her *what?*" the other man choked out, incredulity filling his tone.

Ryker remained silent. He'd grown up on the life lesson that to say too much and to speak too loudly found you gutted on the streets with a blade in your belly. Instead, he studied three vacant places at a hazard table, and frowned.

There was no place for anything less than excellence.

"I am not telling Helena *that,*" Calum said, flexing his jaw. "I may be your second, but I'm not your blood lackey, *my lord.*"

Ryker's hackles went up. With those taunting words, his brother plucked at a frayed nerve. After saving the now Duke of Somerset from death in the Dials, Ryker had been duly rewarded for his efforts with a bloody title from the Prince Regent. A bloody title his brothers had found great humor in, and never lost an opportunity to have fun at his expense over. "Tell her whatever you wish, then," he said icily, not rising to Calum's baiting. He'd not allow himself to be distracted by what had brought the other man over to his side.

Then, Calum and the others had always coddled Helena. The only sibling to share Ryker's blood, he'd rescued Helena from the streets when she'd been a child of six. But not before she'd been scarred by life on the streets. Years later, she'd risen from master bookkeeper of the club, to now Duchess of Somerset. Ryker peeled back his lip. For all Helena's loathing and disdain for the nobility, for having seen their mother whore herself to a duke, she'd ultimately chosen life amongst the haute ton.

A loud shout went up, and Ryker looked to the roulette table where a cheering dandy was being slapped on the back by a fellow patron. Ryker scowled. Where the patrons reveled in their wins, there was not a sound the owner of a gaming hell detested more.

"You sent her away," Calum pointed out, refusing to abandon their argument. "You were the one to send her away from Diggory's clutches, and now you'd punish her for making her way in a new world?" There was a sharp accusatory edge there.

Diggory, the late owner of their rival club, The Devil's Den, had been a thug who'd tormented them all on the streets. He'd extended that warfare years later, into their gaming hells. Having learned of Helena's skill with the books, Diggory wouldn't have rested until she was dead. In the end, Diggory had paid the ultimate price for his greed, and Helena had carved out a life amongst polite Society. Ryker rolled his shoulders. "She chose," he said, the matter at an end.

"She is one of us," Calum retorted. He lifted his gaze to the glass panel that only the proprietors knew of that oversaw the gaming floor. "You owe her."

That handful of words left a charged tension in their wake. For in a world where he was not driven by emotion, feelings, or any sentiments that could weaken, Ryker did honor the code of the streets. For the decision she'd made to join the *ton*, Helena had once been a member of their street family. She'd scrapped and clawed alongside them. And more, when he, Calum, Adair, and Niall, the other members of their clan, had struggled with the skills needed to survive in their new world, Helena had proven adept in ways they never had, or would ever be able to. Her business acumen had singlehandedly helped build their empire. With a silent curse, he stalked off.

"Adair showed her to your office," Calum called after him. Since Helena had left, Adair looked after the books. On a good day, Adair could never be Helena with numbers on a bad day.

Gaze trained forward, he marched through the clubs. Averting their gazes, lords hastily stepped out of his path.

No, Ryker didn't welcome, or accept, interruptions to his daily routines. Helena had been schooled in that. They all had. And yet, something brought her here.

He exited the gaming hell floor, and made his way up the stairs to the offices. The wood stairs groaned in protest at his shifting weight.

Had Diggory's men, bent on revenge for Helena's act that day against their revered master, found their way into polite Society? He reached his office and froze.

A tall, broad figure stood outside his doorway. Arms clasped at his back, his brother-in-law, the Duke of Somerset, waited. "Black," he greeted solemnly, this man who belonged to a people Ryker despised, and yet who'd also stepped in to save Helena. For that alone he had Ryker's respect.

Ryker inclined his head.

"Helena is inside," the other man murmured.

Ryker reached past him and pressed the handle. They may be joined as families now, but he'd never call Somerset brother. Wordlessly he entered the room and closed the door.

From where she sat perched on the edge of a chair before his desk, Helena jumped up. "Ryker."

"Helena," he said tersely, and made for the sideboard. Grabbing a bottle of whiskey, he poured himself a glass. "What do you want?" he asked, carrying his drink to his desk.

"It is lovely to see you, too," she said with a wry twist of her lips. Unhurriedly, she reclaimed her seat.

Ryker sat behind the cluttered mahogany piece and got to the heart of it. "Diggory's men?"

Her smile withered. "No. It is not that. *Them*," she amended.

Some of the tension left his shoulders, but he remained tightly coiled. To let one's guard down meant a man's ruin. That *wariness* went for those you called family, and the thieves on the street.

Laconic as she'd always been, Helena smoothed her gloved palms down the front of her skirts, drawing his attention to the new attire she wore—elegant blue satin skirts adorned in crystal beading, befitting a duchess.

He peeled his lip back in a sneer.

Bringing her chin back a notch, she held his gaze. "I require a favor, and know the rule on the element of surprise."

So that was why she came at this late hour. Cradling his glass between his hands, Ryker leaned back and inclined his head.

"I have not been . . . completely welcomed by Society."

Burned on one cheek, the bastard daughter of a duke, and the sister of a club proprietor, had she expected she *would* be? "Oh?" he drawled.

Her frown deepened. "I didn't expect it would matter to you whether I find my way amongst Society."

She was only partly correct. Part of him, a weak, pathetic piece deep inside he'd sooner slay himself than admit to, did care. Still, he said nothing. You didn't show your weakness. Not even to a sister, begging a favor.

"Questions surround our family," she went on when he still said nothing.

He arched an eyebrow. "When did you ever give two damns what anyone said about us?" He'd raised her better than that. Disappointment filled him.

"I don't," she said pragmatically. "They can all go hang."

If he were capable of smiling after all the sins he'd ratcheted in his life, this would have been the time for it.

"Society wonders about you," she explained. "You are a duke's son."

"A bastard," he said, bluntly. "I am a bastard." He lifted his glass in salute. A child who hadn't mattered a jot to the man who'd given him life. How easily his sister had forgotten *that* key distinction of her own blood, too.

Helena drew in a deep breath, and then spoke on a rush. "They also talk about my husband. Speculate there is bad blood between you."

Ah, so this is why she is here. The Duke of Somerset. When he'd sent Helena away for her safety, never had he believed she would bind herself in name, forever, to one of those fancy toffs. "Ah." Ryker turned his lips up in a humorless smile.

"He did not ask me to come," she said, hurriedly. "Robert said the *ton* could go hang with their opinions." The duke rose another notch in his silent estimation. Helena scrambled forward in her chair and turned her palms up. "But *I* care, Ryker. I love my husband, and they are saying rotten things about him." Her mouth tightened. "They say he is ashamed of you because of your birthright and role at the club."

When in actuality, it was Ryker who had no interest in any dealings with Somerset, title of brother-in-law be damned. Ryker took a bored sip of his whiskey and studied Helena over the rim. "What do you want?" The curt question brought his sister's lips together, tightly.

"I am throwing a ball."

A goddamn ball. How could she endure the *frivolity* of her new life? In running the hell, they'd created wealth and work here for many . . . where was her purpose now?

"I want Calum, Adair, and Niall there." She paused. "And you. I want you to attend as well, Ryker."

Ryker stilled. He'd misheard her. He'd not been paying attention beyond her mention of those frivolous entertainments.

"I want you there," she repeated, with a quiet insistence. "I wish to show a—"

"No."

"United front," she continued over him. "I want the world to see we are *truly* a family and have them know Robert and I are proud of you."

"A family?" he scoffed. Is that what she believed he was to the Duke of Somerset? All because she'd married the gent?

"Yes," she said with a nod. "You are my brother, and Robert is now *your* brother."

"He is no brother of mine," he growled, and Helena jerked, her cheeks going ashen.

Taking another lazy sip, he arched an eyebrow. "Do not demand a meeting, enter my office, and feed me lies that this is for me," he said coolly. This was for her husband, and her.

Proving her mettle, Helena went toe-to-toe with him. "Very well, this is not solely for you. This is for all of us." She skimmed her gaze about the room, and lingered her stare on the cracked, framed piece of art that hung above his desk; the only adornment to grace his room. "You have never truly trusted anyone, Ryker," she said, pulling her attention away. "Oh, you may say you trust our brothers, but you do not truly. You keep us at arm's length, questioning the motives . . . of those who would lay down their lives for you." She gave him a long, meaningful look. "My motives are true. There is no lie in them. I'm not capable of that. But neither will I beg you to attend."

He met her words with more silence. Silence was always far safer. It allowed a person composure of his thoughts and an opportunity to gauge and assess his opponents.

Helena glanced down at her toes, the first to break the impasse. "I'll simply ask, and hope you see that I need you to be there for me . . . and my husband."

Ryker withdrew his watchfob and consulted the timepiece. "I've to return to the floors."

Helena came to her feet. "Of course." She picked her reticule off the floor and fished inside. Leaning over, she set something on his desk.

Ryker froze, and stared blankly down at the words on that thick vellum. "It is Friday," she clarified. "Consider this your formal invitation. I do not ask you to come for the entire event, but if you'd stand beside us for even a short while"—she held his gaze squarely—"then I would be forever in your gratitude."

She could have reminded him of the years of service she'd given the club, and how she'd helped build this empire . . . but she'd not. It was a sign of her weakness. "Helena," he said, lifting his head.

"Ryker." Helena dipped hers in return and proudly marched out of his office.

As soon as she'd closed the door behind her, he let loose a curse. She'd ask him to step out of the only world he'd ever known and enter hers. To what end? To help Somerset. A sound of disgust escaped him. Though she'd not pleaded or reminded him of past favors she'd done the club, they lingered there.

His sense of street honor, where you paid your debts and did your due, was ingrained into him from the moment he'd been old enough to walk, and learned his place in the Dials.

A knock sounded at the door. *What now?* "Enter," he barked.

Calum stepped inside and looked around. A frown settled on his lips. "She's gone already?"

"Yes." Ryker downed the contents of his drink, welcoming the fiery trail it blazed down his throat.

"Is it Killoran?" Diggory's number two, now in command of The Devil's Den, had yet to attempt his revenge for Diggory's death. The time was coming, and Ryker braced for it. Welcomed it. It was the ruthlessness he knew.

"You want to know the matter of *urgency* that brought her here?" Ryker swiped the invitation from his desk and shoved to his feet. Calum stalked over and grabbed the invitation.

As he skimmed the page, his brow furrowed. "A ball?" the other man asked skeptically, turning over the invite.

With a biting laugh, Ryker tossed it atop his desk. "That is the pressing matter of business you called me away from the floors for." He narrowed his eyes. "You're growing weak," he cautioned.

Calum flared his nostrils. With his volatile displays of fury in the streets against their enemies, and his worrying over Helena, he had always been vulnerable in ways Ryker never had been, nor ever would be. "Why does she want you there?" Calum asked, relentless.

"To silence the gossip about me and Somerset." Registering Calum's pointed stare, he snapped. "What?"

Offering an infuriatingly nonchalant shrug, Calum said, "Oh, I would simply expect given that Somerset watched after Helena and followed after her, taking a bullet surely meant for her, that there would be *some* sense of obligation."

A thick, tense silence fell.

Goddamn it all. Where any bloody duke, baron, or any lord in between could go hang on any other day, Calum was right on this. Somerset had selflessly returned to St Giles, to come for Helena when Diggory had snatched her. It mattered not whose bullet had ended the bastard . . . but rather, who had taken a bullet that day.

Swallowing another curse, Ryker strode for the door.

"Should I send round your acceptances?" Humor laced the other man's tone.

"Send my goddamn acceptance," he bit out, as Calum's laughter trailed after him.

Ryker stalked through the halls, and marched an angry path to the observatory that overlooked the casino. He'd survived more blades in his person, gunshots, and street fights than any man had a right to live and tell of. And he'd welcome any one of those tenuous situations to entering London Society.

Cursing his sister, Ryker found his place at the window and stared at the drunken dandies stumbling about his club.

Yes, Ryker had survived life on the streets. He could certainly survive an evening with these same brainless fops and their equally brainless ladies.

Then his debt was paid to Helena and Somerset, and Ryker was free to carry on an existence where the only need he had of the peerage was the coin they tossed down at his tables.

About the Author

Photo © 2016 Kimberly Rocha

USA Today bestselling author Christi Caldwell blames Julie Garwood and Judith McNaught for luring her into the world of historical romance. While sitting in her graduate school apartment at the University of Connecticut, Christi decided to set aside her class notes and try her hand at tales of love. She believes even the most perfect heroes and heroines have imperfections, and she rather enjoys torturing them before giving them a well-deserved happily ever after.

Christi makes her home in southern Connecticut, where she spends her time writing, chasing after her feisty young son, and caring for her twin princesses-in-training. For the latest information about Christi's releases, future books, and free bonus material, visit www.christicaldwell.com and sign up for her newsletter.